*W*e departed London on the Winchester Royal Road riding
ten abreast, a royal guard in smart scarlet, helmets and swords glittering in the low winter sun, and my spirits suddenly burst with
happiness. I'm not called "Joy" for nothing, eh? I loved being in
open air again, loved the jingle of harnesses and clop of hooves,
even loved the bright crimson standard with its three lions bobbing
ahead of me; most of all, I was happy that it was necessary to move
me. We must be winning—otherwise, why whisk me out of the
White Tower without the other women? Why send me to the great
palace at Winchester? For where else did this road lead?

We stopped about an hour short of Winchester at the river ford.

"Perhaps they're worried about the ice," I said to my handmaid.

Amaria's green eyes slid toward the wood. "Or those men?"

At first the branches looked bare, but gradually I saw men as
alike as mushrooms crouched silently on the limbs, men with
shaved pates and legs, white tunics with green sashes, toes curled
around icy bark.

"Welshmen! God's feet, what are they doing here?"

I spurred my steed to the front of the line where Ranulf de
Glanvill was talking to a dour middle-aged Welshman with a scarlet cape over his white tunic.

"Why have we stopped, my lord?" I demanded.

Glanvill's darting black eyes avoided me. "Queen Eleanor, may I
present Lord Ciarron ap Dwyddyn?" He raised his arm abruptly
and shouted, "Reverse direction!"

The lines of ten abreast turned smartly around and began trotting back to London with their jingling harnesses and standard. Instantly, I roiled my horse to join them, but Glanvill and Ciarron crowded my mount on either side and I found myself splashing across a shallow ditch directly into the forest with Amaria beside me. I was too shocked to be afraid, but I certainly recognized the danger.

"Stop at once!" I jerked my reins. "I'll not leave the road!"

Ciarron grabbed my bridle.

"Lord Glanvill!" I cried.

He stared straight ahead, and I knew my fate. Who hasn't heard of the forest executions of political prisoners? We rode deeper and deeper into the bare trees in the company of the ghostly Welshmen, until the tangle became so thick that we were forced into the river, riding in icy water to our hips, with our longcarts floating behind us. Amaria reached for my gloved hand.

Then the ring of an ax. Again I looked at Glanvill's profile. Malevolent he might be, but I could hardly believe that such an important officer would do the bloody deed, a job fit only for an anonymous brute. The sound of ax blows came closer.

Suddenly we entered a small clearing where woodmen were felling trees, some chopping limbs off trunks to make palings for a wall almost fifteen feet high, looming before us. Above us on the guard platform, Welshmen sat dangling filthy feet. The gate swung open.

We entered a broad compound covered with a light fall of snow. Ice-crusted sheep cast long shadows across the yard. Workmen rested on their tools to stare with open-mouthed curiosity. In the distance, over the tops of brown trees, I spotted Clarendon Lodge. I'd gazed down on this clearing many times from above and so knew exactly where I was: Old Sarum, an ancient Saxon tower, a square, squat donjon constructed of crumbling dry wall atop a steep motte encircled by a wide weed-choked moat. It had been uninhabitable for centuries, but now the new huts and fences told another tale.

I was so angry that I could hardly speak. "Lord Glanvill, is this a joke?"

"King's orders. Dismount, if you please."

"I'll not spend ten heartbeats in that windy ruin. Depend on it!"

His eyes ceased darting. "Must I force you?"

I reared my horse and crashed down on the nearest guards.

A hundred men fell on me. From the icy ground, I bit every dirty ankle I could reach, fought my way to my feet, scratched bare scalps, stamped on Welsh toes with my golden boots. One churl put his hand across my mouth, and I bit his thumb. Blood spurted everywhere. I clung to my horse's neck.

"Help me!" I cried. "Someone help! I'll reward—"

At least twenty men dragged me to the moat bridge. I reached out my foot and tripped a guard, who fell backward through the thin scum of ice. I went limp, made them carry me up the motte, through the tower door into pitch-blackness, up a dark stair, where I banged my head on low beams, then up again to the middle room, up a third stair to the uppermost level of this bat-filled eyrie.

Glanvill stood on the top step, panting. "With the Devil as my witness, I'm enjoying this."

"Even the infidel doesn't enjoy killing women!"

He bared his teeth. "No one's killed you."

"No, nor given me a trial! How dare you, a man of the law, treat me like a common criminal! You think I don't know the purpose of Old Sarum? First Saxons, then Normans incarcerated ruffians here to die a cruel death, but no one—I repeat, no one—ever tortured a woman thus! Certainly not a queen!"

"You will have a trial."

"You take me for a fool? After a year? Capture me, hide me, and maybe I'll cooperate by expiring 'naturally' because your king lost his balls after the Becket scandal. Aye, and he'll weep over my grave as he did over Thomas's! Hypocrite!"

"The king wants to be lenient."

"Ha!"

"He offers you a fine position: You may become abbess of Fontevrault, with all the perquisites of your station, a worthy end to your life."

"If I what?"

He came closer. "Recant your orders to your sons."

"So that he can punish them?"

"The king is prepared to be lenient there as well. He loves his princes." He came closer still. I could smell his sour stomach. "Recant, Queen Eleanor."

"I'm tempted . . ." I groped, as if for my kerchief, and found my quoit.

In a flash I whipped him across his eyes. Again! Again! He stumbled backward. Down the stairs: *Thump! Thump! Thump!* I ran down after him, hitting on his face, his ears, his throat. "Are you dead, Lord Glanvill?"

He groaned.

"Still alive? Pity." I kicked him in the ribs.

He rolled to his stomach, then to his knees. I followed as he stumbled to the bottom of the tower and out the door.

"Lord Glanvill!"

He paused.

"I will make your king the Pope—a fitting end to his life!"

I returned to the top floor, where Amaria crouched by a stone latrine carved in the wall.

"He means us to die, Am."

"I know." Her teeth chattered.

"Stay here while I examine our great hall."

The tower was built of large uneven stones without mortar and would have fallen long ago except for a tough woody vine snaking around it as support. I could put my fist through the spaces between stones; wind whistled through in strange harmonies, and snow was fast piling at the base. The roof and flooring had once been of wood; since the roof was long gone, I could only surmise that the floors had been replaced, though they were far from secure. One space between stones was larger than the others, pos-

sibly an arrow slit. I gazed down on the moat we'd just crossed and saw a suspicious mound beyond it, which might be a mass grave. Then, as I turned, a skull rolled at my feet.

I went back to Amaria.

"Follow me."

I led her down the stairs, where they bisected the middle floor, down to the bottom in the dark. There we huddled on bare ground under the steps, the warmest place in the tower. I hastily felt with my hands for more gruesome souvenirs of the past so that my handmaid might be spared. Then I wrapped her in my sables. Our soaked tunics were fast turning to ice.

We heard Glanvill's fanfare and horses.

"We're alone with all those savages," Amaria whimpered. "What will we do?"

"We'll survive." My voice shook with rage. "My sons will rescue us." I hugged her close.

The door opened; a shaft of icy air blew inward. "Queen Eleanor!"

"Here!"

Lord Ciarron carried a lantern in one hand, a smoking pot in the other. "I've brought your food." At least the churl spoke French, albeit with a goatish Welsh tongue.

Stiffly, Amaria and I became two people again. Lord Ciarron placed the lantern on a step while he unwrapped his packet. Instead of bread, we had thin pancakes to dip into a hot gruel, and the wine had likewise been heated. We gulped eagerly. I didn't recognize the mess, though it certainly contained a little lamb gristle. Never mind, it was hot.

Ciarron's lean wolf face watched us without expression, yet even curs respond to gratitude, eh?

"This is delicious," I lied. "Is it Welsh fare?"

"*Lagana*," he said, pointing to the pancakes.

Amaria was more direct. "Do you plan for us to freeze tonight, my lord?"

He shifted his weight. "You have furs."

"But no roof, no walls." She pointed to snow falling through the open space above, to small drifts piling along the dry walls. "We're not bears, my lord."

I said bluntly, "We'll be dead by morning."

"Help us!" Amaria pleaded. "I've heard that the Welsh are the most hospitable people on earth."

Wordlessly, he took his lantern to leave, when the beam suddenly fell directly on Amaria's face. My handmaid has never been beautiful, even when she was young, with her red hair and freckles, but in this pale glow, her delicate features with their green eyes had a poignant appeal, enough to make him hesitate. I held my breath, but he turned and we were plunged into darkness.

"You know, Am, that the Welsh are last in hospitality, not first."

"He seemed a little more civilized than the others."

We wrapped ourselves against the snow.

"Listen!" Amaria stirred.

Steps, then two lanterns. Between them, Ciarron and another Welshman carried eight sheepskins, smelling like glue and crawling with maggots, but welcome as fine down. Weighting two pelts with rocks, they formed walls against the steps, then piled the rest inside.

Again the lantern caught Amaria's face—deliberately?

"Thank you, Lord Ciarron," I said.

After they'd left, we squirmed onto our rough hides, snug as wood lice.

I had never been so cold. An icy gale howled unimpeded across Salisbury Plain, past the flapping sheepskins, to bite the very bone. The dark was a feral presence, enhancing the cold. My jaw ached in an effort to control my chattering teeth; I tried to warm my hands with my breath; I couldn't feel my feet. *Eeeeeoooo! Eeeeoooo!*

"Was that a wolf?" Am cried.

"The wind, dear."

"I don't want to be eaten!"

Nor did I.

"Come closer. We must warm each other." We rearranged my sables so we could slip our hands under each other's tunics.

8

The low mournful tone resumed. Elegiac. *Tomorrow never comes,* a voice from my past. Was this my last night on earth? Would Ciarron discover Amaria and me in a deathly embrace? Then, to be flung into a common grave, perhaps with victims of the Black Death when the spring thaw came. *Stay awake,* I ordered myself; *don't succumb.*

1 **woke with** a start. Disoriented. Where was I? What was that peculiar glow on the beam above? Heart tripping, I slipped out from my sables. The glow had a shape—a naked man's shape! Long pale hair, eyes like blue lances, an apparition to be sure, but familiar. I chilled in a different manner.

"*Grandfather, is that you?*"

He mocked gently. "*Joy, is that you?*"

I licked my cold lips. "*I'm not going with you, Grandfather. I'm not going to die!*"

"*Of course you are! We all die, eh?*" He somersaulted through the air to a lower beam. "*Oc, the same azure eyes, cherry lips, cheeks round as peaches, golden hair—the wintry wind makes merit grow—come while you're still young, dear. Five is a delicious age.*"

"*I was five when you died; I'm fifty-two now.*"

"*And still delectable! You take after me—you know they called me 'Junior.' Did anyone ever tell you why?*"

Had he really been so vain? "*Junior for Juvenile, eh?*"

He leapt again; something brushed my cheek. "*And Joy for passion! Aren't we a pair?*"

"*No, Grandfather, we're not! I won't die!*"

He reached a delicate hand. "*You have no choice, Milord.*"

"*You couldn't take me before—remember?*"

"*In laudes Innocentium! Sallat chorus infantium!*" he chanted.

"*Please, Grandfather, I'm determined to live. Survival will be my revenge for this slow execution! Tell me how—you're the wisest man I ever knew!*"

"*Am I truly?*" His hair rose in a cloud. "*Well, perhaps I am, though the competition was dull.*" He covered his eyes, laughing

silently. Then he became serious. *"Life is love, my dear, my song and my wisdom. You learned my lesson the best."*

"But the world prevailed against us, eh?" A wave of deep despair clutched my vital spirits. *"If life is love, Grandfather, than I am truly dead."*

"You don't yet know the meaning of death, Milord. You breathe, you experience time, and therefore you yet have hope of love."

"Hope in this windy spike? Of love?"

"You're asleep on your horse, not yet asleep. Carpe diem! Make a tryst, darling!"

"Would you have me seduce a sheep in its pen?"

"Many a man wears a sheepskin as disguise!" He pulled his lower eyelid. *"Use your furry flower—you know the tricks!"*

"Grandfather! I'm an old lady!"

"Still young enough to be a trickster! However, I grant that your opportunities are limited." His cloudy hair drooped, then rose again. *"But not your memories, eh? If you insist upon living, let your gaudy flowers bloom on your vellum! Remember how I scribbled my verses well into my dotage? Love is in your heart—now make it your art!"*

With an eerie laugh, he shot straight up and disappeared.

"Levis insurgit, *William,*" I whispered.

I lay under the sable again, colder than ever from my *mesclatz* conversation with a ghost. I closed my eyes; something struck me on the nose! Grandfather being playful? I was struck again—on the forehead this time. Cold, wet. Ice! I sat upright. Heaven help us, the snow had changed to hard pellets. Hail? No, this ice cut; it was sleet! Huge shards, like glass tinkling and banging noisily. I pulled the fur over Amaria's head, which left me exposed.

Surely the rattle and banging would wake her. The cacophony rose to a friendly racket: *Tic! Tac! Hic! Hac! Tiket! Taket! Tic! Tac!* Down the stone steps marched the pellets, like horses dancing

across cobbles, while on the rotting beams *tee, tee, tee* echoed the beat of the clappers, of the tambors, and a lusty voice rang out:

Time may come and turn and go
through days and years, sun and snow
[tic, tac, tee, tee, ton]
While I am dumb
With desire, ever new;
My senses numb.
I so want you!
[Ticket, tacket, tic, tic, tic]
Yet the season goes apace
Will nothing halt my heart's mad race!

Aquitaine! Hugh and Guy and Aimar and Achilles cantering down the summer paths, ready for war and love, Cercamon strumming his lyre, Marcabru!

"Did you feel that, Joy?"

"It's only sleet. Try to sleep."

"*You* sleep! I'll place the fur over your head."

"I dozed a bit; I'm awake now."

And curiously excited. We might be lying in a grave, the sleet might be our final shroud, Grandfather might yet have his way, but I felt alive. My vital spirits leapt to the hot Aquitanian rhythms. And Grandfather was right—I did remember!

"Listen, Am! Did you bring vellum in your longcart?"

"Of course." Her voice was concerned. "Do you think this is the time to write a *lai*?"

"That's for you to decide, dear. I have my own project. May I borrow a few pages?"

"If I can reach the cart, of course." Now her voice was worried. "To write troubadour songs?"

As if talent ran in the blood. As if this setting could inspire licentious verse!

"Oh no, something more mundane. I must send letters abroad."

"Of course." Her tone filled with pity.

My brain grew more fevered; my heart raced to the drumming around me. While I drew breath, while memory was still alive, let me record my tale. *Oc,* let the winds taunt, the sleet cut, but let me not slide mutely into my pauper's grave. Let my words live on; let the record relate *how he so doted on me that he must have me dead.* No doubt he, too, would take up his stylus—or hire some fawning prelate to echo his lies—but somewhere in the crevices of this ancient tomb would lie another story, one of a king's hypocrisy, duplicity, murderous cruelty. He would accomplish my death, no doubt, but never avoid his own guilt, *testa me ipso.* I laughed aloud—and felt Amaria start.

"What amuses you, Joy?" She thought me mad with fear.

"I was trying to recall that verse from Edras, something about victory."

"Edras one, three: ten: 'Truth beareth away victory.'"

"That's the one—thank you."

Tic, tac, tee, tee . . .

And my tract must also record the secret heart that beat under my royal vestments. What mattered a scandal after my death? The royal scribes would deflate my worldly accomplishments, no doubt, but no one could challenge my private feelings. Not for nothing was I born granddaughter of the first and most famous troubadour of them all, Duke William IX, infamous for his own scandalous life. Not that my passion ever became the stuff of common gossip, nor were the manufactured rumors ever close to the truth.

Amusing.

Yes, I would tell my dual stories, both the public and the private, with a dual purpose, as Grandfather suggested. "He who writes of his life of passion lives two lives." There, I'd made myself smile, for the true maxim is: "He who writes of his life of *virtue* lives two lives."

My life of virtue would make a short book.

Shall I begin with my birth in Aquitaine? The misery of my parents? The internecine warfare between my aunts and my mother? My father's dour fate? So much, so much. All poignant to me, the rich soil in which I was nurtured, but it was their story, not mine. My childhood was paradise, as I remember it—did the adults shield me from their misery and resentments? I doubt it. I think rather that they all loved me, whatever their other allegiances and resentments toward one another, for love is what makes a child happy, eh? I hoped my own children would remember that. No, my own tale began when I was fifteen, the night when I stepped center stage in the world's drama.

The north wind soughed again, and now it sounded friendly, like the *autun* wind of the south blowing when I became duchess. *Oooo, oooo,* the sigh carried me back, and I slipped into the skin of the earlier Eleanor.

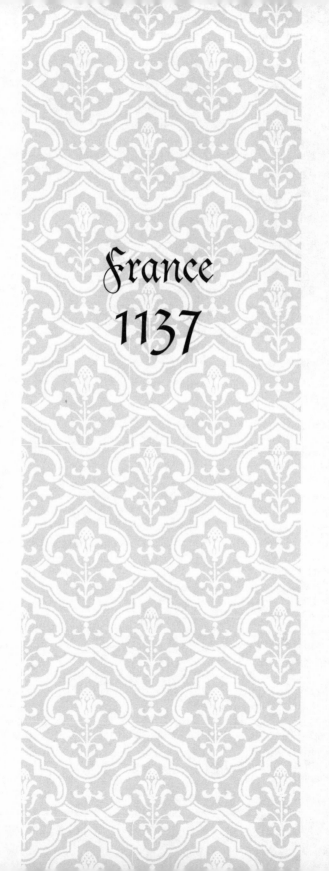

France
1137

1

"Eleanor, run to the tower!"

Who? What? A clatter of hooves on the moat bridge, men's shouts, pounding at the gate.

"Quick!" Aunt Mahaut screamed.

I groped in the dark across snoring bodies.

"Watch where you're stepping!" Petra pushed my leg angrily.

I streaked across the sharp cobbles to Crossbowman Tower.

"Who are they?" Petra sobbed behind me.

"Someone trying to abduct me. Oh!" I stubbed my toe.

Up and up the twisted stair, onto the platform with its crenelated wall, the *autun* wind whipping my braids and tunic. A dust-blurred gibbous moon hung at half-mast.

"Pull down the gate!"

"Wait for your aunts!" Amaria cried.

My aunts and grandmother crowded to the top.

"Everybody, take hold!"

We hung suspended, until gradually the sharp spikes creaked to the stone. I ran to the outer wall to look down.

Aunt Audiart screamed, "Come back! You'll fall!"

Aunt Mahaut pulled my braids. "Pray, Eleanor, pray. Ask God for help!"

"Oh, my heart, I'm too old for such excitement. I can't breathe." My grandmother Dangereuse clutched her chest.

"Father's back! I see Sir Lucain." I shouted. "Father's back from Compostela!"

The rusty gate was harder to push up than it had been to get down.

"Father!" I ran down the treacherous stairs. "Father, I'm here!"

Two hissing pine torches revealed knights in various stages of collapse. A page offered flagons of wine.

"Father? Where's Father?"

Sir Lucain placed his drink on the ground. "Lady Eleanor, greeting."

"Sir Lucain. How did you get back from Compostela so quickly? I didn't expect you until . . . Where's Father? Can you believe, we thought you were knights come to abduct me!"

His head drooped. His voice, raw with wind and dust, was hard to hear. "Lady Eleanor, call Archbishop Geoffrey, if you please."

"I'll go for him." Amaria scuttled into the palace.

"Where's Duke William?" Aunt Mahaut demanded. "Why are you riding in the middle of the night?"

"Yes, why?" I grew chill. "Is something wrong?"

Sir Lucain, eyes black hollows in the flickering orange light, didn't answer.

Archbishop Geoffrey, struggling into his cassock, entered the courtyard.

"Greeting, Sir Lucain. You gave us quite a turn."

Sir Lucain knelt on one knee. "Your Excellency, the duke of Aquitaine is dead these three days. His last words were to protect Eleanor, his daughter and heiress; he said you had instructions."

Amaria swiftly put her arm around me: my aunts pulled Petra to their circle.

"God be merciful," the archbishop murmured. "Dead, did you say? I'm utterly . . . How did it happen?"

"From a polluted stream, just inside Spain."

"No!" Coming out of my trance, I beat on Sir Lucain. "No, it can't be! He couldn't have! I don't believe it!"

Then I became quiet. Of course I believed it, had grown accustomed to the idea since last autumn in Parthenay, when he'd been struck down by a Templar. Abbot Bernard of Clairvaux had met

with Father about a bishop's appointment, and before Father could even present his argument, he'd been attacked like a common criminal. They'd carried him unconscious into the sanctuary, where he'd hovered between life and death for three days. Though I'd nursed him all last winter, he'd never fully recovered from the blow; this pilgrimage had been a futile effort to reclaim his life.

As my aunts gasped and wept, I gazed upward at huge fuzzy stars, white as spots on a peacock's tail, a pulsing red moon, and between Castor and Pollux I beheld a wide silver band, and on that heavenly path, my father trotted slowly on his white destrier. For one poignant moment, he smiled down on me.

"The duke wanted his death kept secret until Lady Eleanor can be invested as duchess," Sir Lucain rasped.

"Yes, of course. Otherwise . . ." The archbishop agreed, horrified.

"She'll be abducted and raped for her lands and title!" Dangereuse screamed.

"She's quite safe here," the archbishop assured her. "Duke William himself noted that the walls of Ombrière Palace are six feet thick."

"Abduction and rape are the ambitious man's way to seize power," I said, echoing my father's warnings. "He wanted me to marry when he returned from Compostela. We discussed it shortly before he left."

"Did he have someone in mind?" Archbishop Geoffrey asked.

Of course he did, and so did I, if only the intention had been formalized. "Yes, except that . . ." My throat tightened. "I understand that I must wed . . . one of our own, a baron here in Aquitaine. Someone—"

"But first the investiture," the archbishop cautioned, "at once, before the barons learn about the death. Somehow we must get her to Poitiers for the ceremony."

"You'll need a strong guard." Sir Lucain ran his hands through his stubbled hair. "Duke William said to ask your overlord, the king of France, to protect her until her husband can do so. Of course, he must approve her choice."

"A formality," the archbishop said stiffly. "As her guardian, I believe I have some say as well."

Their voices bounced in my head as if we were in a hollow well, echoing and repeating.

"Nevertheless, we ride to Paris yet tonight." Sir Lucain refused our hospitality. "I'll return as soon as I have the king's word. My lady Eleanor." He bowed.

Again the gate opened, fresh hooves pounded on the narrow bridge, and we were alone.

Within a few hours, I noticed that everyone had become suspiciously deferential. Because of my grief? Even Petra let me win at parchisi. "Will I continue to live with you?" she asked casually.

"Of course." I smiled at her pinched face. She was a sweet thirteen-year-old, except when she was worried. "You're still my sister."

"Your father was most generous to my convent at Maillezais," Aunt Agnes injected stiffly from behind me.

"I'll continue to support Maillezais, Aunt, provided you cease beating your novices with chains."

She flushed. "They flagellate themselves as they wish; I certainly make no such demands."

"Of course, Maillezais is hardly more than a grain mill," Aunt Mahaut noted, "while my abbey at Fontevrault attracts the greatest ladies of Europe."

Provided them sanctuary when their husbands discarded them was what she meant. Aunt Mahaut was the abbess of that well-endowed abbey.

"I suppose I'll continue to live in Maubergeonne Tower?" Dangereuse asked.

"Where else would you live?"

Surely she couldn't go back to her real husband after all these years. She'd been my grandfather's concubine.

Then suddenly I comprehended: I was the sole caretaker of these ladies, all of them unmarried, unlike my five other aunts;

even my friend Amaria had asked me this very morning if she could be my handmaid.

I'd hardly understood her. "You mean you want to be my marriage prize?"

Amaria's father was poor and he had six older daughters. I would happily give her a dowry.

"No!" She'd spoken intensely. "I want to stay with you always; that way, I can write verse."

"What kind of verse? Troubadour songs? Romances like *Tristan*?"

We'd both been thrilled when Béroul had sung his famous tale of tragic lovers in Poitiers last summer.

Her flush had deepened. "I'd like that, of course, but I thought at first shorter romances, what they call *lais*."

I'd touched her braid. "And I'll be your sponsor. I'd be honored to take you as my handmaid, Amaria."

Now my female entourage became quiet, secure in their new overlord. Together, we huddled against the fierce wind; together, we watched the moon wane, the stars shift ever so slightly in their dusty field, and on the fifth day, Sir Lucain returned.

This time, he arrived in midday, more dead than alive. His horse stumbled across the half-empty moat, where a mule's carcass had become visible. Again he slumped in the courtyard, and again we gave him wine.

He raised bloodshot eyes. "You're going to be married."

"But first the investiture," Archbishop Geoffrey said. "We've been working on the ceremony."

Sir Lucain held his cup for more wine. "Married at once. Then the investiture."

The archbishop raised his brows. "Should I send for Baron Hugh of Lusignan? He's a competent administrator, and marriage might cool his rebellion."

"He's fat!" Petra scoffed.

"No," Sir Lucain answered, "you're marrying the prince of France, Lady Eleanor. Louis, prince of France."

I was too dumbfounded to speak.

"He's on his way at this moment," Sir Lucain continued, "with a huge army. France will take Aquitaine under her protection. That's King Louis the Fat's decision."

"No!" I shrieked. "I won't marry anyone but a baron of Aquitaine—my father wanted it!"

And I fainted dead away, thereby gashing my head badly. No one thought to catch me; I'd never swooned before and was not given to vapors. And perhaps this wasn't a real faint, for I continued to hear their voices.

"It's a belated reaction to her father's death."

"*Oc,* that must be it. They were so devoted, so close. After Anor and young Aigret died—oh dear."

"Someone fetch water!"

Their voices became faint, then faded altogether. The dull gray sky brightened and began to flutter. Round-winged white butterflies filled the heavens in a nervous search, and gradually they parted, revealing a vale of deep, furry green. My breath caught—I knew where I was—on that last *chevauchée* with Father, when we'd visited the castle at Taillebourg.

"Oh look!" I'd cried. "On that scarp—could it be a castle?"

"Taillebourg, the strongest fortress in all Aquitaine, owned by my captain, Baron Richard of Rancon. He's expecting us."

The valley had rung with the clash of stags' horns, the splash of hooves in olive green water, and the scent of lavender had filled the air. Baron Richard of Rancon had ridden forth to greet us, tall and sinewy in his short brown tunic emblazoned with the studded lion of Taillebourg. His unruly hair had fallen across eyes glittering like black diamonds.

"Greeting." He'd taken my hand, and my heart had stopped.

In single file, we'd followed him up the tortuous path, now dark as death, now a blinding gold against the setting sun. Later, high in the small great hall, with windows open to a cerise sky and the blue curve of the Atlantic in the distance, he'd taken his lute. I

could no longer meet those hot eyes; my gaze lowered to his blunt, calloused fingers, then to his boots, laced to his knees.

> *Joy hurls daggers at my heart—*
> *Blood flows freely from each chamber—*
> *While I breathe I use my art*
> *And hurl my song to claim her!*

He's singing to me! My heart had thundered in my ears.

Then those calloused fingers had again taken my hand; he'd wanted to present me with a special gift and, with my father's permission, he led me higher still, to a tiny stable with only three stalls.

"I bred this filly just for you," he'd whispered.

"An Andalusian?"

"Crossed with an Arab. I call her Iseult—remember?"

How could I forget that magic night when we'd listened, side by side, to Béroul strum his famous romance?

"She's beautiful," I'd murmured, "only she deserves a more honest name."

"You don't believe that love is honest?"

I couldn't meet his eyes. "*Oc*, only in the romance, Iseult must drink the magic potion before she knows she loves Tristan, whereas—"

"True love needs no potion," he'd agreed ardently.

And he'd kissed me, again and again, branded me with his lion studs forever.

"Don't look at me," he'd groaned. "Your eyes impale me."

Then the gloom had enclosed us; no image had remained but our fiery lips and our whispers to love forever, to be together for all time, fated lovers.

When he'd ridden out with us upon our leaving, he'd held my hand brazenly. After he'd left, Father had smiled.

"Is it Rancon, Joy?"

"Yes!" I'd looked on him fearfully. "I hope you agree! Ever since he came to train with you, since we were children . . ."

He'd stroked my cheek. "I'm glad, my best knight. It's what I always wanted."

Water struck my face. A hand stroked my brow.

"Joy, dear, are you all right?"

Aunt Mahaut wiped blood from my wound.

I struggled upward. "I'm fine, thank you, only . . ."

Sir Lucain's voice resumed its argument. "Forget Hugh of Lusignan or anyone else. You can't deny an army of five hundred. They'll be here within days."

Archbishop Geoffrey strongly protested that the French prince would bring political disaster to Aquitaine.

"Frenchmen are papists at heart, and therefore against female rule," he warned, "which means that Lady Eleanor may be deprived of her sovereignty."

Sir Lucain remained silent.

"Louis the Fat kept the rightful heiress of England from taking the throne," the archbishop reminded us.

"Matilda of Normandy," I concurred. "The French, the duke of Champagne, all the northerners were against her."

"Perhaps the prince is more tolerant," Sir Lucain finally muttered.

"And perhaps not! In any case, the government is in the hands of Abbot Suger of Saint-Denis. The king and surely the prince are his pawns," Archbishop Geoffrey warned.

I shuddered. Another abbot.

"Suger, like his name, sugar-coated! Beneath, he's a nougat of pure poison! Don't let him beguile you, my lady."

He went on in the direst terms about how this ambitious little abbot had risen from a dung heap to the topmost position in France, and how he'd long coveted Aquitaine, the richest duchy under France's rule.

Arguments were bootless; an army was on its way.

"As we are seen, so are we esteemed!" Grandmother Dangereuse held a diaphanous green tunic to her face. "Does it bring out my eyes?"

As if she were the one going to the hanging tree.

"Not at all. Your eyes are blue, Grandmother."

"Like yours, only not so dark. Nevertheless, place it to your face and look in Junior's mirror."

I picked up my grandfather's silver-backed mirror, brought back from his Crusade.

"The image is blurred."

"The silver's worn, I grant you. Tilt it so you see the upper-right corner."

A single eye, what my father had described as deep and blue as the Atlantic in August and what Petra said was the shape of a scarab. I held the glass lower: a round polished cheek, rosy as an apple, but the green managed to make my skin appear sallow, not that I cared. A pox on being "esteemed." In any case, Grandmother was a better guide to my appearance than a dull glass, since everyone said we looked exactly alike. I hoped so. She'd been the most beautiful woman in the duchy, maybe in the world, with vivid coloring, high cheekbones, pursed red lips always turned in a faint smile, which some thought enticing, others lascivious.

"Try another, Grandmother, and I'll look. We're the same height and coloring."

She held a creamy sendal tunic with an *orofois* band at the pointed neckline and rose brocade inserts to the waist.

"No wonder Grandfather stole you from your husband. I would, too!" I said.

She laughed. "He stole you, as well—he thought of you as our daughter. How he doted on you!" She held a triple strand of pearls against the tunic "Too bad he died before you developed your voice."

"What voice? I don't sing."

"When you speak, my dear, I hear the rich string of a viol. The voice runs in your family, all of you descendants of Orpheus. Yes, this is better, and an eagle brooch at your shoulder to represent Aquitaine, and to fasten this drapery from Rome. Hold it to your eyes!"

Midmorning, and I sat stiffly on the cushioned bench in our great hall, surrounded by my five aunts, my sister, my new hand-maid Amaria, my grandmother Dangereuse, Archbishop Geoffrey of Bordeaux, and assorted functionaries from Poitiers. I pressed my pounding temples.

"Careful, dear!" Dangereuse rearranged my lace mantilla. "Turn your face this way." She smoothed my brows with a bit of spittle. "You would be the most beguiling young lady in the universe with just one pretty smile. Try?"

I withered her with a scowl. Archbishop Geoffrey gave way to a fit of coughing. Soon everyone in the great hall was hacking in chorus.

Aye, well may they choke, I thought, to see Aquitaine sucked into the greedy French maw, not to mention my own bleeding person.

Suddenly, the coughing stopped, as did breathing. In the distance, French fanfare sounded, then the wooden horns of Aquitaine, the slow creak of gates, the mumble of foreign voices, the hiss of drag-ging trains, the soft thud of velvet boots. Dangereuse quickly knelt before me to spread my skirt. I cast my eyes downward to a crack in the tiles, where a small lizard flicked his tongue.

The French party entered the hall in a cloud of rancid armpits, bad breath, and mildewed silk. One sword rattled in a scabbard redolent of oil and rust. Then a line of velvet boots obscured the crack.

Everyone bowed and muttered fawning greetings; my family and counselors answered in kind, but I remained silent. The shoes to my left, actually rope sandals, stepped forward. By the gray linen tunic, I knew it must be the infamous Abbot Suger of Saint-Denis, seneschal to Louis the Fat and the true ruler of France. I looked

upward, and for a long moment we appraised each other. He gasped, no doubt surprised at my reputed beauty, then frowned at my expression. No fool, this abbot; I clapped my eyelids together like the covers of a book. But not before I'd noted his face—a heart-shaped triangle with a broad forehead, pointed chin, luminous eyes, round pink cheeks, and a benevolent smile. Though not young, he had no wrinkles and his brows were dark.

He began to speak over my head. "My dear Eleanor . . ." And I looked upward again; he was addressing Archbishop Geoffrey, clearly doubting that I could follow his Vulgar Latin.

". . . soon to be duchess and princess of the fairest land in all the world, and to all her learned counselors and family, greeting from King Louis the Fat of France, who regrets he cannot be here in person. He sends condolences for your recent loss, which was our loss as well, for Duke William of Aquitaine was ever a valued vassal of France."

The man at the opposite end of the line cleared his throat—*ahem*—in obvious disagreement. Now who would that be?

Suger hastily continued: "We have prayed for him daily at Matins and Vespers as we rushed with all due haste through these perilous lands to claim the lily of Aquitaine. . . ."

Long-winded hypocrite. Vain little popinjay. Look at the fit on that tunic, tailored by the best, I trowe, and the jewel in that sand-colored turban. A real topaz?

"Braving the broiling sun and the equally broilsome Aquitanian barons, we have traveled only at night and hidden like fugitives during the daytime hours, but at last we have arrived, exhausted perhaps, but even more exhilarated by the momentous event before us, the uniting of your duchy with the glorious dynasty of France, which traces its lineage to the great Charlemagne himself."

I bristled. Wasn't my family also descended from Charlemagne? Suger instantly amended his words.

"Two equally great houses made one."

He turned to his neighbor; his sloping forehead and chin created a profile sharp as a chisel.

"I present Raoul, count of Vermandois, the prince's cousin and political seneschal of France."

Dressed in watered sendal shaded in orange and gold, Raoul of Vermandois radiated youth, charm, and sophistication; black waves fell across his forehead, and he had a dimple in his chin.

"My lady Eleanor," he said in honeyed northern French, "may I add my personal regrets for your irreparable loss; I can only hope that, in the days and weeks to come, a new happiness may gradually erase the corroding effects of grief. My own daughter Leonore is marrying this summer, and I often advise her that marriage is the balm of life, for a wedding gives you a new family to sustain you. I promise you, my dear duchess, that we of France will do all we can to make you welcome and happy within our embrace."

I was mildly surprised that he had a daughter old enough to wed, and some overemphasis made me wonder if his marriage was the balm of his life.

Next to Count Raoul stood my future husband, but Suger blessedly didn't introduce him yet, and I was able to pass over his inert figure with glazed eyes.

In another wordy speech, Suger was extolling the great French dukes, and there followed a catalogue of reasons that none but Thibault of Champagne had been able to attend.

Thibault of Champagne was the man who had cleared his throat at the mention of my father's name. Now he bowed slightly, swinging his heavy jeweled cape, which matched the jeweled hat hugging his head like a glove. He wore a large cross sparkling with rare rubies. An impressive figure, if his expression had not been so dour, his eyes so unforgiving.

"I had the honor to fight against your father," he said dryly.

I stiffened; surely he meant *with* my father.

"In Normandy," he continued, "when he followed the misguided policy of aiding Geoffrey of Anjou in his bootless quest for power for his son Henry."

"Bootless," because the claim had been based on a woman, Matilda of Normandy. I listened to his tone, not his words, the cold mettle of the man.

"However, such issues were before your time," Thibault ended with a poor attempt at a smile. "We are delighted to enfold the daughter of our former adversary, for we understand that no *woman* can be held responsible."

Meaning women were not fit to reign, not in England, not in Aquitaine. Poor Thibault, he would have to make a volte-face when I took over.

Suger's voice brought me back to the drooping plant in the middle of their group.

"And this, of course, is Louis of France, one day to be King Louis the Seventh, with you as his queen."

It took all my training and a clear sense of protocol to refrain from bolting at once. God's feet, what a disaster, worse than I could possibly have imagined. Quickly, I tried to find arguments in his favor, for this mooncalf was my future husband! He wasn't fat, though he was stooped and hollow-chested as an old man; he wasn't bald, though his hair was dank as seaweed; his eyes seemed sincere, though red-rimmed and bleary; his glistening pale skin was blotched—no doubt the sun; his tunic was a rich blue silk, though with a stain in front shaped like the state of Denmark and an unraveled hem; he had teeth in his loose mouth, though they were uneven and slightly brown. Then, breathing hard, he began a constipated mumble through a clenched jaw.

"Because my father is ill with the flux which might have been brought on by eels which he eats in quantity though the doctors have told him not to because, you see, his stomach has been delicate ever since his stepmother tried to murder him with poison when he was a boy . . ."

Dangereuse gasped in astonishment.

"So because of the flux he can't sit on a horse, you see, but he sent you these."

The French made way for a page to place an open casket of uncut jewels before me; the lizard, I noted, scuttled toward a potted hibiscus.

There was a long, awkward pause as I waited to see if Louis was finished. He was.

"We thank you and your lord father the king. I shall treasure them always," I said in bell-clear classical Latin.

I saw Suger start.

I gestured to the palace. "You must want to see your quarters after such an arduous journey."

Suger shook his head. "Not at all. We can wait a little longer, I assure you; we couldn't rest properly until we settle the time and terms of the coming nuptials. If you please."

A French page produced a scroll, which Suger gave to Archbishop Geoffrey. "That is our wedding contract, which we trust you will find acceptable."

I gestured to Bishop Peter of Poitiers, who likewise produced a scroll. "And these are our terms, Abbot Suger," I said sweetly.

Suger smiled. "I have no doubt that the two papers are identical." He glanced at Louis, who was swaying with fatigue. "All we need to settle is the date. When are we to be joined?"

As if we were oxen. "Two weeks hence. When we spied your campfires across the Garonne last night, we sent runners to my barons—everything is in readiness." I, too, stared at Louis.

"Perhaps we should discuss the contract now," I added. Deliberately, I unrolled the French document, leaving him no alternative but to look at ours. The hour rang once, then again, before I raised my eyes. The weary French guests shuffled from one foot to the other, leaned on one another, half-asleep.

"Very few differences," Suger said again.

I disagreed. "Though I am political vassal to King Louis the Fat, my possessions and wealth far outstrip those of France. Therefore, I cannot accept the prince as duke of Aquitaine. I am the duchess, he my duke consort, and I will control my duchy absolutely."

"But when you're in Paris . . ."

"My uncle Ralph of Châtellerault will be my seneschal."

"I was not aware that you had an uncle."

Liar.

"I have two uncles; Ralph is the son of my grandmother and brother to my dead mother; my father's brother is Raymond, prince of Antioch."

"Antioch?"

"In the Holy Land," I said dryly.

"Nevertheless, Louis must rule your duchy." Suger drew himself up. "I myself have trained the prince. . . ."

"As my father trained me. I signed my first legal paper when I was eight."

"But to lead an army . . ."

"I have my own captain, Richard of Rancon, baron of Taille-bourg. Furthermore, I shall control tallages, rentals, water rights, shipping, agriculture, as well as the appointment of bishops, plus absolute control of my treasuries here in Bordeaux and in Melle. Is that clear?"

He fanned himself with my contract. "Splendidly. Oh dear, I'm not as green-tailed as I once was; I must concede to your youth. At least you'll indulge me on the religious portion, which is my special domain. You will be wed at Saint-André's Cathedral, I presume?"

"No."

"It's a hideous old pile, I agree, nothing like my new chapel at Saint-Denis, but . . ."

"Not in any church at all, Abbot Suger. Marriage is a civil cere-mony."

His little mouth fell open. "Then Aquitaine is far behind France in this matter, for marriage is a sacrament recognized by Rome. Your marriage will be sanctified, I assure you, or I shall see that the king assigns you to someone else."

A threat—this slippery elf would happily send me to some remote northern stretch with a rough oaf wearing bearskins. Well,

what did it matter? The ceremony would be over in a moment, while the civil portion would last forever.

I conceded "Very well."

He glanced at his company. "I like your spirit, I truly do, and I know you'll make France a great queen. Now, however, if we might retire . . ."

"Your chambers are prepared." I summoned a page, then rose. The French gasped as I expected them to. I wore the creamy sendal, but it was my Roman scarf that took their breath. A silken fall, it was embroidered with the lily of France, but in the center a huge fierce seed-pearl eagle of Aquitaine clutched the lilies in his talons. I turned slowly on floating steps and faced Prince Louis of France.

I paused in dismay.

His eyes, on a level with mine, pooled with water, while his blotches deepened to a dangerous magenta. His shallow breath rattled, his head drooped forward and his knees gave way. Count Raoul barely prevented him from falling, while Abbot Suger propped him from the rear.

"He's tired!" the Abbot gasped.

"He's never done this before," Raoul apologized, "except under certain trees, such as the helm oak, where he usually has his visions."

Visions? Under helm oaks? As if they were the helms of ships? What did he mean? My groom gasped like a fish, his lips round and bubbled; mucus dripped from his nose. And I had my own vision of a succubus. Quickly, I turned away.

Oh Father, I thought, help me! With all our lessons, you never taught me how I could bear what lies ahead. Palaver and jousting, contracts and armies, kings and dukes—what does all that matter when we are naked in the bedchamber? Who will instruct me how to bear the carnal act with this damp scallion?

"I won't marry him!" I screamed. "I'll kill myself before I let him touch me!"

"Marriage is the balm of life," Aunt Isabelle crooned, forgetting how she'd been beaten by her harridan of a mother-in-law.

"You fall in love after marriage," Aunt Beatrice concurred. "And the blessing of children, oh my dear."

"My children can share their father's chamber, where they can all wet the bed together!"

"Leave her to me," Dangereuse ordered. "I'll bring her around."

My aunts shuffled out.

"Now, Joy," my grandmother said sternly, "who is he?"

"You saw—the prince of France. I wager he'll become fat, on top of everything else!"

"Don't pretend you don't understand. You love someone—his name, please."

"Oh, Grandmother, you're the only one who understands love, the only one in the whole family. I can't give him up! I won't!"

"Give up whom, dear?"

But something in her voice warned me. "Never mind his name. A baron."

"A baron? When you have a future king in your palm? How far has it gone?"

Slowly, with many tears, I confessed my poor truncated affair, though I omitted how it had begun even in childhood. I'd always loved Rancon; he was like the famous mote in the eye, never to be removed.

"Like troubadour love, the way Grandfather felt when he abducted you from your castle."

"Note that you speak of how Junior felt about me, not how I felt about him." Her still-luscious lips curled.

For a moment, I was startled out of myself. "You loved him, didn't you? Why else would you . . ."

"Certainly I loved him, but I tell you truly, my dear, that I wouldn't have left a count if William hadn't been a duke. No woman can afford to be careless."

"Grandmother!"

She shrugged. "Oh, I know he wrote poems of troubadour love, always adulterous, but you note that he wrote from a man's point of view. A woman who is rapt by a married man must be vigilant on her own behalf."

She then recounted how she'd applied the same lesson to her daughter Anor, whom she'd forced to marry the duke's son, my father, so her own position couldn't be challenged by the duke's jealous children. I'd heard the tale from my mother, who was that same Anor, of course, but never in this context.

"And now you're my security," she finished. "The powerful future queen of France."

I pulled away, sorry I'd confessed as much as I had.

"Don't despair, sweets," she comforted me. "You'll learn to love Louis and forget your silly childish affair; the bed is a great persuader."

Dully, I realized that my fate was sealed. There would be no grand rescue from anyone, no help from my own family. Yet I knew I was right: Love existed, and the emotion couldn't be denied. Arranged marriages were uniformly disastrous, witness my father and mother. Yet if infidelity was the answer for men, why was it not the same for women?

2

*W*ithin days after the French had arrived, my vassals began to ride into Bordeaux. The townspeople were deliriously happy at the celebration which would make them rich. A succulent pall of smoke hung over the streets as pigs, chickens, and ducks turned on the spits, pastry hawkers put up booths, and houses hung newly painted signs offering hospitality; hundreds of people would press through the streets for gaiety and profit.

Three days before the wedding, my uncle Ralph of Châtellerault galloped at breakneck speed across the moat.

"Eleanor, the Lusignan brothers are planning to abduct you!" he shouted.

To rape me in order to force a marriage and seize Aquitaine. Even Louis was preferable.

"They plan to attack the wedding party when you leave the nuptial feast. Your marriage will never be consummated."

"Call Suger," I ordered a page.

The small abbot listened attentively. "How long is the feast intended to last?"

"All night for the guests. I had thought our party would ride away shortly after None."

"How much time would we gain if you left directly from the church?"

"Perhaps five hours."

"And is there a fortress nearby where you could be housed? We mustn't stay in open camp."

"Richard of Rancon would give us hospitality, I'm sure," my uncle said quickly. "Taillebourg Castle could hold off a large army."

Suger was watching me. "Didn't you say he was your captain?"

I could barely speak. "Of course, you're right." His frown deepened. "It's just that . . . the last time I was in Taillebourg, I was with my father."

"Then I advise that you arrange it. Call Raoul of Vermandois."

Raoul arrived, was introduced to my handsome uncle, and we all sat to take our instructions from Abbot Suger: No one but present company was to know of our scheme, except my sister Petronilla. The wedding feast would be arranged here in Bordeaux as planned, but the bride and groom would not attend. Raoul of Vermandois and Petronilla would stand in for us while Louis and I rode straight to Taillebourg, where another feast would be waiting, and where I would spend my wedding night.

Petra was extremely excited about her share in the plot. "Is there anything you want me to say to your guests, Joy?"

"Ask them to pray for me, that's all."

"Maybe Louis won't be so bad."

"So bad as what, dear? Vipers are better than cobras, I believe; they take less time to chew their victims."

"I grant you that he speaks strangely, but he's somewhat handsome."

"We must test your eyes."

"Joy, since Father died, am I your marriage prize?"

I pushed her golden braids, a shade lighter than mine. "Why yes, I suppose you are. And a very desirable one, too, since he left you rich Burgundian estates." She was also an exceedingly pretty damsel, a creamy rose, if you could avoid her prickly thorns.

"Promise you won't make me marry against my will."

"Never! You know I won't, on our mother's soul. You'll tell me when you're ready."

"And I can choose my own groom?"

"Didn't I just say so?"

"Thank you, Joy. I feel better."

Better than I did, certainly, and I would find her someone better than Louis, drier anyway.

◆

My wedding day, when I would turn from a maid to a wife, second only in importance to the day I turned from a wife to a mother. I hardly recognized myself in my grandfather's crusader's mirror. Grandmother Dangereuse had matched my bruised eyes exactly with a light brush of heliotrope on my lids—though these eyes would never follow the sun—and the rose of the mallow faintly flushed my high round cheeks and lips. *Oc,* a transplanted garden, concealing the wormwood within.

Below in the courtyard stood a gilded longcart with wheels covered in flowers and sides draped with white satin fringed with pearls. On the back, the same fierce eagle that I wore on my headpiece spread his golden wings protectively. Pages hoisted me upward, where I held carved ivory lilies for balance. Before me, four white horses were richly caparisoned with swan feathers, as if they might soar over the city.

When the gates opened, a vast roar of voices drowned the bells and panicked the horses. Guards struggled to hold the animals, and I calmly studied the outline of the low buildings above me, which, by a curious trick of light, appeared blood-red and throbbed in the same rhythm as my own heart. Incredibly, as the sound grew and the cart moved, the red turned to sea green; I rose and fell in waves, sucked out to sea. From all sides, my name swished in my ears, but I kept my eyes forward, as befits a lady going to her own execution.

In the church square, the crowd threatened to become a mob in its enthusiasm. Everywhere I heard "Joy! I love you, Joy! I pray for you!" For a few giddy moments, I thought I was back on a *chevauchée*

with my father and I was happy. Surely his spirit hovered somewhere in the angel gauze above me. Then an aisle was created by
my guard, a stairs was brought forth, and I descended to the long
velvet carpet leading to the church doors.

I paused under the tympanum, then plunged into chill air and
darkness.

Gradually, my eyes adjusted. The crowd inside the sanctuary
almost rivaled that in the square, and I was aware of familiar faces,
the Faidit brothers, Lord Aimar from Limoges, the lords of
Angoulême, all of them either related or seeming to be related, for
the men had been boys in our palace, under the tutelage of my
father, and my brothers; my own vast family, my childhood female
friends—none of them yet wed—the good people of Poitiers,
Baron Lézay from Talmont, the natives of Melle, of Parthenay,
everyone it seemed I'd ever known in my entire life, except Hugh,
Guy, and Geoffrey, the Lusignan brothers.

But there were also the five hundred Frenchmen who'd taken
the long journey, most of whom I'd not met. A large area had been
cleared and blocked off by flowers for the wedding party, and here
were Frenchmen I did know, among them, foremost in the center
and turned to me, the man who was to be my husband.

I hardly recognized him. I still would not say he was handsome, but neither was he the freak I'd met in the great hall two
weeks before. Standing straight and tall, he appeared the seventeen years he was, not an old man, and his blond hair was shiny,
his face clear, his costume of white and blue pressed and clean.
Only his eyes remained the same, filled with incredulous pleasure
and panic.

Behind the altar stood Archbishop Geoffrey of Bordeaux in his
white-and-gold surplice. He conveyed reassurance.

Scuffing on my jeweled slippers, I took my place beside Louis. A
tiny silvery tinkle signaled that the ceremony had begun. Archbishop Geoffrey's right eyelid twitched nervously, for he was as
concerned about this strange ritual as I was. I'd told Suger the

truth when I'd said that we didn't consider marriage a sacrament here in Aquitaine, partly because the Church itself felt that the sexual joining of a man and a woman was an inappropriate event for holy blessing, partly because a marriage is obviously a *dispensatio*, a civil arrangement between two families.

In fact, I wasn't sure that the tiny abbot had been so forthcoming in his claim to the contrary; the French priests accompanying the royal party knew of no marriage Mass, and Archbishop Geoffrey had been forced to create his own ritual from bits and pieces of other Masses. First, however, we would dispense with the civil portion, which by rights should have been performed at the church door. I'm creating precedent, I thought; my wedding will be the model for all to follow. I could not say the same for the married state—a chill pricked my arms.

"Bless you, my children." The archbishop made the sign of the cross before my face, then Louis's. He read from the redrawn contract: "By the grace of God above, His Son, Lord Jesus, His representative on earth, the Holy Father who resides in Rome"—I winced, for my family no longer recognized the Pope in Rome—"I hereby state that you are absolved of the sin of incest, and though you are cousins to the fourth degree and the Church prohibits the marriage of cousins to the seventh degree, I waive the prohibition; consanguinity can be no issue between you for so long as you both shall live."

Thank God Louis was not my blood relation. I'm proud of my family, both those living and all my forebears.

"We hereby acknowledge Eleanor, duchess of Aquitaine, to be the sole sovereign in her duchy, to rule as she sees fit, with no interference from outside influences, howsoever they may be related to her by this marriage. Furthermore, her progeny shall be the sole heirs, or, if she should die without issue, her rights will revoke to her nearest of blood kin without challenge. Louis, prince of France, hereby waives all claim to Aquitaine."

He glanced up; Louis murmured that he agreed.

"Furthermore, all incomes derived from the duchy's enterprises remain solely in the hands of said duchess to dispose of as she sees fit."

Louis once more agreed. Everything sounded correct. Why did I feel apprehension?

"The vassals of Aquitaine owe homage to the duchess, not to France; only she owes homage to the king of France."

This ended the civil portion.

Again the bell rang, and Louis and I knelt at the altar for the Mass. A single male voice chanted as everyone prepared for the religious ceremony.

"*Domine Jesu Christe,* I give you my peace, I leave you my peace, and I pray instantly that Thou wilt unite these two in holy matrimony after Thy will. . . ." The archbishop kissed the chalice. "Teach them and show them through the holy passion of our Lord the peace given by God and all human lineage."

Though I knew well that "passion" referred to the death of Jesus, I objected to the word in this setting.

"Will you each kiss the corporal, after each other, in a token of love and concord to the end that even as flesh joineth itself to flesh, and spirit to spirit, let you be united in the virtue of love."

With another chill, I kissed the wafer.

The archbishop beat his breast. *"Domine, non sum dignus et intre sub tectum meum."*

"Amen," Louis and I repeated, which meant that we were not worthy to have the Lord enter our house. A strange statement—was this part of the archbishop's improvised service?

The priest dipped his finger in wine and sprinkled it before us. "Peace be with you in love. Peace be with you in the glory and bliss of paradise."

Which was an orison for the dead. I had an unholy impulse to laugh.

And so it went for an hour, more and more disjointed in meaning, and my attention wandered. I thought of my aching knees on the hard stone, listened to the pleasant coo of pigeons in the

rafters, wondered at Petra's strange radiance today, as if she were the bride herself, and tried not to envision the wedding feast at Rancon's castle.

A Gregorian chant brought me back to the present. Louis rose, but I remained in my same position.

"As man is subject to God, so is woman subject to man. A submissive wife is the root of a happy household. To symbolize her willingness to follow God's will, which is to say her husband's will, the bride will herewith prostrate herself before her new lord and master."

Petra and Amaria helped me stretch myself across the cold stone. A column of ants climbed over my eagle headpiece, carrying crumbs from Christ's body. More Latin was intoned and Petra touched my shoulder. I rose as gracefully as I could.

"To signify the husband's possession of his wife, he shall place a ring on her finger three times."

With my eyes down, I held out my left hand. I could feel Louis's cold sweat even through my glove.

"With this ring, I take thee as chattel and promise to govern and chastise thee as I see fit," he said through tight jaws.

He slipped the ring on and off my forefinger.

"With this ring, I take thee as my conjugal partner, for the Lord has ordered us to wax and multiply."

The same ring on and off my second finger.

"With this ring, I thee wed and promise to be a good and faithful husband until death do us part."

This time, the ring remained on my third finger.

Next, the gold. Louis turned to receive a small sack from Suger, which he then offered to me.

"According to Salic law, I purchase you with thirteen dinari, the gold in this bag."

I passed it to Bishop Peter to be distributed among the poor. Another movement from Suger, and Louis pressed a key into my palm. "Accept this as my wedding portion, a castle in the county of Berry."

We were pronounced man and wife.

Outside, the skies had become overcast. Listening to the jubilant cries of the crowd, looking at the city now leached of all color, I wondered at the changes two short hours could bring about. Aquitaine, like my girlhood, seemed a receding port—I was on a blank sea.

We rode briskly toward Ombrière Palace, but at the last moment, the French—now including me—veered from the main party and crossed the bridge spanning the Garonne River. As Petra and Raoul of Vermandois took our place at the head of the guests, I caught the startled reaction among my vassals, but it happened too quickly for anyone to comment. On the far side of the river, we were joined by a large army of Aquitanian knights, some from Rancon's fortress, others from Niort and Angoulême.

Then suddenly, Rancon pushed forward, the baron of Taillebourg in his rich brown tunic with its snarling golden lion. One glance at his tragic face told me I was not alone.

Beside me, the limp celery stalk clung desperately to the mane of his horse, let flee strange gurgling pops like bubbles bursting in a moat.

I fought faintness and wondered if my humors had changed as a result of this odious marriage. We sped across the landscape, crossed the narrow Roman bridge spanning the Charente River, descended briefly into the verdant vale, where we faced the forbidding scarp of Taillebourg. Again, Rancon led us up the narrow ledge carved into the rock, straight up to the hot howl of wind. My headdress rose and pulled my hair upward, my skirts flew, grit filled my eyes and mouth, and everyone seemed without color or substance. Then we reached the small perch that served as a courtyard.

Suger hurried us to an inner courtyard surrounded on four sides by the castle itself, where we were able to straighten our tunics and hair. I bathed my hot face and wrists; Amaria pinned my headdress in place, for the eagle was slightly askew. The French fanfare summoned us to the feast—our last Station of the Cross. Inside the

same courtyard, tables had been set in tiers. For the first time, I took my place beside Louis, with Amaria on my left. We were inside a hot, still cocoon with *autun* winds raging above and around us. How could we hear anything in the midst of this shriek? How I missed Petronilla, who was even now playing hostess to a similar feast in Bordeaux, with Raoul standing in for Louis. Tears of self-pity stung my eyes, as if being without my sister a few days was the worst calamity I faced.

Abbot Suger droned interminable prayers, which gave me ample time to scan the table setting. The purpose of the feast was to tit-illate Louis and me for our first conjugal night together. To our right stretched a long forest with miniature trees and caves filled with wood-carved satyrs and naked ladies. The ladies were sup-posed to be fleeing the satyrs: Run, damsels, run!

Suger's drone ended; Louis's hand reached to accept the ewerer's towel.

The first course was a gluey boar's head. I turned away, sickened.

Louis, however, devoured every morsel. Before each bite, he whispered, *"Sanctus, sanctus, sanctus,"* and made the sign of the cross before his lips, which should have impeded his eating but didn't; he seemed ravenous.

The second course reeked of pig bladder.

"You're not eating, Joy," Amaria remarked. "Are you not feeling well?"

I shot her a withering look.

The third course was comprised of rank tunny. Was this some subtle plot to nauseate us?

At last, the table was cleared—I breathed again—and, with a great show of silver plate, the wine was wheeled on. On a cart stood a miniature mountain with caves spouting streams of wine, except that the spouts were carved suspiciously like male members, which dispensed blood-red claret. This was the beginning of the tit-illation.

Then I heard a familiar *STRRRM*. Before me stood Rancon, now garbed in the white and green of the troubadour; his dark features

curled like a wildcat on the attack. I clasped my hands tight under the table to conceal their trembling, but I couldn't conceal a rush of tears or the flush I could feel rising to my cheeks. He flourished low before me, so close I could have touched his tumbling hair. I was entranced by his long black lashes and the juice of his lips. For three heartbeats, he looked at me, sick soul to sick soul.

Oh mirror, once I saw myself in you,
Heard my sighs echo like a fool;
But when I leaned to do what I must do,
Like Narcissus, I perished in my pool.

He turned in a circle as his deep basso echoed through the hall. Then he strummed before us again, his voice now raised in a haunting countertenor.

Thus do I fall into despair,
Into disgrace;
Was I a fool to cross the bridge?
Did I mistake my place?

No, you did not! And for one glorious moment, our eyes held. Louis turned to me. "Is that man your lover?"
My heart fluttered and my breath grew shallow. "N-no! Of course not. His song—his song is merely the troubadour convention." I was frightened by Louis's cold, sanctimonious face, then wild with rage. What had I done except to sacrifice my happiness forever?
Suddenly, everyone jumped at the deafening clatter of the wooden clappers from all sides, and here came the dwarfs. Naked to the waist and painted blue, with their lower halves in animal skins, these little men made a living going from wedding to wedding; they were highly skilled in naughty gestures and lewd remarks. Although normally I shrieked with laughter, today I found them repulsive. Did every bride feel so? They mixed with the

guests, stroked their own parts, leaned forward, and let go farts to the bleat of a sour horn. Everyone laughed—even Abbot Suger wiped his eyes with mirth.

"*Sanctus, sanctus, sanctus,*" Louis whispered. His face was again blotched.

Round and round in circles ran the misshapen satyrs, until they had cleared an arena for the main act, and here they came, the principal actors, playing Louis and Eleanor. "Louis," in white and blue, had silver spangles where his eyes should be and high, astonished black brows. His vision was further impeded by a huge pink sausage rising from his crotch and striking him in his nose. He aimed it wildly and whined:

> Now what be this?
> Is it a club?
> How can I kiss
> With such a drub?

He stroked the member.

The crowd roared with laughter.

"Eleanor," with a drooping dead eagle on her crown, grabbed the member and beat her groom about the head.

> You silly beast,
> This is our feast!
> We have pig's meat,
> It's time to eat!

She took a huge bite from the member.

Again the crowd howled.

"*Sanctus, sanctus, sanctus,*" murmured the real Louis. Amen, I wanted to add.

"My turn!"

"Your turn—I mean my turn!"

The lewd couple ate the sausage voraciously. Suddenly, the mock Louis found himself with an empty crotch. He clutched himself and howled.

O mun be sick!
I have no prick!
How can I fuck?
I have no cock!

"Eleanor" doubled in laughter.

Your silly greed
Has made you feed
Upon your tool!
How can I bed
E'en though I'm wed,
With such a fool!

A trumpet bleated and a dwarf rode forth on a two-manned "horse," with a sausage held up like a sword. "King Arthur to the rescue!"

At last, the travesty was over; the final subtlety was brought on: a huge cake depicting a wedding bed, with bride and groom stretched naked—though I noted that the baker had not added a cock, only breasts to make the distinction—and dozens of babies crawling on the floor.

My moment had arrived.

The clappers and troubadour players, the dwarfs, the mock Louis and Eleanor, all filed to our trestle with bags of flowers in their arms. Three prelates, Abbot Suger, Archbishop Geoffrey, and Stephen, the archbishop of Chartres, lined beside the players and gestured that we should rise. We both stood to follow.

As when I'd entered the church hours ago, now, before climbing the narrow stone stairway, I looked back on the bespattered court-

yard in a sad farewell to my maidenhood, for the deflowering ahead settled my fate more than any Romish litany.

Up the twisting stairs in the wake of our sweating counterparts, the dwarfs, and the priests who were to bless us; we entered a small chamber with a bed strewn with wilted flowers. I lay down on one side, Louis on the other, our bodies inevitably touching. For a few moments, the clappers hushed and the priests began their windy ablutions.

That, too, came to an end. A chalice containing holy water was brought forth.

Archbishop Geoffrey sprinkled our faces. *"Benedictio thalmi,* may there be no curse against fertility."

The chalice was passed to the archbishop of Chartres; water struck my eyes. *"Benedictio thalmi,* may the wife be cleansed of any former adultery."

For a moment, I was jarred out of my desolation. How odd that he should say the wife and not the husband. Was Louis so obviously pure? Was I so obviously not? Neither, I concluded, except that no female with all her wits would bed Louis.

"Benedictio thalmi," intoned Abbot Suger finished. "Henceforth, may the Church govern all your acts, both public and private."

I glared directly into his bland face. Was this in our contract?

Now they all muttered in Latin and swayed back and forth. The room filled with incense; the sign of the cross was made again and again. Suger seemed determined to remain until we consummated our marriage—to be sure I didn't escape? Or was he simply an old voyeur?

Just when I was about to order them out, they each bent to kiss our cheeks and left. The door closed, the clappers began their beating outside, and the crowd shouted lewd wishes at such a pitch that conversation was impossible. I closed my eyes for a moment and must have slept.

"Lord Louis, Princess Eleanor, open at once!"

I sat upright. Had the night passed so quickly? Louis snored heavily.

"Louis!" I shook his arm. "Suger's shouting to get in."

I opened the door. Though the sky was still a dull gray, torches formed halos around Suger, Thibault, other officers, and—in the back—Amaria.

The tiny abbot shoved me aside to embrace Louis. "Oh, my dear prince, steel yourself for terrible news. A messenger has just arrived—your father is dead!" He turned to me. "Both of you, meet me below as soon as you can."

Before we could even respond, he was gone. Amaria quickly thrust an armful of riding clothes into my hands and then she, too, ran down the steps.

Louis stood like a gravestone.

"My father's dead?" he said to me, seeking confirmation.

"Yes, both of our fathers in one summer. I'm so sorry, my lord."

"Yes."

I waited for tears.

"You'll come down to the courtyard?" he asked, dazed.

"As soon as I'm changed."

Grabbing his blue cape, he ran after Suger.

The courtyard was crowded with jabbering men; horses snorted in the background and servants passed cups of wine and bread. Louis was already mounted by the time I arrived.

Suger pushed me toward my own steed. "Hurry—we must be off."

"To Paris? But I . . ."

"You'll go to Poitiers, of course. Be invested by your barons as planned."

I hardly knew him in this martial role.

"I've sent a runner to Bordeaux to instruct Lord Raoul to meet you in Poitiers, where he'll stay with you until we summon you." He paused for breath. "As soon as Louis is crowned."

"Why the hurry, Abbot Suger? Shouldn't we all go to Poitiers and then . . ."

His mouth twisted cynically. "You have much to learn about succession. Louis's younger brother, Robert of Dreux, is probably

assembling his own court even as we speak." He turned away. "Are you ready, my lord king?"

Louis didn't realize he was being addressed, nor did I. *King* Louis must mean *Queen* Eleanor.

Suger spoke to me again. "We'll ride together for a short way, then split the army into two parts. Raoul of Vermandois will stand in for the king as your duke consort during your investiture."

"And who will stand in for me as queen?"

It was asked innocently, but Suger drew himself up. "After Louis is crowned in Paris, you will both have a formal coronation in Bourges at a later date—but we must assure—"

"So you told me."

We plunged down the precipice at a dangerous speed. I became aware of a familiar scent, a musky smell that quite overwhelmed me. Rancon rode beside me on the outer edge of our narrow mountain path. Our knees brushed, then pressed in rhythm.

"Thank you, Lord Rancon, for your hospitality."

He didn't answer.

"I hope you'll accompany me to Poitiers for my investiture. All my lords will be there and . . ." My voice piped most piteously.

"I must ride to Aragon." His scent became stronger. "To bring back my future wife, Lady Arabelle of Aragon. I'm sure you will indulge me in this important commitment."

If I hadn't been on the inside of the path, I would have plunged to my death. Before I could even reply, he was gone.

The French army beat our way through the valleys, across rivers, and there at a curve in the River Clain, we reached the parting of ways, where I turned to Poitiers and the French went on to Paris. Louis and I were permitted a few moments together.

"I'm sorry . . . I wish . . ." he stammered.

I controlled a shudder. "We'll be together soon."

His pupils were small, his whites enormous, like the eyes of a wild animal that's just been captured. Then the French went one way, my party another, and I completely forgot Louis.

Poitiers was looped in black crepe and wilting flowers in honor
of my father. Though the people gave me a warm welcome, all of
us turned our attention to the great man who'd departed. I worked
late into each night with my double purpose, to honor my dead
father and to establish my own government, but over all was my
deep personal grief. Though I'd thought I'd known what it was to
lose a father after that terrible scene in Parthenay, I'd deluded
myself. What can prepare one for the finality of death? Duke
William X of Aquitaine, a tall, handsome man with a deep, melodious voice in the fashion of our family, with his own laughter, his
marvelous horsemanship, his uncanny grasp of governance, soon
to be immortalized in the statue of a hunter I'd ordered, then to be
put in the annals of Aquitaine history, then—as I and my generation joined the vast company of the dead—to be forgotten.

Concomitant with my duties and grief, I wallowed in nostalgia.
Not only was I becoming a duchess, and soon a queen; I was saying farewell to girlhood. I roamed through our garden down to the
River Clain, past the apple tree where my father had discovered me
reading Virgil when I was only six, past the hummock where my
beautiful young mother had leaned, laughing. For a moment, she
lived again, with her fine dark hair flying free, her pansy purple
eyes sparking as she spoke of the arts of love. As if she knew! The
young girls from all over the duchy who lived with us for her
instruction—my friends Faydide, Florine, Mamile, Toquerie, and
Amaria—had giggled and nudged, eager for what lay ahead, but I'd
been perplexed. I slept in the same bed with my mother in the
women's quarters and I still remembered the night my father had
visited. Aunt Mahaut had pulled me roughly from Mother's arms to
lie with her on her mat in the corner. All the other ladies had likewise huddled against the walls, listening, and finally I, too, heard
the slow tramp of Father's boots on the stairs. With Aunt Mahaut's
hand across my mouth, I'd listened to his grunts and her moans
from the bed. When he'd gone and I was again in her arms, I was
offended by the wet spots at my hips and her tears on my cheeks.

That was the last time, I believe. Nine months later, my brother Aigret was born; Father's mission had been accomplished.

Now I knew the bitter secret between them. Grandfather had discarded his wife, Philippa, my other grandmother, though she'd given him five daughters—my aunts—and two sons, Father and Uncle Raymond. Grandmother Philippa had become a religious zealot under the spell of Robert d'Abbrisel at Fontevrault Abbey, so said my grandfather, but his children claimed he'd been seduced by the beauteous countess of Châtellerault. Whatever his motive, he'd stolen Dangereuse from her garden for a wild ride along the Clain, with her husband in pursuit and my mother in Dangereuse's arms. Dangereuse, seeing angry children around "Junior," had insisted that her Anor wed Duke William's heir, my father. Mother had adored him, I believe, and he may have secretly cared for her, but he'd never shown it in public. For him, she was the daughter of an ambitious whore who'd ruined his mother's life.

Hard to believe, but in the midst of such angry crosscurrents, I'd come into the world bursting with joy, and my love for life had never abated. Was I stupid? Insensitive? Did I—as he'd claimed— take after my incorrigible grandfather? My grandfather had instantly declared me his own, and I could still remember his lusty songs, his jokes, his naughty, ironic jibes. I'd ridden with him on the float on Saint-Radegonde's Day the day before he'd died, then lay beside him on his bed during that last long twilight.

My own father had then replaced him both as duke and as my constant companion. I believe I was daughter, wife, and perhaps even his lost father to him. We hunted together, fished together, but mostly he shared his books with me. Then came that fateful summer when Mother and Aigret had departed to our summer home at Talmont-sur-Mer, leaving Petra and me behind in Poitiers, sick with the chickenpox. I wandered now into our great hall, reputed to be the largest in Europe, and seat of our governance, where I sat in Father's chair, and could still see his finger with its large carbuncle ring tapping on the table as he'd whispered, "Lady Anor and Aigret have succumbed to malaria." He'd covered his face

with his hands. "I've had their bodies burned on the shore to prevent contagion." I'd realized with wonder, even as I sobbed myself, that he was weeping for my mother as well as for his only son, the future duke of Aquitaine. Within a single day, I was sitting before him again, both of us wearing white for mourning, and he'd explained his dilemma. The future duke of Aquitaine must be replaced, and there were several possibilities: As a still-young man, he could wed again, or he could summon his younger brother, Raymond, from England.

"However," he'd continued after a pause, "what say you to a duchess in place of a duke?"

Only today did I fully appreciate his courage in naming me his heir. At the time, there had been indignant shrieks from my aunts, who loved me but hated my mother and grandmother, hot condemnations from Rome, and the virtual insurrection of lords all over Aquitaine. How he'd quelled objections, I still didn't fully comprehend, but I knew how he had trained me. I would be not only the first woman to govern my duchy but also the best-informed, the wisest, the most dedicated lord in my distinguished family. I'd learned Latin and Greek from Father Anselmo, astronomy and philosophy from Rabbi Isaac of Montpellier, and literature, governance, strategy, and history from Father himself. We both slept short hours, and I was tested constantly for my comprehension and memory.

Most important—and most complex—was the tangle of warring factions that made up Aquitaine itself. While seeming to hold a light rein on rival claims, we subtly coaxed, cajoled, and, if necessary, insisted that all fights end with the kiss of peace. While no baron was satisfied, none was dissatisfied, either, and we all lived in freedom.

Father also sponsored songs, festivals, and a general celebration of life in our realm, and our subjects took pride in their poets and romancers. Such a vibrant culture was the natural outcome of our history, for the Roman province of Aquitania had never been fully subjegated by the invading Goths, nor later by the Holy Roman

Empire. Many considered us shockingly licentious, if not heretical, but we knew that we were, in fact, the last vestige of civilization in an uncouth, superstitious world.

Oc, Father, I vowed, I won't fail you.

After the final funeral Mass, I accepted the oaths of fealty from all my counts and barons, all save Rancon, who at least had the grace to write. Knowing I would have to be in France a few weeks before my crowning, I appointed officers to begin my rule, foremost, my uncle Ralph of Châtellerault as political seneschal, and Archbishop Geoffrey for the religious sphere. I then sent out seneschals into every section of my duchy and appointed the baron of Taillebourg in absentia as my military captain.

And with that appointment, I faced another grief, combining past with present. The poignancy of that song in Taillebourg, as well as the memories swirling around every blade of grass, every bowl at the table here in Poitiers, devastated me. When my girl-friends had come to be instructed by my mother in household arts, a similar covey of boys had arrived for instruction from my father, first in chivalry and culture, then in the arts of war. I'd first noticed Rancon when he was a small boy jumping on a wine bag. He'd displayed the same exuberant joy I felt, my male counterpart. From that day forward, memory became a series of Rancons: Rancon without his front teeth, Rancon cleaning the mews, Rancon bending over his lute. One day when he was ten and I was eight, I'd carried an empty jug to the wine cellar, and on my way back to the palace, I had happened on a ring of boys squatted around their trained badgers. With long metal sticks, they'd nudged their beasts to a race. "Get away!" Hugh had shouted at me. "Stupid girl! You've made me lose!" And he'd raised his stick against me. "You're stupid yourself!" Rancon had cried as he beat with his fists. "She's ugly! Her eyes are purple like a walrus's!" Hugh had bawled. Rancon had wrestled him to the ground. Then, panting with rage, he'd reached his grubby hand to my face. "Pay him no heed, Lady

Eleanor. He's a beast! And your eyes—your eyes are like gentians. You're beautiful!"

It had been a declaration for both of us.

That same night, while the boys were serving us our food at the trestles, their instruction in household courtesy, Rancon had accidentally poured wine down my father's back. After the shouting and japes had subsided, our eyes had met over the table. Yes, he was as nervous as I, and both of us exhilarated.

And here, sitting in the crook of the linden where I'd once been strictly forbidden to come, I'd watched the mature Rancon on the fighting field. I thrilled anew at the memory of his metal form charging swift as an arrow toward the quintain, his morning star swinging in lethal circles. Then the heavy lance lifted as if it were a feather, the broadsword, and finally the long bow, the most gifted fighter Father had ever trained, dubbed at fourteen and gifted at strategy—no wonder Father had made him his captain.

Memories flooded, even in the sanctuary of the great hall, where Lord Raoul of Vermandois sat beside me, listening and suggesting, and I recalled beams loaded with branches and flowers, torches sending round halos of light onto the walls, and young men and women pretending to be older in their finery, all entranced by the visiting minstrel, Béroul, who'd strummed the tale of Tristan and his beloved Iseult. How we'd wept at the story of fated love and death, how hot eyes had mixed with hot eyes at the thought of what lay ahead, how Rancon and I had been locked in the bliss of anticipation.

At last, the time came for my friends, now my ladies-in-waiting, to load our longcarts for Paris. I would leave as a maid, return as a woman, and I prayed, with no hope whatsoever, that the event would help me to forget Rancon. Yet I wept inconsolably as we crossed the Clain and my friends whispered how I grieved for my father.

We reached the outskirts of Paris a month later.

Raoul pushed to my side. "We'll wait here, milady, while I send a runner to inform the king of our approach."

"Thank you." I smiled falsely at this handsome courtier, for the sense that he was always acting forced me to act in return. During the month in Poiters, however, he'd been discreet in his business, and had left me with my uncle Ralph to arrange the affairs of my vast duchy. Furthermore, he'd been courteous to my family; I was the only one who seemed less than enchanted with his person.

My sister, grandmother, Amaria, and my ladies walked with me into a wood to repair ourselves, then sat in the shade to wait. Two hours later, we heard the French fanfare, and then a small line of horsemen appeared on the wide Roman road in the distance.

Duchess and soon-to-be queen, and here came the impediment to my good fortune.

Except that the small bouncing figure wasn't Louis at all; it was Abbot Suger. He dismounted.

"Ah, my dear Eleanor, venerable duchess of Aquitaine, and queen to our new king of France, greeting."

"Where is the king?" Raoul demanded. "I sent a runner to tell of our approach two hours ago."

"Such an unfortunate coincidence: He had to attend a Mass for his dead father."

"There are Masses every day," Raoul countered, "and only one arrival of his wife."

"I believe this was a special occasion, something about the roll of necrology."

"I quite understand," I said. "We had many such Masses for my father in Poiters."

Suger glanced at me, but spoke no more. His head drooped; he gave forth an aura of melancholy, dense as a cloud. All my ladies sensed it and all tried to counter it, especially my grandmother.

"What a charming vista! So Roman, and I believed France to be modern!"

Suger seemed not to hear.

We prepared to enter Paris. I rode between Suger and Raoul at the head of the line, and now I was grateful for the seneschal, whose smooth monologue made Suger's silence less apparent. Where exactly was Paris—beyond that island?

I was looking at all there was.

"You mean those few spires?" Soon-to-be-queen of a sand spit.

"There are still some Roman ruins on both banks," Raoul said, defending the city.

Suger was more forthright. "The area is compact, I grant you— the city retreated when the Vikings poled up the Seine in their long blue boats—but the population is sophisticated, I assure you."

I regretted my lack of tact. "And, of course, the Vikings are no longer a threat—certainly it can expand."

Suger raised his pointed chin. "The Vikings quelled? Not at all! The Normans are vicious descendants of the invaders."

"Yet civilized," I said, smiling.

Suger remained grim. "Young Henry of Normandy is a red star of malice. So long as he lives, France is not safe."

That same Henry invoked by Thibault when he'd spoken of Henry's mother, Matilda. Well, each country has its own enemies; in Aquitaine, we liked the Normans.

We reached the Châtelet protecting the bridge to the Ile de la Cité; the Seine River had seemed wide and empty from a distance, but close up, eel boats banged and scraped solid as a floor. The top of the Petit Pont, which the bridge was called, was crowded with vendors and young men in student gowns milling before rows of tiny houses that served as schools and stores. Talmelliers hawked savory morsels while professors hawked knowledge in joyful cacophony.

"The university!" Raoul shouted.

I was astounded that Paris didn't collapse under the weight of sheer numbers. Houses built on top of houses met overhead, while in the streets flotsam flowed sluggishly with dung and human waste. Everyone shouted and every shout echoed against the urine-stained walls, like pigs squealing in a pit. Yet the exuberant cos-

tumes, grins, darting eyes, and swinging hips made me laugh aloud—I immediately caught a large horsefly in my mouth. What excitement, what energy, eagerness, even danger! I gazed directly into rooms occupied by startled students and, in one case, busy lovers. Lascivious eyes turned in my direction—one Russian squeezed my knee as I passed.

We rode through a vegetable and flower market, then stopped before a gate. Again fanfare blasted, and we entered a minuscule courtyard layered with horse dung. To avoid the filth, my page led my horse to an ancient olive tree stump, where I could leap to the steps of the palace. God's feet, this was the royal domicile? Built in the Merovingian style, a low stone hovel without windows, it looked a perfect retreat for feral cats.

Holding Amaria's hand, I stepped into pitch-darkness. Gradually, high arrow slits revealed an octagonal room, and vague rustlings indicated that it was occupied. I was assailed by a stench that made me reel, as if we were standing atop a grave.

"This is your new family, my dear duchess," Suger said, taking my hand.

My eyes adjusted. Queen Adelaide, my mother-in-law, a defeated, withered woman who looked to be a hundred, and why not? Louis the Fat was reputed to have had forty bastards. Louis's sister, Constance, a heavy, sullen princess who obviously took after her father. Leonore of Vermandois, Raoul's wife, imperious, condescending. With her hawk nose and meeting brows, she appeared old enough to be Raoul's mother. Robert of Dreux, the brother who'd not achieved the throne.

Their hands were uniformly cold and dry, their voices whispers.

Then Louis appeared like a ghoul rising from the tomb. He was dressed in black, smelled wormy, had tonsured his hair. Had he taken vows?

"Dear wife, I have waited since that day when first we met and my father had the flux, and after our wedding there in Bordeaux, I have waited and wanted for you to meet my father, my spiritual adviser, Count Thierry of Galeran."

A great ghostly hulk of a man stepped forward and bowed shortly, a Templar in his white tunic and blazing red cross, a fleshy face, hard pewter eyes, a devil's mole sprouting on his lower lid. I peered intently, for I thought I knew him. It was a Templar with a devil's mole who had beaten my father in Parthenay at the behest of Abbot Bernard, but I wasn't certain in this dim light, so I held my peace.

I turned again to Louis. "Have you been ill, my lord? You look much thinner than I recall."

"I'm fasting."

"Why?"

"And it's made him tired," Suger interjected. "He needs rest, as I'm sure you do, too."

At this obvious thrust, Louis twitched. "Wife, I must speak to you privately."

"Be merciful, my lord. Let her refresh herself," Suger ordered.

"Talk to her at once," Thierry countered in a high falsetto.

Louis brushed through a door, and I followed. To my surprise, Thierry came as well, and we all three huddled under a stair in the dark.

"Wife, I am in mourning for my father, as you must be for yours."

"He's taken the vow of chastity for the mourning period," Thierry added.

"As I'm certain you have for your father," Louis said.

I hadn't thought of it. "For how long?"

"A year."

"For each parent," Thierry said sternly.

"Two years . . ." I gasped. Louis and Thierry were gone.

Shock gave way to outrage. Turn from a maid to a woman? Turn from a maid to a withered crone! And what was Thierry of Galeran's influence? As I moved to follow, Abbot Suger touched my arm. "Well?"

"Who is this Thierry of Galeran?" I demanded.

"A count. A Crusader. Why do you ask?"

"Is he connected to Abbot Bernard of Clairvaux?"

"I believe he is at times. Yes, he's his acolyte."

"His butcher, you mean! I've seen him with my own eyes. My father—" I choked.

"Butcher? Your father?"

I explained in detail, including the rain pounding on the portico in Parthenay, the puddle into which my father's head had fallen, the way the monks had beaten me back when I'd try to assist him.

Suger appeared appalled. "Does the king know? What did he say?"

"I don't know; we didn't discuss it. Only I could see that Thierry of Galeran is Louis's main counselor. He ordered him to abstain from the wedding bed for two years!"

"*Two years!* Why?"

"So that we may mourn our respective fathers."

"I'll absolve him of his mourning duties."

For a moment, I was stopped. "You could have done so before I arrived. However, you miss my point."

"Not at all. A young bride has a right to expect her husband to do his duty."

"I don't care a fig about Louis's duties!" I cried. "*Dex aie*, listen to me! I will not enter a union with the murderer of my father!"

"Louis never met your father!"

I leaned against the cold wall and breathed deeply. "Very well, Abbot Suger, be obdurate if you will, but hear me well. This marriage cannot be. I understand your interest in Aquitaine, but you will have to take it some other way. Raise an army, bring Thibault of Champagne again, but I warn you that we shall be ready this time. I'm returning to Poitiers first thing in the morning."

He took my hand in his warm claw. "With God as my witness, I admire your spirit! You would relinquish a crown to be independent!"

"I have no personal interest in your king, nor in France. I obeyed my overlord Louis the Fat when he was alive, but neither Louis nor I wanted this marriage. I'm certain Louis will be happy to release me. As for me, I might still tolerate your reluctant king if he were not under the influence of my father's murderer. How could I ignore such a deed? How could I betray my father by

accepting his killer? Therefore, I'm leaving! No, don't argue. I mean this! We can arrange an annulment later, but I'm needed in Aquitaine at once! I want to begin my governance!"

Suger put his arm around my shoulders. "Look you, of course you can leave, and I'll write the Pope myself for an annulment. I had no idea of this unfortunate connection with Count Thierry, believe me, but you can't leave in the dark. And may I beg one more day? Do me the favor—nay, the honor—to first visit my abbey tomorrow, where I can discuss my architectural theories with a worthy audience. Meantime, you must be tired."

His arm held me upright or I would have collapsed from astonishment. I well knew that this was no small thing I was proposing, and I was prepared to argue for days if necessary. But he'd said I could leave—I could have an annulment! Oh, bless Louis and his murderous adviser! They'd released me to be myself, Duchess of Aquitaine.

And to be with Rancon—where was he? Belatedly, I recalled Arabelle of Aragon, then shrugged. If I could annul nuptials with a king, surely he could do as much with the puny Arabelle.

"We've prepared quarters for you and your entourage."

I came back to the present. Of course I was weary, and my ladies were exhausted.

"I'll call someone to take you and your ladies to your chambers. You need not return to your French family now."

We climbed up a stair narrow as a ladder to a room too small to stretch our pallets, but never mind. My heart sang: Tomorrow I would see Suger, and the day after that, I would be on my way back to Aquitaine.

3

*L*ed by a dozen French soldiers in a westerly direction, I trotted beside the foul ditches flooding the Paris streets. A steady rainfall cooled my fevered brain, which had kept me from sleeping, tired though I was, for I must resolve my situation with Rancon. What if Arabelle wasn't puny after all? What if she was a sultry beauty of the Spanish type? What if he loved her? Then the skies rumbled and we were in a torrent. Following my blue-garbed guards, I pressed my steed to a canter. By the time the rain eased, we were in a narrow strip of open country enclosed on both sides by impenetrable forests.

We turned into a lane through gnarled apple trees and suddenly came upon a clearing filled with scores of men working in the light sprinkle. Some chiseled at blocks of stone while others stripped branches from felled trees. Behind them rose a giant scaffold where foolhardy churls hoisted heavy beams with chains, then wrestled them onto precarious perches.

Riding through still another apple orchard, we approached a low ancient building at the far end, which needed remodeling more than the church: Moss and lichen clung to the stone facing; weeds and nests and saplings sprouted in the thatch. At least the windows had glass, and there were three chimneys on the outer walls, indicating fireplaces instead of greasy fire pits like those in the palace in Paris.

I pounded with my open palm on the heavy door. Then again, and when it opened, I almost struck a novice on the nose.

"Abbot Suger, please."

"Your name?"

"Eleanor, queen of France."

Which I was for today. He backed inside, gesturing that I should follow, then left me in a dark, low-ceilinged vestibule redolent of beeswax and mildew. Monks were chanting in the distance.

"You're early! Welcome, my dear." Abbot Suger beamed. "Each time I see you is a revelation. Such fresh young beauty!"

I couldn't return the compliment. He looked like a rough peasant in his short woolen tunic, which hung above his thick, hairy legs and boots.

"Shall we walk?" he asked. "It's a glorious day!"

"It's raining."

"Hardly at all."

Which I took as a comment on French weather.

He smiled exuberantly. "I've ordered an excellent repast for us— we can eat under the trees."

He opened the door and my muddy boot slipped on the slanted floor.

"Careful! I just laid those planks—you wouldn't think they would buckle so soon, eh? Still, it's an improvement, both here and in the choir. My poor monks were suffering from rheumatism after kneeling long hours on stone. I don't believe that suffering elevates the spirit, do you?"

He was already wading through the orchard, with the novice struggling to keep pace.

"Abbot Suger, wait!" I called, also struggling.

"You must see what I'm doing with my church." He headed back the way I'd just come.

I stumbled after him.

Vain old popinjay; a pox on his new abbey. I waded through mud and building debris, then scrambled under ropes to the inner area. There, to my astonishment, an entire building lay half-buried in mud. I thought it must be the crypt, or perhaps the original Saint-Denis, built by King Dagobert in the seventh century. I followed

Suger down crumbled steps to the interior. Instead of a dim cave, we were inside a shell without a roof; above us, men pounded on the distant scaffolding. At least the noise was muted.

Suger pointed upward, his face beatific: "God is Light, Eleanor! Let Him suffuse His own Church with holiness!"

I was dumbstruck. I would have believed anything about this devious politician except that he was a religious mystic, which is to say mad, in my view.

"God and everything else." I pointed at pigeon droppings. "Without a roof, you'll have more than light."

"Oh, I'm building a roof—you see it all around you!"

He pointed up to the scaffolding.

I forgot Louis for a moment. "So high? Roofs have to be supported, Abbot Suger."

"Ours will be supported by glass."

"A glass ceiling?"

His smile was strained at my slow wit. "No, a stone ceiling; glass walls."

"Very original, Abbot," I humored him.

He recited:

> Bright is my Father's home;
> Bright the mind who Him beholds;
> Brilliant the walls of my holy dome;
> More glorious than the costliest golds.

He continued: "The glass walls will be buttressed by piers slanting outward, so that the base rests several feet from the walls, like arches under a bridge. The weight will travel outward, you see? It's a principle of engineering."

Suddenly, I wondered. "Has it ever been tried?"

"Never! It's *my* creation!" he cried immodestly. "Of course I've built small models, and there is something similar, I hear, in the cathedral at Durham, but in truth I'm inventing a godly architecture!"

"A stone ceiling supported by glass windows?"

"And not simple clear glass, Eleanor. I'm staining small segments in brilliant hues, then assembling them in lead frames into cunning illustrations of the life of Saint-Denis." His voice trembled. "When sun penetrates the color, God will truly be among us. I shall greet Him with treasures to rival those in the Hagia Sophia."

Abruptly, he exited through the portal under the scaffolding, passed the abbey, and entered into a bog covered with hidden holes and thorny brush, moving toward a faraway copse, where the novice was laying out our meal. I dodged after him. I was covered with sweat by the time we reached the tall old poplars, one of which was already turning a rich gold.

"There, now, this will do very well." He dismissed the novice, then sank onto a log under a small fiery sumac, which served as a partial shelter. "A glorious prospect of the valley of Chevreuse, eh? Let's see what the porter prepared for us. Ah, honeyed ham, bread, goat cheese, and potted duck. Simple fare, but wholesome. Shall we pray?" He did so. "Here, dear, this apple cider is new this year."

I lifted my flagon. "To our friendship, Abbot Suger. I admit that I had the wrong impression of you; you're a most reasonable prelate."

He sighed. "Yes, I'm reasonable; now I must persuade Louis to be likewise. I spoke with him last night."

I felt charitable. "I'm certain your king is a virtuous lord, though perhaps not suited to the crown."

"Nor was he his father's original heir. He had an older brother, Philip, who was king designate. As a child, Louis was placed in a monastery, where he quickly found a vocation in God; he took his vows as a monk."

"An appropriate choice, it would seem."

"Perhaps, except that Philip was killed when his horse reared at a runaway pig. Louis the Fat then removed Louis from the monastery in order that he could fulfill his royal duty."

"Yet he had another son, who obviously covets the throne. Why not Louis's brother, Robert of Dreux?"

"Louis was next in age, and he's gifted, more than he may seem."

"I suppose a celibate king may be effective."

"He's not celibate!" Suger cried.

"I'm sorry. It's just that he said . . ."

Suger sighed again. "He's fallen under the influence of that Thierry of Galeran."

I shook my head. "A dangerous man, Abbot Suger. Take care." Once again, I recounted the scene in Pathenay. Though I'd had months to anticipate Father's death after his wound, and weeks to accept it after the fact, my voice still failed. I couldn't describe Abbot Bernard in his brick-colored turban, holding his cross before him, or the horror of Thierry rushing forward with his sword upraised, then the slow trickle of blood from my father's head, staining the puddle below his helmet.

"He lived a few months," I sobbed, "though he was never the same. I dream of that Templar, Abbot Suger, with his devil's mark."

Suger patted my hand. "Try to forget, my dear. Your father is with God."

My tears dried, to be replaced by a dull throbbing in my head. "You must dimiss the Templar, Abbot Suger. For France's sake, for Louis's sake."

"I agree."

"If Louis is as gifted as you say, why does he permit such an obvious villain to influence him?"

"I don't see any signs of his influence as yet."

"What about the period of mourning? The sacrifice of—"

"That may be his original vows as much as Thierry. As you know, men of the Church are celibate."

"Not in Aquitaine," I retorted. "Many of our priests marry. My own Father Peter has six children."

Suger hastily crossed himself. "May he be forgiven. Our Pope has proclaimed—"

"*Your* Pope, not mine."

"A heresy."

The subject was not relevant. I smiled. "Well, Abbot Suger, I've enjoyed seeing your new abbey, and I'm especially grateful for this opportunity to converse, but . . ."

"Lust distracts men from their duty to God." The little abbot refilled his flagon. "I daresay Louis fears his passion for you. No man can serve two lords."

"Nonsense! Men visit the women's quarters to produce sons, nothing more!" I rose, lifted the muddy hem of my tunic. "I must go before the rain increases."

Suger gazed at me quizzically. "Are you certain? I'm told that most men covet the carnal act."

How would I know what most men felt?

He continued staring. "I thought all Aquitanians believed in love."

"Not within marriage!"

"Of course, I'd forgotten your grandfather's famous adultery."

I didn't point out that my grandmother Phillipa had forced him by following God into sexual abstinence. An odd reversal of men's attitudes, if Suger was right.

"Ah well, be that as it may, you make an excellent point: Indeed men must produce heirs, especially when that man is a king." He cracked a stick over his knee. "I agree that Louis must be separated from Thierry, who plays on Louis's natural fanaticism, which might be admirable if he were still a monk, but is death to a king. The Capets are famous for producing male heirs." He sighed. "As a Templar, Thierry fought for the Kingdom of Jerusalem, you know, where he was captured by the enemy. The Saracens castrated him, and made him a guard in their harem."

"He's a eunuch?" I gasped.

"Yes."

I fought to control laughter. In Aquitaine, eunuchs are considered a joke. "And he was in a harem?"

"Eunuchs are safe around naked women, you see. Thierry claims that the experience taught him firsthand the evil wiles of the meaner sex. He's a dangerous man."

Thierry amid naked women—I couldn't restrain my mirth—wicked though he was, this picture made him ludicrous.

"I wouldn't laugh, dear. Have you met any of our soldiers for Christ?"

"My grandfather was on the Crusade you know. He became lost on the desert and wandered in a wadie for days, an amusing tale. However, he lost Toulouse for my grandmother Phillipa by being away so long."

Suger waggled his finger. "Your grandfather wasn't a Templar. These men use our gentle Savior as an excuse for the most brutal savagery. And they're ambitious! Yes, we must release Louis from his influence!"

Why did he say "we"? I had nothing to do with Louis's release from Thierry or anyone else. Louis Capet would have to decide his own destiny, with Suger's help of course. I glanced at the sky— what hour was it? The clouds had settled into a gray lid; the rain was again steady.

"Thank you for your hospitality, Abbot Suger, but I really must go."

"The King of France must produce a son, my dear Eleanor," Suger continued, as if he hadn't heard. "I know you think I chose you as queen for your lands, partly true, I admit, but your female charms were the greater lure. I needed the most bewitching beauty I could find to offset the influence of Louis's spiritual adviser."

"Your scheme misfired." I tied my shawl under my chin.

He looked up innocently. "How has it misfired?"

"Because I'm leaving tomorrow morning for Aquitaine, as we agreed."

"Why are you leaving?"

Was he so dense? "Abbot Suger, you admitted yesterday and again today that the marriage was a mistake, so we will have it annulled as soon as possible. Meantime, I have work to do in Aquitaine. I must begin my governance."

"Aquitaine will do quite well under France's control."

"Aquitaine is not under France's control! We do homage of course, but we're quite independent!"

"Indulge me a short time more, and sit down. We've spoken of Louis's vows to the Church, his need for an heir, and while these are political issues, I would like to instruct you more broadly."

He looked again like the duplicitous gnome I'd met in Bordeaux. However, I sat a little farther away, where I had more shelter, and waited.

"As you say, Aquitaine does homage to France and our relationship to your dukes has always been amiable. . . ." I stopped listening. I'd told him that my father had instructed me, but any child knows the system of homage and overlords. My father used to call it a pyramid, with the king at the top, and it held the social body intact with its ancient system of fealty to the immediate overlord. The Catholic Church, with the Pope as its peak made a similar pyramid, and most of the kings' troubles came from the Pope's power, which was greater than theirs. Aquitaine itself has several counties that do homage to it, and we do homage to France, which was the cause of my present catastrophe.

"My father has told me all this," I said icily.

"However, I believe your father fought with Count Geoffrey and his son Henry in Maine, did he not?"

"Yes, against France," I concurred. "France wanted Count Geoffrey to swear fealty directly to France, not to Aquitaine. My father was coming to the aid of his vassal."

This was ancient history. Again I took a step forward.

He caught my skirt. "Your father misread the issue. Ever since Duke William the First of Normandy conquered England, the Norman dukes have wanted France's fiefs along the Atlantic seaboard to change allegiance from France to England. Do you follow me?"

"Of course, you're saying that Maine was about to switch allegiance. I think you misread, Abbot; my father said that Maine refused to give homage to France because Aquitaine was its overlord. Now I must insist—"

"Maine is insignificant, but Aquitaine isn't."

I smiled with pity. "If you want to guard Aquitaine from the Normans, save your breath. I just reiterated our allegiance to France,

didn't I? And I'll brook no interference from England, although I believe there may be more to fear from France. The present English king, King Stephen, is from Blois, I believe, put there illegally by the French. Matilda of Normandy is the rightful queen."

Suger clapped his hands. "*Benedicite,* you are a wonder! I should have gone directly to the point."

"Then do so," I demanded. "I must be on my way."

"Well, Empress Matilda is a formidable woman. Did you know she raised her own army for an invasion?"

"Yes."

"And she failed, of course. Her son Henry is a different matter. When he becomes king of England, he'll seize those counties and duchies that rightly belong to France. He's a determined enemy."

I became impatient. "I know of your obsession with 'the red star of malice,' Abbot Suger. If you're concerned that Aquitaine might fall under his influence, I've just assured you that we're loyal to France."

He beamed. "Then you won't mind that France controls Aquitaine!"

"Not control. I put my uncle Ralph in charge in Poitiers, Archbishop Geoffrey in Bordeaux, my captain, Rancon, to lead our army. I have officers in every major city. And now I shall assume my own duties." I smiled to soften the acidity of my tone.

"Poor Eleanor. Raoul of Vermandois replaced all your appointments with Frenchmen. Not one Aquitanian appointee remains."

I was too shocked to respond. All my misgivings flooded back, about him and Raoul both, but how could I have imagined the depth of perfidy? I began to run. "Good-bye! I'll ride this very night!"

"Wait! We still have much to discuss."

I turned. "No discussion! Recall your officers at once!"

He merely stared.

"By God, Abbot Suger, bring them back or I'll take you to court! You signed our civil contract!"

The man of steel emerged from behind the wispy gnome. "The civil contract isn't worth the vellum it's written on."

"Of course it is! There were many witnesses!"

"You've made your marriage vows to the most powerful entity in the world, the Church and its Pope in Rome. The Church controls you."

"Controls me if I stay in France, and I'm not!"

He smiled with pity. "You should have left yesterday, instead of giving me warning. Every bridge across the Seine has been closed, every guard alerted; even when you came here, the French guard came with you. You cannot leave Paris."

I collapsed, beyond shock. "Are you so greedy for power, Abbot Suger?"

"Louis needs an heir."

"Find someone else to further your ambitions!"

For the first time, he became angry. "You see me only as the ambitious counselor of kings. How do you suppose that happened, my grand duchess? Did I have your birthright opportunity to rule? To marry greatness? Did my father instruct me in history and policy? I was born a lowly peasant, Lady Eleanor, and my father was beaten to death by his master. I dreamed of becoming a military commander—ah yes, I have a soldier's gifts—but how can a poor peasant find a sponsor to provide horses and arms? Or I could have become a famous architect, if someone had accepted me as his apprentice. No one would, my fine lady; no one cares for a rough, short peasant who can't even read. Thousands of talented young men live and die like animals within a mile of where they were born. Then the Church offered a way; in the Church, I could receive an education and develop my natural talents, so much so that I attracted the eye of King Louis the Fat. With his help, I finally had my horse and sword and fought by his side; with his indulgence, I began the rebuilding of my abbey. Do I want to protect the French king? Yes! I owe France and its royal family everything! Can you understand?"

"I understand that you had one advantage I lacked, Abbot Suger. You are a male. Where does a female rule, no matter what her

birth? Where does a female peasant receive an education, no matter what her brilliance? Not in your beloved Church, my dear Abbot, which doesn't even underwrite convents, only monastaries. Can you appreciate my father's courage? I owe my father everything!"

"He gave you Aquitaine. I'm offering you France!"

"You're offering me Louis's bed! Is that France? Have you ever looked at his mother, the former queen?" I shouted. "I won't become a shriveled, defeated wretch like her for you or anyone else!"

He lowered his head in prayer. "Sit down again, dear. Let's dispense with choler and speak dispassionately. Listen to me, Eleanor. I suspect that you have some young knight you long for, eh?"

My heart raced. He sounded like Dangereuse—was I so transparent?

He patted me gently. "And you must forsake him—I'm sorry. For your father's sake and for the trust he put in you, you must act like the ruler you are."

"My father wanted me to rule Aquitaine."

"France will expand and eat your beloved Aquitaine in a gulp. France will be the supreme power in Europe, and you can share that power."

"You can't force me, Abbot Suger."

"Can't I?" His benign expression now seemed malevolent. "Why do you think Thibault of Champagne came to Bordeaux? To study your fortifications, my dear, and he has the greatest army in Europe."

"It's against your vaunted canon law to invade my duchy— France is supposed to protect us!"

"Thibault and the Pope are like brothers." He smiled sardonically. "The Church and the army are the same power, like a hand and a glove."

"I have an army! A captain!"

"Hardly a united army," he countered. "Your barons fight one another all the time. They're notorious for their petty feuds."

I couldn't deny it. Thunder grumbled in the distance.

"Is there no way I can make you change your mind?" I beseeched.

"You will wear the crown of France, Eleanor. And I'll not change my mind."

The beautiful view of Chevreuse disappeared in a sudden torrent and with it my brief delusory moment of hope. "I accept the crown, then, but not the royal bed."

"You don't want to rule Aquitaine? Or even to see it again?"

I stared into his cold gray eyes.

"If you take Louis to your bed, I'll permit you to rule in Aquitaine."

"May I live in Aquitaine as I rule?"

"During the summers, yes."

"And keep my uncle as seneschal in Poitiers?"

He considered. "Yes."

A pain stabbed my heart. "I have no choice, then."

His face lighted up. "You won't regret it!"

"I must leave, but I expect your promises in writing." I drew myself up. "And you will obey your queen's orders."

Before he could reply, I ran—across the field with its black suck of mud, under the apples trees and into the building area. Here, I slowed to avoid falling timbers and suddenly tripped. For a moment, I lay sprawled in wood chips and mud, so desolate that I wanted to die.

"Be ye all right?" a voice called.

I looked up at a carpenter barely visible on the scaffolding.

"Fine, thank you!"

I struggled to sit, and winced. *Dex aie,* my foot was trapped under a timber. A pox on Suger's stained window and the lunatic king who had financed it. I doubted if Louis would . . . and I became very still. The rain increased, then suddenly stopped, and still I sat. Sunlight shone among the high timbers as if seeking the colored pictures of Saint-Denis. I pulled my boot free.

Suger was still sitting under the sumac. "Forget something?"

"You don't care a fig about an heir, Abbot Suger."

"What do you mean? I assure you that I—"

"Want to hold on to your power. You and the abbot of Clairvaux are struggling for the soul of France. Am I right?"

He took a deep breath. "Yes. I commend you upon your—"

"Forget compliments. What do you really want from me?"

Our eyes held.

"Your Aquitanian culture," he said so softly that I forced him to repeat it. "Oh, I know that Champagne and even France at this point wouldn't agree with me, and I myself have been critical of your grandfather and his followers. Nevertheless, you have superb architecture. You value art, don't you? You value learning—you must have heard of the great Abelard—and France should be in the forefront, the envy of all nations. Or it could become a narrow, cruel theocracy."

"I'll be happy to help you from Aquitaine. I'll send troubadours, architects, even scientists from Montpellier to Paris."

"You'll summon them from your throne. I mean that, Eleanor."

I studied his adamant expression. "Because," I said softly, "you can't control Louis. Without me, you'll lose him to Thierry."

He straightened. "That's one interpretation."

"That's the truth. Therefore, you owe me much more than you've offered."

He frowned. "Take care; I've been generous."

"Not considering the stakes. And your weak position. When Louis the Fat died, your good fortune expired."

"Yes." He rose like the fighting cock that he was. "You saw yourself how Abbot Bernard seeks control through force. You just described how your father—"

"Is he raising an army against France?"

"He's more insidious. He blankets the country with dire warnings and threats of God's vengeance. He's indefatigable in his efforts to change the very fabric of the country!"

"He needs Louis."

"Yes."

"And if he wins—through Thierry—you will be out of power."

Tears filled his gray eyes. "Abbot Bernard is trying to stop my new abbey, Eleanor. Art and beauty are not Christian, he claims, falsely of course, but he has the Pope's ear. I hope that you can—"

"Seduce your impotent king so you can have your stained glass?" My voice shook. "My life for a window!"

"A window unto God, Eleanor! You should understand—you know better than anyone the connection between art and life."

"Oc, and my understanding has a price. If I'm to facilitate your vision, I want to rule France."

He blanched. "I rule France!"

"Temporarily, unless I help, eh? But if I must learn to substitute power for personal happiness, then I will have the power. Think fast, Abbot Suger. You may keep me as captive, but you can't force me to seduce your king."

"I concede," he said. "When Louis becomes your husband in fact, you will rule Aquitaine and co-rule with me in France. So be it."

"In writing."

"No."

"Then what guarantee?"

"My word."

"You understand that I can do nothing with Louis for at least two years—he's mourning both our fathers," I hedged.

"You'll consummate on the night of your coronation three months hence, in Bourges," he ordered. "If you want to rule Aquitaine . . ."

"You'll have your heir within a year."

What more was there to say? Abbot Suger, still talking enthusiastically about his great abbey, accompanied me back to the French guards. The sun was already low, the days getting shorter.

I prepared to ride back to Paris.

When I was mounted, Suger held my bridle. "Queen Eleanor"— I caught the flattery—"may I prevail on your goodwill in still another matter?"

"You have no goodwill from me, Abbot Suger."

"Please, we're friends, partners for the good of France." He waved his hand. "You're from the richest duchy in Europe and a

lady of impeccable taste." He smiled again. "Would you send a contribution to help me pay for my stained glass? It's outrageously dear."

What a shameless old beggar.

He smiled, reading my thought. "I told you how I assumed power, Eleanor. You must learn to use your own weapons."

"Which are?"

"Beauty and riches."

Another sudden torrent on the return trip concealed my tears, the thunder my howls of anguish. What did it matter if I'd outfoxed this cunning rogue in our bargain? I was still captive to France and I'd lost Rancon. Another few miles and my howls ceased. I'd lost Rancon in any case. Might as well cohabit with Louis as any other warthog. Then I howled anew: I wanted Rancon! I couldn't live without him! Grandmother was wrong about love! King Louis might have a worthier title than Baron Rancon, but not for me! My heart, my mind, my burning flesh all said otherwise! Rancon plus Aquitaine equaled Eleanor.

Futile arguments. Rancon was married; I was married. I'd had no choice with Suger, except to make him give up his own sovereignty in return.

When I reached Paris, I sent Suger a generous bag of gold. Whether he knew it or not, this was a bribe—the first of many. My two assets, wealth and beauty. I truly doubted if I could seduce Louis with either, but I was well on my way with Abbot Suger, partly because he'd forgotten my third asset: intelligence.

4

Three months later in Bourges, when I was crowned Queen of France, Rancon was among my guests.

I knew it well before Mamile sidled close with her delighted whisper, before the coronation began in the great chilly church. While I never looked directly at him or his lady, the corner of my eye was ever on his tall, commanding figure in its floor-length formal tunic of rich brown. I absorbed the new short trim of his curls, the pallor of his skin in winter, the cherry fullness of his lips. Most of all, the musky incense of his person made my senses swim. Of the slighter female figure at his side, I paid no heed.

Then the ceremony was finished, the crown heavy on my brow, and I must greet my guests. With difficulty, I performed the obligatory courtesies with our French nobles, the prelates, and finally my lords and ladies of Aquitaine, all preamble to the greeting that mattered.

"My lord of Rancon," I murmured.

"My queen, greeting." He bent his face for the kiss of peace. It took all my strength to restrain myself. Let our lips cling forever! "May I present my lady Arabelle?"

"My queen!" She knelt to the floor, then rose.

Neither a smoldering Spanish beauty nor a puny witch, she had a sweet, bland face with pale skin and eyes. She appeared frail. And Rancon was protective. Weak with jealousy, I forced myself to move to the next lord and lady.

Thereafter, I avoided Rancon's person, though I was still dominated by his presence.

The dinner was over, the festival of the Nativity finished, and at last I climbed the steep stair in the royal castle to await my lover-king. This was the night abstinence would end, so the great god Suger had ordained.

"You looked beautiful today, Joy," Amaria remarked as she followed me.

"*Dex aie*, Am, don't flatter me; it's not required. I hate myself in purple." Which brought out my "walrus eyes."

She took my long cape from my shoulders. "I don't agree. With your eyes and rich coloring . . . In any case, it's ungrateful to complain about a shade so hard to achieve, eh? Think of how many oysters and murexes had to die for this color."

"Had to *dye* for this color." I corrected her, then chanted:

> Pity the poor oyster
> Who lost his cloister
> In order to tint
> The queen's purple lint.

Amaria laughed.
I went on:

> Pity the murex
> Who despite her pure sex
> Is forced to bleed
> To fill the queen's need.

"You're in manic disposition, Joy. Why so hilarious?"

"You misread me: I'm in panic disposition."

Let her believe I referred to Louis. I removed my crown, which was long and narrow, more fit for a horse than a human.

"Draw the arras along the sides of the bed, Am, but leave the end open."

I walked to the window and undid the shutter; snow fell in soft wet balls.

"Won't you be cold?"

I turned and grimaced. "I'm expecting Louis."

"Of course. Should I . . ."

"Yes, help me prepare; then leave."

After we'd put tapers around the altar, she undid my hair and braided it loosely; I stepped out of my stiff garments and into a soft pink robe edged with vair. Amaria gazed at me wordlessly, kissed my cheek, and left.

Instantly, I picked up my discarded purple and held it to my face before a mirror. It *was* becoming, yes. My eyes looked violet, and my cheeks glowed. My manic disposition dissolved into melancholy. I must keep my bargain, but, oh, at what cost.

There was a faint rap at the door.

Louis, still in full regalia, registered my loose robe with panic. Then Thierry appeared at his side.

"May we come in?" Louis stammered.

"Both of you?"

"If you please," Thierry said in his high, thin voice. "We need an audience."

I drew myself up. "Hardly in my bedchamber, Count Thierry."

"Please . . ." Louis beseeched his adviser.

"I'll wait for you here at the door, my lord."

"All night?" I challenged him.

"We shall see." He smirked.

I closed the door. "Welcome, my lord Louis."

Sidling like a whipped hound, he searched for a place to put his crown and his cape. Gently, I lifted his heavy mantle from his shoulders and dropped it to the floor. He lurched away from my touch as if I were a leper. Scripture warns us not to cast our pearls before swine, but how much more degrading to cast them before reluctant swine.

"Would you like to pray, my lord?"

"Yes!" He crawled eagerly on his hands and knees to the altar. *"Sanctus, sanctus, sanctus."*

I knelt beside him. I became colder and colder, until my jaw hurt from trying to hold my teeth steady. There was no fire in the room, and I must have left the shutter slightly ajar; an icy draft fanned the rushes. Would he never cease?

The bell rang Matins by the time we rose. Then without warning, Louis clutched at his stomach and bent double.

"Are you ill?" I cried, alarmed.

"No, it's just—may we sit?" He perched on the end of the bed, his head bent to his knees. "Give me my cape," he muttered.

I began to place it on his shoulders, but he pulled it to his lap, then sat straight. His face was stricken.

"I've failed you, Joy."

Failed Suger, not me.

He continued: "I can't—I hoped, but I can't—can't have sexual concourse."

Like a thunderclap, I understood! Louis was trying to tell me that his member would not rise.

"You're tired, my lord, and frankly, so am I. Perhaps we should just rest."

"No!" His lips twisted with horror.

What a miserable oaf. Louis couldn't abhor the prospect of sexual congress as much as I did, but at least I had the courtesy to conceal my repugnance.

"Do you want to leave?"

"I want to talk."

I pulled a small faldstool from behind the altar and sat opposite him.

His brows rose over red eyes. "Tonight I'm supposed to . . . Suger said . . ."

I knew well what Suger had said. "Follow your own heart, Louis."

"My heart! Oh, oh, oh, my heart, yes," he blubbered, his nose a bright red. "My heart, love you, Eleanor, how I love you, if you

knew, a sin, perdition"—his voice dropped to a whisper—"more than I love God."

So Suger had been right about the reason for celibacy.

He pressed his hands against his temples, again heaving and weeping. "And I . . . want you . . . desperately."

"But you took a vow of chastity?" I suggested, as if Thierry were at my shoulder instead of just outside the door.

"What? What vow? Oh, when I was a monk of chastity, you mean, when I was in the monastery school, chastity. You know about that? No—I wish it were so simple. This is profound, wife."

Profound? A titillating word. Surely Thierry hadn't castrated him, but what did I know of eunuchs? Perhaps he considered it a purification. "Did Thierry . . ."

"Yes! Oh, how Thierry comprehends my spirit, my soul—oh and yours as well. He instructed me—may I begin at the beginning?"

"Please do."

To my amazement, he began with the story of Lord Adam and Lady Eve in the Garden. Though I knew the story well, I listened attentively. After a long discourse, he finished.

"Do you understand their sin, Eleanor?"

I thought carefully. "Disobedience to God. Eve was the real sinner, of course, because she tempted Adam. Women are ever the source of all evil."

"Quite true, yet Adam disobeyed God as well."

"No, he was tempted by Eve," I repeated humbly. Proving she was the smarter.

"Adam was made in the image of God, and his disobedience was more serious."

"Yes, I grant you; men are created in the image of God and women have no moral character." Speak of recanting!

"No moral character," he repeated gratefully.

Meaning that I had no moral character, further meaning that he wanted me to tempt him? So he—unlike Adam—could reject me? I toyed with the concept.

Also by Pamela Kaufman

Shield of Three Lions
Banners of Gold

D0122489

In Carcerem
1174

The
BOOK
of
Eleanor

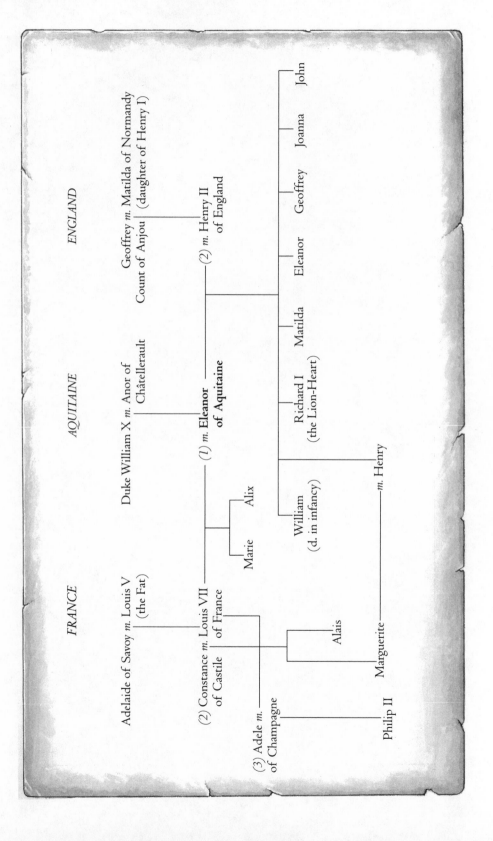

FRANCE   AQUITAINE   ENGLAND

Adelaide of Savoy *m.* Louis V (the Fat)

Duke William X *m.* Anor of Châtellerault

Geoffrey *m.* Matilda of Normandy
Count of Anjou (daughter of Henry I)

(2) Constance *m.* Louis VII of France

(1) *m.* **Eleanor of Aquitaine**

(2) *m.* Henry II of England

(3) Adele *m.* of Champagne

Marie

Alix

William (d. in infancy)

Richard I (the Lion-Heart)

Matilda

Eleanor

Geoffrey

Joanna

John

Alais

Marguerite — *m.* Henry

Philip II

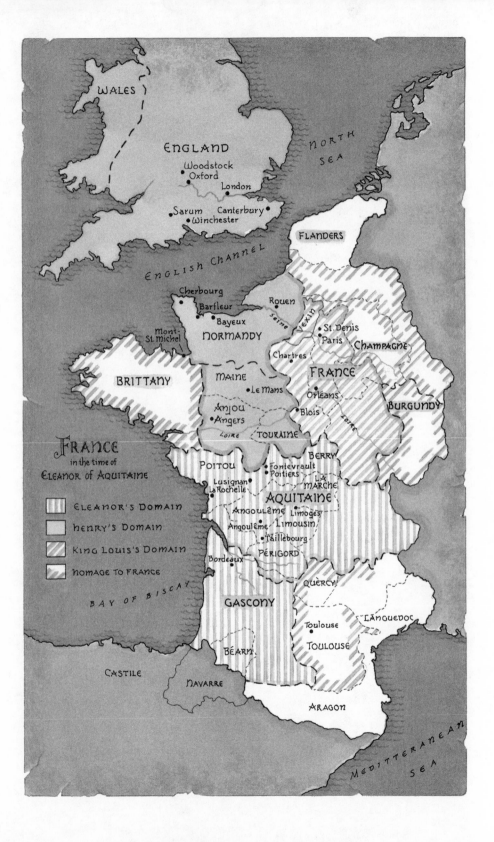

WALES

ENGLAND

Woodstock
Oxford
London

Sarum   Canterbury
Winchester

NORTH SEA

ENGLISH CHANNEL

FLANDERS

Cherbourg
Barfleur
Bayeux
Mont-St.-Michel
NORMANDY

Rouen

Seine

Vexin

St. Denis
Paris

Chartres

Champagne

FRANCE

BRITTANY

MAINE

Le Mans

Orléans

Blois

BURGUNDY

Anjou
Angers

Loire

TOURAINE

Loire

FRANCE
in the time of
ELEANOR of AQUITAINE

POITOU

Fontevrault
Poitiers

BERRY

ELEANOR'S DOMAIN

Lusignan
La Rochelle

LA MARCHE

AQUITAINE

HENRY'S DOMAIN

KING LOUIS'S DOMAIN

Angoulême   Limoges
Angoulême   Limousin
Taillebourg
PÉRIGORD

HOMAGE TO FRANCE

BAY OF BISCAY

Bordeaux

GASCONY

QUERCY

Toulouse

LANGUEDOC

TOULOUSE

BÉARN

CASTILE

NAVARRE

ARAGON

MEDITERRANEAN SEA

To my sons, Bruce and Ted

Published by Crown Publishers, New York, New York.
Member of the Crown Publishing Group.

Random House, Inc. New York, Toronto, London, Sydney, Auckland
www.randomhouse.com

CROWN is a trademark and the Crown colophon is a registered trademark of Random House, Inc.

Originally published in the German language by Scherz Verlag.
Copyright © 1997 by Pamela Kaufman.

Printed in the United States of America

DESIGN BY ELINA D. NUDELMAN
MAP AND ILLUSTRATIONS BY DAVID CAIN

Library of Congress Cataloging-in-Publication Data
Kaufman, Pamela.
    The book of Eleanor / by Pamela Kaufman.
    1. Eleanor, of Aquitaine, Queen, consort of Henry II, King
of England, 1122?–1204—Fiction. 2. Great Britain—History—
Henry II, 1154–1189—Fiction. 3. Henry II, King of England,
1133–1189—Fiction. 4. France—History—Louis VII,
1137–1180—Fiction. 5. Louis VII, King of France,
ca. 1120–1180—Fiction. 6. Queens—Fiction. I. Title.
PS 3561.A861786 2002
813'.54—dc21   2001032506

ISBN 0-609-60906-8

10 9 8 7 6 5 4 3 2 1

First American Edition

The BOOK of Eleanor

A NOVEL

Pamela Kaufman

CROWN PUBLISHERS
New York

"A man must resist and—oh, oh, God cursed us. . . ."

"How so?" I prodded after a silence.

"He made us—that is, we can say no with our hearts and minds, but he made us, he willed us Adam's rebellion in our flesh!" Again he wept.

I waited for his tears to subside. "Can you be more specific? I don't understand."

He sighed deeply. He was the least coherent man I'd ever met, even when his grammar was fairly straightforward. "His—his—my—member!"

Ah, I understood; I'd been right: He couldn't have an erection. "I believe, my lord, that there may be a physical as well as a moral cause for your . . . problem. You've had a long, trying day."

"During which my member stood stiff as a ramming rod," he said miserably.

Now I was confused. "Then surely you are prepared to—"

"How can I?" he cried, appalled. "Do you want me to *enjoy* the act?"

Frankly, I thought he would; I was the one who would suffer.

He arranged his cape frantically. "If I—sin to—oh, oh, my God which art in Heaven, help me! I do not want to commit adultery!"

"Adultery?" I was dumbfounded. "Louis, I'm your wife!"

"To cohabit with lust—I'd rather cut it off!"

So Thierry *had* suggested he become a eunuch. I must tell Suger—this was serious.

"How do you know you will enjoy the act, Louis? Perhaps you'll hate it." I realized I was arguing against my own best interests in this case, but I was intrigued.

He gasped, "Because . . . because . . . the act, Thierry said, when I'm near you, my . . . grows very long!" Again he sobbed. "I want you! I desire you carnally and I mustn't! Therein lies adultery! My member betrays me!"

I couldn't conceal my astonishment. "Do you mean that you could do your duty if you had *no* erection?"

"Yes!" he cried gratefully. "Yes, if I . . . soft . . . small . . . no pleasure."

"Well, my lord, as a maiden and a virgin, I know little of men, but I've been told that the swelling to which you allude must take place before a man can . . . do his duty."

"You've been told wrong, my dear wife," he said earnestly. "The member should be flaccid; the conjugal act should be like a handshake."

"How can I help you?"

"You!" He reacted with unflattering horror. "You can teach only disobedience—you are Eve!"

Meaning that Eve gave Adam an erection?

"Yet I have no rebellious part," I pointed out. "I can be indifferent." The first absolute truth I'd spoken.

"Your entire body is rebellious; you're totally polluted," he explained. "You swill in carnal sin."

Only my determination to rule Aquitaine made me swallow my outrage; I must play this game to the finish. "We both took a vow to wax and multiply, which is even more necessary because of our positions."

"There you go!" He held up his hands in horror. "Trying to tempt me!"

"*Tempt* you—by referring to our wedding vow?"

"By begging for babies."

In short, the more I "seduced" him, as Suger had ordered, the more I would succeed in repelling him.

"Louis, dear husband," I said softly. "I do want your love; I can't help myself. You're so . . ." So what? I slipped my hand under his cape and touched his knee.

"Stop!" He rolled away. "Don't thrust your body at me! It's the sepulchre of *my death*. I must remember that! Filled with phlegms, excretions, and odorous oozings. God give me the strength to despise you as you deserve!"

"I deserve love, not hatred." I stroked his back.

"Thierry is right. . . ."

Then I made my first error. "You won't do your duty because of a eunuch!"

He flushed dangerously. "Thierry knows women, believe me. He's told me of their wiles . . . methods with hands, rubbings, tongues, things practiced in the harem baths."

"Are you saying I'm a concubine?"

"You're all sisters."

"You dare say that to me! You love me? Believe me, if I loved you . . ."

I stopped myself—too late, my second error. He seized my arm. "Who is he?"

"Who's who?"

"The man you love. Thierry warned me—"

"Let go, you're hurting me!"

He twisted, bringing tears. "I saw you mixing eyes all day with one nobleman after another. With Aimar of Limoges—"

"Don't be absurd."

"You rolled your hips, lolled with your open rictus . . ."

Another twist of my arm.

"I warn you, Eleanor."

"Warn me of what?"

"You will not take a single step, draw a breath, speak or write to any man without my knowing."

"Is that a threat?"

"Thierry will be behind you every move you take, every thought you have."

I wrenched free. "Then let me warn *you*, Louis—keep that eunuch out of my sight."

He smiled—no, sneered. "He will murder any man who comes too close to you. Upon my orders."

We were getting dangerously off the subject. "Louis, this is not like you. You're a gentle soul, a . . ."

He bowed stiffly. "Seduction again. You waste your time, milady."

I should have been pleased; even Suger couldn't fault me for my conduct. Yet I recognized my real jeopardy with a chill, which had nothing to do with the open window. I looked at Louis with new eyes, no longer seeing a buffoon, but a dangerous man, trained for power, as Suger had told me, and warped by religious fanaticism, perhaps more intelligent than he'd seemed, and—above all—in conflict between desire for my body and his pledge of celibacy. He loved me? Not as much as he hated me.

"Wait, Louis!"

He stopped, but didn't look at me.

"You say Thierry will spy on me?"

"Yes."

"And you'll believe whatever he tells you?"

"Of course."

"And murder any man he suspects?"

"Must I repeat myself?"

"And what about me? What happens to me if he says I'm unfaithful?"

He turned, his eyes flooding. "I have no choice, have I? An unfaithful queen must be put to death."

He opened the door; Thierry immediately joined him and both looked back at me, then disappeared.

Well, I hadn't bedded with that fiend and his beloved stiff worm, thanks be to God. I was still a virgin, and probably would remain so as long as Thierry lived.

I walked to the window again and opened it to the cold air. How white and still, *deathly* still.

No, not so still; revelers were singing in the tavern across the way:

> *Oh mirror, once I saw myself in you,*
> *Heard my sighs echo like a fool;*
> *But when I learned what I must do,*
> *Like Narcissus, I perished in my pool.*

Rancon's song, though not Rancon's voice.

I wiped my face with snow. So be it; through this wretched marriage, I'd lost all hope of personal happiness. At least I still have Aquitaine, I thought bleakly. And I would govern. Aquitaine and part of France. Yes, Suger would have to stay with his bargain.

Cold compensation.

5

$\mathcal{S}$uger assured me first of all that I wasn't going to die at Louis's command.

"What errant nonsense!" he snorted.

I just looked at him.

He waved a hand of dismissal. "You have my word."

I still looked.

After a long silence, he conceded, "Take care." Then he added, "Patience, dear Eleanor; all major changes require patience."

We set up a schedule for my instruction.

Suger was an excellent teacher, no better than my father, but he touched upon different areas. My father had specialized in culture, foreign trade, and the delicate balance of political power among our barons; Suger was interested in French expansion, military games, and Church diplomacy. In fact, we taught each other; I took Bordeaux grapes to the outskirts of Paris (they needed more sun and better drainage—we tried seedlings from Burgundy), and I let him use my new port at La Rochelle. To show his gratitude, he helped me plan a palace for Paris; then we had meetings for a new cathedral. We met every morning.

I helped France with trade, but I helped myself as well. I passed seventeen sea laws to facilitate exports, I doubled our sales of salt and wine, and I experimented with new crops in freshwater clams (black diamonds), nuts, and cheeses. As a result, I tripled my own income. I saw more and more clearly that riches were indeed my source of power.

Yet, despite our exchange about policy, Abbot Suger couldn't give me the power in France that he'd promised. In fact, he had very little power himself. He could suggest his ideas to Louis, and often Louis would listen, but Count Thierry of Galeran's influence continued to grow. As for me, I could suggest opinions to Suger, who—in cases of economy, such as the cultivation of grapes—could occasionally bypass Louis, who wasn't interested in his income, but Suger rarely relayed my suggestions to the king, and never in my name. My real power was in Aquitaine. I visited my duchy many times during the winter months, as well as spending my summers in Poitiers, and controlled every aspect of governance through daily runners from Poitiers and Bordeaux.

Nor did I neglect the Aquitanian culture or my other asset: my beauty. First, however, I protected myself with a female barricade around my person—childhood friends, aunts, cousins, visitors from abroad, and new friends in France. Within this army of women, I felt safe from Thierry, safe from Louis, from curious males of all stripes, and possibly from myself. Yet I took care to elevate my own reputation for beauty in the center of a glittering court, offering my troubadours, poets, and romancers festivals for every saint's day, brilliant opportunities for flirtation, conversation, intrigue, and scandal, while at the same time remaining as remote as an ice princess. I invited comment; I tweaked noses—even the hawklike proboscis of Abbot Bernard—with my fashion designs: long snaky trains, low-cut bodices, earrings that dangled to the shoulder, peaked hats and wimples, side seams that revealed tempting flashes of flesh. I became famous, sought-after, and notorious. Once, I almost went too far with Hugh of Lusignan; we'd always flirted—half seriously—and I found him difficult to control.

Was my heart in my role? Only in my waking hours. I stopped sleeping in order to avoid dreams: Amaria provided me candles so I could peruse accounts through stormy nights. More revealing: I never invited Lord Rancon to Paris.

I derived real pleasure, however, from Louis's frustration. Of all my audience, he was the most tantalized. While he sang in the choir at Notre Dame or studied catechism with Thierry, he yearned for the half-dressed queen who'd flaunted her charms the night before. It was a delicious game: Though I was highly visible, I was inaccessible, and therefore he could desire me all he liked without consequences; on the other hand, the very fact that he so desired me protected me from his odious advances. He wasn't prepared to "shake hands" in the bedchamber just yet. But it didn't protect me from his mounting jealousy. He and Thierry followed me everywhere, even to Aquitaine during the summers, when, again, Hugh was a problem, but not Rancon.

From May to September, I went to Poitiers and Bordeaux, where I met with my barons and tried to persuade them to be less bellicose, more centered on our common good. By letter, I appealed to Rancon for assistance, and he responded magnificently. In fact, he was my real seneschal in the south.

One evening while in Poitiers, I left the great hall early and went to my bedchamber alone. The instant I entered, I knew someone was there. No noise, just a presence. I stood very still. Ah! The scent of boiled sweetbreads, and there! A faint rustling behind the arras where I hung my tunics. Very quietly, I sidled to the end of my closet, where the twilight glow revealed Thierry pulling my undergarments from my laundry chest. One by one, he sniffed at the most intimate section. I waited till he was almost finished.

"Is this how eunuchs take their pleasure?" I asked.

His face congealed. "You jest at a hero's wound."

"Is your lack a wound? Since you despise women, it must be a blessing. In fact, it's a blessing for women, as well."

"If you will excuse me." He tried to pass.

"Not until you answer my question, my lord. I do not let my dog sniff at my undergarments, much less a servant."

"I am a count!"

"Since you serve my husband, you serve me."

"I'm serving your husband here, in this manner. Ask him for an explanation."

"First, you will answer."

Again he moved.

"I mean it, Count Thierry. Shall I scream for help? Say that you attacked my person? How do you think the king will respond?"

"What a witch you are."

"Indeed. I have the body of a dog, the head of a wolf, the tail of a lion, and I instruct my tree toad to throw spots on the moon. But even a witch deserves privacy. What were you searching in my undergarments?"

His metallic eyes didn't move. "I looked for evidence of sexual congress."

"Hasn't Louis kept you apprised of our chastity?"

"Not sexual congress with the king."

My breath grew short. "How?"

He leered. "The woman retains the man's seed for hours after the act, and gradually it drips from her privates, leaving a slight starchy stench."

I could hardly speak. "Listen to me carefully, my lord of Galeran, if ever you dare enter my chamber again, I'll have you dead. Tell that to your lord and master."

Still the leer. "I have remedies against your diabolical arts."

"Don't depend on a mandrake root, my lord; expect a dagger between the shoulder blades. You're in Aquitaine now."

He left. Before Compline rang, I'd confronted Louis with the full force of my wrath. He promised to remove Thierry from my sight, but of course he didn't.

In this way, seven years passed.

The seventh summer I was to depart for Aquitaine, a bishopric opened in Champagne, and the Pope wanted to fill it. Suger urged Louis to appoint his own man. Bernard of Clairvaux backed the Pope's choice, however, and Thibault of Champagne agreed with Bernard, as did Thierry. To my astonishment, Louis insisted on his own bishop. Louis could be absolutely intransigent when his will was crossed—because of his weakness?—and he refused to give way. While he and Suger remained in Paris to haggle with Thibault, I went alone with Petra to Poitiers, hardly believing my good fortune. When had I last been free of my gaolers?

One afternoon in Poitiers, I tiptoed from the women's quarters where my Aunt Agnes snored away, stole to my father's library, where I took *Tristan and Iseult*—which I hadn't read for years—then headed out to the apple orchard. One summer yellow apple looked sufficiently ripe; I threw a rock and knocked it to the ground. What bliss, to be free as a girl again. I ran lightly through new grass still damp from morning dew, past the wine house, and toward my secret place where the tributary entered the Clain. Above, the sky was faintly lined with silver, as if an invisible spider spun in the heavens. When I drew close to the old Roman bridge, I paused to catch my breath.

I heard laughter to my right. A familiar voice and yet different—I wasn't certain. One of the servant girls? I bit my lip—I shouldn't, and yet . . . I slipped off my shoes. Now a man's voice, again puzzlingly familiar. I'm like Thierry, I thought, playing the voyeur, but I couldn't stop myself. The lovers were behind a hibiscus bush covered with yellow blooms. I dropped to my knees, then to my stomach.

Slowly, slowly. Their clothes were tossed across a rock. I shouldn't, I thought again as I squirmed forward. Now I could see the lower half of a male leg, well formed, with black hair on the calf. Forward, and there was its female partner. As I watched, fascinated, the male foot rubbed the female shinbone. The intimacy stunned me. I was frightened and fascinated. With a low moan, the male heaved himself on top of the female, and, knowing they were too preoccupied to care, I moved still closer.

In time to see Raoul of Vermandois mount my sister.

I stuffed my fist to my mouth—and watched the entire act. Repelled and astonished by the sheer physicality—his hands searching for the right place to insert his member, the sucking sound, the faint perfume, the huffing and moaning—and then by the searing emotion. I felt the ecstasy with them, forgot questions in the wonder of the act. Oh my God, they were . . . He lay very still, his lips on hers. Her hand, lying on a dandelion clump, opened and closed, then gripped a yellow flower.

"Love you, love you," he murmured ardently.

They became very quiet. A bee buzzed close to his buttocks and crawled up his spine. She moved her hand from the flower to his hair and the bee went to the bloom. I dared not stay, dared not depart. The three of us remained so forever before he moved again. He'd never pulled free of her, and while they twisted and groaned, I quickly slipped away.

I ran to my reading place. *Dex aie*, I'd dropped my book! I ran back—too late. They were dressing. As I watched from behind a tree, they walked like one person, arms closely entwined, across the bridge, and I recovered *Tristan and Iseult*.

I was too agitated to think. Round in airy circles, first thrilling to the hidden scene of love, then shivering at the implications. If she were discovered—worse, if he were discovered—it was too awful to contemplate. I must speak to Petra at once, but how? To say what? To admit what?

A malaise fell on my vital spirits. Whatever the consequences, they knew mature love. How could I bear the sterility of my life? What if I ruled Aquitaine? France? Then I dreamed I was lying under a hibiscus bush with Rancon's weight bearing down. I heard the hum of bees, felt the grope of his fingers as he sought—Oh God, stop this! Hope is gone!

I wanted Petra to have the man she loved—I'd promised her as much—but a man married to Thibault of Champagne's niece? And Raoul was political seneschal of France. No wonder I'd never trusted him.

I summoned Petra two weeks later. "I have good news, darling. I've found you a husband."

Even if I hadn't witnessed her act under the hibiscus bush, I would know now that something was terribly wrong.

She paled, grasped the table; I thought she might swoon.

"I can't—"

"Of course you can, dear. Believe me, your marriage will be better than mine."

She turned away. "Who?"

"Philip, the duke of Flanders. A most admirable choice, eh? You've always liked him, and he's smitten with you. And, more important, I would enjoy him as a brother." I laughed easily.

"No, Joy, really, you must trust me in this. I can't marry."

"I'm your overlord, Petra; you are my marriage prize. I know I once made a promise that you might choose, but you've waited too long. I'm ordering you to marry Philip." I picked up his letter. "He's on his way now."

She rose. "Stop him, Joy! I beg you! You don't understand!"

"Understand what?"

Our eyes held; she looked away first. "I won't be here. . . . I'm going to Sot . . ." Her voice became unclear.

"To Sot? Is that a tavern?"

"Scotland." She no longer bloomed. Never had I seen her so wretched.

"*Scotland!*" I was sure I'd misunderstood. "That barren crag north of England? Where men and women fight naked side by side and paint themselves blue? Is this a jape?"

Her eyes were desperate. "You're mistaken—it's quite civilized."

"Why are you going? Or why do you *think* you're going?"

Her lips moved finally, "To have my baby."

"*Baby!*" I walked to the window to hide my face. Indeed, this complicated my plans for marriage. I turned. "I assume that Raoul is the father."

She gasped. "How did you know?"

"You could be seen from the bridge."

She took it in.

I returned to the desk. "Do you want to tell me about it, Petra?"

"Yes, but could Raoul be with us?"

"Does he know you're pregnant?"

"Of course. He's waiting—I could send for him."

"Then do so."

He was bright red from running when he entered the hall. I ordered we not be disturbed. When I turned back, he was holding Petra in his arms.

"My sister tells me that she's planning to disappear into the wilds of Scotland. Very convenient for you, eh?"

He looked at me steadily. "I can understand your cynicism, Queen Eleanor, and I feel I've been terribly weak in this affair. But you must know that I love your sister—*love her*—and plan to follow her as soon as I can. I'm sending her to my brother in Scotland, who will take good care of her."

"I may be cynical, my lord, as you say, but 'as soon as I can' seems a flexible span of time."

"I must have my marriage annulled, which may be difficult.

"Annulled after five children? How old are you, Raoul?"

He flushed. "Fifty-one. And I'm a grandfather."

"How long have you been my sister's lover?"

"We fell in love at once, Queen Eleanor. When you said your vows in Saint-André's, we said ours silently."

Suddenly, I recalled Petra's vivid happiness the day of my marriage.

"So it's been seven years," I repeated. "And now it's finished. Petra will wed the duke of Flanders. I'm sorry, of course, that she's with child, but it won't be the first time."

He put his arms around Petra. "We'd rather die than be separated."

And so come death. The message resonated; I'd just finished *Tristan and Iseult.*

"Rather die?"

He nodded. "I don't expect you to understand. We both know all about marriages for political and property advantage, but occasionally . . . we've been blessed. We found each other."

For the first time, I saw them as they were, a man and a woman joined as one, beautiful beyond understanding. I had to turn away.

"If you insist, then. I'll help you, except—"

"Oh Joy!" Petra rushed to clasp me.

I held her at arm's length. "Have you forgotten Louis?"

We arrived in Paris, to find the palace in turmoil. Abbot Suger had moved in from Saint-Denis to counsel Louis from dawn to dusk about the appointment in Bourges. He demanded that the king stay with the royal choice for bishop, a man named Joubert, and Louis's anger raised a notch each day.

He was a wild man by the time I saw him. He exploded in a volley of grievances: Pope Innocent had threatened his sovereignty, Count Thibault was committing treason by siding with that charlatan in Rome, and Thierry had shown his true allegiance at last. Suger stood a pace behind him, nodding like a puppet.

I agreed with him, but I had a more important issue on my mind; I asked if we might stroll alone in the garden after dinner, since we'd been apart too long (three weeks). He flushed with pleasure.

I listened carefully to his garbled recital.

"You're more offended with Thibault than anyone else, eh?"

"Yes, because he's my uncle, my father's own brother, and has always loved me and all my family as well." His voice became aggrieved. "You know—Suger says I should appoint the bishop. Why does Thibault defy me?"

I stopped and faced him, inspired. "Louis, I can explain! He doesn't care a fig for the bishop; there's another reason."

"I've never crossed him."

"Raoul of Vermandois backs you in your choice, eh?"

"Yes, and so does Suger."

"But Suger isn't married to Thibault's niece, and Raoul is.

"Countess Leonore? Has she influenced her uncle against me? I'll ask Raoul."

I took his hand. "No need, my darling. Let me explain. You see, Raoul wants an annulment of his marriage."

Louis blanched. "Impossible! He has five children! How can he claim—"

"On grounds of consanguinity; he and Leonore are cousins to the fourth degree. All people of our class are related; even you and I are cousins. And—"

"We had a dispensation."

"Yes, but Raoul and Leonore didn't. Therefore, he wants his marriage dissolved."

With rare perception, Louis saw the flaw in my argument. "Why now? There must be some other reason to make him move now."

"Yes." I drew a long breath. "He's in love with my sister."

"*Petronilla?*" His astonishment was hardly flattering. "But he's married!"

I spoke from experience. "A forced marriage can never produce love, Louis. Raoul's tried—the five children prove that he's done his duty—but he was smitten by Petra from the day he met her, when you and I also met."

Memory shadowed his eyes at the mention of our nuptials. "I don't see it. If Raoul . . . and if God, the wedding . . . his motive isn't pure. . . ."

"It isn't for us to judge the issue of his annulment, my dear; the point here is what Thibault believes. Try to follow. Thibault knows that Raoul backs you in this matter of the bishops. And Thibault may suspect that you back Raoul in the dissolution of his marriage! A quid pro quo."

Louis hesitated, his brow furrowed. "I must think this through carefully."

"Good, that's settled—you'll help Raoul and my sister."

"What? Did I say that?"

"You said you wouldn't give way to Thibault."

Louis rose to anger. "How dare he oppose me on this issue!"

"Issues."

A giant leap. I let the information simmer.

Suger was faster. He cornered me the following morning. "What's this about Raoul and your sister?"

I explained.

"Tell them to stop their nonsense immediately. We don't need a scandal to complicate matters."

"It's too late." I explained further.

"Then I think he has an excellent solution, for both of them to retire to Scotland."

"It might surprise you, Suger, to learn that I believe in *love* between a man and a woman. It's a rare event, I admit; all the more reason to be treasured."

He studied me thoughtfully. "Yes, it does surprise me. You seem so sensible. However, Joy, in this case, you're being unrealistic. Pope Innocent is the last Pope in the world to indulge infidelity— especially with the other complications."

"I know that. Nevertheless, Louis should send a legate to Rome."

"Why, if the outcome's known?"

"For protocol."

"So that you can say to your sister that you tried?"

I smiled. "I shouldn't have to instruct you on religious rules, Suger, but I conferred with my bishop in Poitiers; three bishops equal one Pope. If I can find three bishops to do the job, Raoul's marriage can be annulled and he and Petra can wed on the same day."

"I know the rule very well!" he snapped. "It's meaningless, as three bishops who will risk excommunication can never be found."

"We've already found all three; the bishops of Noyon, Craon, and Senlis will absolve Raoul of his former wedding vows." I added as an afterthought, "The bishop of Noyon is Raoul's brother, you know."

As it turned out, Countess Leonore and her children sought refuge with Count Thibault, and he accepted them with a marked lack of enthusiasm; they were Raoul's burden, not his. Raoul married my sister. The Pope sent his appointed bishop to Bourges, and the city refused to let him enter; Louis sent his own man to Bourges.

Thibault declared war.

⊠

Louis promptly hired mercenaries from Flanders and Brabant, ruthless fighters who lacked all knightly restraints, but it was Suger who helped him the most. Angrier than Louis, if possible, he summoned us to Saint-Denis to demonstrate a secret weapon.

Hidden in one of the groves behind the abbey was a series of cauldrons. "I've only used this once," he cautioned Louis, "and it takes skill. I warn you, it's dangerous. Perhaps I should go with you."

Louis spoke gently. "I can't let you risk your life, dear friend. Instruct me; I'll take care."

Suger sighed. "I used it with your father on the Loire, in a battle that was supposed to last a week and we celebrated our victory dinner within a single day; we quite confounded the enemy. The principle is simple, but I can't tell you why it works, only that it does. I take dry wood chips—here in this cauldron—mix them with grease—here, extracted from the pig—and this cows' blood, which may be the most important ingredient."

The blood was a viscous black liquid with a nauseating odor.

"Put the mix inside tuns—not too large—and launch them from catapults. They seem to explode, though I'm not sure whether it's spontaneous or whether they're ignited from fire that's already burning. But I assure you that they settle the issue very quickly; there's no possible defense against my weapon. Remember that it was God's thunderbolts that won the day over Lucifer."

Louis sent reports of a swift advance. Thibault's army had not yet shown itself, but Louis's spies informed him that they would meet in the town of Vitry-sur-Marne within a few days. Then he wrote from Vitry-sur-Marne that he was camped in the hills around the town and that he'd sent a polite message to the lord of the castle, inviting him to desist from all rebellion and join Louis's cause. Another missive informed us that he'd received no reply and was therefore rolling out his vats to prepare Suger's weapon.

"Against a town?" Suger worried. "I told him to fight in open fields."

Several days passed; our anxiety grew. Then late one afternoon, an exhausted knight rode through the gate; his face was black with soot. He'd come to describe the battle.

The king had mixed Suger's oily preparation according to his recipe, then waited two days for a reply from the lord of the castle; when he had no answer, he'd dipped sticks into Suger's mixture and placed them against the city's outer wall.

Suger groaned. "I told him to put it in tuns."

He'd lighted the sticks; within a few hours, a thick, noxious smoke hung over the town. Under cover of the pall, and with kerchiefs tied across their faces, his mercenaries had hacked their way through the city gates. The city seemed empty, the lord nowhere to be seen. The mercenaries went back to camp.

That afternoon, a wind rose in the west. The flames along the wall suddenly became an inferno. Again the air became black, this time with a blizzard of ashes.

"The area was dry," the knight croaked. "We had to stamp out small blazes around the king's testudo on the hillside. Then there came a sound—we thought it was the wind's shriek. . . ." His red-shot eyes were glassy.

The soldiers had heard a dull thud. Suddenly, black ashes had mixed with heavier objects, like charred branches. One had fallen almost in the king's lap; he'd pushed it away with his foot. It was a human leg.

Louis had plunged down the hillside to enter the gates himself. Choking and stumbling, he'd discovered that the church had blown up, killing at least two thousand innocent victims who'd taken sanctuary there, old people, women, children.

Suger buried his face on my shoulder; numbly, I stroked his trembling frame.

Then Suger received a letter from Bernard of Clairvaux, a copy of one he'd sent to Louis. I read only part of it: "You are following the she-devil to your own perdition. Heed my words, for the Devil often assumes an alluring female form, but you must resist the demon's spell. Ask yourself if the Father of orphans, the Judge of widows could approve this slaughter. . . ."

"God's eyes!" I cried. "Did he serve in the harems with Thierry? Why this hatred of females?"

"He means me," Suger said grimly. "He knows quite well that the weapon is my invention and that I encourage Louis to resist. Louis has erred in his application, but the principle is right: A king must be obeyed."

"You're not a female, Suger; I am."

"Very well, we're both accused."

But it was Louis who was punished: Pope Innocent excommunicated the French king; an interdict was thrown against France. Even so, Louis continued to fight.

Horrible as the news was, I hardly noticed, for Petra was in labor.

6

istening to poor Petra howl, I thought how mistaken was Louis's claim that God had cursed men with their rebellious members. If God had cursed anyone, it was the entire female sex with the pains of childbirth.

"Push! Push!"

A faint mewing cry, and a tiny bundle was pulled free. Now the women worked frantically; they snipped the cord.

"Want to hold him?" the midwife asked me.

I had the waxy lump in my hands before I could reply, while the women continued to coax the afterbirth free. Then he opened his eyes. I'd been informed that babies can't see much, but his eyes, dark as the Atlantic at dusk, were intelligent. We perused each other in silent greeting.

"He's smiling," I said.

"Gas, my lady."

A warmth flooded through my chestspoon; this was my nephew, baby Raoul. He was alive, a real human being, when only a few moments earlier he'd been nothing. Where had he come from?

"A miracle," I whispered.

"Aye, all babies is miracles," agreed the midwife. "Us women make miracles."

I looked at her in amazement, grasping this fundamental truth as if it had just been invented. There was a wisdom there somewhere that I could hardly comprehend.

The new infant interrupted my reverie with a series of angry bleats.

The wet nurse tickled his lips. I watched him take her nipple, kissed my sleeping sister, and left.

Outside, I slumped to the floor and leaned against the cool wall. Weak tears coursed down my cheeks. I must have my own baby! God's heart, hadn't I sacrificed love in my life? Must I also be deprived of the fruits of love? I was a woman with a woman's yearnings, a baby of my very own, someone to love and who would love me without guilt or judgment, but I was already twenty-two. Was it too late?

I was obsessed with my new plan, which must include Louis. Could I persuade him to cooperate? From a distance, he seemed to have changed; he'd become militant—dare I think manly?—he'd defied the Pope, Bernard of Clairvaux, Thierry. I prayed for his victory and for his swift return to Paris.

We heard from Rome that Pope Innocent had died, to be replaced by Pope Celestine II.

"A new Pope couldn't be worse," Suger assured me.

"Indeed."

Another week brought the news that Pope Celestine had raised the interdict against France, had restored Louis to the Church, and was willing to discuss the matter of the bishop in Bourges. Louis had won! He immediately ceased fighting and went to the peace parley in Corbeil, only to storm out when Bernard of Clairvaux sneered that I was leading Louis around by his nose. Better and better; my husband was showing his mettle.

While there was no peace, neither was there war, for Louis saw no purpose in fighting solely for Raoul and Petra. Instead, he wrote, he was returning to Paris. Heart pounding, I gowned myself in rare silks, dowsed my body with attar of roses, had Dangereuse arrange my hair, ready at last to consummate my marriage.

And to become a mother.

When I heard fanfare, I went to the courtyard, shy as a girl, to greet my victorious hero. His knights entered the gate, his pages and standard-bearer, but where was the king? Then I saw him skulking through a side entrance. Ashes dripped from his straggly hair; his face was rubbed with soot; he wore a hair shirt and walked on bloody bare feet. Indeed, he tottered and fell as soon as he saw the door—obviously, he'd been fasting.

"What's wrong, my lord?" I rushed to help him. "Why this penance?"

He glared from the cobbles. "You who know of Vitry dare ask me that?"

"Yes, but I thought . . . You yourself said that it was necessary. You were so brave, I thought . . ." I reached to help him.

"Don't touch me!"

"Allow me." Thierry of Galeran pulled Louis upright.

Suger and I stared at each other across the yard.

The months that followed marked a new low in my existence: I lived with a verminous ghost who squatted on the floor and melted into the walls, his eyes rolling like a madman's. This was the man who must father my child if I were ever to have one. The case seemed hopeless. He was killing himself with penance; I despaired that he would have the energy—let alone the will—to do his duty. Yet he remained jealous; he followed me like a vengeful wraith.

Suger was equally disturbed because of France. If Louis continued his obdurate self-punishment, his brother would surely try to seize the throne.

"Then what would happen?" I asked.

He glanced sharply. "You mean to your marriage? You would drag Louis back to Poitiers to live out his days."

"Which couldn't be long."

"It won't come to that; I have an idea. He can't be at peace with himself until he's at peace with his vassals. I think we need to call a peace conference."

"With Thibault of Champagne? Save yourself embarrassment; Louis would never come, assuming that you could persuade Thibault."

"Oh, I think I can persuade him, yes, and the villain Bernard, even the Pope if I time it correctly. And Louis, too. See if I don't. I'll make it the centerpiece of my dedication of Saint-Denis."

He showed he had more understanding of Louis than I did, for Louis immediately agreed, if the others were willing. Suger wrote long and diligently: Pope Celestine was too ill to travel, but he would send a surrogate; Thibault was willing, providing that the issues were settled to his liking; Abbot Bernard of Clairvaux was eager to address the recalcitrant king.

As Suger trumpeted his victory, I dandled Petra's baby and pondered. I studied the participants' records for help, discounting Pope Celestine, who wouldn't be there. I explored Thibault and his tangled relationship with Raoul with little hope, then turned to Bernard of Clairvaux, my most powerful adversary. His record was ghastly: Bernard so hated women that he refused to speak to his own sister because she had a baby, a legitimate baby, but it meant she'd sinned instead of becoming a nun as he'd advised.

Yet I must try.

The dedication took place on June 11, the feast day of Saint-Barnabas, and Suger had carefully planned to transport the precious relics of Dionysus the Areaopagite to the new reliquary of his choir, an irresistible event for the religious community. No one was happier than Louis, for it suited his hope and his humility to participate in this observance.

Everyone gasped in awe at the glorious jeweled light blazing through the holy scenes, spilling on floors, walls, and uplifted faces. God had entered Saint-Denis. At last it was over, and the participants of the peace parley assembled in the vestry, a coven of enemies. Amaria and I followed the men inside, though we weren't invited. Abbot Bernard Clairvaux was the centerpiece, a dark gnarled little monkey—smaller than Suger—in scarlet robes. He started at my presence but said nothing.

The men involved stood in a line behind the negotiating table. At last, Louis had shed his verminous shirt; he wore the French blue. His hair and nails were clean.

Thibault, the first to speak, requested that Louis restore Champagne's ravished lands; the king agreed. Further, Louis must permit the Pope's man to take his post in Bourges. Again Louis agreed.

I was disgusted.

Abbot Bernard then denounced the king for his defiance of Rome in the harsh invective I knew so well, and I had to look away to control myself. Finally, the abbot gave Louis the kiss of peace; it was over. The company filed past me as if I weren't there. I waited until Abbot Bernard came at the end of the line.

"Abbot Bernard, I must speak to you privately." I took his arm.

Horrified, he struggled as if he were in the coils of a cobra. "Unhand me!" he gasped.

I gazed down on his swarthy scowl. "You have enormous powers, my lord abbot; everyone knows your ability to prophesy—and to place curses."

"God exerts His own will. I am the instrument of God; the miracles are His." Though his tone was still harsh, he was flattered; I had him.

"You underestimate yourself, my dear abbot. I doubt not that you're a saint in our midst. You can do infinite good, and of course your curses are meant to bring sinners to their senses."

"Get to your point, my lady."

"I'm thinking of my husband, the king of France."

"We've just settled our differences."

"Except that he believes that you have placed a curse on him. A private curse."

He was honestly shocked. "I have never cursed King Louis! Who told him such a demonic lie?"

"I don't know, but he believes . . . He thinks that he mustn't . . . that you refuse him a prince for his realm."

"What do I have to do with a royal prince?"

"He says he cannot, he will not—" I choked a sob.

His eyes narrowed. "Tell the truth, my lady; you plea for yourself. You're barren, aren't you?"

"I don't know; our marriage has never been consummated."

My tone must have convinced him.

"Because the king . . ."

"Thinks that you wish him to remain chaste."

Abbot Bernard actually blushed. "Then you may inform him that he's wrong. After all, he's not a churchman; he's a king."

"I've tried—I knew you would never do such a thing—but he doesn't believe me. I think someone must be using your name."

He opened his mouth to ask who, then closed it again; he knew very well whom I meant.

"Speaking of names"—and here I lowered my gaze modestly—"if we do have a son, which I know we will if you intercede, may I name him Bernard? I know it's bold to ask, but I like to think of King Bernard. Perhaps you could even be his private counselor."

He nodded. "I'll do what I can."

"You'll let Louis know personally? You'll pray for him?"

"I gave you my word, which is the word of God."

I removed my hand from his arm.

After he'd left, Amaria and I walked slowly through the translucent shell of light. My heart beat so I could hear it; for the first time in years, I was filled with hope. I would have a son!

I never saw Abbot Bernard's letter to Louis, but I knew when it had arrived.

"How do you feel, Joy?" Louis asked after we'd supped.

"About what?"

He rolled his bread into tiny balls. "I meant, are you in good health?"

That night, he came to my bedchamber.

Of our sexual congress, the less said the better. I removed all my ladies from the women's quarters so we would have privacy, only to face Thierry of Galeran in Louis's company. Thus our intimacy began with a heated quarrel.

"I will not permit a stranger in my bedchamber!" I burst into tears. "How can you be so unfeeling?"

Louis gasped his usual religious nonsense.

"Get out, both of you!"

In the end, I succumbed, to the extent that Thierry stood just outside our open doorway. It seemed his purpose was to guide Louis in the use of his *cajoule,* a robe with a hole cut to accommodate his member, though in his case, it was too high and too small to do anything but frustrate his purpose.

On the third night, he arrived alone and flung off his chemise. As I had suspected, he enjoyed the act; I did not, in good part because, in spite of his obvious excitement, he prayed for forgiveness the whole time.

Fortunately, I was able to tell him within two weeks that I was with child, then to withstand his pleadings that we should continue love to be absolutely sure. Alone again, and holding my abdomen with two hands, I whispered to my son, "See what Mama will do for her boy? I love you, baby!"

I worshiped my expanding abdomen, oiled my skin, which didn't break as Petra's had, constructed my own slings, found the right wet nurse. And waited. One magical morning, I discovered a blood-stain in my bed and summoned Dame Jenette. There was no one in the family to help me; Petra was in Vermandois and Louis was visiting in Senlis, but I didn't mind.

I wanted to savor every moment alone.

To my astonishment, the birth gave me no pain whatsoever. It was, in fact, much more pleasurable—even erotic—than conception had been. Like Petra, I pushed, pulled on ropes, breathed deeply, but I didn't need to bite on the towel. I wondered, between sleeps, if Petra had been unduly frightened, to produce all those screams, or if I was just lucky, or if I wanted my baby more than she had. Eagerly, I slipped onto the birthing stool and bore down. I heard a plop, a faint cry.

"Give him to me!" I gasped, reaching for the waxy bundle.

"Her," the midwife corrected me. "It's a girl."

A heavenly angel. Even before she was bathed, I remarked on her silky curls, her white skin, her fat, round cheeks.

"Isn't she exquisite? Did you ever see such a perfect baby?" I asked the women, even as I bore down again for the afterbirth.

"She's the finest baby I ever saw right after birth," Dame Jenette assured me. "What will ye name her?"

"Only one name suits, eh? Marie, mother of Heaven."

I refused to permit her to be strapped to the cradleboard, for I couldn't let her out of my arms except to be fed. How I cursed the rule that forbade me to offer my own seeping breast, as if it were necessary for me to be fertile for Louis's next visit.

When Louis arrived from Senlis, Marie was three days old, and I was glad he hadn't seen her before because she was improved. She opened her eyes, blue as one of Suger's stained-glass windows, and smiled when tickled. Louis had been informed, of course, and I dressed her in fine chantilly lace to meet him.

He entered the nursery in the late afternoon. I'd put a curtain at the window to protect Marie's eyes, so he was only an outline.

"Greeting, my lord. Come look! Isn't she a miracle?"

His voice was sepulchral. "God has bestowed his wrath on me, Eleanor," and he broke into deep, heaving sobs.

For the first time, I realized that he was again in haircloth, with ashes on his head.

"God's feet, Louis! What's wrong? Did the Pope—"

"You can't look at that . . . *female* and ask?" His trembling finger pointed to Marie.

"Female? You call her a female? She's your daughter!"

"God help me. God forgive me for my transgression." He fell to his knees.

"How? Because you produced an heiress for France?"

His face, almost level with mine, twisted to a vicious leer. "A girl, a *female,* wife. Can't you understand? Abbot Bernard promised me a son! He prayed to God to give me a son, and this is God's answer. A demon!"

I cupped my hands over Marie's ears. "Dare you call this angel a demon?"

"When a she-babe emerges from the womb, the tongue of the ancient serpent licks her perspiration and marks her as a demon. Let me see—I'll show you the mark."

Quickly, I carried my precious babe to a corner. "Leave this room, Louis, and never come close to my person again or to Marie's—or I promise you that I personally will mark you with a hole to your heart, if you have one. You are a superstitious fool, but worse, you're evil! God makes half the population female—do you claim they're all demons? I think, rather, that it's people like you and your Bernard and Thierry who are demons. You were born without souls, without compassion or the ability to love! I hate you forever! From this point forward, you are my enemy!"

His jaw fell open.

"Don't sit there another moment, hear me? Out! Out of my sight!"

And he crawled away.

Via Crucis
1147

7

On a balmy afternoon, Petra, young Raoul, Marie, and I sat dangling our feet over the side of an old Roman embankment where the Seine divided at the foot of the garden. I held my father's copy of *Tristan and Iseult* in front of Marie.

"Now listen!" I instructed Petra. "I swear I haven't ever shown her this before. Can you read this for your aunt, Marie?"

My charming princess bobbed her blond curls and pushed her nose with her forefinger. Slowly, she lisped the first six lines.

I took the book. "Now do you believe me?"

"Remarkable," Petra admitted. She hugged Raoul close to her side protectively. Raoul wasn't exactly slow—boys are always behind girls—but he was worrisome. He whined and cried too easily, as if he were Louis's son, and he was physically too thick in the middle, his knees were knocked, and one foot turned inward. Whereas my miracle child . . .

"Joy."

I leapt at Louis's voice behind me.

"Announce yourself!" I cried. "*Dex aie!* We might have fallen into the water from alarm."

"I didn't think it necessary in our own garden," he apologized humbly. "I thought . . ."

Petra rose. "I'll leave you, Joy."

"Take Marie with you."

Louis watched them hurry toward the palace. "I sometimes think that Marie doesn't know I'm her father."

I studied him suspiciously. "Have you bathed?"

"How can you tell?"

"A rotting whale has been washed back to sea." I was on my guard.

"Yes! Joy, I am myself again!" He held up an enormous scroll wrapped in silk. "This document—this papal bull—just arrived from Rome." He knelt to the grass. "I'll roll it out and read it to you. Can you help me?" He tried to upend the slippery missive.

"Just tell me what it says."

"Very well. It begins with a *Quantum preadescessores* about my courage, my glory as a Christian king, my close ties to Rome, my faith, my exalted position as leader of the Christian world."

"What does Pope Eugenius want from you?"

His voice was awed. "To lead a Crusade to the Holy Land."

"Because Edessa fell to the infidel? That's only a small kingdom."

"Edessa is one of the five kingdoms established on the first Crusade."

"Yes, I know, Louis." My grandfather had become lost in a wadie in Edessa.

"And Jerusalem may be next." He placed the scroll carefully on the grass. "And I'm to lead an army for him."

Was the Pope mad? After what had happened at Vitry?

"When we arrive in Jerusalem, I'm to kneel before the holy relics of our Lord and beg for absolution for Vitry. The Pope has promised me that I'll be absolved."

So he had heard and was still mad. Louis's eyes glowed; I had to look away.

"Do you realize what that means?"

I was afraid I did.

"We can be husband and wife again. We'll have many children, Joy—what you've always wanted—and sons for France." His voice was thick.

I would never have another child. Marie would inherit both France and Aquitaine. I knew at last how my father must have felt: My daughter was worthy. "When do you propose to leave?"

He laughed jubilantly. "First I must preach the Crusade throughout Europe in order to enlist a Christian army."

If there was one thing Louis could not do, next to leading an army, it was to preach. He could express only one straightforward idea: jealousy.

"How many soldiers for the Lord do you expect to persuade?"

"Here in France, a hundred thousand, perhaps half that number in Aquitaine—with your help, of course."

I didn't comment.

"And the Pope wants Germany to join us, which might be another hundred and fifty thousand."

"You will lead *three hundred thousand men?*"

"Yes! I've been elected, Joy! The Lord has chosen *me* above all other men. I feel—oh, I cannot describe it—humble, grateful, and elated. I've been reborn; my whole life is ahead of me!"

Three hundred thousand doomed victims. My skin pricked and my breath grew short. I couldn't recall a like disaster in all history. I moistened my lips.

"How many Saracens will you be fighting?"

"Hard to estimate. They're fierce beyond their numbers, in any case. Their leader, Zengi, executed every man still existing in Edessa, then rounded up the women and children to sell into slavery."

"Try to give me a number."

"Eight hundred thousand, perhaps a million!"

"Three times your army. Then you'll need Suger's weapon, eh?"

His tears flowed; his voice choked. "How can you ask? I will never throw a tun of living death again, Joy. If you could have seen—"

"But the odds, Louis."

"We have God on our side!" His tears dried, and his voice was sweetly sepulchral, though his nose was still red.

Tales of my grandfather's Crusade rose vividly to mind, the rivalries and treacheries among factions. A strong leader was the first requisite—witness how Louis himself had cited Zengi for the Saracens.

I could have wept at the tragedy ahead, except . . . Louis would be away. Oh, no doubt I would weep bitter tears with the rest of Europe as the cost of this travesty drifted back, but in the meantime I would be without Louis for years. Perhaps forever? Suger and I would reign; I would teach Marie about statehood. Hastily, I crossed myself.

Louis noted my gesture. "Dear Joy, you're as moved as I am, aren't you? I can see it in your eyes! Oh, my dear, my darling, what a marvelous adventure we'll share!"

I shrank from his reaching hand.

"Together, we can tread the Stations of the Cross. Together, we can worship—"

"Wait, Louis, are you suggesting that I go to Jerusalem?"

"Do you think I would leave you alone in Paris?"

"Hardly alone."

"Away from me, which is alone," he said stiffly. "We are one soul, one flesh, and no one can tear us asunder."

"We are apart every summer, Louis, and not torn asunder."

"Aquitaine is hardly Jerusalem. I'll not leave you in France for every man in Europe to prey upon."

"You just said that every man will be on the Crusade! We'll be a continent of women."

"Who is he, Joy?"

"God's feet, be reasonable."

"Don't make me put you in a cage and carry you!"

"I certainly would never make you do such a demeaning act."

"If it's the only way I can be sure of your fidelity!"

"Louis, I swear I'll be chaste! By holy Saint-Radegonde, I swear it!"

"The saint of carnal love!"

"The saint of Aquitaine!"

"The saint of your grandfather! The saint who permitted your father to wed his own sister! You're a child of incest!"

"They did not have the same parents!" This was old territory. "Bring relics from Notre Dame! Any saint you choose! I'll take a vow to be faithful before God!"

His voice dropped. "You'll swear on the relics?"

"Yes! Yes!"

"Then you'll do it before we leave. Only then can I devote myself to God's work!"

But I was accustomed to his leaps. "Before *you* leave, not *we*.

"You'll go! I insist!"

"Insist all you like! I'm staying with my child!"

I ran from the garden.

"We'll worship in Jerusalem together, Joy!" he shouted after me.

Within hours, Suger was shaking his finger at Louis. "You can't leave your country on some wild chase for penance!"

"It's not wild, Suger; I must recover my life."

"Your life is France!"

"God will protect—"

"No, *you* will protect!" Suger's voice rose to a squeak. "Even as we speak, Henry of Anjou is massing his army to attack Paris. Henry's your true enemy, not Zengi! And Henry's *here*! Are you aware that he took the Vexin last week?"

"The Vexin?" Louis seemed befuddled. "But that's France."

"Not anymore. And when he learns that France is without a king—"

"Without a king or queen. Eleanor is going with me."

Suger's shock was almost comical. "*You're* going on this mad venture?"

"Yes," said Louis.

"No!" I cried. "Louis has one of his fixations! You try to explain, Abbot Suger!"

And Suger did with his usual long discursiveness, to the effect that if Louis persisted in this fanatic adventure, then I must be his regent in France because, bluntly, Marie needed one parent as regent in case she inherited the throne.

"You must name her as your heir," I told Louis, "at once."

"I'll name her," he said slowly, "if you go with me."

I smiled grimly. "If you name her, I promise to swear on your relics."

When Louis launched the Second Crusade at his Christmas
Court in Bourges, he failed to attract a single recruit. He then
moved to Orléans, to Limoges, to Poitiers, and still no one took the
cross. When pressed, nobles claimed they'd suffered disastrous
years of drought, or there was a family problem, or an old wound
that prohibited action. After Vitry, no one wanted to follow Louis
into battle.

Of course Louis could have corrected that difficulty if he'd confessed that he had no intention of leading the army, that he himself was going as a pilgrim seeking religious salvation and would
lead other pilgrims, not the fighting men, but he was ambivalent on
this issue. With his usual muddled purpose, he clung to the pres-
tige of being the Pope's appointed leader and reserved the right to
assume military authority if he so elected, yet he would try to avoid
fighting. Just how he could conquer the infidel hordes without
doing battle remained unclear, though I suspected he harbored a
secret scheme to convert them, and how he would accomplish that
was an even greater mystery. In short, he reveled in the honor while
squirming away from responsibility. Perhaps, I mused, he was right
not to disclose his inner uncertainty after all. No need to expose a
deranged purpose along with his military confusions.

Weeks passed, and it looked as if Louis would raise his fiery
sword alone against the Saracens. Pope Eugenius was wild with
anxiety; he exhorted King Conrad of Germany, but since Conrad
was warring fiercely against the papal state for territory in Lom-
bardy, he didn't even reply. The kings of Hungary, Norway, and
Denmark were equally indifferent, though I never heard their pre-
cise excuses. It was easy to imagine that they—along with every
ruler in Europe—resented Rome's assumption of world power with
the concomitant wealth collected in taxes. Of course the one ruler
Rome needed the most, Emperor Manuel I of Greece, was beyond
the Pope's influence. Though the Eastern Empire was more immediately threatened by the Turks than Jerusalem, its brand of Byzantine Christianity might not be Christianity at all, and they were

known to traffic with the infidel. They were, however, strategically located, and therefore indispensable; they were also very rich.

Then Pope Eugenius found a way out of his dilemma: He assigned Abbot Bernard of Clairvaux to aid Louis in his recruitments. Bernard flew on his broomstick over the entire continent, preaching, threatening, prophesying doom, and generally creating panic among the masses. A few great lords took the cross, but most of the recruits were "pilgrims," meaning adventurers at best, prisoners bargaining away their gaol terms at worst. Then in a weak moment during the Nativity, Conrad of Germany took the cross— a promise he immediately sought to recant, but Bernard would not release him. After that, the Crusade caught fire everywhere but in Aquitaine. For us, there was still the problem of Louis.

To my infinite relief, Bernard of Clairvaux strictly prohibited women on the Crusade. He pointed out with no confusion whatsoever that we were not soldiers, or pilgrims, or God's creatures— but in fact, an embarrassing anomaly of the race.

Yet even Abbot Bernard needed wealth, for Crusades were expensive. His pilgrims, drawn from the desperate rogues of Europe, had to eat, knights had to be paid, and lords had to be compensated for lost incomes. France had no money to spare for the journey, nor did Conrad of Germany, who planned to leave ahead of the French in order to scavenge the countryside for food, leaving the French in a quandary.

The entire Crusade was in financial ruin before it started.

Suger levied a Crusader's tithe against the French populace, but it was still not enough. Then Bernard of Clairvaux reluctantly gave permission for me to march with Louis, *if* I contributed huge sums to the Crusade.

I refused the honor.

8

$\mathcal{I}$n the middle of a stormy night, February 5, a letter addressed to me and marked "Personal, urgent" was delivered to my bedchamber. I called for candles and read it while I lay in bed under piles of furs. My first thought was that someone had died, perhaps my grandmother Dangereuse in Poitiers. But no, it was written in Latin, obviously by a scribe.

"To Eleanor, duchess of Aquitaine, countess of Poitou, and queen of France, greeting."

The odd arrangement of my titles made me flip the pages for the signature: "Raymond, prince of Antioch," my uncle Raymond, the first time I'd ever heard from him; I went back to the beginning.

"I am mortified that I haven't written before, either on the occasion of my dear brother William's death, or then on your accession to the throne of France. By the time I heard of either event, more than a year had passed. Please believe that I still light a candle for William every day of my life; I loved him most dearly, for he was always kind to me, a younger brother, which is rare in our time. I'll miss him forever."

I felt a surge of grief, for he'd also been a kind father to his daughter. After my experience with Louis and Marie, I realized anew just how unusual it had been for a man of power to be generous with a female, more so than with a younger brother.

"I'm sure that you, too, share the generosity and loyalty to family so marked in your father. Although we hear little of France here in Antioch, we know that you are reputed to be the most beautiful and wisest woman in Europe."

Flattery. To what purpose?

"I don't know how much William told you of my situation, so I beg your indulgence if I repeat what you already surmise. I was sent to England while you were still a child, there to play the prince to King Henry I, who'd lost his own son at sea. After Henry I died and the great battle for the throne commenced between Matilda and Stephen, I was at a loss. Then the patriarch of Antioch approached me: They were looking for a younger son of a great house, someone lusty enough to have children, a strong knight, adventurous, intelligent, devout but not narrow, for Antioch embraces many faiths, to come be prince of that great city."

Obviously, modesty was not one of the required virtues, nor was literacy. I recalled my father's pain that Raymond had never learned to read or write.

"The prince of Antioch had just died, leaving his eight-year-old daughter Constance as his heir. The prince's widow, Alice, however, had seized the throne for herself. Alice was an Armenian by birth and sister to Melisende, queen regent of Jerusalem, but she had no blood ties to Antioch. The plot was to bring me to Antioch, ostensibly to wed Alice so that I would be accepted; once there, however, I would marry the child and heiress, Princess Constance, instead. The adventure was full of risk, especially since Emperor Manuel I of Constantinople planned to seize Constance for himself, and thus annex Antioch to Greece. I accepted, my heart confident of success.

"I wed Constance in secrecy, as planned; her mother, Alice, ran to Jerusalem, where her sister Queen Melisende swore eternal enmity. I defeated the Greeks, and Manuel Comnenus, too, is my enemy. I go into this background so that you can better understand my present isolation.

"When Zengi and his hordes of Saracens attacked Edessa, he announced that Antioch would be the next to fall. My knights are brave, although outnumbered, and neither Jerusalem nor Greece will come to my rescue. I am not worried for myself, only for my people and my family. Constance and I now have three daughters; the oldest and our heiress is called Eleanor after you. Did you know?

"The case is desperate, niece. My only hope is that my own country, Aquitaine, will rally to my cause. I know the Pope has summoned King Louis of France to aid Jerusalem, but Jerusalem is less at risk than I am here in Antioch. God willing, I pray that you will lead our Aquitanian lords to Antioch, to fight back the infidel, which I know we can do together.

"Please let me know your decision as soon as possible. I will fight to my death if need be, but my case is desperate."

My tapers flickered; I sank deep into my furs, remembering the handsome uncle of my childhood. Raymond. *Oc,* I recalled riding the float designed as a ship with Grandfather on Saint-Radegonde's Day—I could have been no older than five, because Grandfather had died that year—how we'd both watched Uncle Raymond charge down the hill to Saint-Radegonde's Church, a handsome, laughing young man with an eye for the ladies. Then, much later, the day he'd left for England to replace the drowned English prince; he'd been full of hope, but the ladies he'd left behind openly wept. I'd liked him—everyone liked him—and he was my father's only brother. But liked him enough to go on a Crusade? With Louis? That miserable meander to Hell? What about sending money? I threw off my furs and another letter fell from the packet. From Rancon. My heart stopped.

"To Eleanor, queen of the French, greeting. Forgive me, I have read your letter from Prince Raymond. As you can see by the date, it was sent eighteen months ago, and I took the liberty of opening it, fearing some catastrophe."

Eighteen months! God's feet, what must Raymond think of my long silence?

"Lady Eleanor, I have taken the further liberty of doing an informal survey of your barons' opinions in this matter. If you will lead us, we're ready to fight for Prince Raymond. Most of us remember him as a true Aquitanian, and a chivalrous member of your family.

"I must emphasize, however, that we are not volunteering to follow King Louis on his Crusade. We will march to the Holy Land with France for expedience, but our purpose is to aid Raymond and only Raymond, not to fight the Saracens otherwise. Furthermore, we need you as our titular head.

"Are you willing? I assure you that I look forward to working with you, as we once discussed years ago when your father still lived. Yours, etc., Rancon."

"Amaria!" I called. "Quick, bring writing materials! We're going on the Crusade!"

Suger fought against me like a wild boar. Though he acknowledged my genuine concern for my uncle, he pointed out with many sarcastic barbs that if I truly cared, I should do everything in my power to abort this disastrous march. Send Raymond money, let him hire mercenaries, let the men on the spot fight at once; after all, it was their own fate at stake. Not when that man is an Aquitanian, I argued; he'd asked for help and, God willing, we would supply it. Then the old abbot shrewdly suggested that I attend the counselors' meetings before making a final decision.

I leapt into a pit of adders. Never had I heard such hissing, seen such spitting of vitriol among "friends." Worse was their *mesclatz* decision to elect a new leader each morning. To replace Louis might make sense, but to lack any leader at all? Nevertheless, I remained firm.

I left at once for Poitiers to meet with my uncle Ralph, my seneschal, to be certain he could attend all business in my absence. Two weeks later, I attended another meeting in Paris, where I had to battle against the greedy bishops. Aquitanian gold would be held strictly apart from the Crusader's tithe, as I would need it for my army. In revenge, Abbot Bernard of Clairvaux proclaimed that, although I could follow my husband, no other ladies were permitted, no extra horses, no hounds for hunting, no falcons, no finery. I must go as a supplicant with my ashen staff.

I summoned the women of my inner circle at once—Florine of Burgundy, Mamile of Bouillon, Toquerie of Guyenne, Faydide of Berry, Amaria of Gascony—and invited them to attend me. All were now married, all except Amaria had children, and all agreed. We then enthusiastically collected the best hunting gear, steeds, dogs, and birds; I summoned my own special designers to make us becoming armor in case of attack. In fact, I designed special costumes for our entry into Greece, our first Station of the Cross; we would be decked as fierce Amazons.

Of course I said nothing of the captain who would lead our army, nor did my ladies ask. How could they? Each of us had formed childhood attachments in Poitiers, and we were all discreetly silent.

Che plan: Che Germans would leave in May, a month ahead of the rest of us, which gave them an advantage, for they could ravage the countryside for food. In return, they were to perform engineering tasks for us—specifically, to build strong bridges across the various rivers. After the Germans had left, the rest of us would meet in Metz, including my Aquitanian army, and follow their path through Germany, into Hungary, thence to Bulgaria, which was part of Greece, then down the peninsula to Constantinople. Conrad and his Germans would await us there.

From Constantinople, we would march together across Anatolia to Jerusalem.

The only sane voice in the babble of idiots was that of Bishop Arnulf of Lisieux—miraculous, considering that he was papal legate and came from Normandy, France's enemy. I liked him at once; he was an urbane classical scholar of wit and sly humor, and, thanks to his exalted position, I was able to express my warmth without incurring Louis's wrath. Even so, I had to be careful, for I learned that Bishop Arnulf was the spiritual adviser of young Henry of Anjou, who was fighting to become the duke of Normandy. I especially took care not to reveal this connection to Suger. The entire company was rife with such small concealments and intrigues.

At the beginning of Lent, Louis and I crossed our foreheads with ashes and rode the soft Burgundian roads to Vézelay, there to take the cross from Bernard of Clairvaux. Thousands of Crusaders met us there, among them my Aquitanian lords and knights, except for Rancon, who had taken his vows in Bordeaux. The wooden platform where Abbot Bernard stood to deliver his exhortation collapsed midsermon, which many took as an omen of disaster. Though I secretly agreed that the Crusade was doomed, I now clung to the hope that my Aquitanian army could rescue Raymond.

I rode alone to Vermandois, where Petra was caring for little Marie. My princess loved the countryside around her aunt's château, and she said her farewell impatiently, for she wanted to ride in her pony-cart.

Petra watched me curiously. "Don't concern yourself, Joy; Marie will thrive here with Raoul."

"If anything should happen to me . . . ," I choked.

"When do you see Rancon?" Petra asked.

It was on my lips to protest that I didn't know, but her eyes stopped me. "In Metz."

She threw her arms around me. "Oh Joy, have courage! Life is so short!"

I bent, sobbing, to clutch Marie, whom I loved better than anyone, and yet I leapt to my horse and left, still weeping.

My ladies and I rode to Saint-Denis on June 17, 1147, the day after Pentecost, the day of the Lendit Fair, for the official launching of the Crusade. Though it had been raining for ten days, the morning dawned brightly—a good omen, according to Mamile—and we donned white linen tunics, bound our hair in white coifs, and hung heavy crosses on our necks. We silently trotted through the empty streets of Paris.

Louis had left the night before for Vespers and was presently breaking bread with lepers in a lazar house, so we were the first to arrive in Saint-Denis. Booths were being raised for the fair, and the fields were filled with merchants and buyers who gazed at us curiously. We entered the brilliantly glowing edifice and took our places on benches at the back of the nave.

Soon after, a line of monks walked to the altar and chanted softly before the tall bejeweled cross. As I listened to the echo of voices wafting from the high arches above and beheld the shards of living color, I knew that nothing I experienced in Jerusalem could be more holy. How prescient Suger had been to recognize that art serves God, *is* God. Gradually, the sanctuary filled with clerics and great nobles; then Suger himself walked down the center aisle to take his place before the altar. His face was grim.

French fanfare sounded from the court and, with a rustle of excitement, the Crusaders looked back to the door. Louis appeared framed in a blaze of light. Shining with sweat and tears, holding aloft his ashen pilgrim's staff with the empty bucket swinging in its crook, he shuffled down the aisle in his new rope sandals. His gray pilgrim's tunic, I noted, was already stained on the back side, as if he'd sat in verjuice.

Abbot Suger tersely presented the king with the pilgrim's wallet, sign of Jerusalem, and the French oriflamme, which he'd removed from the wall. Blinded by tears, Louis stumbled solemnly back down the aisle and out the door. After the church had emptied, we ladies followed.

The men had already disappeared into the refectory, where they would be given a light repast, followed by a night of prayers. Since we were excluded from this portion of the ceremony, we walked to the apple orchard behind the church, where we ate a meal prepared by the monks. When the heat of the day had passed, we mounted our horses to ride directly toward Metz, ahead of the others.

We were forced to proceed slowly because of our heavy longcarts filled with our wardrobes and the cages of hooded falcons, and we must pace ourselves to our loping hounds.

At the front of the line a single voice sang out:

O Knights, if you would serve God well
And save your souls from burning Hell,
Then fight the fiends who seized His fief
And torture them with pains of grief;
   Knights who ride with Louis, France's king,
   Shall surely with the angels sing!

Fireflies sparkled in the pungent wild carrot growing beside the path and the soft *clop-clop* of the horse matched the beat of my heart. Two nights later, when Venus rose on the pale horizon, we crossed the Moselle River, opposite the walled city of Metz, where we would meet my barons with their knights.

And their captain.

The following morning, when Amaria and I climbed onto a crag to seek our army, we gazed over a sea of improvised campsites inhabited by toothless, unsavory churls stripped to the waist, women suckling their young, old men with rag crosses pinned to their chests, and fancy women laughing raucously, but no Aquitanians. In the other direction, close to the river, brightly colored army pavilions waved banners of a great duke or baron or king. Lords lolled under trees, laughing and talking.

The lords and rabble had one thing in common: They were hungry. Metz refused to sell any Crusader food. By the time Louis arrived that night, the pilgrims were threatening to attack the city. Louis called a hurried meeting. To my delight, I learned that Thierry of Galeran had been assigned to negotiate with Metz before we came.

"Everything was arranged!" he cried angrily. "They promised in the name of Jesus to sell us meat and bread. Not to give it away, of course—I offered them good money."

"Then what happened?" Louis asked.

"It's a conspiracy," Thierry claimed. "King Conrad of Germany must have ordered them to withhold food!"

"Conspiracy to what purpose?" Bishop Arnulf of Lisieux asked. "And even if you're right, shouldn't you have learned about it earlier? Conrad left a month ago."

Thierry's face darkened. "Not if he instructed them to remain silent." Bishop Arnulf waited. "If it wasn't the Germans, it was the Greeks," the Templar muttered.

"From such a distance?" Arnulf raised his brows.

Louis whispered a prayer.

As the clerics indulged in wild accusations, the lords and knights listened quietly. Thibault of Champagne was represented by his oldest son, Henry, a brilliant young knight; George of Burgundy sat with his hand across the lower part of his face, his pale eyes skeptical; Robert, Louis's younger brother, was in attendance, along with Alphonse-Jordan of Toulouse, William of Nevers, Thierry of Flanders, and the usual Templars. The most interesting lord, unknown to me except by reputation, was Louis's own uncle, Count Philip of Maurienne, who was the oldest except for Burgundy; he had brought fully half of the French fighting force. With his heavy thatch of dark red hair growing low on his forehead, his pale, bristling brows over small brown eyes, his collapsed face, he looked more like an old sailor than a great noble. Though he listened intently, he didn't make a single comment.

I excused myself from the meeting, and Thierry of Galeran slipped out behind me.

My army still hadn't arrived.

As the bells struck Sext the following day, Thierry of Galeran appeared before my pavilion to tell me I must return at once to the council—there was a life-and-death emergency. Inside Louis's hot blue pavilion, the clerics frothed with rage.

"Attack!" screamed the Bishop of Langres, who was Abbot Bernard's cousin. "They've undermined the Lord's mission!"

Thierry snarled at Bishop Arnulf. "Now perhaps you'll believe me when I say we were betrayed!"

Louis was too stricken even to pray.

I tugged on Arnulf's tunic. "What happened?"

"A murder," he whispered. "A young man called Robert stole a dory early this morning to go to Metz to buy bread. Either he sneaked through the gates or he was attacked outside the wall—

I'm not clear—but the armed guards hacked him to the ground without mercy."

I looked to see what Maurienne's response might be; to my surprise, he wasn't present. Nor did I see any reason for my being there—surely today my army must come. I told Arnulf that I was leaving.

I paused on a mound to shade my eyes. My Aquitanian lords sprawled on the grass beside the river: Hugh, Geoffrey, Achilles, Guy, Aimar, sitting with legs spread apart, whittling on sticks. My blood froze before, gradually, I beheld another form as it turned in the shade of a willow, and I breathed again.

"Greeting!" I called gaily.

Rancon rushed forward. Before I could prepare myself, I was in his arms, receiving the kiss of peace from the juicy lips I remembered so well. "I must speak to you alone. At once," he whispered.

I nodded, too agitated even to reply, and briefly noted the specks of sky reflected in his dark eyes. Then I was in the arms of Aimar of Limousin, now a stodgy, self-important viscount, who pressed my lips briefly, leaving the sensation of cold, moist skin; his younger brother Achilles followed, and laughed aloud, his eyes dancing; Hugh of Lusignan, who was losing his hair, wrapped me tightly against his soft girth, crushing my breasts; his brothers Guy and Geoffrey were leaner versions of Hugh and less ardent. Rancon hovered close as the men went back to their whittling and japing.

"Would you excuse me, my lords," I implored, smiling, "if I steal your captain a few moments? We must discuss strategy."

Eyes glassy with disbelief stared upward before Amaria said staunchly, "Please do as you must, Queen Eleanor."

Rancon nodded. "My request. While we talk, my lords, I suggest you hunt for our supper. I hear that the good people of Metz have refused us hospitality."

"It's too early to hunt," Hugh protested.

"Not at all! I'll show you the best feeding grounds," Toquerie offered.

I smiled at Rancon. "We could stroll by the river, except . . ." I didn't want Thierry to see us.

"Where's your pavilion?" he demanded.

"It's much too hot," I protested feebly.

Much too dangerous.

"I'll open the fenestrations."

"But . . ." Our eyes met. "Well . . ."

I led him to my huge salmon-colored pavilion with dark blue eagles embroidered on its sides, and the banners of Aquitaine and France flying above.

Inside, Rancon swiftly opened the flaps; from behind him, I peered in all directions, then closed them just as swiftly.

He grinned quizzically. "I thought you feared it would be hot."

And it was, twice the temperature of the air outside, and stuffy. "You said you wanted privacy."

"Yes, it's urgent. Did you see anyone?"

"No." I gestured to my table and we sat facing each other. For the first time, I really looked at him. He'd changed since my coronation, subtly filled out from a boy to a man; his neck was thicker and more muscular, his hair cropped short in military style, his frown lines now permanent. He was tanner than when I'd last seen him, or perhaps it was the reflection of my salmon tent that gave him that golden glow. His features had deepened in inexplicable ways, the nose bolder, the lips redder, the eyes hotter. His creased forehead beaded with sweat and his short white tunic became damp. In this cramped oven, the closeness, and perhaps my own sensitivity, intensified his male fragrance, making it almost overpowering.

I tried to be businesslike. "What's wrong, Rancon?"

He frowned. "You don't know?"

"How could I? Has something happened to Raymond?"

"No, closer to home."

The pulse in his jaw beat rapidly; his eyes burned. He moistened his lips. Oh God, please let me conceal my own feelings better than he does, I thought. To reveal himself so soon, so boldly—I felt giddy.

"What is it, then?" I asked faintly. As I lowered my telltale eyes, I suddenly noticed his tapping finger. "Did that carbuncle ring belong to my father?"

"Yes, he gave it to me on that last *chevauchée,* when—" He stopped, confused, then pulled the ring free. "Take it; it's yours."

"No, he wanted you to have it." I pushed it toward him.

"No, he would have wanted you—he couldn't know he was going to die."

"Even if he'd known—keep it, Rancon!"

We pushed the ring back and forth over and over before he finally put it on. Both of us were breathless, as if we'd fought in a tourney. His eyes now caught the topaz glow.

"This morning as we approached Metz, we came upon Philip, count of Maurienne," he announced somberly.

With an effort, I focused on his words. "I noticed that he didn't attend our meeting. Was he out hunting?"

He gripped the table. "Joy, he's leaving the Crusade."

"What?" I was stunned. "But he can't—he took the cross! He has half the army! What will the French do?"

"Forgive me, I misspoke; I should have said that he's decided to go by sea instead of land. Over the Alps, down the boot, and out from Sicily."

"Has he told the king?"

"No, we're the first to know."

"I'm amazed. We discarded the sea route long ago. Why did he change his mind?"

I thought he wouldn't answer. The silence grew; he tapped his finger again. "He said that the clergy are an incompetent, quarrelsome lot who know nothing of the military, or even the routes. Yet they make the decisions."

"That's true."

"Worse, the king is a fool." Beads of sweat ran down his forehead. "His words, not mine."

"Yet Louis is his nephew." And Louis wasn't *just* a fool—a dangerous perception.

"And he hated to say it for that reason—I pledged secrecy."

"It won't be a secret long—that he's leaving, I mean."

"Listen! This is what I want to say. Maurienne invited our army to march with his. He admires our fighting force and wants to help us. He says that the sea route makes more sense."

I felt an ominous stirring. "For the Aquitanians perhaps."

"That's what I told him! That we'd gladly accept his offer! I knew you would agree—knew it!"

I cleared my throat. "*Oc*, the right strategy by far. When does he leave?"

"We must join him yet tonight! I'll tell our men!" He pushed from the table, then noted my expression. "Forgive me, I should give you ample opportunity to inform the French."

"I can tell them at any time. Go while you must."

His gold outline doubled.

"Surely the French won't protest. After all, our objective is Antioch, not Jerusalem. They know that."

"Yes, they know." I shrugged. "They need my financial support, which I've given to a point."

He bent over the table. "Don't rush, Queen Eleanor. I understand that there's dissension at the moment concerning Metz, and Count Maurienne knows it as well. I'll send Hugh to ask him to wait a few days. To give you opportunity to make your arrangements."

My arrangements, what a travesty; he had just doomed me to join the bootless trudge with stumbling pilgrims through the wilds of Europe after all, then the scorching wadies of Anatolia, just what I'd sworn to avoid, while my real purpose flickered like an elusive fox fire before my eyes, then disappeared. My life was over. Why had I agreed to come on this miserable, fruitless quest?

"No, go at once."

"Something's amiss, Joy." Rancon's face bent close. "Is it the count? You know Maurienne better than I do."

Let me behave like the queen and duchess I am, I thought; let me spare my favorite people—Rancon—my dismal fate. "So far as I know, he's a most honorable lord. The French will be disappointed, but, after all, he'll be waiting for them in Anatolia, eh?"

He didn't move. "I have the impression that you don't plan to come with us."

"No, I can't, Rancon." I attempted a smile. "I'm the queen of France and have my obligations. . . ."

"You're duchess of Aquitaine, damn it!" he shouted. "By God, I have your commitment in writing! You promised to lead us to Antioch! To fight for Raymond!"

"Please lower your voice!" I jumped up in alarm. "Yes, I did commit myself to Raymond's cause, and I mean to fulfill my vow. But I must march to Constantinople with my husband, Rancon."

He leaned on the table and dropped his head. "I'm sorry, forgive me. Of course you want to be with your lord."

"No!"

"Then?"

"He—he wants to be with me."

"But it's my understanding that you're not . . . that is, you don't share his tent."

"Oh, Rancon," I pleaded, "please try to understand what I say. This isn't easy."

He looked sick. "Perhaps I know. There are rumors. . . ."

"Rumors?"

"Scandals. I don't want to repeat them."

"But you believe them?" Never had I felt such outrage.

"No, I do not! I know you wouldn't be unfaithful!"

"Others do, eh?" The irony, that I had become Bernard's instrument in his struggle with Suger. "Scandals about me are a political weapon."

"How political?"

"Two abbots are vying for power over France. Louis is the real target, not me. However, Louis is vulnerable where I'm concerned. He quite . . ."

"Adores you," Rancon finished bitterly. "We've heard that, as well."

Why burden Rancon with the rivalries between Suger and Bernard of Clairvaux or the many other players in this game? "His twisted moral judgment makes him vulnerable—and dangerous. That's why it's just as well you go with Maurienne."

Rancon's hot temper flared again. "Danger to me? When have I ever offended the king? Have I ever approached you?"

I reached for his hand. "Rancon, Louis is not logical. You are a man, which is enough."

His fingers laced with mine. "And your protector. By God, I won't permit such lies. . . ."

"Thank you, but you don't know what you're saying. This is beyond your protection." I smiled to remove the sting. "And as your overlord, I believe that I'm the one to do the protecting. Therefore, leave. You'll reach Raymond sooner."

"Yes, we would reach him sooner"—his fingers tightened—"and no, I won't leave you."

Such commitment alarmed me into a deeper truth. "Listen! Louis is obsessed, Rancon, even mad, and extremely dangerous."

His brows raised. "Dangerous?"

"Not personally—he claims to be mild, Christ-like—but his henchmen obey his orders."

"Henchmen can't manufacture evidence."

"Yet you believed the scandals about me, didn't you?"

"I just told you that I never—"

I stopped him with my hand. "And they have their instructions to kill on such evidence. I tell you, Rancon, that anyone who comes close to me—"

"Your king controls you with threats," Rancon interrupted angrily. "You have no reason to fear!"

"Depend on it, I have. Ultimately, he'll win, I know that. I just don't want you—or any of my Aquitanians—to be his victim." I should have thought of that earlier, I realized.

My tone, if not my words, reached him.

"I find this incredible."

"Nothing is incredible, my lord."

Then we both heard a slight scraping.

"Hush!" I moved to the window.

He followed. "What do you see?"

"Look!"

We both watched Thierry of Galeran sidle along the opposite pavilion.

"Louis's spy. He follows me everywhere."

"Is he the one who threatened you?" Rancon whispered.

"Among others."

I turned. Our faces almost touched. "Go to the opposite side of the door and loosen the ropes. There's an opening between the wall and the floor of the tent where you can escape."

He kissed me—another kiss of peace? "I'll protect you, Joy; *teste me ipso.*"

"You'll go with Maurienne. Please."

"No, I disobey my lord."

I watched him wiggle, slippery as an eel, on the canvas floor. He had a scar on the back of his right knee.

I gave him a few moments—no, gave myself a few moments. His lips, his perfume; I closed my eyes. And he was going to stay on the Crusade—he and all my friends. I was faint with relief, then angry with myself. Was I now the one assuming too much? I'd spoken honestly about Louis—why had he not mentioned Arabelle? No, that was *mesclatz.* When has any wife, queen or otherwise, influenced the behavior of her own husband? Yet he had feelings—did he love her?

As I stepped outside, Thierry of Galeran slithered from the shadow of my neighboring pavilion.

"Who was that man who just left your tent?" he asked.

"My lord Hugh of Lusignan," I answered without hesitation.

At the same moment, I saw Rancon on the mound, watching us. I shook my head.

"You had your flaps closed."

I took Thierry's arm to pull him away from Rancon. "Only now, after he left. We deliberately opened them so that you might better hear our conversation."

His eyes narrowed. "I never eavesdrop. What did he want?"

"Why, to know if I could tell him the whereabouts of Philip of Maurienne. Unfortunately, I have no knowledge of the gentleman."

Thierry apparently believed me. "You left the meeting before we were finished."

"There was no point in my staying."

"The king wants to talk to you about money."

"My favorite topic. Well then, of course I'll return."

So, the French knew about Maurienne's departure, which relieved me of a burden. And the Aquitanians were going to follow their captain, who would follow me. The pathless forests of Europe now beckoned; the desert wastes seemed mere sand castles in Anatolia! Apprehensive as I was, I couldn't wait to embark on the great adventures ahead.

9

wo days later, we left. During that period, I spent more grueling hours in Louis's tent as the bishops decided irrelevant details, and when they were finished, in the late afternoon, I watched my Aquitanian lords from a distance, but not Rancon. Toquerie informed me that he'd gone with a few men to collect more grain for his horses. Perhaps, but he may have been avoiding me, which meant he'd grasped my message.

I'd warned Rancon with good reason, but the very first day on the road, all of us were reckless as children. Who could resist the sunny skies, the swaying green-gold boughs, the charming rustics cheering us along the way? In late afternoon, Amaria and I rode along the entire line together: At the head was George of Burgundy, elected by the council that morning, with his knights, squires, keepers of the horse, and foot in the rear, carrying bows, arrows, spears, and maces. Then came his litters and wagons of supplies. We were next, then other French lords, with the same general order, and, finally, the pilgrims, followed by the riffraff. And Louis, of course, who walked barefoot at the rear.

Louis's beatific affectation aside, the pilgrims and their unsavory neighbors worried me. Though a few carried ashen staffs and were undoubtedly sincere, many more appeared to be outright scoundrels, with their hard eyes and scarred bodies. The women were divided between gravid drones and camp followers, euphemistically called "washerwomen," and neither type carried food or livestock. Still, they were Louis's responsibility, not mine; he'd offered to feed them if they came, which was probably incentive enough.

"There's nothing approaching three hundred thousand men," Amaria informed me. "I would say twenty thousand at most."

"Did you count?"

She was excellent at calculation.

"Not each person, but, look you, if we carried grain for even a hundred thousand horses, our line would stretch over a hundred miles."

She was right. Not that every man was on a horse—far from it—but every knight who used horses had at least twenty trotting beside him. And knights were punctilious about feeding their animals. Of course, our line didn't include Maurienne's men, now marching across the Alps—another twenty thousand?—or the German army. But, at the most sanguine estimate, the number fell far short of Louis's original number.

As the days passed, a pattern set in. Since the Aquitanians didn't have to attend the morning election of a leader, they used the time to hunt game for our Haute Tierce meal, rode during the afternoon, then did military exercises during the long twilight. I did have to attend the morning meetings, and I also sent runners to France and Aquitaine almost daily, for Suger and my uncle Ralph had to be kept apprised of my decisions, and, of course, I also wrote to Petra and Marie.

Yet I managed to go to my own people by late afternoon, where I joined happily into a celebration of life. Flirtation was our southern way, a hot sauce to disguise the humdrum flavor of duty, eh? All the Aquitanian lords and ladies sang and shouted and laughed as they jostled one another, slapped thighs, and created minor mayhem. And so did I. Thus the first days passed, and I had no contact with Rancon, not even to speak. I saw him as he dashed from one French count to another, conferring and gesturing toward the lines. This, I learned, was to be our pattern.

Fortunately, Louis was also blissful. Two Crusaders conveniently expired in hideous pain the first week, giving Louis the sublime opportunity to succor their agony, then to anoint them for burial.

Using Suger's Crusaders' tithe, he bought expensive food and fed thirty hungry pilgrims each morning before he broke fast himself. Best of all, his acts were publicly acclaimed. No longer the bumbling monarch or warrior, Louis became the holy martyr, virtually a saint. Everyone was happy.

Though the clerics pretended to know our route, in fact we simply followed rivers and streams flowing south. Thus we kept our animals supplied and avoided undue climbing. We made wide swaths around towns, partly because of the ill will created by the German army, partly because the water was polluted by human waste and tanning factories. We had to stop at borders, of course, to negotiate free passage with kings.

Several evenings during the long twilight, I watched my lords work their animals in mock battle. All were skilled and fierce, but all paled when Rancon took the field. The boy I recalled so vividly had matured into a thrilling professional fighter. Though he used reeds instead of lances, a stone on a cord in place of the spiked morning star, he became one with his horse as he charged forward with wild eyes, both man and beast a single deadly machine. I became breathless, watching.

"Take care, Joy," Florine's soft voice murmured beside me one evening.

I started. "Take care about what?"

"Your face. Do you not carry a mirror?"

"Of course I don't!"

"Then let me inform you of what others see. You've changed, blossomed. Your cheeks are vivid as apples, your lips cherries, and your eyes glint like the sea in sunlight."

I laughed easily. "*Dex ai,* friend, you make me sound like a fruit orchard."

"You're a hot flame," she rejoined. "Especially when you watch him." She nodded toward Rancon.

And I chilled.

"The same might be said about you," I retorted lightly. "This is a great adventure, eh?"

"Everyone's noticed," she warned.

I turned away to watch the end of the exercise, then strode quickly to my tent. There I sat in the dark, clutching my hot cheeks. Florine was right: If I looked what I felt, I was again putting Rancon and myself in danger. Yet what could I do? I couldn't change my heart, could I? No, I admitted, but in the past I'd become the mistress of deception. Except that in Paris, even in Poitiers, I'd not been exposed to such daily temptation. Well, I must hone my skills, try harder. After all, both Rancon and I were wed to other people, and, in his case at least, I'd had no hint that he was anything but happy with his choice.

Florine was wise to warn me.

Except for a few showers, mostly at night, we had good weather until we crossed the border into Hungary where it began to rain day after soggy day. We slogged through flooded fields, up hills and down into bogs, making little headway. When we came to the Druze, we stopped altogether. A fast current in the middle defined it as a river, or we might have been gazing across a lake. And where was the bridge that the Germans were supposed to have built? Had it been washed away? We considered boats, except that the opposite bank was too steep for landing.

Louis conferred with his engineers, who discouraged him against attempting a bridge. We sent scouts up and down the river, looking for a narrower crossing, but to no avail. Louis decided to ride to Budapest to ask for King Gêza's help. Surely the young king could suggest some alternate route into Bulgaria. Louis departed with his great lords, including the intrepid Thierry, to seek the king, saying he would be back within two days.

The morning he left, a strong wind blew clouds away; the sun came out.

"Lady Eleanor! Joy!"

I stepped out of my pavilion to face Rancon.

"Come for the hunt, my lady! Your minions are ready!" he cried. His eyes danced and he was garbed in his hunting green. Behind him, all my lords and ladies sat on their small hunting steeds.

"We're going for the blue heron! Tell your venerer to fetch your falcon," Hugh called.

I laughed. "You're *mesclatz,* all of you! It's too windy for the hunt!"

"And too beautiful not to try!" Rancon reached for my hand.

I studied his face. "Can you wait? I'll order our dinner!"

Hugh guffawed. "Christ! We'll eat our birds! Haven't you seen them, Joy?"

Achilles raised his fist. "Don't tarry, Joy, or we'll miss them! I swear if you come, we'll have a feast tonight!"

Rancon still held my hand. "They blacken the sky."

I pulled free. "I'll be right with you!"

When I emerged from my tent in due time, the Aquitanians were arguing in excited voices.

"I think the wind's changed," Mamile warned, holding up a wet finger. "They'll hear us!"

We hesitated less than ten heartbeats.

Aimar tapped his black hunter. "We'll catch the afternoon feed-ing!"

Rancon, not yet mounted, took my hand to assist me. He'd pro-vided me with one of his fine sorrels. "Are you comfortable?"

I nodded.

"I've sent Rimbault ahead."

His steed bumped mine; he put his hand on the small of my back. "Are you all right?"

Feeling Florine's eyes upon me, I didn't answer.

Rimbault, our master of the hunt, had struck out with the vener-ers and our falcons to await us at our rendezvous. Now our horns sounded, and we loped slowly toward a low line of wooded hills. Hooves splashed through puddles; mud flew upward. Rancon, now at the head of the line, slouched lazily under scudding clouds. I loved the hunt, loved the day, loved our truancy. Except for the landscape, we could have been in Aquitaine.

Hugh suddenly burst into song in his hoarse, guttural bray, soon to be joined by all the men. It was my grandfather's verse:

> I take great joy in love and war
> And don't wish to confuse 'em;
> Just because my groins are sore,
> There's different ways to use 'em!
> Lord!
> > God!
> Give me adventure in the fields!
> Be it the enemy or the lady who yields
> 'Tis all the same!
> I have a good name
> Straddling my battle steed
> Or my lady in the mead!

Hugh waved his fist: "Everybody!"

Raising our voices to the robust tune, we joined in the second verse. The wind blew harder; we raced after fleeing cloud shadows, leapt over logs and brooks.

Suddenly, rain fell in a solid sheet!

"Take cover!" Aimar shouted.

I spurred my sorrel to a nearby chestnut, where I jumped down and pressed against the trunk.

"Now watch!"

Rancon was on the other side. In his hands, he displayed three chestnuts, then began to juggle them swiftly. And, *plop, plop, plop,* they fell into his open mouth as he leaned this way and that. He swallowed them.

"Are you mad?" I cried, horrified. "You'll choke!"

Crack! Lightning jagged across the sky.

Without a word, Rancon came around the tree.

"You swallowed them, you fool!" I repeated.

"No, you swallowed them, I saw you! Now close your eyes."

I did so.

Hot lips pressed mine.

"See?" He drew back and showed me the chestnuts, as if they'd come from my mouth.

"You're a trickster!"

"Am I?"

Was he? Was this a jape, or had he kissed me?

"How did you do that?"

"Shall I do it again?" He reached for chestnuts. But before he could repeat his trick, the sun broke through.

"Look, it's stopped raining!" I said.

"I can do the trick in sunlight." He began to juggle.

"Ride!" Aimar called.

Rancon threw the nuts to the ground, dashed to his steed, and leapt into his saddle without touching his stirrups.

I raised my skirt, streaked across the grass, and leapt into my own saddle with equal ease.

He laughed. "You've just earned your spurs!"

"I'm a trickster!"

He rode ahead of me and I studied his back. A kiss or a jape, which? Take hold, I warned myself; this could have happened with Hugh or any of my lords.

We climbed through a tangle of roots and rocks to a small rise where it was completely dry. Now we descended into a grassy dell, also dry, a perfect place to wait for the heat of the day to pass. Our servants quickly sank wine into a stream to cool, then set up trestles under dappled shade. Soon our party ate voraciously of grouse, trout, pork, and sweetmeats, all washed down with Aquitanian red. All except me. I couldn't eat, speak, or look at anyone. I fought for composure, though I had no way of knowing if my cheeks were apples, my lips cherries.

Finally satiated, the company sprawled under the trees. I leaned under a myrtle and spread my skirts apart from the others. Instantly, Rancon stretched on the grass and rested his head in my lap. Not daring to move, I smiled at Florine, who watched me. Her shoulder rested against Guy's. In fact, everyone was paired with someone.

"Go for a new flask, Rancon," Hugh said, yawning. "When I get hot, I get thirsty."

Rancon didn't open his eyes. "Go yourself. I'm asleep."

Guy laughed. "Balls about wine cooling you, Hugh; wine heats your blood."

"You're wrong; wine cools me, brother."

Guy punched Hugh's padded hip. "Not the other night. Made you hot in your pants, in your libido, brother. Jug-bitten as a mouse when you chased that half-naked Gitano wench all over the camp." He rolled away before Hugh could hit him.

"You sound jealous, Guy," Mamile observed.

"Of that tawny thief? Ask Hugh what she took from him, besides his seed, I mean!"

"I'm still thirsty!" Hugh stood up.

"I'll go with you," Mamile offered.

"I feel like taking a stretch, as well," Guy said. "Coming, Florine?"

Soon they all drifted into the greenery in pairs. Rancon opened his eyes wide and smiled.

"Seems we're alone," he said.

"Except for the bees."

He sat upright. Bees buzzed over empty flasks and bits of meat. "An erotic beast, the bee."

"Erotic? I would say they're scavengers." Yet I recalled the bee on Raoul's back long ago, my sister's hand groping with a yellow flower, and my heart thumped.

"They follow love. Can sense it even when they have no evidence. Then they give their lives to attain it. Is that not erotic?"

"Somehow, they lack the melody, the appearance—"

"Listen!"

I did. A steady happy buzzing, the sweet waxy perfume of honey. We must be near a hive.

"Well?"

"I grant you, they're troubadours. Never mind their fat striped tunics."

"Ouch! What the—" Rancon sat up suddenly. "My God, I've been stung!" He tried to reach behind him.

I began to laugh. "Stung by love!"

He turned so our eyes met. "Yes."

"Does it hurt?"

"Yes. But I love my pain,"

"May I help?"

"Please. You're the only one who can." He pulled his shirt up. "Can you see the stinger?"

I could see his smooth back, the undercoat of muscles.

"Close to the spine, about midway down."

"Yes! Sit very still."

Carefully, carefully, I curved my finger and thumb. "It's out!"

"Christ, is it?" He glanced over his shoulder. "But it still pains. They say that saliva . . . if you could . . ."

Slowly, I put out my tongue. Was this a kiss or a treatment?

"Have my wine!" Hugh called from the bush. "Want some?"

Rancon adjusted his shirt. His face was flushed, his eyes bright.

"What happened?" Florine asked.

"I was stung by a bee. Joy removed the stinger." Deliberately, he leaned close, and in front of all of them, he kissed me lightly. "Thank you, my lady."

A courteous kiss, nothing more.

When the shadows became long and the air cool, we mounted for the hunt. Below us, pools of trapped water flashed brilliantly into our eyes; our grooms and venerers moved stealthily among our hooded falcons tied to their perches.

When Master Rimbault signaled, we descended into the dark green dell. The herons would be flying directly over our heads within the hour, returning from their feeding grounds, we were told. We all sought out our birds.

Mine was the last in the row. I slid on my arm guard, reached for my Jeté, a handsome Welsh white in his feathered and belled cap.

"Would you like to ride first?" Master Rimbault asked me courteously.

"Why thank you!"

"Choose a partner."

"I'll go!" Hugh offered.

"Sorry, we'd already agreed," Rancon said, smiling.

Master Rimbault approved. "You have the Norwegian white? Excellent, a snowy team is good luck."

Rancon jostled against me.

"You smell of honey," he murmured.

Without looking at him, I undid my bird's bells and gripped its talons. He jumped to my lower arm, heavy as a rock, his claws deep in my arm guard.

"Falcons, an erotic symbol." Rancon grinned at me.

"Except that they eat meat, not honey."

"They're ready to die for it, though." His voice dropped to a whisper. "So am I."

"Are you a symbol, then?"

"Your horse, my lady." The groom handed me my reins.

"Let me." Rancon hoisted me up on the hunting side.

I smiled down. "Have you forgotten that I've earned my spurs?"

"A momentary lapse." He mounted, himself.

"The herons will soon be here," Rimbault warned in a low voice. "Best watch your groom."

As if he were a warrior on the field, Rancon now gazed intently at our lookout in the distance. And so did I.

The groom pointed silently to the northeast.

Behind us, voices called softly, "A flight!"

In a vee formation, necks outstretched, our prey etched black against a deep vermilion sky.

Our horses moved like one.

Rancon whispered, "There!"

"Yes!"

"A kingly bird, eh? Let's take him!"

A breakaway piece of the sky. Over our heads and he was three hundred yards beyond us.

"Now!" Rancon shouted. "To flight!"

"*A vol!*" I sang.

Swiftly, we cast our birds to the air. Up they flew, instantly on target. Bleating in terror, the heron climbed higher.

"Go!" Rancon spurred his horse.

Together, we soared as if on wings ourselves.

"*Huunnggooo!*" The heron honked.

"Watch out!" Rancon shouted. "He's going to drop his gorge!"

I veered to miss the crop. Now lighter, the heron spiraled upward, the falcons close behind it, and it was suddenly trapped in a downdraft. Jeté stooped and struck! Blood hit my cheek. The heron dodged, feinted, took another strike.

Now it flew directly toward our falcons, but the falcons weren't fooled. The Welsh struck; the heron jinked and fell forty feet. Bleeding heavily, the wounded prey dropped low to fly for water and safety.

Too late.

The Norwegian struck a wing and bonded; then the Welsh had its throat. Rancon and I galloped to be there for the fall. Feverishly, we pulled dead pigeons from our bags. Just before the three linked birds struck the ground, we tossed the pigeons to the falcons. They dashed for the bloody bits, releasing the heron. I grabbed the falcons' jesses as Rancon caught the bloody bird.

He quickly slipped the beak shield over the sharp bill, then a hood over the heron's head, and with a quick twist of its neck, the game was over.

"*Asusée!*" cried the crowd.

"Perfect!" I echoed.

Rancon gazed over the dead bird. "Do you feel as I do?"

I nodded.

He whispered, "A kingly bird, Joy, a blue kingly bird. Brought down."

We rode in single file under an umbrella of dense trees which created an artificial night, though above us we caught glimpses of a bright twilight. Our progress was slow, our path rugged. I was behind Rancon, Amaria behind me.

Rancon sang softly:

> *Who cannot hunt has no heart,*
> *Who cannot sing has no art,*
> *Who cannot love has no Joy!*
> *Let no man wonder at my state*
> *If I love her, do not berate,*
> *My heart joys in no other love,*
> *Not here on earth or Heav'n above,*
> *Blows of Joy do me slay,*
> *Which love alone can allay;*
> *I fall in dizzy circles from the sky*
> *And swoon in Joy before I die.*

Joy, the key word on which the song turned, and used as my grandfather had always intended, a play on the similarity of religious exaltation to sexual ecstasy. Had he been right? How would I know? I'd never experienced either. Yet he'd been the first to dub me "Joy," a prophecy, he'd said. He was a better poet than he was a prophet.

But the word had taken hold, both as my name and as a symbol in song. Which way did Rancon intend? He'd been attentive today, but no more so than any of my lords would have been if they'd chosen me. I mustn't assume, just enjoy the moment. I tried to memorize the soft *clop-clop* of our horses, the even softer squeak of our saddles, the heavy perfume of wet foliage. A thin gold moon hung like a scimitar against the lapis blue, cradling the evening star, the emblem of our Saracen enemy. Oh God, life was so fleeting and we were riding so swiftly—to what?

We ambled for hours under the descending dark, everyone now quiet. Our horses snorted, stumbled in ruts.

A voice called from the gloom. "Is the queen of France among you? The king is seeking her."

"She's perfectly safe!" Hugh called back.

We stopped.

"Tell her to come forward," the guard ordered.

I flicked my roan to move.

"Queen Eleanor!" The guard's voice was closer.

"Here, my lord!"

Torches illuminated Louis's pale figure among his counselors.

"Greeting, my lord," I said. "You're back soon."

"Sooner than you expected," Thierry of Galeran replied. "Queen Eleanor, we demand to know where you've been throughout the day and into the night."

"Why with me, with all of us," Hugh said belligerently from my side. "We used our day of leisure for the hunt, and became lost in the unfamiliar wilderness on our way back to camp."

Amaria added more pleasantly, "We have a brace of heron for the king's table."

"The king doesn't eat flesh," Thierry snapped, "which the queen well knows. Queen Eleanor, answer my question if you please: Where have you been?"

"Lord Hugh just answered." Rancon pushed to the front. "Do you doubt his word?"

"The question was for the queen."

I quickly edged between them. "On what authority do you challenge my captain, Count Thierry? You wear no crown, nor are we wed. Now, out of my way."

Louis spoke from his halo of light. "Answer to me, Eleanor."

"You heard Lord Hugh."

I brushed haughtily past him. Louis was ever the odorous ferret.

The following morning, I took my place at the back of the line with Louis among the pilgrims. Though I wore shoes, I walked.

After our midday dinner, I rode with Bishop Arnulf of Lisieux, who happily pointed out botanical specimens along the way. I listened attentively; I was his best student, he claimed, since he'd taught young Henry of Normandy, who knew every type of genista that bloomed in that fair duchy. I smiled politely; to be compared to Henry was only slightly better than being compared to Louis.

10

Thus, once again a queen of the French more than a duchess of Aquitaine, I rode into Bulgaria, a part of Greece that we quickly learned was enemy territory. Never once were we permitted entry into Greek towns; rarely could we purchase at any price food or grain. The Greek excuse? The brutish Germans had taught them the character of Crusaders, and they would not be robbed a second time. With hunger came open defections among the riffraff, who became dangerous criminals in our midst. All of us suffered; the land was sparsely forested, and the game nonexistent. We ladies donned our Amazon costumes nevertheless—we were in Greece, eh? The Greeks never saw us, but Louis was appalled: How dare we ride with bare breasts? (They weren't bare, though our tunics were cut low.) How dare we lace our legs with golden boots? (I admitted our fault, and we quickly discarded the "Greek sandals," as the straps cut cruelly and there seemed no purpose without Greeks to see us.)

We were all relieved when French pages called from the front of the line: "Constantinople!"

I pushed past the French knights to join Louis and his closest advisers where they sat on a rise overlooking a strait. On the other side floated the fabled Constantinople, an iridescent jellyfish with a hundred spindly arms stretched to catch unwary ships.

"We're waiting for our guide, Demetrius," Arnulf informed me. "We sent him ahead two hours ago to alert the emperor of our approach."

Rancon rode up beside me.

"There he is!" Thierry shouted, pointing to Demetrius as he approached by boat.

Louis recoiled. He despised the obsequious Greek with his short tunic fluttering around hairless oiled legs. The messenger threw himself on the ground before Louis's horse.

"Most holy king, leader of the Christian world, greatest monarch in all Europe, and hope of all humanity against the ravagers of the Holy Land, greeting. Emperor Manuel, ruler of Byzantium and the holy Orthodox Church, humbly extends his welcome to his Christian brothers."

A horse snorted.

"He bids you and your gracious queen to accept his hospitality in the Phillatium, his hunting lodge."

I groaned aloud. Louis and I had never shared quarters.

Thierry interrupted. "Surely you must be mistaken. The Phillatium is outside the city walls, Lord Demetrius. We're to meet with the German king, Conrad, inside Constantinople. Place us close to Conrad, if you please."

Demetrius raised enigmatic black eyes. "The Phillatium is where King Conrad stayed while he was here."

"*While he was here?*" Arnulf repeated. "Where is he now?"

"King Conrad left three weeks ago."

Voices exploded, but Demetrius didn't know why Conrad had left or where he was going. He did, however, know why the emperor kept the Crusaders outside Constantinople: The Germans had defiled the city with their criminal behavior.

"How dare you call the Germans criminal?" Thierry cried, though he'd said the same thing not two days before.

The Germans had stolen from the great bazaar, had shown contempt for the temples of the faith, and, worst, had murdered two priests.

The uproar hushed. Murdered *priests?* Indefensible!

"Tell your emperor that we are French, not German; tell him that our king is a saint," Thierry said, his voice trembling.

Demetrius became even more unctuous. "The emperor's first obligation is to protect his city."

We all heard the duplicity.

Rancon pushed close to the Greek. "If the emperor won't extend hospitality as he should, Lord Demetrius, what about the other provisos? Will he give us grain and food for our long march?"

The black eyes became more evasive. "I don't know."

"Then I suggest you find out at once," Rancon said coldly. As he returned to his place, he said through his teeth, "Watch your gold."

"We must consult," Thierry ordered.

I silently joined the huddle of advisers, but the conversation was the usual chaotic jumble; We should attack Constantinople at once (we had no boats to do so); we should return to Europe and let Conrad perish; we should go forward and hope to prevail over the emperor. Despite hot words, the last suggestion was our only choice.

As we loaded our supplies onto barges to make the crossing, Rancon again sidled close.

"We'll camp on the beach, close to your quarters. We must confer."

"Take care," I warned him. "Demetrius just told us that the hunting lodge is surrounded by the emperor's private wild-game park, filled with lions."

His teeth flashed.

An hour later, I found that the lodge had separate quarters—one problem solved. All night long, Louis conferred on his side with his counselors while I lay listening to animals roar outside my window.

In the morning, I discovered I had a letter waiting from Raymond.

I ran along the protected walkway to the sea to seek out my barons.

I thrust the letter at Rancon. "Read it, please."

Still in Latin, and still obviously written in a scribe's formal diction, it nonetheless sounded a shrill alarm. Under no circumstances were we to trust Emperor Manuel, the most perfidious Greek ever to sit on the throne. Our very success depended on a healthy suspicion. "Do not trust the Greeks," he wrote. "Take nothing from them; beware of false friendliness."

"Have you shown this to the French king?" Rancon asked.

"No. Should I?"

"Since he has no interest in Antioch, we have no reason to share Raymond's intelligence." His voice was cold.

Aimar took the letter. "Conceal what we know from the Greeks, as well. Play their game."

"If we ever see the Greeks," Hugh said.

Rancon came close. "You'll see them, my lady, if anyone does. When you do, try to purchase supplies. Here, I've made a list of what we need. Keep it on your person."

I glanced briefly at the items. "Why so much, Rancon? This is enough to take us to Antioch and back again."

Rancon leaned back on his elbows. "Better too much than too little."

"Why not buy along the way? Save our beasts of burden," Geoffrey suggested.

Rancon frowned. "We're going into a desert wilderness with no forage for our horses, and there may be no place to purchase supplies. I just hope we find enough water."

I tucked the list inside my bodice. "I'll do my best."

It was the first time Rancon and I had spoken since the hunt.

Within that very hour, a messenger delivered an invitation for the great European cousins to enter the city at Sext to meet with the emperor of all Byzantium, and thereafter to see the city and dine as his guests in the royal palace.

Bells rang Sext, gates opened, and we urged our steeds forward, only to be stopped.

Greek grooms ordered us to dismount and ride steeds worthy of our procession, compliments of the emperor. All of us were insulted—even the clergy on their nags—for we took great pride in our beasts; we in Aquitaine rode only the finest Spanish sorrels.

Our new mounts had short legs and short necks, like ponies. Their faces were painted with wild eyes and flaring nostrils, their manes and tails pranked with ropes of glittering brilliants, their legs wrapped with strips of contrasting silks in diamond patterns. As we started to move, they pranced and bobbed as if dancing.

We forgot our mounts as we gasped at the blinding square white buildings, the lush gardens, and—most of all—the huge statues looming every few feet, depicting the pagan gods. The priests covered their eyes against the graphic carving of male parts, and then female. Traces of gaudy paint showed they'd once been even more natural, and their eyes were still inlaid with lapis.

The wide streets were so clean that I studied our fancy little animals. Yes, they were firmly trussed under their tails. We were flanked by a solid line of guards standing along the curb who looked less human than the statues, for they were as alike as a swarm of bees: bronzed, hairless bodies oiled to a high gloss, short purple tunics, gold breastplates and helmets, gold sandals laced to their knees, Roman noses, brown eyes, and chiseled chins.

We were now on the Mesê, the famous market street. Behind the guards was an active bazaar of booths and hawkers selling tapestries, brocades, goldwork, brass and copper artifacts, silver-backed mirrors, sofas, cushions, and tables. There were also myriad animals, ranging from domestic beasts—camels, horses, goats—to white eagles, and even a small antelope, which appeared to be a unicorn.

We reached Blachernae Palace all too soon. The courtyard was filled with fountains, tiles, more statues—busts of human rulers—and gardens. We entered an enormous audience chamber dominated by a long golden table laden with encrusted gowns, scrolled swords, lamps, saddles, even two large spotted cats with ruby collars. The officer in charge told us in Latin that we were to select gifts from the display, as many as we liked, with the emperor's apologies that there were so few. I took one of the hand mirrors set in gold. Florine had been right, I conceded. Despite my hard self-discipline during the last few weeks, my face still glowed with tell-tale light. Had I achieved nothing? I glanced over my shoulder, where Rancon was examining a lamp. Yes, I'd spared my captain possible death. Pray God I could continue to protect him from my folly.

When we were finished selecting, we entered a chamber where a purple curtain hung from ceiling to floor. Trumpets sounded, a deep gong rang, and bronzed soldiers slowly pulled the curtains apart. There, on a purple dais ten feet high above golden steps, stood Manuel Comnenus, emperor of all Byzantium, and his wife, Empress Irene. The clerics hissed through their teeth.

Emperor Manuel was twenty-seven years old and in prime condition: His superb athletic body, erect and tall, was cunningly displayed through a series of slits that reached from ankle to hip. He had startling blue eyes (I recalled that his mother had been Hungarian), which seemed empty holes in his dark face, as if the sky were showing through, compressed lips, a low forehead, and a chin like a heel. His tight tunic was a field of flowers embroidered in jewels, his crown a high mirrored series of enameled plaques. His facial expression had cultivated remoteness to a fine art.

I saw Louis through Manuel's blank blue eyes, for he was twenty-seven as well and presumably a great monarch. His stained pilgrim's tunic was almost transparent from wear, his beard as long and ratty as a hermit's, his hair crawling with lice. His body was in fair condition from the march, but who could see it? At least he wasn't weeping.

Empress Irene of Byzantium was the most beautiful woman I'd ever beheld. I knew she'd been born Berthe of Sulzbach, that she was a recent bride, and that she was related by marriage to King Conrad of Germany, but I'd never expected such a mysterious face. Her eyes, also blue, were strange and enormous, almost uncanny, her skin like dazzling white porcelain, her polished pink lips curled like a flower; her blond hair, under an enormous gold filigreed fan, cascaded in scores of curls and braids to her hips. She wore a deep purple silk tunic, elaborately draped over her arm in the Roman style. She gazed down on us with no expression whatsoever.

In a rich, soft baritone, Emperor Manuel addressed Louis in Greek. To everyone's amazement, the empress immediately translated his words into Latin with schoolgirl precision, her voice high. The king and queen of France were most welcome, and the emperor gave his permission for them to prostrate themselves before him.

For once, Louis and I had the same reaction: Never! We were not his vassals or his inferiors, but Bishop Arnulf whispered in Louis's ear, Louis glanced at me, and we stretched ourselves along the cool marble tiles. Such was the price of my little mirror.

Again the speech in Greek, then Latin, and I understood that Emperor Manuel would take the men to view the True Cross as well as other wonders while Empress Irene accompanied me and my ladies to her quarters, called the *gynaikion*. The rulers then stretched out their arms to be guided down the steep golden steps.

Irene passed us without so much as a glance, but a guard in purple indicated that we were to follow. My friends and I trotted after our hostess who clutched her servants for balance, trailed through a maze of palaces within palaces, each large enough to enclose the entire palace in Paris: ceilings high as elms, mirrored walls doubling the space, chandeliers wrought of amethyst and pearl, tiled floors depicting scenes of warfare and love. Hundreds of intrepid bronzed soldiers lined the walls.

Finally, we stood in a garden of roses before a garish purple palace, and the empress paused. Speaking with her back turned, she announced in her fluted Latin that my ladies would turn to the right inside the palace, and I should follow her.

The empress led me to her own apartment, lined on floor and walls with purple-and-gold tiles and decorated with at least a dozen lion skins, which doubled as rugs and robes. Fifty bronzed soldiers stood on guard.

"Bring me a white robe," the empress ordered, still in Latin.

One of the soldiers produced the loose garment. Then, while she stood like a doll with her arms outstretched, the men undressed her. Two lifted off her tall gilded headdress, and her blond braids went with it, leaving a normal head with dull brown hair wrapped in gauze. Next, they supported her as she took a step forward and left high-platformed shoes behind her. No wonder she had to be led. Then her tunic fell in piles at her feet and she stood stark naked! The men were unfazed. One held a tray of unguents while another gently swabbed her face. Off came the porcelain skin, the flower pink lips, the artificial brows. Her body was rosy and soft, her breasts especially pretty with their shiny pink nipples. I waited for the nipples to go the way of the lips, but no, these had been bestowed by nature. The white robe fell over her head—the hemline was right for her real height—the band came off her hair, and her locks fell to midback. She waved the servants away and turned in my direction.

"Are you there?" she asked in French. "Give me your hand."

"Can't you see?" I gasped.

She laughed. "Not until the belladonna wears off. I use it to make my eyes look larger; you must try some."

I took her fingers and together we sat on a lion skin.

The empress touched my face. "Are you as beautiful as they say?"

"It depends on who's speaking."

"Well, I'll soon make my own judgment." She clapped her hands and gave an order in Greek. Two of the soldiers disappeared, soon to present a tray of sugared figs. The empress talked without cease, mostly questioning me about the outward journey, about Aquitaine, all very trivial.

"I can see you now," she said suddenly. "Yes, you are!"

Her tone made me drop my eyes. She'd seen what Florine had, no doubt about it.

With the return of her sight, her manner changed. Again she clapped her hands, and all the men left the chamber.

"Eunuchs are supposed to be entirely trustworthy, but you never know, and I want to talk privately."

"Eunuchs! Is that what they are? But so many!" I shuddered involuntarily. For me, eunuchs would forever be associated with the murderous Thierry.

"More than any other sex here. Ambitious men want to be eunuchs—they have special opportunities in the military, the church choirs, and, of course, to staff our great houses. They're incorruptible, and their loss is compensated by material gain."

"Men, women, and eunuchs," I said in disbelief. "At home, we—"

"Men, women, eunuchs, and pederasts," she corrected me. "And a few women from Lesbos who prefer women, though they're usually discreet about it."

She knew well the society in which I lived, since it had also been hers. Did she accept Byzantine morals? Of course, fully half the men where I lived were also "eunuchs," only by choice, and we called them monks, and they were also well rewarded, though they were hardly incorruptible. The difference in our countries, I suspected, was how women lived. In a place where men must abjure their normal urges, women were called evil, which made the sacrifice easier. It also worked the other way. If passion was evil, some women denied their own bestiality in the wan hope that they would escape the awful image. We had nuns and a few professional women among the poor, but the vast majority were frigid wives. How often I'd heard the tale from Dangereuse, who claimed that Grandfather's wife, my father's mother, had been such a woman.

Was Irene happy with Manuel? I couldn't ask her directly, but I queried nonetheless. She'd come here two years ago on trial, then married last year. Yes, her sister was married to King Conrad of Germany, but she'd never met the king.

"Even when he was here in Constantinople?"

"The emperor had no reason to confer, and I dislike him sight unseen. He's over fifty, and my sister is sixteen."

The thrust of my questions changed. Conrad hadn't seen Emperor Manuel? How had the German king purchased supplies? Is that why he'd left so suddenly?

But she had her own reasons for our conference. "I have a business proposition, my dear queen. You rule in your own duchy, don't you?"

"Yes." With Suger's considerable interference.

"And you have a trade with the East through Bordeaux?"

"Yes, though less than I would like."

"Would you buy silk from me?"

"You mean from Greece?"

Her voice edged. "I said from me; I have my own mills. Don't look so shocked—every empress before me owned and managed her own enterprise, and I love my silk. I've worked hard to import the finest worms from China. Are you interested?"

"Trade goes both ways, Empress Irene; I'll buy from you when I return if you'll sell to me now." I rattled off the lists of grains and supplies Rancon had given me.

She leaned back, her eyes glazed—and not from belladonna. "I'll have to confer with the emperor. You're Prince Raymond's niece—and you must know that my lord may have reservations."

"Unquestionably the king of France would look askance at my dealing on my own, but you'll note that I'm not asking his permission. Why must you? I thought you said it was your own mill."

She hesitated. "Can you keep it a secret?"

"Absolutely. I have good reason."

Her eyes, now sharp as needles, studied me. "My position in Greece is a little different from yours—I must pretend at least to confer with my lord. I think he may sell you some, though not what you ask; I'll simply make up the difference."

"How soon?"

"Day after tomorrow."

I would send Rancon to the appointed warehouse. I wrote a promissory note to buy silk, a sum that was greater than the figure for the grains and food, but no matter.

Then she surprised me. "You haven't ordered nearly enough for your needs."

I'd ordered exactly what Rancon had recommended, which was already more than I'd thought necessary. "To cross Anatolia? I've been told it's only four weeks' travel at the most to reach Antioch."

Her shrewd look held. "Let me be the judge; you'll receive more than you demand, and without pay. I'd rather not have it on record. Now, may I offer you a bath before we dress? And come, let me select a robe appropriate for the banquet."

As she dressed me, I congratulated myself. I'd accomplished Rancon's assignment in a single day, and I'd learned that the powerful Byzantine Empire was a new, more tolerant world than I'd known in Europe. However, there was Raymond's warning. Much to ponder.

11

When I entered the banquet hall, my appearance sent Louis into paroxysms of crossing himself. I was painted to be Irene's twin (sans the belladonna), my hair had been teased and stretched to form my own cascade of curls and braids, and pearls fell in heavy strands almost to my knees. My gown, created in two layers, was actually modest, but the gossamer red silk of the outer garment was slitted in the Greek manner over a tunic of palest pink, a flesh color; from a distance, I appeared to be naked. Though I took perverse pleasure in tweaking Louis's nose, the French king was not my chosen audience.

The solid gold table was shaped like a T, with the rulers placed where the two bars joined, the ladies to Irene's left, Louis and the French lords to Manuel's right, the clergy at the long center bar.

The banquet began with a tedious prayer in Greek by the patriarch of Constantinople, followed by a strange minor chant in the eunuchs' thin voices; having paid homage to religion, the dinner became a Dionysian revel. Behind each guest, a eunuch leaned forward to place plates of rare gold, wineglasses of crystal delicate as bubbles, crystal finger bowls, gold spoons, knives, and a peculiar pronged instrument called a fork. Most of the clerics disdained the fork in favor of fingers, and a knight broke a crystal glass with his teeth.

The food on this fine service, however, was almost inedible, and I wondered if there was a shortage of game in the area. The lamb, served with savory and a grain called rice, could be eaten, but not a black gluey mess called caviar, which was too salty and fishy for consumption, nor long limp stems called asparagus, which smelled as if they'd been boiled in urine, nor heaps of tasteless grass called lettuce, nor fried frogs in goat cheese—I'd as soon eat snakes. I was relieved when a heavy gold basket was released on a trolley over our heads and each in turn could help himself to wondrous new fruits, including bananas and pineapple. Each course was accompanied by a change in wine.

Emperor Manuel leaned forward to speak to me through Irene. "Tell me the truth, Queen Eleanor, how do our wines compare with your product in France?"

"Yours are better than those of France, but don't ask me about Aquitaine."

He smiled and nodded; I suspected Irene had censored my words.

Louis leaned forward on the other side of Manuel and frowned menacingly. Did he think I'd insulted French wines?

The entertainment began. Turkish women danced on their hands and wiggled their talented toes, then danced upright with licentious torsos; new musical instruments, the zither, a peculiar pipe, accompanied polyphonic singing, the first I'd heard. Most intriguing was a performance of mechanical toys, the emperor's private collection, and we marveled at silver nightingales, jeweled larks and canaries, soldiers with drums, even an automatic organ. They had been designed by the Romans, Irene told me, and so far no one had been able to duplicate their mechanical secrets.

Irene drew my attention from the toys to the emperor.

"He wants to give you a rare copy of Galen, the famous physician," Irene told me. "He has the finest medical library in the world."

I nodded my gratitude to Manuel.

At last, we left.

Louis ignored me until we reached the hunting lodge, where he coldly ordered my ladies to depart at once, he needed to confer with his wife alone.

He spoke through his tight jaw as if choking. "How dare you disgrace our Crusade? Do you realize you have sullied our reputation forever?"

"I don't know what you mean," I said warily.

"To walk into the banquet hall half-naked! To flaunt your bosom before our enemy! Have you no respect for me whatsoever? Or for our holy mission?"

I heard the salient message. "Why do you call the Greeks our enemy?"

He pretended shock. "You know exactly what I mean, my lady. Anyone so familiar as you are with the emperor must have heard of his treaty with the Saracens!"

"What treaty? Stop acting, Louis, and tell me what you've learned."

Through his petulance, he managed to say that three months before our arrival, Emperor Manuel had signed a peace treaty with the Turks, in which he'd agreed to concede portions of the Anatolia Peninsula. The Greeks had simply capitulated to the enemy. More damning: Manuel had promised the Turks that he would not aid the Crusaders.

"So you see, all those excuses about the German army's behavior were pure deception."

"Did the Greeks give any reason for their perfidy?"

"Of course, if you want to believe liars. They claim that the Crusaders came too late to help them; they were losing everything to the Turks. To cede some land was an effort to save what remained."

"And you don't believe them."

"Never! Trust a Greek? Then to watch you, the queen of France, make such a display of yourself. How you slavered over that Byzantine traitor!"

"I was courteous, Louis, nothing more. If you wanted me to be otherwise, you might have told me beforehand of the treaty."

"When have I ever been able to control you? But that gown! Your nakedness!"

"Irene insisted on dressing me."

"You didn't want to charm the empress! Those veils were meant to attract Manuel! I'm surprised you didn't dance!"

"If I ever play Salome, my lord, your head will be on my tray!"

I pushed him out of my chamber.

Two days later, Emperor Manuel summoned the crusading leaders to Blachernae Palace to make a serious announcement. Though everyone claimed the meeting must be a trap, everyone attended. The emperor entered briskly, without fanfare or pomp, and informed us that he'd just received a runner from King Conrad.

Our company was surprised—this was the last thing we'd expected.

King Conrad had chosen to follow the shortest route to Jerusalem, which took only a week, across Mount Cadmos. At the foot of the mountain, he'd met the Turks and engaged them in fierce battle. The Germans had slaughtered fourteen thousand Turks, virtually a rout, and suffered few or no German casualties. The king of Germany had won a major victory; the Crusade would soon be over. As we lingered in Constantinople, King Conrad was marching toward Jerusalem to strike the final blow.

The Crusaders greeted this news with a roar. Hadn't the Pope demanded that all crusading nations march together? That all share the glory? Why had they not taken Conrad's first treacherous act—to leave Constantinople without the French—more seriously?

"How many Turks are still in Anatolia?" the duke of Burgundy asked Manuel.

The emperor conferred with an officer. "We don't know, but not many. Turks usually refuse to engage after such a defeat. You should have no difficulties."

"We'll march to Jerusalem at once! Prepare to sail to Asia Minor yet today!" Burgundy ordered.

Shouts rang through Blachernae Palace.

Manuel agreed to lend us boats to cross the Dardanelles.

"We'll overtake the Germans yet!" someone bellowed.

"Glory be to God!"

I moved to my lords, who stood in the rear. "What do you think?"

"I hope Conrad waits for us in Antioch," Hugh said.

Rancon frowned. "Better hope he goes to Antioch at all."

I studied his face. "Uncle Raymond warned us against the Greeks. Perhaps he didn't know about the Germans."

It took all day to drive our herds of horses to the pier, then wagons of supplies collected at the last moment. Once we'd crossed to the other side, where the peninsula would still be Greece, though the hills beyond might be Turkey—the borders were vague after Manuel's treaty—we stretched out on our mats under the stars. As I looked back across the black water, Constantinople, with its towers and minarets, was clearly outlined in moonlight. I'd hardly seen it; I'd missed the Hippodrome, the True Cross, Manuel's library, so many wonders.

I was wakened before dawn. "Our Lord God in Heaven, who rewards the meek and loves the poor, we beg that You listen to our humble prayer. . . ." Louis stood on a crate of grain to address the pilgrims.

As he mumbled, we prepared to ride.

An hour later, the king finally crossed himself and said, "Amen."

"Horses to the van!" Rancon shouted. Aimar's men led our saddled mounts forward.

"Wait!" Louis held up his hands. "Stay as you are! We have to elect a leader!"

Hugh rolled his eyes.

After another hour of pointless wrangling, Louis climbed back on his crate. "We're not riding today!" he bawled. "Raise your tents! I must wait for the arrival of my uncle Philip, count of Maurienne!"

What was this? With Conrad racing toward Jerusalem, we were going to *wait*? I fought my way to my lords, who were surrounded by the French and the Templars, all talking earnestly. Before I could hear their opinions, Thierry tapped me on the shoulder: Louis demanded that I raise my pavilion close to his. Vexed, I gave orders that the Aquitanians should camp in a circle around me.

When I finally returned to my lords, Geoffrey, our master of supplies, was conferring with Rancon. "God alone knows what this delay will cost us in grain."

"If Maurienne comes within two weeks, we'll be all right," I pointed out. "We have six weeks' supplies, and if we go by way of Mount Cadmos, we need only a week's."

Rancon shook his head. "Assuming Maurienne comes at all."

"You think he defected?"

"He claimed that the Mediterranean was the faster route. Why isn't he here?"

And how long would we wait? The unspoken question.

"If King Conrad bypasses Antioch and dashes straight to Jerusalem, Prince Raymond's a doomed man," Hugh interjected.

"We're all doomed if we wait too long, and not just because of grain or King Conrad," Rancon warned ominously. "This is the third week of October."

Hugh shrugged. "October's different here. We're far to the south—surely winters aren't so fierce."

"Or they may be more fierce," Rancon countered. "We'll be in high mountain passes, where it may be winter all the time."

None of us knew; none of us could act, in any case.

Rancon constructed a fighting field the next day, enclosed with boulders and displacing a shepherd with his goats. Every man in the Aquitanian army from that day forward had to fight, feint, push loaded horses up steep slopes, shoot arrows, and do hand-to-hand combat. Soon the French, seeing the virtue both of keeping men battle-ready and free from malaise, made their own fields.

Two weeks later, a ship arrived without Maurienne, but it did bring letters. Suger wrote that he could send no more money to Louis; he'd already raised enough for the entire journey—what had happened to it? Louis didn't tell me this, of course, but Suger also wrote me, adding that Marie missed me. Why didn't I sail back to Europe while I could? Archbishop Geoffrey of Bordeaux sent a large iron box of treasure to help me—which Louis saw unloaded from the ship.

Rancon and his barons were dejected at the further delay and beset with a growing pessimism about Maurienne, when, three weeks later, he arrived with his army. Nothing had happened to delay him; it had simply taken longer than he'd anticipated. Louis was overjoyed. God had vindicated his patience! Maurienne shrugged off divine intervention and took Rancon aside. Wasn't it too late to cross the Anatolian mountains? Rancon admitted that he was worried. The concern was moot; we were going.

But first we must buy new supplies: We'd bought for a month; we'd waited a month. The French were especially needy, since Louis fed the pilgrims every day, but we all prepared to return to Constantinople. Louis sent buyers, including Arnulf of Lisieux, and I sent Lord Geoffrey; everyone returned empty-handed. Manuel had doubled the price of his goods! The French didn't have enough money, and I'd not sent enough.

"Call everyone here at once," I ordered.

My barons arrived within a few heartbeats.

I pushed a packet of my new gold into Rancon's hands. "Take this to your tent, hide it in the ground, and then come back for more."

He took it without a word. I gave Guy a like amount. When I'd disposed of all my new packets, I pointed to a heavy chest. "Pull out my treasure."

Hugh and his strong brothers obliged.

"Now, everyone, take as much as you can carry concealed on your person, and don't be modest about where you hide it."

The women slipped coins into their bosoms and cinched their belts so the coins wouldn't fall to the ground, then raised their skirts and loaded their tights where it wouldn't show. The men did the same, and filled their boots and helmets, as well.

Finally, everyone minced slowly from my tent. Rancon returned just as Louis and Thierry entered.

"I'm requisitioning your treasure, milady, which properly belongs to France," Louis announced without looking at me.

"By our wedding contract it belongs to me," I reminded him.

Paying no attention, Thierry raised the lid of my cask; half the coins were gone.

"Have you spent so much?" Louis asked, frowning.

"Like you, my lord, I had to provide for my army this month."

"But you contribute nothing to our devoted pilgrims." He gazed at me quizzically. "Where's the money you received from Bordeaux?"

"What money? I sent for wine, which was packed in crates."

Thierry snapped his fingers and several underlings came with bags for my coins.

I watched coldly. "Am I to assume, my lord, that henceforth you'll feed the Aquitanians as well as the pilgrims?"

"God will provide."

"Which doesn't answer my question."

His jaws were tight. "You may line up with the beggars, my lady."

"Better a beggar than a thief!"

"You're my vassal! What's yours in mine!" The shrill note had crept in.

"Since when is a queen a vassal?"

"Henceforth, you're forbidden to attend our meetings of policy. In this treacherous country, we must keep tight security."

Rancon pushed between us angrily. "You can't cut us out! The Aquitanians must know the orders of the day, my lord!"

Louis squinted at him. "Who are you?"

It was dark in my pavilion, but it was possible that Louis had never before registered Rancon's person.

"Richard of Rancon, the duchess's captain of the Aquitanian army, and I insist—"

"You will follow your leader!"

"If I must follow you, you must inform me of your strategy!"

"You must follow God! God is our leader!" Louis looked from Rancon to me and back again, then left the pavilion.

"God's heart, Rancon, why did you argue?" I asked.

"Because isolation is intolerable! Damn him! We have to know the plans!"

"I suspect the clerics have taken over."

Rancon stamped his foot. "Is there no one to stop this madness?"

Geoffrey took Rancon's arm. "Henry of Champagne told me that the king plans to go by way of Mount Cadmos, the shortest route. Short or not, we have to buy supplies."

I sat at my table. "Listen! I have an idea!"

Quickly, I wrote a note to Empress Irene, offering her all my new gold, my jewels, to be sold in the marketplace, and asking for credit beyond that.

That evening at sundown, Rancon and the Lusignan brothers disguised themselves as pilgrims and boarded a small bark to sail for Constantinople. In their bags, they carried heavy gold and jewelry; in their hands, they held Angevins for bribes. They returned just before dawn with a fleet of fishing boats loaded with supplies. We did this for three nights, and on the last night, they brought two small Arabian horses as a gift from Empress Irene.

"Raymond would appear to be wrong about the Greeks," Rancon said wearily.

"Except that Irene's not Greek; she's from Sulzbach," I pointed out. "And women don't necessarily follow their husband's policies."

"Thank God," he agreed fervently.

"In fact, she shortchanged herself, Rancon. I still have half my treasure left. She might not be Greek, but she likes a profit. Are you certain you toted the amount correctly?"

"I knew she was making a gift." He paused.

"And? You're holding something back."

His face was worried. "I hope it's not to salve her own conscience."

Two days later, our lines formed once again, with Louis in the lead. The half day we'd wasted formerly in choosing a leader was now wasted in prayer, and it was almost time for None before our horses climbed slowly into the first low foothill. At the crest, I glanced over my shoulder for my last look at Constantinople, the last touch of Europe. The city glittered from afar, then slowly dulled. I blinked my eyes.

The pall deepened. I heard anxious comments: What was the hour? Was it going to rain? Mamile pushed beside me on the narrow path.

"The sun's disappearing, Joy. Oh, God, it's a terrible omen, soothly!"

Shading my eyes, I looked upward and saw a curved shadow on the edge of the white orb. I looked away.

"Be careful," I ordered, "you'll injure your eyes!"

Priests cried in terror that it was Judgment Day! Everyone wept, begged for mercy, confessed sins. Mamile's eyes rolled back.

"Achilles!" I called to my nearest lord. "Help me!"

He clutched Mamile's waist just in time.

"Prepare to die!"

"Pray for your souls!"

The panic grew. Stars appeared in the blackened heavens; the Crusaders became disembodied voices.

Rancon pushed up the path. "Are you all right?"

"It's an eclipse, isn't it?"

"Yes, it won't last long." And he was gone.

A natural event, but the groans, the sighs, the desolation, the uncanny darkness revealed the demonic side of our quest. For the first time, I was afraid, not of the bleak wilderness around me, but of man's nature. When, an hour later, a pale, sickly sunshine emerged and priests thanked God for His mercy and climbed back onto their nags, my melancholy held.

Someone at the front began to sing the Crusader's hymn, only now there was no fragrance of wild carrot, no soft clop of horses on friendly turf. Only the occasional dart of a lizard while above buzzards circled, waiting.

Louis might be right; we might need God to lead us.

12

Following Emperor Manuel's advice, we planned to purchase food in Nicaea before we started on the long march across Mount Cadmos. Though Manuel had assured us that the small city was rich and friendly, no one came to greet us. Nor did we see any sign of life.

"Where is everyone?" Mamile asked fearfully. "Struck dead by the dark?"

"I would doubt that, dear," I consoled her. "They're probably herding their goats, or hunting."

By the time we crossed the entire city, we all knew that the inhabitants had fled and taken every valuable item with them. We saw not a horse, not a goat or chicken; even the wells had been capped.

"Raymond was right about the Greeks," Rancon murmured caustically.

On the far side of the city, we found a lake where we could fish for our supper. In our Aquitanian camp, we raised only my pavilion so that my ladies could rest, especially Mamile.

Later, we ate silently around our fire.

"Still," Hugh said, spitting out a fish bone, "we can stand anything for seven days, eh? If Manuel was right about Mount Cadmos."

"I have to believe him; I spoke to our guide Titos this morning," Rancon assured us, "and he says that there's a well-traveled road over the summit. Springs and rivers abound, and grass grows in the high-mountain valleys. We should be in Antioch in seven days."

"Manuel said Jerusalem," I reminded him.

"Antioch is on the way." But he seemed unconvinced.

"What was that?" Mamile called from her mat. "Listen! Do you hear it?"

"Nothing, darling; have a bit of fish and bread," Amaria begged.

"I hear it, too." I rose uneasily. "Listen!"

A low howl, rustling.

"An animal," Geoffrey said. "Some form of wolf, I would guess."

"It's human!" Rancon pushed to the pile of arms outside the tent.

All the lords rushed for their arms. Inside, we listened in dread for the clash of battle. Had the Saracens attacked? Oh God, we were so ill-prepared.

"It's all right! They're friends!" Rancon called.

"Stay here," I ordered my ladies.

I struggled through pilgrims, half-armed knights, slapped horses' rumps to make my way to the front. There, in the dim twilight, Louis and Thierry were talking to a figure in white. Rancon and the duke of Burgundy stood next to them.

Behind the figure, a hundred or more bearded men in tattered white tunics swayed back and forth as if about to faint. Some were bandaged; all were bloody. They were eerily silent.

The old man in front spoke in a low, guttural voice, *"Ist hier Frankreich?"*

"God help us, that's German!" Bishop Arnulf shouted. "King Conrad, is it you?"

It was indeed the victorious King Conrad, our intrepid German ally, who'd slain fourteen thousand Turks at Mount Cadmos.

Now the true story emerged. The Germans had been told that the journey to Jerusalem would take seven days, which was a lie. It took seven days to reach the first river! Since they carried no water (nor did we), they were parched and near death. They'd rushed forward to drink.

And gone to their deaths! Thousands of Turks had charged from behind the rocks. By the time they rode away, 150,000 Germans lay in a bloody pool at the foot of the mountain. Only the pitiful number now in our camp had survived. By God's grace, King Conrad had been spared.

Had the Greeks conspired with the Turks? Had the Germans been led to their ambush deliberately?

King Conrad became vehement. "*Ja! Ja!*" There could be no doubt whatsoever. Their Greek guide had fought with the Turks.

"Where's Titos?" Rancon whirled around. "Titos! Titos!"

We searched the camp; our own Greek guide had disappeared.

Deliberately excluding the Aquitanians, Louis led King Conrad to his tent, where he and his advisers would make new plans. I started after Louis, but Rancon held me back.

"There are limited choices. We should be able to guess the route at this point."

Inside my pavilion, Rancon drew a crude map on the floor while Amaria held a rush lamp high: If we didn't go over Mount Cadmos, there were only two alternative routes.

"The seacoast," Rancon concluded quickly. "Longer but safer, and with the possibility of provisions."

"*If* it's Greece. Don't forget that Manuel ceded Anatolian territory to the Turks," Hugh said. "How do we know which territory?"

"The Greeks would hold the seacoast for economic and strategic advantage. I can't imagine what the wilds in the middle would do for them, except as means to appease the Turks. Look here, though, how the coast twists—can you see?" Everyone bent close. "It doubles our distance. If we take the longer route, Geoffrey, do we have supplies?"

"Five and a half weeks' worth. And that's stretching to the limit."

Rancon's tone had a nervous edge. We would ride in tight formation: Rancon in the van with half the other lords and beasts, the women, the longcarts, then foot and a second mounted army in the rear, led by Aimar. Rush lights flickered, and Amaria moved to replenish them. Our voices grew gravelly with fatigue. Hugh stood and stretched his arms.

"Are we almost finished?"

Before we could answer, a man burst through the door!

"To arms!" Rancon cried, baring his dagger.

"Where's the queen?" Louis's voice demanded in the dark.

Amaria relighted the lamp.

"My lord." We all bowed.

The light flickered upward on Louis's mad, fixed eyes, his slack lips.

I edged toward him carefully. "What's wrong, my lord? Take care that this crisis doesn't—"

His voice was a hoarse growl. "Traitorous cunt!"

Everyone cried out.

Rancon rushed between us. "Apologize at once! How dare you call our duchess a traitor? Or a . . ." His voice failed.

I pulled him back. "I understand that you're upset, Louis. We all are—and with reason." I took Louis's arm.

He jerked free. "Don't ever touch me again, whore!"

Rancon shouted from behind me. "By God, I'll not tolerate insults to my lady!"

"Nor I!" Aimar cried.

Then a chorus of male and female voices.

"Hush!" I tried to be heard. "He's not himself; he's raving!"

"Raving, am I?" Louis screamed. "I have proof! You were seen sailing back to Constantinople in a fishing boat to bed with the emperor, the enemy of God! You were willing to sacrifice thousands of Germans to satisfy your unholy lust! Yes, and to sacrifice us as well—for you put the lie in his mouth about the German victory! A Jezebel! A traitor!"

He slithered out of the tent.

Rancon charged after him. "Not so fast!"

We all grabbed at him. Mamile, lying on her mat, clung to his foot.

"Let go!" He kicked to free himself, but Louis had disappeared. Rancon whirled on us. "Damn all of you! Why did you stop me? I'll throttle that slime!"

Hugh's hoarse voice sounded. "By God, we should have let him do it! The king of France is a raving maggot! Why didn't you tell us, Joy?"

"God damn, he's insulted Aquitaine!" Guy cried.

"Let me meet him on my own ground! The next time he's in Aquitaine . . . ," Achilles chorused.

"Leave me with our duchess," Rancon snapped. "Everyone!"

A silence fell. The men shuffled uneasily. Then Aimar opened the flap. "We'll be just outside." All the lords and ladies scuttled after him, even Mamile.

Rancon's breath was rough. "Very well, you warned me, I grant you, but I had no idea. . . . Listen! I'm going to protect you from that worm! Don't ever stop me again!"

"You can't reason with a demented man."

"My fists can reason! Or a knife in the ribs! He'll see reason when his head is bloody!"

"Calm yourself, Rancon."

"Be calm when he called you a whore and worse?"

"Words, nothing more." I put my hand over his. "Listen! You say you remember, but I fear you don't. I'm not in danger—you are."

"For my chivalry?"

"Forget chivalry. Louis lives by a different code."

"And what code is that? He's a madman, Joy!"

"Even madmen can be predictable. Your chivalry was misplaced. I told you before that he will never harm me. He will harm you, though, Rancon, and he has the power."

He fought for control. "And you think that an insult to Aquitaine doesn't harm you! What about the rest of us? We have a stake in Aquitaine as well, you know. In you!"

"Words can't hurt Aquitaine," I repeated.

"Words precede acts, by God! Can't you see the danger? Don't you know why he married you?"

He was gone before I could respond.

The next morning, Louis foundered into a gully that led toward a mountain range, the opposite direction from the sea, a baffling mistake, since everyone could see the sun rise and set. After two days of meandering, we finally looked down on a blinding glitter with a narrow path along the shore.

"If the Turks decide to attack from where we stand, we achieve instant martyrdom," Rancon commented in the bitter tone he'd used since Nicaea. He spurred his great stallion down the slippery slope; the rest of us followed in our assigned order. Maurienne pushed forward to ask if his army could follow ours, which Rancon granted. Our progress thereafter was so tortuous—moving in loops so close that men could touch one another across deep drops into the sea—that we hardly advanced at all. Aside from enduring the topography, we had to wait again and again for the pilgrims to catch up. They whined for food, rest, shoes for their bleeding feet; they refused to carry armor, which the knights were then forced to wear. Although it was winter, the sun was merciless and there was no shade; under their helmets, the knights boiled in their own sweat. The first evening and every evening thereafter, we fed our beasts and went hungry ourselves. On the third day, Greek boats bobbed along beside us, offering fish and bread at outrageous prices. Though we kept out eyes stolidly ahead, we noticed that our pilgrims became fewer in number; they'd joined the Greeks in their boats. Meantime, we sat on the rocks ourselves with improvised lines and hooks. Thus, we survived.

"How long before we reach Antioch?" I asked Rancon one day.

"At this rate? Six months."

It was now November.

We arrived in the Greek city of Ephesus in time for Christmas. For once, the Greeks were hospitable. We put our tired horses out to pasture in a rich water meadow. One unexpected bonus in Ephesus was that King Conrad decided to return to Constantinople. Our sympathy for his terrible defeat had worn thin as we got to know him better. Pompous, whiny, sly, critical, he made us appreciate Louis, who at least was fairly quiet. We were amazed, however, to learn that Emperor Manuel had sent a ship for his "brother" Conrad to transport him back to Constantinople so that Manuel personally could tend his wounds. Manuel, who had betrayed the German, was now his doctor? Even more odd was the fact that Conrad gladly accepted.

The day after the Nativity, we had our first rainfall, a deluge. After a week, the skies cleared and we prepared to ride again. When we went to collect our horses, we found several hundred bloated carcasses floating in the flooded field. Only sixty-two superb coursers had survived. Rancon, tears streaming down his cheeks, waded among the corpses, seeking a sign of life. All the knights wept like children; these animals were their friends as well as their security in battle. Rancon then bargained with the Greeks for new mounts, testing each one under the load of heavy armor. Though I was willing to give all the gold I had, he could purchase only small Arabians—swift and dextrous but not trained for combat.

Louis called a meeting soon after the tragedy.

"My fellow Crusaders, God has warned me in a dream to reconsider our route. We can no longer afford the longer way beside the sea; we will march over Mount Cadmos."

His announcement was greeted with absolute silence.

Slowly, we followed the swollen Meander River into the foothills. At last, the Turks showed themselves. From high ridges, they berserked, taunted, and shot small bone arrows, which fell short of their mark. All the leaders warned us to keep faces forward, not even to look upward. Nights were the worst. We dared not light fires, which would mark our position, and we were forced to sleep in our furs, close as wolves in a litter. Even during daylight hours, Florine had trouble breathing, and all of us tired easily.

We reached the foothills of the famous Mount Cadmos; though very high, the actual peak rose from a tableland and therefore did not appear dangerous, especially since the Turks no longer threatened us. We rode ten abreast in the shadow of a sheer cliff. Suddenly, there was shouting at the front of the line. We'd come upon the slaughtered German army! Thousands of young men lay frozen, as if they'd decided to rest after dinner; unarmed, dressed in light linens, they would have seemed alive except that their faces had been eaten away.

"I'll give them a Christian burial," Louis sobbed. "Bring me a spade."

"The ground is frozen, my lord; it would take weeks," Arnulf argued gently.

When Thierry hastily agreed with Arnulf, Louis settled for a Mass. By the time the priest finished, snowflakes pricked our skin. Late that afternoon, camped in the foothills, we listened to Louis's plan for crossing the peak.

"A broad road above is visible," he said, pointing, "and it winds around to the very top, where there's a wide plateau suitable for camping. Please look before it becomes too dark."

We all stood obediently and looked upward, though dusk was too advanced to see much.

"This is the order of ascent," he continued. "Aquitaine will go first"—we stirred nervously, knowing that Aquitanians would take the brunt in any ambush—"followed by Champagne and his knights, then all our carts and supplies, then the French knights, and finally my pilgrims. I shall bring up the rear."

Then Maurienne spoke. "If it please your lord, I should like to combine my army with the Aquitanians."

"At the front?" Louis's consternation revealed that he had deliberately put us in danger.

"Yes, I would prefer the front."

"Very well," Louis said stiffly.

Bishop Arnulf's was the only dissenting voice. "I think, my lord king, that you should ride in a more protected position. The rear is vulnerable."

"I put my trust in God."

In the morning, the line quietly formed as ordered. We women put on our leather skin guards, our helmets and mesh, until Rancon suggested we remove the heavy mesh; the leather would suffice.

He also instructed us to ride close to the inner edge of the path and, if we were attacked, not to look up.

At first, the rise was gradual, then became narrower and steeper. The destriers panted under their heavy loads; the Arabians were staunch, as were the mules pulling the carts. Our pace slowed as we pushed ever higher, and although the light snowfall continued, we were all hot with the effort. It seemed very dark because we were on the north side of the mountain. When we emerged onto the plateau, the brightness hurt my eyes.

We instantly thanked God.

Maurienne climbed back onto his horse. "This part of the plateau is too exposed. Shall we explore?"

While the others sat and waited, I followed Maurienne and Rancon to the other side, where we would descend the next day. There, just out of sight, was a lower shelf, protected on one side by a small cliff and covered with gnarled, windswept trees. Charred fire pits confirmed that it was the usual campground. We agreed that it was perfect.

"Good cover in case of an attack," Maurienne said, "and protected from the wind." An important point, since we'd agreed not to build fires, and the wind here was more biting than below.

We went back for the others. Soon we'd laid our mats, put up linen windbreaks, and freed our horses to graze in some unexpected stubble.

Now we waited for the French.

"I'll go to the top of the path to show them the way," Rancon offered.

Maurienne joined him. When darkness descended and the icy wind howled, I followed across the barren plateau.

"Rancon!" I called.

My voice echoed off the rocks.

Then in the distance and far below, I heard, "We're coming."

Their mounts suddenly became visible in the dusk.

"Where are the others?"

"After half a mile, we felt it prudent to return," Maurienne replied.

Rancon dropped down beside me. "I'll escort you back to the camp, milady. Maurienne and I will keep watch here through the night. If anyone comes, we'll call out at once."

"You promise?"

"My word as your captain."

"Do you think—"

"Don't think."

Rancon didn't shout until dawn. "Come! They're here!"

I was in time to see a few knights stumble onto the plateau, where they fell to their knees, weeping. I couldn't believe my eyes—Walter, Jurgen, Edwin—knights I'd known well in Burgundy's army, brave soldiers all, now reduced to tears.

They'd been ambushed, they cried with rage and astonishment. Waiting on the mountain above the narrowest part of the path, thousands of cowardly Turks had rolled huge boulders down on the army. The Crusaders had been like so many ants being crushed— they'd never had a chance. Where was Saracen chivalry? To attack like snakes coiled in their holes!

"When did they hit?" Rancon asked.

"After you Aquitanians passed, when the carts had appeared. The most defenseless part of the line, where else?" Horses and mules had flown into the abyss; carts had rolled. The path turned into a wall of rubble. Marching behind the carts, the Burgundians had come abruptly upon a crush of dead animals and spinning wheels. They'd turned in horror to face Crusaders singing the Crusader's hymn, and now men as well as horses joined falcons, dogs, and supplies in a horrible dive to their common grave.

Walter sobbed into his hands. "They'll be like the German soldiers, with their eyes pecked away and—"

"Are you the only survivors?" Rancon asked.

"We don't know," a Burgundian baron replied. "I don't think anyone fought. We were armed, but you can't shoot arrows straight up.

The only thing that stopped the bastards was the coming of night. We'll just have to wait."

Slowly, more weary men appeared up the path, some still on horses, as the remnants of Burgundy's army, then Champagne's, and finally the Templars reached us. Not all were wounded, but all were profoundly marked. So far, we'd seen no pilgrims, and everyone had the air of tragic expectancy. Then Burgundy, Henry of Champagne, and Master Barre of the Templars arrived; all the leaders were accounted for, save one. If Louis didn't appear by sundown, it was agreed, a small contingent would go looking for him.

So long as I could work with the wounded, I could avoid thought, but there weren't many living casualties—this "battle" had produced survivors or corpses, nothing in between. Finally I could work no longer; I huddled apart from the others to wait. Louis dead assumed a more benign image.

"Pilgrims!" someone cried.

A few embattled men collapsed at Burgundy's feet, weeping.

Behind them, supported by Thierry, Louis stumbled into our midst, still carrying his pilgrim's staff. Gutted with dust and mucus, his smile was beatific.

"I have been saved," he murmured. "God has preserved me from the Antichrist."

"What happened, my lord?" Maurienne asked. "How did you escape?"

Everyone hushed to listen. At the rear of the line, Louis began, the Turks had attacked the pilgrims face-to-face. Louis had scrambled up a scrubby tree growing out of a rock, where he could not easily be seen. Two infidel warriors spotted him nevertheless, and they made desultory passes at him, but he was obviously unarmed and looked to be an ordinary pilgrim, so they left him.

"My humility saved me from human foes," Louis declared proudly, then his voice dropped in awe. "There in the dark, after the Saracens had departed, the worm sought me; I could hear it hissing in the dark, hear rocks tumble to its slashing coils. At the first light, I looked down and saw it in a pit at my feet, the dragon of the Antichrist surrounded by its slithering progeny, earth, air, fire, and water. I looked into the yellow eyes of Hell without fear, for my God was with me.

"The dragon spat fire and the rats of death scurried from the brush to the root of my tree. With their long fangs, they gnawed and gnawed—I shall never forget the sound—and I knew that if God wanted me to die, my time had come. I prayed in the name of His Son, in the name of our holy Saint-Denis that His will be done and I would abide, and when I raised my eyes, the rats had departed, the dragon was gone, and I was saved."

"Amen, amen," the pilgrims murmured zealously.

"You climbed God's Tree of Life." Thierry dropped to his knees. "You have undergone a miracle, my lord; no doubt you will be canonized one day."

Maurienne took Louis's arm to lead him to his own pavilion.

I stepped close. "I'm so grateful that you escaped, my lord. I can't tell you . . ."

Louis made the sign of the cross. "In the pit, I saw you at last in your natural shape, milady, and I have prevailed."

He hobbled away.

13

*L*ouis called a meeting on the open plateau at None. Standing in the exposed windswept bowl surrounded by sharp brown peaks, we all gazed anxiously above us, searching for Turks. But no, the sky was bleached, the slopes bare; even the buzzards were gone, feeding no doubt on our dead soldiers. Louis sat on an improvised platform of dark rocks, his clergy and Templars closely huddled around him. To his left, I caught the movement of Bishop Arnulf's arm. I watched his lips move but couldn't catch their meaning.

Thierry whispered with Louis, then stepped in front to make a brief announcement: We would return to the sea route at once, veering westward toward the city of Attalia, reckoned to be four days' march. Master Barre of the Templars would be our leader; there would be no fires, no pavilions—though we could use small tents—no talking. "Be prepared to depart tomorrow at daybreak." He returned to the huddle and there was a long silence.

Louis called out, "Will Richard of Rancon, baron of Taillebourg, step forward, please?"

Rancon pushed into the open space in front of Louis.

"My lord Rancon, you were assigned to lead our climb over Mount Cadmos. Is that correct?"

"Yes, Your Lordship."

"And you stood with me when I pointed to the top of the mountain where we might camp?"

"I did, Your Lordship, along with many others."

"But the others were not in the vanguard. Isn't that true?"

"The Aquitanians rode in the van, that's true."

"You heard my orders; you saw the area where I pointed. Why, then, did you deliberately disobey?"

Rancon cocked his head. "I don't understand your question. How did I disobey?"

"You were told to camp on the plateau. If you had done so, you could have heard—perhaps have seen—the onslaught on the soldiers of Christ. Yet you took it upon yourself, *against my orders*, to camp on a distant shelf."

"The whole mountaintop is out of earshot and out of sight! You pointed up and we came up! Did you expect me to expose my own army to the Turks?"

Louis rose to his feet. "You committed treason!"

Rancon's neck grew red. "I did what any general should do; I protected my troops."

Louis sank back to his rock, his hands on his knees. "You lost contact with our troops, which a general must never do."

Rancon's temper flared. "What about a king? Do you have no responsibility to this army? You split the line! You put the carts in the middle, a vicious design! You wanted everybody to be crushed like so many vermin! By God, I *should* have disobeyed you, but I didn't!"

Thierry called out angrily, "The carts were loaded with female frippery! Abbot Bernard prohibited falcons and finery on the Crusade, but the women disobeyed!"

Racon lashed back. "The carts also carried arms and supplies. If the line had been properly organized, if knights had ridden with them, if scouts had been sent ahead as is customary, none of this would have happened!"

"Do you defend the women?" Louis asked almost pleasantly.

I saw the thrust. With all my will, I tried to signal Rancon to be quiet.

"I defend them against false accusations. It behooves a knight to take responsibility—and a king."

"Do you defend the queen in particular?"

"Are you accusing the queen in particular?" Rancon parried coldly.

The question hung. Louis turned again to his advisers, then spoke to Rancon. "To defy my orders is to defy God! Since I am king by the grace of God, I *am* God here on earth! In my living person, you see His will! He willed that I survive!"

Rancon paled, but his voice remained strong. "By God's will, I, too, survived the massacre!"

Louis stood. "Before the sun sets this day, you will hang by your neckbone until you are dead."

The entire company gasped. I strode to join Rancon.

"Prepare two nooses, my lord Louis. I gave him the order where to camp."

"She's lying to save me!" Rancon shouted.

"I gave him the order," I repeated.

Louis's face crumbled in the manner I knew so well. "Joy, think again, I beseech you; you give me no choice."

Rancon bellowed, "She's lying! I found the camp! I told her she must bring her ladies! I admit it!"

"Rancon argued, but he had to obey." I looked straight at Louis. "I alone lead the Aquitanians, no one else."

He rubbed his brow as if ill. Thierry leaned and whispered. Louis could hardly speak. "Joy—think of the consequences."

"*You* think of consequences for a change. You brought the charges—you want to hang someone? Hang me!"

Maurienne pushed to my side.

"My dear lord, my own nephew, son of my beloved brother Louis the Fat," Maurienne said, "you mistake the villain, if there be one; neither Lord Rancon nor your queen gave the order to camp on the other side of the plateau; I did. I rode out to find the best grounds; I insisted that the lower ledge would be safer and more hospitable. If that was against your orders, then I misunderstood, and I humbly apologize."

I looked on Maurienne's crushed, homely features and thought I'd never seen a more beautiful man. His devotion to the truth, his courage simply overwhelmed me. I would forever be grateful.

"I rode with you, Maurienne," Rancon protested. "I gave the order."

Maurienne continued to look at Louis. "As we all know, women have no jurisdiction over the military, and my rank is superior to Rancon's. Besides, I have the added authority that I am your close relative."

Louis rose unsteadily. "My uncle Philip of Maurienne and Baron Richard of Rancon have committed treason against the king of France. They should die, but God has told me to be lenient in gratitude for my own deliverance. Therefore, you are both declared unworthy to serve in God's Crusade. When we reach Attalia, you will return to Europe on the first ship that sails."

A murmur of relief swept across the plateau. I, too, was relieved, but also wild at the loss. To send Rancon away before we saved Raymond!

I ran after Louis as he disappeared inside his tent.

"I must speak with you."

He looked up from his furs. "Be careful, milady; if you so much as mention your lover's name, he's a dead man."

"Do you refer to Emperor Manuel?"

"Don't be facetious."

"It's no joke to follow your aberrations, I assure you."

"I refer to the lover you just defended in a most grievous public display."

"He's not my lover!" I cried hotly. "Nor did I call for a public trial to air childish jealousies. You live in a murderous fantasy!"

He looked away. "Thousands died last night. Was that a fantasy?"

"As you so often proclaim, God and only God decides who will die."

"And God condemns adultery! Do you know the punishment for an adulterous queen?"

"You've reminded me often enough. If you want to rid yourself of me, my lord, why didn't you hang me when you had the chance?"

His face became cunning. "I can't harm you, Joy, no matter how much you deserve it; you are my reward."

"Reward for what? Tree climbing?"

"While I was in the tree last night, I had another vision, which I didn't confess in public. A flock of golden birds sang in a joyous chorus that I was being saved, that I might worship in Jerusalem, that I would be absolved of all sin and thereafter might enjoy the bliss of conjugal love." His eyes fixed on mine. "And for that, I must keep you with me. We will come together in the City of God."

"God spoke to me as well, Louis. He told me that I was too weak a vessel for His great enterprise; I should go back to my child, where I belong."

"Don't mock me!" Louis thundered. "You will stay with me! Furthermore, you will remain unsullied. If Rancon or any man should touch you or even look at you with lust, that man is dead. Do you understand me, Joy?"

"Your words are clear."

"And next time, there will be no trial."

I walked swiftly from his tent, then broke into a run.

I stepped into my dark tent. "Amaria, go fetch Rancon! I must warn him—quick!"

A shadow moved. "She can't hear you; she's keeping watch."

"Rancon, go!"

"I won't go unless you give the order, *test me ipso!*"

"For God's sake, I'm giving it now! Louis will kill you if he finds you with me—he means it!"

"Then come with me!"

"I can't . . . I can't." I was near tears of vexation. "Please be reasonable, you most of all."

"Is it unreasonable to want you to live? To want Aquitaine to survive? Christ! You've lectured me often enough. Now it's your turn
to listen! He may be besotted with mad love, uxorious as a mouse,
torn between religious fanaticism and his own balls, I grant all
that. But that's just the surface, Joy! He and Thierry and Suger
back in Paris all want the same thing—they want Aquitaine! And
you're playing their game! Can't you see it?"

"You must leave! At once!"

"Only with you. Damn you, I'll save you in spite of yourself. Save
Aquitaine. That's my duty! Your own father—"

"Nothing's going to happen to me or to Aquitaine!"

"You still believe he won't harm you?"

"He didn't, did he? He went through the motions of threatening
me, as usual, that's all!"

"Tell me, what would have happened if Maurienne hadn't
stepped forth?"

My heart skipped a beat; I lost my breath. What was wrong with
me? In an instant, I faced the truth. Yes, Maurienne—without that
timely confession, Louis would have kept his word. Hadn't he said
as much? He might regret the act, might weep tears of self-pity
that he hadn't enjoyed my body after all, but Rancon and I would
now be hanging side by side in the dark.

"Well?" his voice prompted.

"Give me a moment."

"Moment's up."

I spoke slowly—ironically, if he'd known it. "Good policy is compromise." Suger's words. "I'll leave Louis, I promise; I'll go back to
Aquitaine and rule alone. Only you must let me find a way. To leave
now, with you and Maurienne, is sure death for all of us."

"Seek an annulment! Ask Raymond to help you!" His voice was
jubilant.

"Yes, I will, only go!"

He pulled back the flap to the howling dark, and paused. Then
he was back.

"Christ, Joy, this is *mesclatz*! You know what I want to say above all else! I love you! Love you!"

And he kissed me deeply. Not with the boy's sun-warmed lips of Aquitaine, but with the hungry mouth of a grown man, sure, insistent. And again, and again. I clung to him for support.

"Oh God, Rancon, we mustn't! This is exactly what he suspects!"

"For once, he's right! Do you love me?"

"Yes! Always, I always have. Always will."

"I love you, I love you. Oh Lord, how I love you! Here, take this for fealty." He pressed a ring into my palm, my father's ring. "Return to Aquitaine—we'll be together. Forever!"

He left; I collapsed to my furs. Forever. Together, not married. Tristan and Iseult? But I wanted . . . I buried my face in my hands, kissed the ring. Even to be Iseult, I had to leave Louis. He was no benign King Mark, would not tolerate an affair—he'd made that clear.

But what about Rancon? Could he pledge "forever" when he was still with Arabelle?

14

$\mathcal{J}$ stood in my new role as Iseult, watching my lover sail to his sure death. Love and death, the leitmotif of Tristan; this time, the hero will rest on the bottom of the sea.

How could I believe otherwise? Rain had poured steadily on our long march to Attalia, where we'd found a soggy city gripped by the Black Death. There had been only a single ship in harbor and everyone had wanted to sail, but Louis's position gave him first choice, which meant Rancon and Maurienne. Through the silver sheet of rain the ship was barely visible, tilted to the side. My heart stopped; then it righted itself and disappeared.

When would I see him again? In Aquitaine as a free woman, according to plan? I shook my wet furs. He will become fodder for fish, and I will surely expire in this pissmire of a city. Tristan and Iseult, a short romance in our version. Faydide had died that morning of the Black Death, to join hundreds of others in a shallow grave. The sick city reeked of oozing buboes and vomit, and, here on the upper more habitable tier of the city, of corpses. Even in this downpour, Louis's pilgrims were digging shallow graves, which barely accommodated their inhabitants. I now made my way carefully to the lower tier, where we squatted in royal misery with the rats.

Ten days later, the waterlogged graveyard collapsed, carrying a mud slide filled with corpses to our very feet. Equality in death; the living now shared the sea spray with floating skulls, detached arms and legs with rotting flesh.

For once, Louis's prelates grasped that we must leave Attalia at once. We were ordered to prepare to march: We would return to Mount Cadmos! Everyone shrieked, and Louis lost all authority. Then, almost casually, a sailor remarked that Antioch was only three days distant by sea.

Since the sailor was Greek, we suspected his motives, until a man from Cyprus confirmed the time, then another from Lebanon. Louis sent word by a commercial boat to Emperor Manuel to name his price; we wanted to rent ships for transport. Manuel sent three dilapidated ships, all listing dangerously, their decks missing several boards, their sails tattered, but what could we do? Louis ordered that we make ready.

Knights objected that there were no holds to transport the few horses that were left. Louis ordered doors cut in the sides so that the huge destriers could be carried belowdecks, and we prepared to leave. Then Louis was forced to make another choice. Three ships would barely hold the lords and their knights and horses; there was no room for the thousands of pilgrims and foot who had survived the Black Death. Eyes rolling wildly, Louis proclaimed that God had ordered him to convert the pilgrims into foot soldiers, and he ordered them to march forthwith over Mount Cadmos and meet us in Antioch, where we would await them before proceeding to Jerusalem. In a pathetic but grandiose gesture, he gave them as their military pay the last of the gold he'd stolen from me.

We climbed onto our dismal barques. As the oars struck the water, I stood on the deck, next to the hanging buckets for our wastes, and looked back on the doomed city. Within an hour, a gale took our tattered sail and both city and shore disappeared behind high waves. Our leaky tub pitched and turned helplessly; sails ripped, waste buckets clattered over the deck, and boards groaned. Tied to iron pegs on the deck to keep us from being washed overboard, we rolled back and forth, our skins raw where the ropes cut, our bones bruised.

By midday, we realized that our freeboard was getting lower, the sea closer—we were sinking. Sailors shouted that the doors in the horses' holds hadn't been caulked—the ship was a sieve. While sailors rushed to stop the leakage, desperate knights fell down the steps to rescue their beasts; hours later, the knights climbed back up, their faces ashen. Carcasses sloshed back and forth in regular rhythmic thumps as the ship rolled. The odor of dead animals, while noxious, was still better than the sickening sweet stench of human decay.

Our three days turned into a week, then two weeks. Several people died, and Toquerie began to vomit. The ship didn't yet sink with its cargo of death. The third week, I woke groggily with delusions of sunlight and flowers. Like Louis with his visions, I thought; I'm near death. Then Amaria undid my ropes; I stood upright. We were floating close to a field of bright anemones. No wonder Louis had been so certain of his golden birds and worms—this seemed real.

The captain called that we would be putting into the port of Saint-Simeon within the hour. Saint-Simeon, the port for Antioch.

Che sea was now afloat with flower petals, and small boats bobbed close, filled with cheering knights. With wonder, we gazed down on the faces of our own lords, who'd sailed on the ships ahead of us from Attalia. Henry of Champagne shouted that they'd made the trip in three days, as promised, and had given us up for lost. God be praised for our delivery! We must have appeared as wraiths, but thanks to the constant rain, we were at least clean. Oarsmen pulled us slowly to the hook of concrete extending into the water.

I squinted anxiously at the hordes of shouting people, seeking my uncle Raymond. The Crusader's hymn sounded from our right; crowds pushed people in front into the water. Where in this mass of humanity was Raymond of Antioch?

Florine saw him first. "There, Joy, that officer dressed as an Arab!"

Standing at the exact point where we must disembark, he was handsome as a Greek god with his sleek bronzed body. He wore an *orofois* turban clasped by a cluster of glittering rubies, a very short embroidered tunic hasped in emeralds, with a gold saber hanging from his hip; his long, elegant legs were wound with gold thongs. An Eastern exotic, and yet he was familiar. Louis walked first down the plank. Raymond gave him the kiss of peace, then looked upward expectantly. I put my foot on the shaky board. Within moments, I was crushed against my own father's chest, was looking into his deep blue eyes; the two brothers could have been twins. I began to weep.

"Welcome, Eleanor."

He tenderly wiped away my tears. The balmy air, the cleanliness, healthiness, enthusiasm, the faces of old friends and my uncle, who seemed to be my reincarnated father, were miraculous. A glance at Louis punctured my euphoria. Yet even my husband seemed less threatening in this hospitable land.

Raymond provided horses to transport our company the ten miles to Antioch proper where his wife, Constance, had prepared a feast for us. We rode into the hills along the Orontes River on a narrow road neatly paved and walled by the Romans. Antioch itself was a miniature Constantinople, touched with the antique patina of Ephesus, and more beautiful than either. Built of whitewashed stone into the side of Mount Silipus, it was covered with hanging gardens, flowering vines spilling over the walls, and shaded by trees heavy with purple blooms like lilacs. We stopped in the main square.

"My palace is straight ahead, my lord king," Raymond told us. "I've prepared a villa for you and my niece next door."

"The king and I are residing in separate quarters until we reach Jerusalem," I said easily. "I would like to stay with you in your palace, if I may. I can come to know my young cousins."

Raymond agreed readily, and Louis's only comment was, "You live better than we do in Paris."

Raymond laughed. "You have a fine wit, King Louis, and you know how to flatter. Paris is the jewel of the civilized world."

Raymond's palace, like the Blachernae in Constantinople, was ancient and elaborately appointed. My aunt Constance, who was a few years younger than I was and the mother of three young daughters, was a graceful Armenian beauty with penetrating green eyes. With exquisite tact, she prepared perfumed baths for me and my women, then laid out dazzling robes for our pleasure. We were tended by women in the baths, which was fortunate, for we were all weary to our bones and in danger of falling asleep in the water. By the time we attended the feast, we were no longer capable of even pretending to be awake, and we went quickly to our beds. Before I drifted off, however, I reconsidered Rancon's word—*forever*. Was it possible? Yes, if he'd survived. I smiled. In this setting, I thought surely he had.

Rancon had appointed Hugh of Lusignan as my new captain. Hugh, though not my own choice because of his wayward amibition, took his assignment seriously. "Prince Raymond believes that the decisive battle against the Saracens will be fought in Aleppo," he reported. "They have a new leader, you know."

"I thought Zengi was supposed to be unconquerable."

"Zengi was killed this winter. Nur-ed-din is even a worse foe. That's why Raymond believes our best chance is a preemptive attack at Aleppo. I'm going to ride out with him to determine strategy."

"When will you attack?"

"He thinks we should wait for Louis's seventy thousand foot soldiers from Attalia."

"Soldiers!" I grimaced.

Hugh grinned. "Listen! We need a fleshy wall to soak up arrows. They go in first; we follow."

"Can Aleppo wait for the pilgrims?"

"Good question."

As we tarried in Antioch, I watched for an opportunity to approach my uncle. We met in my chamber on the third afternoon. Seen close, Raymond looked less like my father, more like my grandfather, with his jaunty élan.

He arranged cushions for us. "At last, we can talk as people. I hate all this protocol."

"I'd never know it; you're unparalleled in the art." I smiled.

"Here in the East, a state runs on protocol. That and fighting. But you didn't ask me here to discuss Antioch. What can I do for you, my dear Eleanor?"

I was too surprised to answer.

"That's another thing we learn here in the Frankish kingdoms—how to smell a request."

"I want to annul my marriage."

His face instantly sobered and he responded slowly, "God's feet! This is serious."

I didn't dwell on Louis's antic mind, especially as it applied to the military. I simply described him as a celibate religious fanatic.

He rubbed his brows. "I guessed, of course."

"How? He hasn't said anything here, has he?"

"I've hardly seen him, but you throw out misery like sparks. Even Constance asked me what ailed you. And then—there have been rumors."

"Rumors from whom?" Rancon had heard gossip in Aquitaine, but this was Antioch, a world away.

"Ships bring local news, most of it hopelessly twisted in transit." He shrugged. "That you were frivolous, amorous—do you want to hear this? I knew it must be a major scandal to reach all the way to the hinterland."

"I've done absolutely nothing!"

"Then I take it that it's Louis who wants to end the marriage."

I started. "Why do you say so? He certainly says otherwise."

"Because when a husband wants to escape, he makes the wife a villain, eh?"

I nodded, though I didn't think Louis wanted to lose Aquitaine.

"Could I stay here with you while Louis goes on to Jerusalem? I need to form my legal arguments."

"After we fight Aleppo, you mean?"

"Of course, after Aleppo. I have no intention of going to Jerusalem; however, if you want to join the French there, I could stay with Constance."

"She'd be honored; we both would."

His face seemed suddenly covered with small anxious lines, as if he'd walked through a spider's web. "However, I would appreciate it if you kept your plans secret from Louis until after we've fought in Aleppo. I need his help desperately—oh, you don't need to tell me that he's a bad soldier, but he has an army, and protocol is all, as I said. It's important that we appear to work together."

"Of course, Raymond. Oh, thank you!"

We then spoke of Aquitaine, our family there, and other interesting subjects for most of the afternoon. He was a charming, generous-spirited, brave, and worried man.

15

While Louis waited for his "pilgrim foot soldiers" from Attalia, he doggedly visited Christian shrines, viewed where Saint-Paul had first coined the word *Christian,* saw the relics, even looked at Roman ruins, but he refused to ride out to Aleppo to study the terrain or to discuss the coming battle with Prince Raymond.

After three weeks, a runner burst into our evening feast, waving a parchment.

Raymond held it high. "A message from Attalia!"

Louis rushed to the front. "That's mine!" He paled as he read it, then croaked feebly, "My pilgrims have deserted! The Turks offered them food, and with my gold . . ."

My gold, I thought.

Louis's mouth worked; his face became ashen. "They went over to the enemy." The rest was a whisper. "They c-converted to Muham-madan-ism."

The guests moaned.

Louis held up his hand. "*Pace, pace,* we came to aid Jerusalem, and that purpose still holds! Even as we've dallied here, King Conrad and Emperor Manuel have sailed to meet us. Therefore, prepare to march at once! Together, we will attack Damascus!"

"*Damascus!*" Raymond thundered, aghast. "Damascus is on our side!"

"You are not an ally," Louis said stiffly. "You can have no opinion."

"Opinion? This is a fact! The Crusade was called because of an attack on Edessa! Antioch is the next goal, not Jerusalem! You came to attack your only Saracen ally? Damascus will fight with us!"

"Wait!" I pushed my way to the front. "Aquitanians came to aid Raymond of Poitiers. When he wrote for help, we answered, and with God as our witness, we will deliver that help. When he fights in Aleppo, we'll be at his side! I order my army to remain in Antioch to fight with Raymond."

"Hear! Hear!" Hugh cheered. "Our duchess has spoken! I echo her order!"

By nightfall, we had the remnants of Maurienne's army with us, but while many French wanted to stay, they dared not disobey their king.

I stretched out on my silken mat, full of hope. Finally, I'd spoken my intentions outright, and while I knew Raymond was disappointed, I knew our chances of victory were better without Louis. Soon, it would be over. Vaguely, I heard Amaria still moving about me, then nothing. Though I closed my eyes, I couldn't sleep. Images played in my head: Rancon in the stable at Taillebourg, his person in my pavilion at Metz, then in the night at Mount Cadmos, and—what was that? Someone in the room. Movement. Could Rancon have . . . No. Amaria? No. There, again, footsteps, breathing. Close.

I screamed! Cloth fell over my face, was forced inside my mouth. I gagged. A hood over my head, hands rolling me brutally, grunts. I kicked, struck out, but I couldn't see, couldn't speak. I heard similar movement from Am's bed—she was being trussed as well. I was rolled to my stomach, my hands bound behind me with rope, my ankles. Again on my back. A boot kicked me viciously in my ribs. I gurgled in pain, was kicked again.

I was slung over a shoulder like a bag of grain. A metal brooch cut my stomach.

By the change in air, I knew we'd left the room, were on the balcony, then going down the stairs. Each step cut me in the middle.

Now where? On the street, yes, I smelled a horse. From the shoulder to the horse's bony neck—at least I was free of the metal torture buckle. We began to ride.

To where? Who were these men? Saracens? Was I to be used as a hostage? Ransomed? To Raymond? Or—oh God—put in a harem. Oh Jesus, help me!

Could I roll? Escape? I tried, but I was firmly tied. Where were Raymond's guards? Dead or bribed. We rode only a short distance. More horses circled, their hooves beating on cobbles. Men grunted but didn't speak. I was shoved into an airless litter. The cart instantly began to rattle over the cobbles. Another body—Amaria's, I thought—jolted next to mine.

The air became stiflingly hot—the sun had come up—and I needed to urinate. I controlled my urge and tried to find a position where I could breathe. Who had done this? I racked my memory for enemy names mentioned by Raymond—I would try to bargain if I got the opportunity.

I was in a stupor by the time we finally stopped. My hands and feet were numb, my throat raw. Then I saw light through my hood. Hands lifted me—gently—to the ground, and someone fumbled with my ropes, removed my hood and gag. I saw shapes but couldn't focus.

"Water!" I gasped.

A flask was placed to my lips. I splashed my face, drank deeply. "More!" I said hoarsely.

"I warned you at Mount Cadmos, Eleanor, but you paid no heed."

I choked. Through a swimming blur, I gazed at Louis! Next to him was Thierry, his tunic fastened by a large brass belt—my abductor—and behind him stood a circle of sheepish French lords.

Louis continued in that sanctimonious piety I knew so well. "I thought that infidelity was the most loathsome of sins in a queen, but you've taught me otherwise."

I gurgled.

He understood. "I refer to incest, wife."

Incest? Had the sun dried up what few vital cells he still possessed? I had no brothers, no cousins, no father.

"You and your uncle Raymond of Antioch have known each other carnally."

Raymond! In an instant, I saw his diabolical scheme. Destroy me, destroy Raymond, the Crusade, everything in that one word—*incest*.

I signaled for more water.

"Incest is the greatest sin anyone can commit. Yet I forgive you your transgression, wife; in Jerusalem, you will confess to God and He will assign you as my beloved mate."

I rolled water in my mouth and stepped close.

With all my might, I spat into his face.

From Jerusalem, I feverishly wrote an apology to Raymond, splotched it heavily with tears, sent the letter anyway by a runner, and wrote again. I couldn't stop my outpouring of horror at what I might have done to his cause and his person by exposing him to Louis. I didn't need to elaborate the damage—we both knew it. If rumors of my "infidelity" had flown all the way from Paris to Antioch, how much more quickly the irresistible scandal of incest would spread. My reputation was already sullied beyond repair, but Raymond had been a shining prince. I was sick with remorse.

And my dear uncle replied—in his wife's hand, instead of a scribe's. Both he and Constance apologized for lax security; it was their fault that I'd been abducted! But who would have thought of warning the guards against the French king? They pitied me, offered asylum if I could escape. Raymond would even come to Jerusalem and escort me back himself if I gave the word. Was there ever such a generous heart? I was proud to be his niece.

As for Louis, I locked myself in my apartment and refused him entry; I preferred imprisonment to his loathsome physiognomy.

A letter from Suger confirmed the swiftness of rumors. He also informed me—to my amazement—that the count of Maurienne and my captain in Aquitaine had returned in record time. He then went on to say that he was appalled that my relationship with Louis had disintegrated to such a sordid level and he had no doubts whatsoever that the fault lay with the king's overwrought imagination, plus the terrible difficulties we had undergone. That said, he also had no doubt as to what my reaction must be, and he begged me, implored me with the weight of France and Aquitaine behind him, to remember the importance of domestic tranquillity for the public weal. "Dear, dear, Joy," he wrote. "I love you as my queen and as the daughter I could never have. I understand your anguish; when you return, I will make it up to you however I can, but do nothing rash while you are so isolated from rational advice. I won't rest until you write me that you heed my warning."

Before I could even answer Suger, I received another letter in Constance's hand. Her words were smeared and almost incoherent: Raymond was dead! Dead? My hands shook so I could hardly read. Had Louis returned to do the deed? Or sent Thierry?

No, he had been more subtle, more oblique. Murder by omission, or, rather, by a series of misguided commissions. If Louis and the French had stayed, if Louis hadn't abducted me and thus put the Aquitanian army in limbo, Raymond might yet be alive. As it was, Raymond had ridden out two weeks earlier to scout the terrain for the coming battle, accompanied by only a small guard. Suddenly, a sandstorm had blown with gale force across the desert and he'd taken refuge in a narrow declivity. Instantly, Nur-ed-din's men had descended, brandishing their scimitars. Raymond had fought fiercely, but the wind was against him; he was blinded by sand. He'd been slain on the spot, then decapitated. His head, set in silver, now rested on Baghdad's gate. Nur-ed-din had done the actual deed, no doubt; but Louis had doomed Raymond to his fate. Louis Capet, king of France, was a murderer. I would never forgive him.

"Forgive me, dear niece, for though I make no excuses for the Saracens, this surely would not have happened if the Crusaders had given Raymond the support he deserved. The king, especially, must be held responsible. I will say no more."

Nor did she have to. I wrote my condolences at once, and I agreed with her conclusions absolutely.

Louis was absolved of his massacre at Vitry; then, by proxy—through Louis—I was absolved of my sins with my uncle. Could we not resume normal marital relations? he wrote. And, oh yes, he was sorry to hear of Raymond's untimely demise, especially since he had planned a trip back to Antioch himself to make amends with my uncle; after all, he knew quite well who was at fault in the matter. I didn't answer, of course.

Bitter and grief-stricken as I was, I could still be shocked at Louis's hypocrisy. He, the most abject pilgrim of them all, the most religious zealot, the most lunatic, dangerous madman, the strictest papist, was still willing to ignore Church teachings and have carnal relations with me, who had presumably committed incest. No, not willing—eager. Surely Adam's worst sin—what had perhaps annoyed God more than his disobedience—was the fact that Eve was Adam's close relation. Incest, the universal taboo. Every Church marriage mentioned consanguinity. Even Louis and I . . .

"Am!" I jumped up. "Go for Bishop Arnulf of Lisieux at once!"

Once that worldly prelate was in my presence, I seized his hands. "What is the one reason a couple can annul their marriage?"

"My lady queen, I beg you—"

"Think, Arnulf! How did Raoul of Vermandois get a release from his vows?"

He frowned. "By Louis's fighting at Vitry."

It had come to that, of course, but the real reason was legal. The bishops had annuled Raoul's marriage because of his relationship to Leonore.

"By consanguinity! Incest!"

His eyes searched mine.

"Louis and I are cousins. And he's just proclaimed to the world that incest is the one sin he can't abide! We're related to the fourth degree! Would you represent me before Pope Eugenius?"

"Send for your genealogies."

We both smiled.

I then wrote to Rancon; Aquitaine would soon be mine again. I'd soon be free; I'd kept my word.

Of course, the Crusade had to be terminated before I could leave Jerusalem. Fortunately for me, it took only three days for the Crusaders to be defeated in Damascus. Louis proclaimed victory, then prepared to depart. By now, Louis knew I was suing for an annulment; he had no choice but to appear opposite me before the papal court. I wisely refused to sail on the same ship with him; I went by way of Sicily; he landed in Brindisi. We would meet in Tusculum, home of the Pope since Rome had ousted the Holy See.

After the grandeur of Eastern cities, Tusculum appeared a primitive village, built around a decaying palace of a sickly mustard hue. Inside, the palace was no better. The edifice was sinking on its foundation at an uneven pace, so that huge cracks jagged across the yellow walls, and there was a pervasive stench of the *garde-robe*. Nevertheless, it was Elysium to me; this is where I would regain my freedom.

On the appointed day, Bishop Arnulf accompanied me into the Pope's chamber. Arnulf had coached me well; I knew that this Pope, born Petro Bernardo, of an impoverished aristocratic family in Pisa, owed his rapid climb up the Church hierarchy to Abbot Bernard and his Cistercian Order. He was a strict constructionist, and we would stay within a narrow agenda. His bias would be against me, but the fact that he had been willing to hear the case at all was encouraging.

The room was cramped, the air heavy with incense and dead gladioli. Louis was there ahead of me. Now washed and garbed in his kingly tunic, he appeared young, vibrant, untouched by the myriad corpses and shattered lives in his wake. His eyes, of course, were filled with tears.

We knelt to receive the Pope's blessing.

Pope Eugenius spoke with a slight lisp, and a thin line of spittle dripped from one side of his mouth. A stroke? Had his mind been impaired? When we rose, I looked directly into his hooded black eyes; no, he was acute.

Nevertheless, his hands shook as he shuffled the papers of my case. He read our genealogies aloud, then turned to Louis and asked if he could rebut our consanguinity. Louis replied that we were indeed cousins, but that we'd received absolution at our wedding ceremony, and thus consanguinity could not be an issue between us. The Pope turned to Bishop Arnulf.

True, said Arnulf smoothly, the wedding ceremony had sought to dismiss the obvious obstacle. But had it succeeded? The ceremony had also ordered the young couple to wax and multiply; yet in ten years of marriage, they'd produced only one child, and that a person of the meaner sex. Was this not a sign of God's disapproval?

"God has His own reasons," Eugenius intoned. "Perhaps a daughter is merely the first in a large family."

Arnulf warmed to his argument. He might agree, except that there were special circumstances; the great Abbot Bernard of Clairvaux had personally intervened with God in this case to bring about the birth of a prince. Certainly no one could question the credentials of Bernard with God; God's refusal was a measure of His wrath.

Then, to my surprise, Louis asked to speak on his own behalf. I'd noticed at once that Thierry wasn't present, but I'd supposed that one of the other bishops would be Louis's advocate. In an intense whisper, which sounded convincing even to me, Louis lamented his own failings in the marriage. "I have loved and cherished my wife as no man before me, but we wed under the shadow of both our fathers' deaths and thus couldn't consummate in the first flush of desire. Then came the tragedy of Vitry, and I became a penitent, and chastity one of my sacrifices. Only now, only since I have visited Jerusalem at your behest, am I free to be the husband I've always wanted to be. I beg you in the name of Jesus Christ, our Savior, who taught us how to forgive, to permit me this second chance."

All true, except that he omitted the seven years of self-imposed chastity between mourning and Vitry—the result of his own monkish convictions—and failed to mention his wild jealousies, his murder of my uncle. Bishop Arnulf moved slightly to keep me silent.

But the Pope asked me directly, "What say you, daughter?"

Bishop Arnulf answered. "She appreciates the circumstances of her marriage, Your Holiness, but the fact remains that she appears to be barren. She approaches the end of her childbearing years"— I was twenty-six—"and believes that for the sake of France, she should relinquish the throne to a more fertile successor."

"No!" Louis cried out.

The Pope folded his hands. "I believe that the king of France wants to fulfill his conjugal duties. I further believe that the long years of abstinence have caused an unnatural strain between the contending parties. I therefore refuse the queen's application and declare again that consanguinity can be no issue between them. However, as your Father here on earth, let me help you further. Tonight, I shall abdicate my own chamber so that you may have your reconciliation under God." He smiled, displaying black stubs. "Furthermore, at the risk of pretending greater powers than those of our revered Abbot Bernard, I shall pray for a royal son."

I rose from my knees. "No one can force me to consummate a union I believe to be a sin. I'll stay in your chamber with the king at your orders, but only as his cousin, which I am, not as his wife, which I am not."

I swept out.

Hours later, I stood beside the Pope, Louis and a host of bishops inside the tiny hot papal chamber. On the wall hung painted effigies of Saint-John the Baptist's head leering from its plate (and reminding me of Raymond); Saint-John the Apostle burning in oil; Saint-Polycarpe going up in flames—none of them more martyred than I was. The high bed was strewn with flowers, and the large altar was surrounded by wilting bouquets. The shutters were closed, the heat from the altar tapers insufferable, the combined stench of decayed plants and human putrescence overwhelming.

Before retiring, Pope Eugenius prepared the sacrament for Communion. I nibbled the wafer, sipped the strong sweet wine, and watched the holy men depart.

"Oh Joy," Louis said, holding out his arms. "If you knew how I've longed for this moment, how much I love you. Please don't resist me. . . ."

"I do resist you," I said thickly. I reached for a burning taper. "If you dare t-touch me, I'll set myself afire as surely as Saint . . . Saint . . ."

I fell forward. Louis's face had halos of light as he caught me.

When I woke, I lay naked beside Louis's naked body. Horrified, I reached for my tunic on the floor and moaned with nausea. I staggered to the door.

"Joy, wait; it's just dawn. . . ."

Thank God, the door was unlatched. I stood in the Pope's rose garden and vomited.

In ten days time, I knew I was pregnant.

16

In France, I went straight to Vermandois to pick up Marie, and to commiserate with Petronilla, who was now a widow. I felt I'd been gone decades instead of years, but my darling princess acted as if it had been only days. We resumed our lessons and play without strain. To my delight, she had her family's gift for poetry.

In April, I delivered a second daughter, whom I named Alix. When I woke from my birthing sleep, Louis sat by my side.

"Next time, we'll have our prince," he whispered.

I spoke to him for the first time in months. "How will you drug me next time, Louis? I'll never take Communion again."

For the first time since the papal fiasco, I wrote to Rancon, a bleak short missive: "I will honor my vows. I beg you to be patient."

Did I have to wait for Pope Eugenius to die? To pin my hopes on another Pope? Perhaps, but Eugenius remained healthy; Abbot Suger became ill. His situation was grave. During a January blizzard, I rode out to his abbey, where I sat by his bed in his mint-laden chamber. I held his dry, hot hand.

"Lean closer, my dear."

I did so.

"Promise not to leave him."

I kissed his hand. "I can't, dear friend. You above anyone know my heart."

"I wonder if I do. Is it your uncle?"

How could I lie to a dying man? "Louis murdered him, if that's what you mean."

He watched me with faded eyes.

"I'd already decided. At Mount Cadmos."

"Then who?"

"Does it have to be another man?"

"For you, yes. From the very beginning, eh? Louis never had a chance."

"I tried, Abbot Suger; you know I tried."

"You're avoiding the question; there's someone. Whoever he is, spare him, Eleanor. There's no one in Europe who has sufficient strength to take you on."

I smiled. "Am I so formidable?"

"You must forget your personal life; as the world judges, you are Aquitaine. I warned you long ago that France and England will contend for the prize, and France will win. Louis will fight, Eleanor. No one in Europe can challenge France."

"You mustn't worry."

He fixed me with his fading eyes. "After all my efforts, such wonderful possibilities. And now Louis has finally come around. He loves you."

"For now, Abbot Suger. That could change tomorrow."

"Use your strength for peace, Eleanor; stay with Louis."

I was moved, and saddened; I loved the old man.

"You and I made a good pair," I said.

"Yes, we should have been married." He smiled, and closed his eyes.

Yes, I thought, we loved each other, but I resented the coercion. Why should Louis continue to dominate my life?

For the next year, I moved from palace to palace, from county to county, and everywhere I went, Louis came after me. Rancon and I corresponded, sometimes daily. My messages were short and oblique, in case they were intercepted. He wrote in the person of an imaginary troubadour, Bernart de Ventadorn, and addressed me as "Bel Vezer," meaning "beautiful vision."

One morning, I thought I was safe in the hunting lodge at Bélizes; sitting on the bank of a stream, I had just finished reading a scorching love poem when Louis spoke behind me.

"Greeting, Joy."

I leapt into the water, where Marie and Alix were playing. "How dare you come on me unawares!"

"It's the only way I can see my own wife," he said humbly.

"I'm your cousin. What do you want?"

"To see my daughters."

"So look at them; then leave at once."

Marie shaded her eyes. "Are you my father?"

Alix, clinging to my legs, began to cry.

He winced, then sat on the grass. "I've brought my court to you, since I knew better than to summon you to Paris. We must try a case."

"I have no jurisdiction in your court."

"This concerns your own vassal, the count of Anjou; Count Geoffrey refuses to put the case to anyone but you. I've called Abbot Bernard of Clairvaux to argue for you, but you have to make an appearance."

"What's the issue?" I asked.

He sighed. "A seneschal called Berlai invaded Anjou from Aquitaine; Geoffrey and his son Henry put him in chains. They won't release him unless you give the order, since you're the over-lord of Anjou—and unless I recognize Henry as duke of Normandy."

"Berlai was your appointment, not mine. And I thought Henry had become the duke of Normandy years ago."

"He won the title in battle," he conceded, "but King Stephen of England holds the legal claim. Ever since William the Conqueror, England and Normandy have always been governed by the same man."

"And France put Stephen on the English throne to avoid giving a woman her just inheritance, eh? And that woman was Henry's mother."

He looked pained. "That was during my father's reign, not mine. I'm prepared to grant Henry his due if he'll do homage to me, which so far he's refused."

"Settle it however you like; I'm not interested." I walked briskly toward the lodge, pulling my princesses after me.

"Where are you going?"

"To pack and leave."

"You can't—everyone's here and waiting."

He was right—the courtyard was full of knights. Oh well, I would sit like a popelote while Bernard ranted, and then I'd depart—best get it over.

The timbered hall was small for a court, but it had to do. I took my place beside Louis on the highest tier; Abbot Bernard spoke animatedly with Thierry as we waited for the plaintiffs. The bell struck None, there was a rustle at the door, and two men strode across the wooden planks, their spurs jangling at every step.

Backlighted by the open windows, the infamous father and son knelt briefly, then stood, as bold as cocks on a dung heap.

Count Geoffrey—my father's friend—was a strikingly handsome man with auburn waves to his shoulders, a rich sendal cape flung carelessly over one shoulder, and flashes of jewels at his waist and wrists. His brown eyes moved audaciously from person to person, and his slanted grin was unrepentant.

His son Henry was as plain as his father was attractive, but that impression was fleeting. Although he was the same height as Geoffrey, Henry's bull neck and deep chest made him appear shorter. His hair, also red, was cut in a copper stubble, his sunburned face was a mass of freckles, his lashes and brows bleached almost white. His clothes, though rich, were indifferent in style, and he wore no jewels. And yet he fascinated every eye in the room. He was called a "red comet" because of his wild streaks and deadly strikes across Normandy; he was reputed to have the black powers of his famous ancestor, the witch Melusine. He was also known to be formidably intelligent and ruthlessly ambitious, but it wasn't his reputation that enthralled our gazes; it was his inner fire. He was a dangerous animal in our midst; he stamped his heels, his muscles quivered, and he seemed barely in control of seething energies. Like his father, he smiled, but his smile struck terror. He had large over-lapping teeth and his protuberant gray eyes had the warmth of hail-stones.

Abbot Bernard began the trial. With much religious convolution, he finally managed to say that the Angevins had seized Berlai ille-gally and must return him forthwith.

"This is not a Church matter, nor a French one, either," Count Geoffrey said in a deep, melodious voice. "We await for our duchess of Aquitaine to hear our case."

They would wait a long time with Bernard at the podium; he didn't even glance in my direction, but continued his harangue. Count Geoffrey looked out the window; his son stared straight ahead, both of them still smiling. Bernard worked himself up into his usual froth, and when he got no response, he suddenly shouted to Geoffrey, "You have insulted God! You have committed trea-son against the king of France with your unlawful seizure of a title! Give in on this matter, or within the month you will die by water!"

The audience gasped.

Count Geoffrey laughed. "You're a famous old fraud, Lord Abbot. You cannot intimidate me with prophecies."

For the first time, I truly looked at him. What a brave man he was.

Lord Henry spoke in a hoarse voice, as if he spent too much time facing the wind. "We would like to put our case to our duchess, Eleanor." Not queen, duchess.

I walked to the front of the tier. "State your case, milord."

I amended my first impression. Seen close, Henry wasn't as plain as I'd thought; at eighteen, he had the shine and confidence of youth, and his animal energies were magnetic as well as forbidding.

"If you will personally take charge of our prisoner, we will put him in your hands."

"Then do so; I accept his custody."

"That's not the only issue," Louis said from behind me. "I demand that you do homage to me."

"Do you recognize him as duke of Normandy?" Count Geoffrey asked.

"That honor belongs to the king of England."

"Which Duke Henry will soon be, I assure you." Geoffrey's voice had a metallic edge.

Henry dropped to his knees. "I acknowledge you as my overlord and vow my fealty forever."

Louis was startled. "Well then, of course you have earned your dukedom."

But Henry looked at me. "As a sign of my troth, I cede you the Vexin."

"The Vexin!" Louis wasn't alone in his surprise—everyone was buzzing. The Vexin, the most strategic strip of land in all Normandy, as astonishing as if Louis had suddenly handed Henry his crown. I was the most bemused of all—I had the distinct impression that young Henry had addressed the words to me. But what did I want with the Vexin?

A month later, Louis caught me again, this time in Poitiers. He was sweating and trembling after a hard ride from Paris.

"Have you heard the news?" he gasped.

"The Pope is dead?" I asked hopefully.

"Not the Pope, Count Geoffrey of Anjou." He covered his face with his hands and began to weep. "You were there; you witnessed it, when Abbot Bernard prophesied his death by water within the month, and it's just a month."

"How did he die?" I asked slowly.

"In the Loire River. He went for a swim—it's terribly hot—took a chill, and died that same night."

I felt a chill myself. "Was the water contaminated?"

"I suppose so, but that's not the issue. Oh Joy, we have a saint in our midst. I've always known that Abbot Bernard was a holy man, but this goes beyond devotion; he has power to work the will of God."

And, as I'd been in Jerusalem, I was seized by an idea.

"Whatever he predicts—whatever he says—must be true," I repeated breathlessly.

"God is never wrong."

Meaning that Bernard of Clairvaux is never wrong. I beat my forehead for the fool that I was. I'd gone to that well once—why not again? I pitied poor Geoffrey of Anjou, I said a prayer for him, and I thanked him for showing me the way. Within an hour, I'd written the abbot and confessed my sin with my uncle. I admitted to being devastated with shame. I repented; I granted that I was unworthy to be the mother of France. Would he read my further confessions? I enjoyed my own lurid inventions—what had taken me so long?

Soon Abbot Bernard of Clairvaux was writing his famous letters to every officer and bishop of France, trumpeting my well-known transgressions: I had a frivolous mind, I was barren, I was a strumpet, and I'd committed the ultimate sin with my uncle. For the sake of France, for the continuation of the Capet line, I must be set aside. I clenched my jaw and let the gossip swirl.

Louis tried to resist, but Bernard was too strong. When Pope Eugenius changed his mind and gave his approval to our dissolution, Louis capitulated; the date was set to end our marriage. Now I dropped my secret correspondence with Bernard, in which I'd confessed my transgressions, and concentrated on the terms I needed to protect my daughters. Louis would be forced to marry again, but I doubted if he would ever produce more children; my Marie must be named his heiress, and after her, Alix. Furthermore, I insisted on the right to see them frequently and to guide their education. Bernard and Louis might scorn at my inability to produce male children, but no one could criticize my passion for my female progeny. I was determined to make them good Aquitanians, and to protect their futures.

On March 21, the Friday before Palm Sunday, in Beaugency, near Orléans, we met to annul our marriage. Abbot Bernard was there, Thierry was there to represent Louis, and I had Archbishop Geoffrey of Bordeaux and Bishop Arnulf of Lisieux in my corner. Abbot Bernard devoted most of the afternoon to listing my sins, but I took comfort that this was the last time I would have to listen to his vicious nonsense. However, he added one surprise: During the Crusade, I'd know Saladin carnally.

"Who's Saladin?" I whispered to Arnulf.

"A Saracen." He smiled. "He would have been eleven years old when you were there."

My case was simple; we answered none of Bernard's allegations, which were irrelevant, and asked for a dissolution because of consanguinity, the proof being that the queen was barren. The conclusion was foreordained, the divorce granted. There remained only the terms: from Louis, that I would not wed again without his permission, that my new husband and I would do homage to France; for me, that our daughters be made France's heirs, and that I retain the right to see them when I wished and could guide their educations.

Louis followed me into the churchyard, where my horse was already saddled.

"Wait, Joy. This can't be all."

"I've heard enough accusations for a lifetime, Louis."

"I don't mean that. Just because we . . . I can't stop loving you." There were no tears; he tried to be manly. "And I don't believe any of what Bernard said."

"That's a late admission, my lord."

He touched my arm. "You're taking my heart with you—I'm not sure I'll live. If you can just give me some hope."

"There's always hope if you trust in God. We are both in His hands."

"I want to be in your hands." He covered his face. "I can't bear this, Joy, please, please . . ."

He didn't just weep—he sobbed the deep, guttural wrenches of a man, such as I had seen when knights lost their friends. I would have felt pity except that he wore a silver collar; I thought of my uncle Raymond's severed head caged in silver atop Baghdad's wall.

"Take care, Louis. The hour's late; I must leave."

I kissed his cheek, a Judas kiss.

Then I mounted my horse and rode slowly away, surrounded by a small Aquitanian guard led by Aimar—I'd not dared put Rancon in Louis's presence, but he would meet me in Poitiers a day after my arrival. My heart was light as a gayberry.

Che sky was a dark blue background to fast-moving cloud puffs; the trees were beginning to froth a pale green. The clop of our horses splashed drops of mud on our finery, but I didn't care. Each step took me closer to home, to Rancon. For the first time, I dared to remember every pressure of that embrace long ago, and I trembled with anticipation. At dusk, we entered the courtyard at Blois, where Louis's sister Constance awaited me. She greeted me coolly, but no matter. Her husband was in England, so at least I didn't have to parry his hostility. I excused myself early so I could make a start before daybreak. In the middle of the night, Amaria squeezed my hand. "Hush, Joy, someone's trying to enter the door."

Thierry again? I couldn't believe it! How could Louis possibly justify this second abduction? Amaria and I silently crept out the window and made our way to the stable. Aimar informed me that the intruder was Theobald of Blois, the duke's younger brother, hoping no doubt to improve his fortunes. We deliberately changed our route in order to leave Blois as soon as possible and enter Anjou, where I would be safe. We were still cautious, however; we rode along the Loire River under cover of woods. We avoided bridges and sought the ford at Port-de-Piles, close to Chinon Castle.

We splashed across quickly . . . and were instantly surrounded by crude mercenaries.

"Let us pass," Aimar ordered.

"You and your men are free to go," a callow young knight replied in a broken voice, "but not Lady Eleanor. I am claiming her as my marriage prize."

He couldn't have been more than fourteen.

"Who are you?" I asked.

"Your future husband, my lady. I'm Geoffrey of Anjou."

"My younger brother," a rough voice said from behind me, "for whom I apologize. He has too great ambition."

I gazed into the glittering eyes of Henry, duke of Normandy. He nodded briefly, then spoke again to his brother. "This behavior ill-becomes a knight, Geoffrey. Now leave before I lose patience."

Geoffrey's boyish voice rose to a screech. "You stole Anjou and Maine from me, but you'll not take Aquitaine!"

Henry drew his sword. "I'll take your life if you don't leave at once."

"My father promised! He said that Anjou was mine, since you had Normandy!"

"Do you want to argue with him in Heaven?"

"By God, I'll fight you!"

At least a hundred Norman knights appeared in the woods, the hedges, on the far side of the river.

"Do you still want to fight?" Henry asked.

"Yes!"

Henry's husky voice was stern. "You're behaving like a child, Geoffrey. Take hold. If you want to fight me about Anjou, well and good, but you'll not frighten this great lady."

Geoffrey looked as if he might weep. "You won't get away with this, I promise you!" But he abruptly spurred his steed into the woods, his small army following behind him.

Henry bowed to me. "Again, I apologize. Your charms must have turned his head."

"As you so wisely surmised, my charms are measured in square miles," I countered. "We thank you, Lord Henry."

"Come, let me escort you the rest of the way. These roads abound with younger brothers looking for opportunity through matrimony."

Which confirmed my recent experience in Blois. "Surely I'm diverting you from your own purposes."

He flashed his huge teeth. "I'm poised in Barfleur, waiting for a fair wind so I may invade England. We've waited years; a few days more won't matter."

"Well then, I accept your offer gratefully."

We roiled our beasts forward.

The situation was ludicrous. The "red star of malice," as Suger had called Henry, had shot from the heavens to my rescue. I wished the small abbot could see us now trotting peaceably side by side through the vernal landscape. I glanced sidelong at Henry's profile: not a handsome man, no, with his protruding chin and glassy eyes, his large nose and small mouth, but one marked for greatness.

"I'm very sorry about the loss of your father, my lord. He was a good friend to Aquitaine."

"Thank you."

"Do you blame Bernard of Clairvaux?"

"For what?"

I reminded him of the prophecy.

He flashed his teeth in my direction; he looked better full face. "God's eyeballs, no! All those charlatans pass out dire predictions like wafers, so they're bound to hit the mark sometimes. I warned my father that the Loire smelled like a pissmire, but he would swim. He could be stubborn."

What a relief to be among the sane again.

Now we were following the Clain, and I could see Poitiers ahead.

"Please let me repay you with a little hospitality, Lord Henry, before you return to Barfleur."

"You're very kind, but only for one night."

Which was all I offered—Rancon would arrive on the morrow!

Lord Aimar then asked if he and his men could be excused from further duty; he needed to ride south. I dismissed him gladly at Pont-Joubert.

"Where is everyone, Joy?" Amaria asked as we entered the city.

"I don't know." Pont-Joubert had been unmanned, I realized, and I saw no burghers in the streets. "Has there been a pestilence?"

Petra and her three children were waiting for me at the palace. Oh God, let there be nothing amiss.

I turned to Henry. "Perhaps you should reconsider my offer of hospitality. If there's cholera or—"

"I wouldn't dream of leaving you to face such a disaster. I'll ride to your palace with you."

We rode silently up the empty streets. I became more and more uneasy. When we arrived at the square of my small new church, Notre Dame, knights lazed in the sun. They carried the banner of two gold lions on a red field—Normandy's insignia.

I stopped my horse. "Are these your men, Lord Henry?

He shrugged charmingly. "Forgive me. I sent a runner to alert my troops of my diversion; a few obviously decided to join me."

With the knights in his train, he must now have a force of over two hundred within the walls, I realized. My heart pounded in cold premonition.

I entered an empty palace. No, not quite empty—four knights lounged in the hall. They bowed to Henry.

"May I present my close friends and counselors, Lady Eleanor? This is—"

"Where is my sister, Lady Petronilla?" I interrupted.

"Quite safe," Henry assured me. "She was called away."

"Called away where? For what purpose?"

"To assure that our plans can be executed without undue difficulty."

"Is she your hostage, my lord?"

"An unkind word. Let's say—"

"What do you want, Lord Henry?"

He shifted his weight. "I want what every man wants, my fair lady. Your charms have quite turned my head."

I'd realized his purpose since I'd seen the knights, but I still couldn't believe it. "You are my vassal; you owe me fealty."

"To which I gallantly add love. And I'm your vassal of Anjou, but not England."

"You're not a king!"

"A technicality; I'm almost a king."

"No king abducts a duchess!"

He nodded judiciously. "And I'm not yet a king. You argue in a circle."

"My lands are not so easily seized, Henry. My barons will not turn tail like your brother."

He smiled. "I could easily take Aquitaine by force, as I did Normandy." Then he shrugged. "And of course they're not here."

My heart squeezed. Oh, why had I told Rancon to come a day after my arrival?

"And to take me by force is easier, eh?"

He grinned. "And more pleasurable. No, you misunderstand me, and I want to be clear. I have yearned for you all my life from afar; my own mother has told me how you are the only woman fit for my bed, and when I saw you . . ." He clutched his heart.

Louis was a better liar.

"You came to France to look me over?"

"And gave Louis the Vexin in exchange for the wife I was about to steal." He laughed.

"You may have the cunning of Proteus, Lord Henry, but you forgot me in your calculations—I will be your enemy forever! Now go while you can!"

"And your sister?"

My heart skipped. "She would be the first to reject your blackmail."

"For herself, no doubt, but she has children. The boy looks

sickly." He licked his lips. "Well, marriage first, and love will come afterward, as they say." He snapped his fingers, and a page left the room.

I clutched his sleeve. "You don't mind that I bedded with my uncle?"

He hooted loudly. "I don't believe it!"

The horror—I couldn't grasp it. Aquitaine spread like a fading feast before me. Rancon . . .

"Lord Henry, I'll share Aquitaine with you, I promise," I said desperately. "I'll cede all territories north of La Marche, only—I beg you—spare both of us this ignominy."

"You'll share my bed and all of Aquitaine in the process. Why should I bargain?"

"Think of your reputation! What the world will say!"

"You'll be blamed, not me. As you say, you slept with your uncle! What could anyone expect?"

"Ask King Louis's permission. You owe him—"

His hoot was now derisive. "Do you ask a baby for his toy?"

"Then think of England. Even now the wind may be rising for your invasion. Don't neglect your greater purpose."

"England will wait."

"No, *I'll* wait! I'll marry you when you become a king, not before," I said tartly. "Why should I demean myself?"

His laughter faded. "You're not demeaning yourself, damn it. I'm the greatest man in Europe, as you well know, and you're fortunate that I chose you. As for waiting, you'll wait as my wife!"

I stared at this freckled travesty of a man, hating his smug self-assurance, his jocular insolence. Was there no way to pierce his cockiness?

I drew myself up. "For the last time, Lord Henry, I warn you that you're making a fatal mistake."

"Are you threatening death by water? Poor Eleanor, you've lived in France too long. You fancy yourself another Bernard of Clairvaux!"

"Bernard invoked God as his instrument; I don't need God."

"Let's get to business." He snapped his fingers.

"I mean it, Lord Henry. You won't take Aquitaine—and you won't take me!"

"I see I'll have to persuade you." He pulled playfully on one of my braids. "You're about to have what you've always wanted, a real man."

The page came back with a priest whom I didn't recognize.

Henry became crisp. "Everything's arranged. I didn't bother with bans or dispensations, but I've taken care of the necessaries. I'm aware of King Louis's tender feelings—there will be no display."

His four counselors surrounded me and the priest read the ceremony. Neither Henry nor I had to make responses; we were pronounced man and wife.

I hadn't lived with Louis for fifteen years for nothing; I knew the vows were not sealed until we consummated.

Our wedding feast was a soldier's lot, washed down with wine from my own cellar. Henry, I noticed, hardly drank anything—a pity. Nor did he appear amorous or even very aware of my presence. Instead, he talked of his coming invasion of England: Lord Huntingdon might be loyal, and Leicester would not.

"Where are you going?" Henry called sharply.

"To tend my own needs."

"I'll go with you."

"My handmaid can attend me."

"Yes, but can she guard you?"

"Sufficiently."

He walked over and put his forehead against mine. "Go make ready, my darling wife. I'll meet you in your chamber for the important invasion."

I sat again. "I'll stay with you here. You were speaking of Vegetius, eh?"

He was surprised. "You know the Roman?"

"I was trained in strategy."

He looked genuinely delighted. "More than I bargained for. Well then, for a little while—if I can wait."

A delaying tactic—I saw no way to escape.

17

*enry dropped his clothing without shame or even much interest, revealing genitals that were disproportionately large. He walked around the bed; I retreated quickly to the window. Thank God I wasn't drugged.

"Eleanor, wife," he said thickly. He fastened me against the sill and pressed his hips into mine. "Feel that?" His face approached.

I bit his nose. "Werewolf!" Blood gushed!

He crashed me to the opposite wall, pressed his lips on mine. I gagged on his bitter blood.

"Take off your clothes," he grunted.

I wrapped my arms tightly around my tunic; he fumbled with the clasp on my shoulder. While he concentrated, I raised my knee hard to his groin.

"Aauh!" He doubled in pain.

I ran to the door. "Help!"

He ripped my tunic from behind.

When I turned, his member extended like a blowfish.

"Henry, I beg you, don't—"

His fist crashed into my jaw, and I fell heavily to the rushes.

"Turn over." He kicked my ribs. Then twisted my arm so I had to roll.

Spraddling over me, he ripped my intimate garments. "There, open your legs, damn you."

I made my legs rigid, crossed my feet. I tried to scratch his back, but he had a leather hide. He pried my legs open with his knee, then leaned his weight on my wrists and arched above me.

He began his deadly stabs.

But didn't penetrate.

"Relax!" he grunted.

He hit me again and again with his sharp tent peg and couldn't enter. I was as surprised as he was; I had no idea I had power in that area. But after an eternity of striking, he prevailed. I bit the rushes.

"There, now it's official; Aquitaine is mine." He lay his large head on my shoulder. "Liked it, didn't you?"

Does a knight like to be run through by a sword?

To my horror, he began again. There was no longer any purpose in resisting—I'd lost. With a curious detachment, I listened to him groan, felt his hands adjusting and groping, was rolled to my side like a dummy, then to my stomach.

Louis had claimed he couldn't perform his conjugal duty if he felt pleasure. Did Henry believe the same? Carnal knowledge in order to have a son, rape for a duchy. Where was love?

Henry snored loudly into my ear, his body heavy as a fallen oak. It began to rain. Through the open window came earth smells of spring.

Henry woke. "Ready, wife?"

And began again.

By morning, each stab was a hot poker. I groaned in pain.

"I knew you'd be moved," Henry whispered. "Granddaughter of the famous troubadour. Am I like his songs?"

"Yes." I sang bitterly: "*'I fucked them, I precisely state, a hundred times plus eighty-eight.'*"

He was delighted. "Did you count?"

"It's a song about a man who rapes two sisters."

He laughed. "You can't rape your own wife." Shades of Louis. "And I won't touch your sister."

Was he japing? No, he meant to assure me.

Henry's face was eager. "No, tell me truly, how was I?"

"Not as good as Louis." I smiled sweetly.

"Oh, come, don't sulk; you know you loved it. Ladies are delighted by rough seduction."

"If you believe Ovid," I said acidly.

His eyes widened. "From Vegitius to Ovid? You astonish me, my dear wife."

"And you astonish me," I countered. "I would think that a man of your stature would have outgrown Ovid's crude advice to the adolescent male, though I suppose I should give you credit for reading at all."

He grabbed me roughly. "I'll match my reading against yours any day, my fine duchess. Do you think me an illiterate brute from the country? This is the happiest night of your life. and the most fortunate; you've married greatness, whether you know it or not, and you'll share my destiny. I chose you because you know how to rule. I meant it when I said I had decided this long ago. In England, a queen reigns with her husband—*regalis imperii participes*—and I'm willing to share with a woman, unlike your former husband."

He hasped his belt.

"And someday soon you're going to beg for a little 'fucking,' as you called it. I recognize a convert."

In midmorning, my sister returned with her children, then my entire household, all dumb with horror. I shook my head in warning: only a few hours and we could talk. Henry, however, declared himself ravished by my charms and decided to stay one more night. My breath stopped: If Rancon should come while Henry . . .

A runner from Barfleur arrived shortly after Haute Tierce; King Louis was leading an army into Normandy! To add injury, Theobald of Blois and Henry's younger brother Geoffrey were riding with him. Henry dropped the vellum and clutched his head. "I should have murdered Geoffrey when I had my chance!"

He staggered forward uncertainly. "I'll kill . . . I'll kill . . . ," he grunted again and again like a stricken boar. My household scrambled away from his path.

"Does he have the falling sickness?" Amaria whispered.

"No, dear, he's been crossed. The terrifying red comet is displaying his two-year-old temper."

Childish or not, Henry's tantrum was both terrifying and dangerous. The volume grew, the staggering became more erratic, his eyes stood forth, and his nose began to bleed again where I'd bitten him. Mucus mixed with blood, his eyes fixed as if he really were in a fit, and his gravel voice howled. I noticed that his knights stayed well out of his way.

"Auu, that!" He kicked the rushes aside and pulled a board free. "That!" He crushed an ivory altar. "That!" he roared, and broke the corner of an ancient chest.

He gnashed at the rushes, swung the splintered board again in his hands. We all pressed ourselves against the wall.

"You!" He swung at a knight. The knight feinted.

"You!" He swung at my screaming sister.

I jerked his arm hard from the rear. Petra fell, unhurt. I crowded my family out the door. We stumbled up to the women's quarters.

Huddled silently, we listened to the smashing and shouting. Then suddenly, everything was still. Someone knocked. I waved my friends away from the door.

Henry's page stood outside. "The duke wants to say good-bye."

Motioning my family to stay where they were, I followed the page to the great hall, where Henry was calmly sipping a cup of red wine. "Ah, my dear wife, I'm sorry to disappoint you, but I must leave at once." He turned to a knight, "Send word to my army in Barfleur—tell them to meet me in Rouen. I'm riding by way of Maine; see that horses are ready as I come through. I'll need at least eleven."

He placed his hands on my shoulders with a gentle smile. The blood on his nose still oozed and a piece of rush stuck to his lower lip. "This has been the happiest night of my life—an excellent omen for our future together. Take good care of yourself while I'm away and don't worry, this shouldn't take long. I'll write you every day; we'll meet in Barfleur."

He then crushed me in a long kiss. The rush was transferred from his lips to mine. "God's eyeballs, what a glorious woman! To think you're my wife!" And he laughed with boyish glee. "Henry and Eleanor!"

He ran down the steps to his waiting steed. His legs were slightly bowed from constant riding, but the instant he was on his horse, he cut a magnificent figure. He waved, turned expertly, and rode away without looking back.

Almost at once, I received my own letter from Louis:

To the Duchess Eleanor of Aquitaine, greeting.

Need I say that you broke every covenant in our agreement? Even Abbot Bernard is astounded at the depth of your depravity. To wed the enemy of France at once! How long have you been plotting this dastardly act? Since the Berlai event? Not only have you betrayed me but you have forsaken your daughters forever. You will never see Marie or Alix again, and I have disinherited them.

If you change your mind, you are still welcome to my bed.

Louis Capet, king of France.

I screamed and staggered in a fit of my own. I would have smashed the altar, would have ruined the chest, if there'd been any-thing left. I was out of my mind with rage! Henry had done this! Did he have no pity for the innocent? No sympathy for children who are disinherited? After all his father had done for him! Yes, and his mother, too, with her vast gift of England. By God, I would avenge my little princesses. I would crush Henry's beloved balls in a garlic pestle! Pluck his icy eyes from their sockets! He would rue the day he'd admired me in France, and he'd never take Aquitaine.

Lai of Amaria of Gascony

When our lord beholds the eagle white as snow,
He carefully aims his trusty bow
And whiz, the arrow strikes a mortal blow;
But her beak like a blade of ice does show,
And quickly she tears his sinews quite apart
To pierce directly to his heart.
He drops the bird, and wavers on his steed,
Falls to the ground, there to bleed.
The wounded bird flutters close to his ear
For she must be certain he can hear:
"You, my valiant lord who aimed your dart at me,
Listen to what your fate may be;
You shall not now die, nor yet be well,
But exist forever in a living hell;
You will suffer unendurable pain
And rue this day again and again
When you followed your trusty eye
And shot me cruelly from the sky."
The lord raised his pitiable eyes:
"A hunter always shoots what flies,
And I had no knowledge that you could speak so well;
You must be a maiden under a spell.
If so, tell me, is there no cure
For the agony that I must endure?"
The eagle lay in a pool of blood,
Her feathers stained in the scarlet flood.
And yet did raise her graceful head,
As our Lord did when He was dead:
"There is only one cure in Heaven above
And that is pure and faithful love;
If some lord will succor me,
And by his love set me free

227

From my spell (as you guessed so well),
We both may on this earth long dwell
In bliss sublime,
If love comes in time."

I was still holding Louis's letter when a dozen knights galloped into our courtyard and shouted, *"Asuseé"*! And there was Rancon in the center, bronzed from the southern sun, his glossy black curls now grown long again. He ran up our steps.

"My lady." He knelt briefly, then looked up.

"Quick, come inside."

"Christ, what happened here?" He took in the smashed altar, the reeds tumbled as if in a storm, then my face. "Who struck your jaw?" He turned dark red. "Who was the bastard? Was it Hugh?"

I burst into loud wails.

"Joy! My God, tell me!" He reached for me; my family entered the *salle*.

"Excuse us, please, we're going to the women's quarters." I pulled Rancon past my gaping sister and household.

In the bedroom, I sobbed uncontrollably.

Rancon lifted my hair. "Before you begin, I want to examine your jaw. Show me your teeth. Does that hurt? That?"

I watched his face through a wash of tears. So near and so far, my entire future blasted.

When he was satisfied that no bones were broken, he leaned against the door, frowning. "Begin at the beginning, Joy. Someone assaulted you for a purpose."

"I can't!" More weeping, but I knew I must confess. Gradually, incoherently, I told the whole sorry tale of being rescued by Henry, being wed to Henry, then raped.

He closed his eyes and whispered, "I'll kill him if it takes all my life."

"No, Rancon, he frightens me—you haven't seen him when . . ."

He's mad, I thought. Not in the delusional manner of Louis; Henry used madness as a weapon. I shuddered at the memory of his temper.

"I saw him in Maine. I fought for him, God help me. Remember?" Rancon's eyes opened.

"Of course." He'd gone to Maine with my father.

"His enemy was France, but he destroyed his own people to be certain of their allegiance. I watched him charge against a helpless countryside. He berserks, slashes, burns—oh, he's formidable when he wants a piece of ground. Now he covets Aquitaine."

"Exactly so."

"Oh Christ, why didn't he attack it directly? Give us a chance to defend ourselves? But to take you . . . to hurt you, to strike . . ." He cried out in his glorious singer's voice, "I'll kill the bastard!"

"Hush! There must be some way . . ." I could hardly speak.

His hand crossed his eyes. "And I thought, hoped . . ."

"I'm not capitulating, Rancon!"

Suddenly, he broke. For the second time within a few days, I was clutched by a weeping man. "Oh Joy, Joy, Bel Vezer, I can't bear to think of you . . ."

I stroked his rough curls, his wet cheeks. What could I say? Except—we looked at each other—I was overwhelmed by his proximity, his fragrance, which I'd yearned for so long, the hard muscles pressing. "So don't think, Rancon. I'm still the same person."

He kissed me. "You may be injured—I can wait—you'll tell me . . ."

I pulled him closer, and we kissed as we had on Mount Cadmos, again and again. Then we were naked on my bed, and dark gradually obscured the walls. Again rain fell outside, bringing the heavy perfume of chestnut blooms, followed by thin moonlight, which made shadows dance on the ceiling. Rancon slept, as did I; we whispered and caressed each other until moonlight turned to sunlight.

"Now!" I whispered.

"I don't want to hurt . . ."

Panting, groping, we desperately sought the solace of love. When we first became intimate, I did have a sharp twinge of pain, but I didn't cry out. Damn Henry! I wouldn't let him rob me of this! The pain passed, and with it, memory. Rancon loved me, again and again and again, and I marveled how the act of love—so repetitive really—can differ so profoundly from man to man. Or maybe it wasn't the man so much as my own body, which opened for my chosen mate like a flower, a "furry flower," my grandfather had called it in a song. My desire grew; I could never have enough! At last, I was under my own hibiscus bush, as my sister had been so long ago, and I, too, wept with happiness.

Yet we found opportunity between kisses and declarations of love to plot. "Tell me exactly, Joy, about the ceremony, everything you can remember."

I did.

Another session of love, and then he told me I must slowly recount the situation I'd found in Poitiers again. Henry's soldiers had been an occupying army? And none of the natives had seen me come home? Or witnessed the marriage?

No, no one except Henry's knights.

The priest was a stranger? No bans? No contract? No papal dispensations? And Henry had left after a single night?

"It never happened!" he cried jubilantly. "Joy, you were never married! Don't you see? It's his word against yours! Surely your sister and aunts will support you!"

"But Louis knew right away," I pointed out. "He believes I am wed."

"May I see his letter?"

I sent a page for it.

Rancon quickly perused the single page. "If he wants you back in his bed, he must believe that you're not married. Louis is punctilious about such matters."

"Then why did he attack in Normandy?"

"My guess would be that Henry told Louis himself before the fact that you were married, in order to reclaim the Vexin in your name."

Good thinking.

"The king of France would never accept a slipshod ceremony. He may be your greatest asset." As he expanded on his theme, I began to hope.

I must act carefully, he said, choose my moment to announce my single state, probably when Henry was absent in England and couldn't defend himself; and, until I was ready to move, I should not alert Henry, who was more cunning than a fox, more ruthless than a lion.

"We'll be together, as we planned, Joy," Rancon whispered against my lips.

"*Oc*," I replied. "Tristan and Iseult."

"You're not going to be married! Not Iseult—you'll be single! We'll live together! Rule Aquitaine together!"

As lovers. Not as man and wife. Still no word of his own marital state.

"Will your lady permit you to live with me?" I asked at last.

He pulled my face to his shoulder. "She knows how I feel, Joy; it was too important to hide. But she's ill; she asked me to wait."

Ill from what? I couldn't contain my jealousy. "Seriously ill?"

"I don't want to talk about Arabelle now. She's joined some cult that demands suicide."

His tone told me to desist. Love and death, her death, not ours.

"Joy." His voice thickened, and we rode our mad way to love once again.

At the end of two days, I was exhausted from love, literally worn to a shadow. I remembered the poem *Tristan,* when King Mark had looked down on the sleeping lovers with pity, for they were thin and haggard from love.

Yet nothing could stop us. Though Rancon's eyes were circled and he hadn't eaten a morsel, he still yearned for love. And so did I. We were fast becoming martyrs to our passion.

I remembered Henry saying that he "recognized a convert" to carnal love. He was right, except that he wasn't the priest who converted me.

We rose at last, smiling wanly, our plans honed. Adultery required strategies as complicated and devious as any battle. Both Rancon and I delighted in the task, and why not? We'd sealed every scheme with the act of love.

Finally, we descended the stairs as demurely as we could, our veiled eyes battling with triumphant smiles, and said farewell in the company of my household. He knelt before me courteously.

"Farewell, my lady; I shall contact you soon!"

And we became lost in each other's eyes.

"The kiss of peace." I leaned forward, and only Petra's firm grip on my arm made me rise.

Even after he'd mounted his destrier, he couldn't leave.

"Joy, I forgot . . ."

And he forgot what he'd forgotten as we kissed again. Finally, I watched him go out the gate.

Το Europe's amazement, Henry had difficulty defeating the French king. Louis, fired by passion, fought like a tiger against my new husband. I prayed that France would win—if I truly was a wife, let me become a widow. Louis retreated, however, when the fighting season was over, and Henry rode directly to Barfleur to wait for the wind. As he had promised, he'd written me every day, and now he summoned me to meet him at his point of departure.

I alerted Rancon.

I took my time riding to my rendezvous, hoping to find an empty harbor, but the wind didn't cooperate. Paused on the hillside overlooking the perfect crescent of Barfleur Bay, I gazed down on a great fleet separated into two parts by an old Roman seawall: To the north were royal galleys with single masts and painted sails now rolled tight with bolt lines. To the south, a mix of dories and fishing sculls banged and scraped in the tide. Even from where I sat, I could smell the rich broth of fish heads and entrails sloshing on their bottoms. I studied the heavens: a sullied day, the sky wrapped in gray gauze, gulls prowling over the pewter swell like hungry rats, and my heart was with the birds. Then my gaze returned to the port, where I spotted his scarlet pavilion on the northern promontory between an octagonal lighthouse and a square customs house.

"Hoyt!" I cried. Amaria followed me on the tortuous descent to the town of Barfleur.

Though the single main street was crowded with sailors and soldiers, it seemed curiously empty; the natives had either fled or been forced out. Without the normal activities, the row of hovels lay exposed like an aging whore's body, rutted, festering with odd stanks of human waste, thatched roofs torn like bad wigs, walls leaning widdershins from the blasts, painted signs clacking like teeth. With people, the place might be happily sinful; empty, it was sinister.

My presence created the small sensation it was calculated to do. From years of practice, I'd honed my appearance to an art, and I wore a winged headpiece of white crane feathers edged with loops of diamonds; my Byzantine silk tunic fluttered from my saddle almost to the ground, now showing ivory, now a pale rose, and was cinched by rubies and pearls; on one shoulder hung a coral cape fastened with clasped hands of gold. My horse was equally splendid from his golden mask, gold bells on his bridle, scarlet silks embossed with lions and eagles, which enclosed his ebony body, to his tail, pranked with rubies.

"Hail Mary, Mother of God," one simple sailor gasped as he crossed himself.

I blessed him with insouciance.

Keeping my eyes on the scarlet tent, I left the dusty road and clopped over a tangle of sea pods alive with fleas. Soldiers ran before me, skirting the line of tents to behind the lighthouse, and at last, here came Henry himself. He bounded lightly over the dunes.

"Joy!" he shouted. "Where have you been?"

He was at my side, gazing upward from voracious grape pulps, his skin spotted like a frog's, only this frog would never become a prince.

"Greeting, my lord."

"Christ, you're like the sun." He covered his eyes as if blinded. "Away from you, I live in the dark."

Very poetic. For a moment, I doubted if I could carry on. In France, I'd despised Thierry of Galeran, though I'd understood that crusading Templars are all narrow zealots and that castration lends another warp, but what was Henry's excuse? The arrogance of power? I hated him to the very bone.

I slid into his arms. My feathered headpiece helped me avoid his kiss. He stared at me quizzically.

"I've fought for you all summer."

I smiled. "And didn't win."

"Didn't I? Louis is in Paris and I'm here with you, which is victory enough. Come, you must meet my mother."

I scooped up my train as we walked along the water. Seen close, the ships were frightening—long, low in the Viking manner, though with ample space for horses; their masts swayed high above like falling trees and each prow was decorated with a hideous carving. Henry paused before a particularly repellent barque enameled scarlet with gold scales.

"That's my *Esnecca*," he said proudly.

"I can see that it's a snake." The prow boasted an evil serpent's head with jeweled eyes and tongue.

In front of the royal pavilion, Henry's mother, the famous Matilda, who'd been used as a political example to me so often, stepped forward, her hand outstretched; she was a formidable figure in a long scarlet tunic emblazoned with lions, and her head was massive.

"Greeting, Duchess Eleanor. We welcome you to our family."

Her manner was so imperious that I wondered if I should kiss her hem.

"Thank you."

"Henry fitzEmpress will soon present you with a crown."

FitzEmpress? Son of an empress? Ah yes, this tall handsome woman with her bright hair and chilly eyes had once been wed to the emperor of the Holy Roman Empire, and apparently she still liked the title; certainly she'd retained the German accent. Broad of shoulder and beam, Matilda was a Nordic goddess; her brow was smooth, her pale eyes penetrating, her chin high, her voice a roll of drums. What an odd mother for the ebullient Henry, an odd wife for his rakish father.

"It has always been my dearest dream to wear the crown of England." My sarcastic tone was lost on both of them.

"He'll land close to Bristol," she said, "where I have many loyal followers. Winchester is still my capital."

Her capital. How ironic, that this vibrant heir to the English throne must forego her rights in favor of her son. France had done that to her—or no, perhaps it was England—or no, perhaps it was the Church, which proclaimed women incapable of ruling. If she'd been held up as a cautionary tale in my past, she was even more so at this moment. I saw a proud, defeated woman who must lean on her son for vindication. Yet he would wear England's crown, not she.

As she and Henry explained their strategy, I tried to recall what I knew of Matilda's marital history. Her father, King Henry I of England, had assigned her as a child to the German emperor, who had died when she was in her mid-twenties. Her father had then found her a second husband in Geoffrey of Anjou, who was a decade younger, fifteen to her twenty-six. Could it be coincidence that Henry was a decade younger than I was? And that I, like Matilda, was a duchess in my own right and had formerly been wed to a king? Had Henry emulated his father and mother in marrying me?

If so, he should have been more prudent; if memory served, his parents' marriage had been one of the most miserable on record. Matilda had left Geoffrey several times, although her father had forced her to return. Had Henry forgotten that I had no father? Once away, I would be gone forever.

Matilda repeated something, her manner meek as a crocodile.

"Yes, I quite understand Henry's claims to the throne," I murmured, "but why does he need to invade? Surely you wouldn't risk killing King Stephen, my lord."

"Never!" Henry exclaimed. "To kill a fellow monarch sets a dangerous example. I mean to parley about my rights—my army at my back will persuade him to abdicate."

The plan seemed simplistic. Why should a king step down just because Henry waved his genealogy? Yet Henry was formidable—I pitied King Stephen.

Matilda put her arm across my shoulder with satisfaction. "You're as lovely as they say, a fit queen for my son."

Had she chosen me? I met her toothy grin which was belied by her hard eyes. Yes, she had chosen me for Aquitaine, not because of my "loveliness"; this woman thought with a man's mind, a fit mother for her rapist son.

Henry smiled. "Too beautiful by far to be listening to military blather. Leave me with my bride, Mother."

She kissed my cheek. "Of course, forgive me."

Henry led me into his scarlet tent; suddenly, I remembered Rancon in my topaz tent and became faint with longing.

"I've had a miserable summer, thanks to you." Henry's voice echoed hollowly.

"I didn't ask you to fight."

"Not the fighting." His husky voice deepened. "I was haunted. Every night I lay with a beautiful vision."

"Yes, I've heard that you are an incorrigible womanizer."

"I didn't mean other women—I meant you!" he snapped. "Can't you understand a compliment, damn it? You're my wife; I wanted you, want you. Christ, you're as creamy as a hawthorn bloom, and your face—I've never seen such a smile, and the way your eyes slide to the side as if beckoning me. I'm undone."

I slid my eyes to avoid looking at him; now I pushed away his groping hands. "Unfortunately, my lord, this is the wrong time for love. I must ask you to abstain."

He froze in the red glow; even Henry shared the universal revulsion against an unclean woman. Would this ploy have worked when he'd wed me? Probably not; ambition overwhelms revulsion. Now he came close and kissed me. "I'll wait here, then, until you're ready. I can't sail without my wife's blessing."

"Nonsense, you must go when the wind rises. You're a future king."

He touched my feathered wing. "You're right, but, God's eye-balls, how I want you. To think we'll spend our whole life together."

I swallowed hard to avoid vomiting.

I saw little of my new husband except in the evenings, when he met with his mother and me to give us our instructions: She was to be his seneschal in Normandy; I was to rule Anjou, Touraine, Maine, and Aquitaine from his county seat in Angers. He'd said I would be given power, but I was surprised at the extent. Yet I sus-pected the real power resided with Matilda, for it was she who would issue most of the orders; we would be in close touch. Though Henry would write both of us, official news would go to his mother. I had Amaria send the news of my assignment to Rancon.

The wind rose at dawn on the fourth day, and the beach became a scramble of activity. The ships had long been loaded with arms and gear; first the horses were pushed aboard, then the men. Henry was the last to climb the plank, and he embraced me in front of everyone.

"I'll bring you a crown," he whispered. "What's your head size?"

"Very large. Ask France."

He laughed and was gone.

I said my farewells to Empress Matilda and was soon on the hill-side again, watching the sails take the wind. Would Henry succeed? He'd tried twice before, but he'd been only a child. I conceded that he was a most excellent leader. His speed and efficiency were mar-velous, and his men seemed to respect him, but I had more weighty things on my mind than Henry's fate. I pushed my steed to a gal-lop toward Angers.

Soon, paused on another hillside, I looked down at the small walled city sloping to the Maine River, where a huge fortress dom-inated the landscape, the castle where Henry had been raised. The edifice was formidable, the moat almost invisible at the bottom of a deep grassy chasm, the bridge narrow and guarded with a spiked gate. Down I went at a dangerous speed.

Inside the crenelated wall, we confronted a large compound surrounded by sharp teeth of stone; my guides led me across the windy court to the domestic quarters, which looked habitable, thank God. A welcoming party greeted me with a deference I'd never known in France, springing, no doubt, from their fear of Henry. I smiled to put everyone at ease. To my delight, many were scholars from the nearby School of Chartres, a holdover from Count Geoffrey's days.

"Has my troubador arrived?" I asked.

One of the scholars from Chartres, Father Gabriel, replied, "Bernart of Ventadorn? He's been here two days."

"Tell him to attend me if you please."

"In your chamber?"

I stared at him. "That's where he may find me, yes."

It was sundown before he rapped; his green cape filled the door, and I was in his arms. "Oh Rancon, tell me how you—"

And we laughed, embraced. Each tried to talk through our kisses, and finally we became coherent.

"Did you do as I instructed?"

"Yes, but—"

"He didn't touch you!"

"No!" I shuddered.

"Thank God!" He wrapped me fervently in his cape.

I closed my eyes. "Rancon, I'm with child."

England

1152

18

"Rancon, I'm with child!" I repeated, my voice trembling.

His body stiffened; he loomed upward in the dark. Then he cried jubilantly in full voice, "I'm a father!"

"Hush! Someone will hear!"

"Oh God, we're to be parents!" he whispered. He kissed me again and again. "Joy, thank you, thank you. I thought I would never become a father, and with you! Ours!"

"It's Henry's."

"Nonsense! I know that I'm the father!"

"Henry is the father."

He drew away. "Why do you keep repeating that? I felt—you must have felt—it's the fruit of our love!"

Indeed, I believed it was, I acknowledged, but generation has nothing to do with possession. I reminded him that I'd just lost two daughters to Louis of France; by law, they belonged to their father, even though he cared nothing for them. My breath grew short. Although I corresponded several times a week with Marie through my sister in Vermandois, I would never accept the loss. I would fight for my daughters forever—could Rancon understand?

"Yes! Of course I understand! I'll never permit Henry to snatch my child!"

Brave words followed by more brave words and, finally, silence. He knew the law as well as I did, and he'd fought Henry in the field. I tried to cheer him: The baby might be a girl, "of the meaner sex," I quoted dryly; if so, Henry might permit her to grow up in Aquitaine.

"I could take her to Taillebourg!" Rancon exclaimed.

"No, to Poitiers, where I could visit. Where we could both be parents."

Another subtle jibe, for I was not eager to have Arabelle become my child's mother. My spies had informed me that she didn't believe in materialism, meaning children.

When he spoke, his voice was tight. "We're avoiding the main issue, aren't we, Joy? You're trapped. My baby or Henry's, you don't dare deny your marriage to Henry now."

"I'm afraid not." The dilemma I'd been facing for weeks.

"My God, you can never be free!"

I put a finger to his lips. "I freed myself from Louis, didn't I?"

"Louis was vulnerable because of his religious bias, whereas Henry—"

"Is also vulnerable. I simply have to discover in what manner, eh?" I didn't add the obvious, that I'd been wed to Louis for fifteen years before I was able to escape.

"I'll never give you up!" he cried, now in anguish. "Oh God!"

"Nor I you, Rancon."

"I can't help myself!"

"Nor I!"

Fated lovers.

And we found solace in love. Then exultation. Then forgetfulness. Until the next day, when I learned that Rancon had continued to think in the midst of ecstasy.

He appeared at midday, dressed for riding. "I've come to say farewell, milady; I'm leaving for Aquitaine."

I gasped—after all our renewed promises of love? "But why now? Later, you'll have to! We have so little time, Rancon!"

"Because I told the barons that the marriage to Henry never took place, no matter what Louis of France thinks. That you were going to expose Henry's claims as false." His tone was flat. "Now I must inform them otherwise."

"And how do you think they'll respond?"

He considered carefully. "Several possibilities. Hugh of Lusignan will be furious that he didn't abduct you himself." His eyes were troubled. "Worst, they might rebel. Most have no love for Henry."

"Nor did they for Louis!"

"They tolerated Louis because he was weak."

Not entirely, I thought; they tolerated him because Suger was clever.

"And because we do homage to the king of France, weak or not. But Henry has no jurisdiction over Aquitaine, not to mention that he's a mere count, not weak, and savage in style." He bit his lips, remembering. "As soon as possible, you must return to Aquitaine, where you'll be safe from that brute. For your sake and for the barons, your personal rule is the best cure."

I nodded. Easy to say or to promise; for the moment, I was in Angers.

"And you must write Henry today, Joy," he added slowly, "about your condition."

I looked up sharply. His eyes were shadowed—had he slept at all the previous night? "I can't, Rancon! After I refused his bed in Barfleur? He'll suspect!"

Rancon was ahead of me. "Tell him you had a show of blood and were afraid of miscarriage."

"I'll send a letter at once."

We stared at each other. He was crisp, almost cold, the soldier Rancon I'd often seen in action.

My voice became thick. "I don't know how long I'll be in Angers. Do you think . . ."

His voice also thickened. "I'll be back as soon as I can, within days. You know what I feel."

Rancon returned the day I received Henry's reaction to my news. He was overjoyed! An heir, he crowed, further validated his claims to England, a thought too horrible to contemplate. We now both followed Henry's daily letters avidly, at each missive adjusting our plans. Henry and King Stephen had faced each other with their armies, outside London, where they had parleyed. Seeing the size of Henry's force, King Stephen had capitulated to Henry's might without striking a blow; Henry was now his heir. So Henry's strategy had been effective after all. He was heir apparent to the English crown.

"How old is King Stephen?" I asked Rancon.

"Mid-fifties, I believe, a vigorous man."

"Who was his heir before he named Henry?"

"His own son, Prince Eustace," Rancon replied promptly, "and he's definitely vigorous. He won't relinquish his inheritance so easily."

Henry went on: He had the king's word, but now he must be sure he had the English lords behind him. He recalled that his mother's fate had hinged on the support she could muster among the nobility. He would now set his sights on courting them.

"In short, he may be in England for years," I said.

Rancon laughed jubilantly.

"Quiet!"

We were in my bedchamber, reading by candlelight.

While Henry courted the English nobility the next few months, Rancon and I participated jointly in the miracle taking place inside my womb. While I'd known that Louis's revulsion towards pregnancy was extreme, I also knew that most men left their wives to the care of other women during this period, so I was unprepared for Rancon's enthusiasm. He oiled my expanding girth, kissed my opening navel, lifted my heavy breasts with awe. At first, I was self-conscious; then I grew to expect and enjoy his ministrations. Finally—to the surprise of both of us—pregnancy stimulated us erotically. We loved fervently, with our child riding between us, tried new positions, fondled our baby and each other at the same time. No part of the other's body was secret; we stroked, sucked, knew each other totally. We entered a delirious world, an *empressement* of love.

We also became slightly reckless. True, "Bernart de Ventadorn" played and sang for our company every evening and set up a music room to train apprentices, but he also attended all meetings at my side, conferred in whispers when the issues touched on Aquitaine, and, of course, slept in my chamber. Did anyone notice? No one said so, but John of Salisbury, a visiting scholar, was reputed to be a gossip.

My first son was born seven months later, with Petronilla in attendance and Rancon outside the birthing door. Rancon's face was haggard when he entered my room. There were tears in his eyes.

"Thank God you're alive."

"Of course I'm alive. It was an easy birth."

"But you screamed—it was awful."

Had I? I didn't remember.

"Do you want to see the baby?" Petra asked uncertainly.

He studied him intently. "He looks like you."

Thank God. If he'd had Rancon's dark hair, his brown eyes— well, my mother had been dark; I could claim her influence.

"And like my father and his father before him. Baby William." I smiled.

"William, duke of Aquitaine."

"And he's your son, Rancon; I know it."

His cheeks flushed. "Are you certain? I see no resemblance."

"I do. Give him back, please." I cradled my baby happily, delicately breathed in his sweet baby odor, already like Rancon's. Rancon's son, Henry's son by law, and my son absolutely. No mother had ever loved her children as I did, and even as I kissed William's soft fuzz, I was remembering Marie and Alix.

Henry wrote: 'To Eleanor, duchess of Aquitaine and Normandy, countess of Anjou, soon to be queen of England, greeting: I am delighted that I now have a prince, that you are well, et cetera. I admit I was offended that you ignored my choice of name, Henry, until I realized that you are a subtle wench; William for William the Conqueror, the first of my family to take this island kingdom. Then William Rufus; he will be William III."

The next letter from Henry didn't mention William. "I make good progress among the nobles here, excepting only Bigord, Leicester, and Hereford, but I am bitterly resented by Prince Eustace. I pass time pleasantly in the great forests that cover the isle; when I am king, I shall claim them as my own preserve."

He made no mention of returning to Normandy. Rancon and I bundled our tiny son to enjoy a pleasant dinner in the garden.

Within a week, however, we had a disturbing missive: "I've made a great discovery! Did I ever tell you how much I worship the great King Arthur? Well, I've been doing some research, and I believe I can prove beyond doubt that he was buried in Glastonbury. I'm having his tomb exhumed at once. You're a student of poetry. Don't you agree that Geoffrey of Monmouth's writings of Arthur's life are unworthy? The meter seems rough, and his characters weak. I hear rumours that you have a most excellent troubadour in your court, Ventadorn. If you think he has the skill, send him at once to England, dear wife. I would pay him handsomely to rewrite the tales of Camelot."

"He knows!" I cried. "Leave, Rancon, save your life!"

Rancon reread the parchment. "Calm yourself. We'll test him by taking him at his word. I'll answer myself."

He wrote that same day and declared himself flattered. Could Henry enlarge on his project? And be more specific concerning his payment?

There followed a little desultory correspondence, which came to nothing. King Arthur wasn't mentioned again. Yet the warning had been raised; I was glad when John of Salisbury sailed back to England.

We had letters as well from Aquitaine, from my uncle Ralph in Poitiers. The Lusignan brothers were savaging the duchy, lusting after more territory and a better title.

"What sort of title?"

"They want to be counts."

In short, they were after my title, for my claim to the duchy rested largely on my title as countess of Poitou. And they were taking advantage of my absence. It was worrisome, but nothing I hadn't experienced before, witness their attempt to abduct me at my first wedding.

Meantime, Rancon and I settled easily into our relationship as mother and father. We both loved the domesticity and doted equally on our charming new member. William proved a chubby, alert baby who said, "Ra! Ra!" at six months.

"No, sweets. His name is Bernart. Say Bernart."

"Ra!" He lifted dimpled arms to a delighted Rancon.

A month later, I received a letter from Henry telling me that he'd declared William to be his heir for Normandy, Anjou, and England. All such inheritances seemed remote. I read on: Henry was returning to Rouen. I was to meet him there within a week.

Suddenly we were frantic. What would we do? How could we avert this disaster? Was there any way Rancon could take Baby William to Aquitaine? To be declared my heir, perhaps? But even if he could, I would still have to join Henry.

Even love couldn't still desperation.

"Come to Poitiers," Rancon begged.

"Every summer, as I did from France." I felt his shudder; it was now September. "And for my Christmas Court. No, more often— it is my home; I have to rule."

"Within the month! Promise! Henry will go back to England— he has to keep the pressure on."

"Yes."

"I can't bear to think of you with that swine!"

Nor could I. Troubadour poets claim that adulterous love is inevitable in a society of loveless marriages, and the poets are right, except they rarely dwell on the end of such affairs. What do the lovers feel when they must return to odious arrangements? Rancon, too, must return to his wife. But how could I complain about a dying woman?

Thus, though both of us seethed with jealousy, I kept discreetly silent.

"Tell Henry you were injured in childbirth, that you can't—"

"I will."

He left my bed at dawn, then returned to my chamber in mid-morning to say a formal good-bye. Dressed in his feathered hat, his swinging green cape, and with the *vièle* flung over his shoulder, he looked every inch the troubadour, except that his eyes were those of a lover and his body, when he sat on his horse, was that of a warrior.

He bent over as if to fix his bridle, and whispered, "Send Amaria to his bed in your place. That goat will never notice the difference!"

In the poem, Tristan has the handmaid Brangien substitute for Iseult in King Mark's bed.

"Amaria lacks the right perfume—I reek of Aquitaine."

I entered the ancient capital of Rouen at midday without fanfare, thus catching Matilda by surprise. Why hadn't I announced myself? Henry was far away, hunting, but she would send a runner at once to summon him. He'd been waiting every day for me, and this was the first time he'd left.

"Then you mustn't disturb him," I protested. The messenger was already riding out the gate. Matilda and I studied each other, our first meeting without Henry. She was physically as I remembered, tall and imposing, and her warm manner seemed genuine. Her eyes again appraised me, though, and her appraisal was frankly political: Was I ruthless enough? Intelligent enough? Did I have the endurance for Henry?

She bent over William with exclamations of delight, and soon I was surrounded by a large chattering family of brothers and sisters—though Henry's brother Geoffrey was not present, thank God—and I noticed particularly two small shy boys watching from a corner.

"Are these Henry's sons?" I asked Matilda.

"Yes, young William Longsword and Geoffrey." She pulled the boys forward. "I wish you had named your boy Henry—it would have avoided confusion."

Henry charged into the *salle*. Covered with sweat, panting from a hard ride, he gripped my arms. "God's eyeballs, you look marvelous! Even better than I remember. Has motherhood brought that sparkle to your eye?"

"Not motherhood, love," I replied demurely.

"Joy!" Then I was in his arms, his large teeth crushing my lips. This was going to be worse than I'd expected.

He seized young William, examined him minutely, then tossed him into the air with an exuberant shout.

"Ra! Ra!" My poor son cried in alarm.

"What's he saying?"

"Da," I answered, taking the boy from him.

"He recognized me," Henry preened. "Did you hear, Mother? Only six months old and he knows my name."

"Eight months old," I said.

I held my frightened baby to my chest, shielding myself against more embraces. But time raced. Vespers were said; night fell like a stone. I marched reluctantly to the bedchamber. Even an obtuse Henry noticed my diffidence.

"Don't be shy," he murmured. "I know I was a little rough the first time, but I'll be gentle."

"Gentle enough to give me a few more weeks?" I smiled.

"Weeks to do what? You're not nursing, are you?"

"Scripture says that a new mother should . . ."

He stopped fumbling my broaches and my cinch. His tone was icy. "Tell me about your troubadour, Eleanor."

My heart stopped. "Peire de Valeria? A likely young Gascon; he has promise."

"Ventadorn, Joy. Where is he now?"

"I don't know." I laughed shakily. "I had to dismiss him."

"Why?"

"He made advances to me," I said boldly. "Can you believe it? I knew his reputation, but with me!"

"You have a reputation, as well," he pointed out. "I should be a deterrent, though. I'm a liberal man in most ways, but not where children are concerned."

"Children? You're confusing me, my lord."

"Am I? Then let me be clear. As you could see downstairs, I'm generous with my own bastards; I'll care for them all their lives, though they will never be my heirs."

No different than most great lords. "Very liberal."

"Because they are my own seed; I have proof beyond their mothers' word. I would never accept another man's seed."

"Why are you telling me this?"

His teeth shone in the moonlight. "You're a subtle woman, Eleanor; you can follow my thought. If I ever believed a woman was trying to deceive me on that score, both the woman and the child would be dead."

"I hope I don't follow your thought, or I would leave at this instant. And take *your* son with me! In fact, I believe I will!"

He quickly grasped my braids. "Not so fast! Tell me now, how are you feeling since childbirth?"

"Exactly the same as I was before."

"Too weak for love?"

"Did I say that?" I turned slowly.

During the act, I found some solace in the immensity of the skies outside the window. What did my little agony signify in the grand macrocosm?

He was finished. "What are you thinking?"

"Of proportion."

He traced the rim of my ear. "What an odd reply, unless you refer to my . . . Are you comparing me?"

To whom? What did he suspect? I must do better! "You're incomparable, Henry."

"Tell me again about your troubadour," he said casually.

I ran my fingers through Henry's stubbled hair. "You sound like Louis, my lord."

"Because we both had the same wife."

"But you are not the same husband. Louis was faithful to me."

"And I'm not?" His voice changed—with delight?

"There's overwhelming evidence that you're not."

"Such as?"

"Geoffrey and William downstairs, and twenty others that I know of."

He laughed.

"I'm serious, Henry. You have to protect your legitimate son."

"Of course." He laughed again.

"Be warned, I will do anything to protect my boy. You know that my daughters were disinherited in France."

"You wrote me," he said wryly, "several times. You can't be worried that William will suffer the same fate."

"At least Louis had no bastard sons."

"You're asking me to be celibate like that fop?" He was amazed—and intrigued. "Do you want me to swear undying fidelity? By God, I'll do it!"

"No, amuse yourself as much as you like. I'm no prude, nor am I possessive"—certainly not of Henry—"but I do demand that you recognize no more bastards. If you become king . . ."

"When I become king."

"When you become king, every ambitious lord in England will await you at the gate with his beauteous daughter in hand. And it's in that situation that I do demand fidelity."

"Mistress of the disputation. Very well, I'll restrict my lechery to the streets. No fine ladies with ambitious fathers and the like. Does that satisfy you?"

"For our son, yes. Do you think you could retrieve my French daughters' rights?"

He raised his head. "Christ! What a demanding wench I wed! Do you want me to take Byzantium while I'm about it?"

I placed my hand over his lips; he bit my fingers gently.

"Or should I just take you," he said softly. "You're a witch in moonlight; I'm enchanted."

The second time was less agonizing physically, and I used all my skills to emulate passion.

Henry stroked my cheeks. "You truly touch me, Eleanor. It's like making love to a melody. So elusive. Are you happy?"

Are tears a sign of happiness? "I have been." With Rancon.

"You've changed."

"How?" I was again alert.

He nuzzled into my shoulder. "You're warmer, more receptive."

More experienced. More duplicitous. And almost discovered. Who had told?

"I can't get enough of you."

And he proved it. How I hated him.

Of course 1 became pregnant again. I cursed my woman's body, which permitted no secrets. I couldn't bear to tell Rancon, though he'd learn soon enough. Even though I felt I'd had no choice, I felt unfaithful, and frightened.

One day, a familiar figure rode into the courtyard, the Bishop of Lisieux.

"Bishop Arnulf!" I cried with genuine warmth.

He dismounted, smiling. "I came to congratulate you on your new marriage, certainly an improvement over France." Henry ran from the palace. "Ah, my lord Henry, you're the one to be congratulated. How did you win this lily of Aquitaine?"

"In a tourney," I replied. "His sword was fastest."

Henry grinned. "Sword being a metaphor."

We called for wine, and soon the whole family was gathered around the popular bishop. Arnulf watched me surreptitiously.

Only at the end of the day could we talk in the privacy of the garden.

"Your son is quite remarkable," Arnulf said pointedly.

"Meaning that God approves this marriage?"

"I can't speak for God, but I approve. And I can see that you and Henry do, as well."

"How so?"

"In Henry's case, it's obvious. He's riding his meteor to power and happiness and the glint in his eye, the pride when he looks at you . . . oh, I know Henry well."

"And me?"

He laughed. "Are you begging for flattery? Very well. My dear Joy, I've known you always as the most beautiful woman I've ever seen, perhaps the most beautiful in all the world. Yet today—now—you have a quality that transcends beauty. You give off a light—I can hardly gaze at you directly, I'm so blinded—and your eyes, the roses in your cheeks, even your voice has a music I don't remember. Oh dear, I have no words to describe what I see; you're a fulfilled woman."

"You do quite well. Thank you, Bishop Arnulf."

We walked on, both of us silent. I must be more careful, I thought; if even a bishop can discern what Rancon has done . . .

"Tell me, how did you finally accomplish your divorce from King Louis?"

I was glad to change the subject. As I told him of my deliberate exploitation of Abbot Bernard's prejudice and vanity, he laughed.

"Of course I knew the truth about the rumors of incest, so I wondered how it could suddenly be accepted as fact."

"It was so obvious, eh? My only regret is the loss of my princesses, but that will change. I'll think of a way."

He laughed again. "I believe you—you're incorrigible. Now, tell me, how did you meet Henry? Everyone wonders; the marriage was so fast."

"Henry is the Devil incarnate!" I said pleasantly.

His smile faded. "Then why did you marry him?"

I told him in graphic detail.

"I'm truly shocked," he gasped. "And sorry. I would not have thought it of Henry."

There was a long silence.

"So the wondrous transformation in your person has nothing to do with Henry," he said quietly.

I was quick. "I've been told it's the way I look after motherhood. But Henry? No." I shuddered.

He took my hand. "Listen to me, Joy. I know you almost as well as I do Henry; I can feel your anger palpably, but take care. Henry is the perfect husband for you, believe me. He has the dash, the

253

masculinity you so craved in Louis. And his intelligence matches yours; you are much alike."

"Alike?" I couldn't decide whether to be furious or just incredulous.

"Yes, both of you born to lead. He knows that, if you don't. And there is no prelate in the world you could manipulate to get rid of him."

Thus he planted an idea: Bishop Arnulf had represented me in my plea for annulment from Louis, and he would do the same with Henry. He'd been shocked at the rape, eh? Arnulf might have loved Henry the boy, but he didn't know Henry the man.

Just then, Henry approached from the far end of the garden.

We continued to stroll, and I became silent, immersed in my own perception. Bishop Arnulf was no Bernard of Clairvaux, not a man to be manipulated through his vanity, nor would I use that approach. If I could get Arnulf closer to the mature Henry, let him see him in action as I did, as France and much of Europe did, he would find his own reasons.

Well, I'd planted a grain of sand with the true account of my rape; now let it grow to a pearl of great worth.

19

Summer came, and Louis struck again. Whatever his motive, he relieved me of Henry's company. His absence, however, forced me to lie to Rancon about why I didn't go to Aquitaine, for I couldn't bring myself to say that I was once again pregnant. God help me, I wrote that William had the chickenpox; I would travel to Poitiers sometime after the first of the year. Rancon's reply was desperate: I must send him daily bulletins of William's condition. As if fate punished me, William did become ill, though I never knew the cause, and it wasn't serious.

Meantime, my own "illness" turned me from a birch into a waddling ball and, without Rancon's loving approval, I hated myself. I vowed to regain my youthful figure and dieted and exercised as rigorously as Henry did to avoid gaining weight, for he tended to stockiness.

Three days after Henry returned from fighting Louis, he received news that Eustace, King Stephen's prince, had suddenly died. "Natural" causes were said to be the reason, though there were rumblings about God's vengeance for his fighting against the Abbey at Saint-Alban's.

"That makes me the indisputable heir!" Henry exulted. "Now, if only King Stephen would expire."

I agreed—if he did, Henry would leave. I prayed fervently it would be so.

To my amazement, another runner arrived with the news that King Stephen had died from eating eels. Was I another Bernard of

Clairvaux manqué? Henry frothed with a jubilance to match his rage in Poitiers: He stamped around the great hall, beating his breast and shouting that he was king of England. It was fate, Fortune's Wheel, wyrd, and vindication of his mother's rights. No, it was my prayers, I thought.

"We should thank God," Matilda said piously.

"Yes, and"—I stopped myself in time from adding "my prayers"—"the eels," I ended lamely.

Though it was now bitter cold, Henry chafed to be going. What if the barons rebelled? Or King Stephen's younger son might claim the throne. I assured him that he was absolutely right. Had I ever told him of Louis's headlong dash to Paris after his father died, when his brother was about to seize the throne?

"When you're safely on the throne and the waters are calm, I'll join you," I said.

His pupils danced like needles in his colorless eyes. "You'll come with me now."

"No, I can't! My condition—I might miscarry!"

"You miscarry?" He threw his head back. "You're tight as my hound bitch."

"I can't leave little William."

"We'll take him with us."

"On the sea in winter? Your only heir? I tell you, Henry, *I won't* go!"

"You'll go, all right. I want those bastards to see a woman at my side. You'll be annointed queen beside me, and you're going to rule with me."

"Good for you, Henry fitzEmpress," Matilda rumbled from behind him. She was not going with us, which may have been why Henry was so insistent; I must be her surrogate.

Heartsick, I wrote to Rancon. Could he possibly join me in England in the spring (I didn't add after my baby was born, for I still hadn't told him)? I couldn't endure to be separated any longer.

We rode to Barfleur in mid-November, where Henry stayed in

one inn with his counselors, his mother in another, and I in still a third with Amaria and my son. On the coast, gale winds whipped the sea into crashing waves, and we settled to wait for a change. Every morning, I stumbled against the hurl of sleet to the inn where Henry, his mother, and his counselors huddled to create his new government, going over endless lists of mysterious names.

"Richard of Luci should be your justiciar," Matilda announced in her deep, mannish voice.

"He's a commoner, Mother," Henry objected.

"Balance him with the earl of Leicester as your second justiciar."

"He backed King Stephen," Henry complained.

"But he is the most intelligent of the earls, and your cousin."

Henry agreed.

"What's a justiciar?" I asked.

"English for seneschal," Matilda explained; "someone to rule in Henry fitzEmpress's absence from the isle, for he'll have to spend much of his time on the Continent."

I looked at her steadily, seeking some sign of duplicity, for "on the Continent" meant Aquitaine to me. Suger's warnings screamed in my head. Matilda gazed back without any sign of duplicity, then continued her recitation of nobles in England.

I listened without comment until they came to the chancellor, when I realized they were talking about the man who would be the royal liaison to the Church. He should be a priest, Matilda declared, or preferably a monk, someone of noble birth who knew the law, yes, a scholar.

"Bishop Arnulf of Lisieux!" I cried.

They turned as one.

"You must find someone like Abbot Suger," I hurried on breathlessly, "someone with a humanist bent of mind."

Henry smiled. "And you think Arnulf is like Suger?"

"He could be! He loves you, my lord, has been on Crusade, knows the world." Which Henry, with all his intelligence, did not. He read, he listened, but he remained a provincial.

Fortunately, Matilda agreed emphatically. "He loves you like a son. He'll be your most loyal support in the balance between Church and state."

"A most excellent suggestion." Henry squeezed my hand to give me full credit. "That will be my first appointment."

"Send for him," I said. "Let him sail with us."

Henry dispatched a runner at once. I was ecstatic; now Arnulf would owe me a favor, and I fully intended that he would repay it by helping me leave my marriage. I told Amaria to find some way to contact Rancon.

When we'd exhausted our lists of appointments, Matilda lectured Henry and me on the basic precepts by which we were to rule. They were simple and cynical.

"Use the tactic of *dangling*," she said. "Hold up rewards as incitements for loyalty—but never deliver, for once they have their reward, they lose loyalty. Use lands, titles, power close to the throne; keep your barons hoping. Make them leap to the lure. *Dangling*."

"Yes, Mother, I know." Her son had obviously heard this precept before. "Dangling."

"Seize all estates and revoke all titles."

I protested. "That sounds like tyranny, Mother. Isn't Henry supposed to be different from King Stephen? Won't he start another insurrection?"

"Not at all. That will give him his instruments for dangling. Believe me, barons have fickle loyalties. They'll forget that he stripped them of their dignities and remember only that they owe everything to Henry. You'll return privileges in your own time, son, after the barons have proved their allegiance. Then they will be beholden to you, not to the former king."

"Good advice, Mother," Henry agreed solemnly.

I was in a school for jobelins: the thief presents the true owner with the stolen goods, then demands a reward.

"In your acceptance speech, announce that you are going to reinstate the laws and customs of my father, the great Henry the First."

"What are they?" I asked.

She sighed heavily. "He ruled in a more simple time, my dear, when kings were kings and the nobles were loyal as one would be to God."

Loyal unless that king happened to be a queen, I thought. She trusted her son as her surrogate—but was he worthy? He gazed on her now humbly, even reverently, but he wasn't yet king. I'd watched Louis change from a bewildered boy to a tyrant when we were on the Crusade. Did the throne always corrupt?

Henry explained to me: "He believed in a rule by law, Joy; I agree with his general philosophy, and I'll learn the particulars in England."

In short, neither of them knew her father's laws.

Matilda smiled benignly. "The noble class will applaud you, for every new reign is a repudiation of the most recent and a return to a golden age. You will wipe away King Stephen's excesses, and . . ."

"And?" he prompted her.

"They won't realize that the excesses include their own privileges until it's too late. He ruled a long time; everyone is tainted."

"A clean broom!" Henry brayed like a child, still not able to believe his good fortune.

I thought of our loose association of barons in Aquitaine, where my family had ruled successfuly for generations by *not* assuming dictatorial rights. Perhaps the English were a different breed.

Arnulf of Lisieux arrived within the week, and he was humbly grateful for the honor bestowed.

"You deserve it," I assured him. "You were a good friend to me in Jerusalem; let me show my appreciation."

His brows drew quizzically. "You suggested me?"

"Of course everyone agreed," I said sweetly.

He nodded slowly. "I'll not forget."

The seed was taking root.

The savage winds increased and snow obliterated the landscape. Each morning, I stumbled through an impenetrable murk from one inn to the other, a scarf across my eyes to protect them from sleet and sand. I had to lean forward like a gnarled shrub to avoid being toppled—not an easy feat for someone in my condition.

Every morning, I also had to contend with my son William's angry howls.

"Why can't I come with you?"

"This is grown-up talk, darling. Be a good boy and Aunt Amaria will tell you a story."

"I want to go on the ship like you said."

"And you will."

"When?"

"I don't know, maybe tomorrow."

"When's tomorrow?"

Amaria stroked his blond curls. "We'll go to bed tonight, and when we wake, it will be tomorrow."

"No!" he shouted. "When we wake it will be today! Tomorrow never comes."

"Worthy of Abelard," I declared proudly.

Henry chafed at the delay. The winter closed in, promising worse gales ahead, and he made a decision. "We'll sail on Saint-Nicholas's Day, for he's patron saint of travelers."

Therefore we prepared to leave on December 6, though no one was happy about it. Who knew how many ships had foundered under the saint's care? We lined up on the beach in a gritty dawn and listened to the surf crash on the sand. My God, this is madness, I thought; what good to claim a throne from the bottom of the sea?

Even the Viking Matilda was rattled. "This is the month that killed my brother," she said, her voice trembling.

A famous and awesome story, a Christmas sailing that had begun present events. The prince of England had sailed on Christmas Day from Barfleur with most of the young nobles of Europe. The ships had foundered and sunk in the harbor, in full view of people still alive who remembered watching the smacks go down on the rocks, then the lifeboats, which were overloaded. The loss of that prince had made Matilda heir to England's throne, and now

Henry. It had also been the reason my uncle Raymond had gone to England and subsequently to Antioch; thus the great chain links us to one another and the dead.

Henry paced back and forth, shaking his fist at the elements, but even he was sufficiently awed to postpone the departure. Then, when the sky was again darkening and we were all chilled to the bone, the wind suddenly dropped.

"Now!" Henry shouted.

Quickly, I took William from Amaria and climbed the slippery plank.

I huddled under the forecastle with my son.

"Like the Crusade," Amaria said dryly.

"Except I don't think we'll wake to fields of flowers," I replied.

"I'll settle for dry land. I never fancied death by water."

For one brief moment, the winds cleared and I saw the poignant figure of Matilda, still waving from the shore. She should be here in my place, I thought; no, in Henry's place—she's the birthright queen. Then she disappeared.

Lanterns hung fore and aft disappeared in the mist. The drums began a steady thump from ship to ship; then the horns bleated mournfully across the sea.

"What's that?" William asked.

"Swans leading us to England," I replied.

"Tomorrow's come."

Four days later, we rode into London. A silver sky illuminated a panoply of glinting spires and amusing houses painted red and yellow or green and purple. Hundreds of bright, smiling faces welcomed us; blond, blue-eyed, red-nosed, plainly garbed in sheep's hides and boots, our new subjects openly hawked goods, native products mixed with wool from Flanders, pottery from Caen, even brasswork from Constantinople. Where were the wines from Aquitaine? Like Empress Irene, I began to plot my own enterprise.

"Waes Hael! Waes Hael!"

I smiled and waved.

"Look, Mama, a dead man!" William pointed to a corpse hanging from a scaffold. "Where are his eyes?"

"See the ducks, William," Amaria called. "What funny prints they leave in the snow."

Animal filth, commerce, death, and burgeoning life, the face of London.

I was almost too heavy to kneel before the altar at Westminster Abbey, the first Saxon church I saw. Amaria stood beside me to help me rise.

Under low vaults, a large congregation of dough-faced males glanced, looked away when I caught them, then glanced again. Had they never seen a pregnant woman before? Or were they impressed by the fine furs and jewels I wore to disguise my girth? I felt like an ungainly magnet before an audience of needles.

Their main interest, of course, was Henry; he, too, was as splendid as finery could make him. Garbed in the English scarlet and gold— unfortunate colors for his rufous complexion—he was another magnet. His energy was palpable, his keen eyes looking everywhere, seeing everything; he seemed as if he might burst into flames.

The ceremony was performed by Theobald, the archbishop of Canterbury, a man I already liked for his urbane manner and his gentle smile; he'd been instrumental in aiding Henry's rise. He reminded me of Suger, except that he wasn't so long-winded, for which I gave fervent thanks. Crowns may be heavy on one's brow, but they don't compare with the weight of a baby on one's bladder.

Henry's speech was so short that the nobles had hardly settled to listen before it was finished.

He held up a parchment. "I am granting in this charter to my counts, barons, and all my subjects the concessions, liberties, and free customs that my grandfather King Henry gave them."

And thereby taking away your present concessions, I thought; you'll lose much more than you gain.

"Likewise, I abolish and outlaw for myself all the evil customs he outlawed and abolished."

Meaning all titles and revenues. Matilda had taught Henry well. But, in my observation, not well enough. Perusing the audience, I caught a few subtle gestures of dismay, and several lords whispered to one another. I recognized their expression, long familiar to me in my own barons, of resistance and belligerence. Who were they? I knew by name only Hugh of Bigord and Robert, earl of Leicester, but I sensed their minds. Like many brilliant rulers, Henry underestimated the intelligence of his subjects.

With Christmas only five days away, it was essential that I put my household in order. I sat in the great hall of our temporary manor in Bermondsey to interview applicants for the royal positions. My back ached and the cold, cramped quarters made everyone seem incompetent.

Though I perched at a low table between my secretary, Sir Matthew, and my English consultant, Sir Nigel, with Amaria to the side, the important presence was invisible, my aunt Mahaut, who'd taught me administration long ago. I remembered especially her instruction that we must arrange our households as if we were queen. Now I was twice a queen.

I heard her ghostly voice. *"Begin with the stewards and be sure to look directly into their eyes as they speak,"* I quickly assembled the stewards of the bread, the sewers, wine and candles, the larder.

"Let your cook select his own helpers so far as possible." My chef from Aquitaine, Ralph de Marchia, grunted his approval for the keeper of the vessels, the scullion, ushers of the turnspit, the butlery, the buttery, then keepers of the cup.

I dismissed him and continued with the horn-blowers, the cat-hunters, the wolf-catchers, keepers of the brachs, keepers of the hearth, up to two hundred in all.

"I thank you for your services," I said, dismissing Sir Matthew and Sir Nigel.

Amaria helped me rise from my bench and walk about the tiny room.

"Who's left?" she asked.

"A storyteller."

She gasped in alarm.

"Not anyone we know," I assured her.

Not Rancon.

Once I was settled again, she opened the door to a cadaverous man with white hair and fierce black eyes. He wore the familiar green and carried a small harp.

"You're Wace of Jersey?" I pulled forth the sampling of his verse. "And you specialize in stories?"

"Yes, Queen Eleanor. I'm a teller of tales."

"And you want to write about King Arthur?"

"Aye."

"Though the life has already been done by Geoffrey of Monmouth?"

"In Latin, not French."

"And you will translate?"

His eyes flashed. "No, I'll reshape the tales entirely."

"Ah." I smiled. "How will you treat Queen Guinevere?"

He hesitated, sensing a trap. "I'll make her more sympathetic."

"But still an adulteress?"

"Perhaps not."

"Oh, I think you must. Arthur's mother was an adulteress, as well. We must be truthful." I cocked my head. "All queens are adulteresses, eh?"

He glanced at my belly. "Among the French perhaps, not in England."

"The point is, her lover must be worthy. I quite dislike her affair with Mordred. Well, go to my master of the scriptorium and say I've taken you on."

His hollow cheeks flushed. "Thank ye, my lady." He bowed deeply.

When the door closed, Amaria said dryly, "That's the fastest appointment I ever saw you make. Why do you think he's the man for King Arthur?"

I ruffled the pile of verses. "He's malleable. I would like to see Guinevere elevated to the position of Iseult. Help me up, dear. We're finished."

Before I could rise, the door swung open and Henry strode in, followed by a tall stranger.

"Well, Joy, are you accustomed yet to being queen of England?" He bent to kiss my brow and ran his hand over my stomach. "And what about you, young fellow? And are you ready to become a prince?"

I pushed his hand away. "Greeting, my lord." His companion was obviously embarrassed. His pallor turned a wine red; his dark eyes darted from side to side. He wore the raiment of a churchman; I might have seen him with Archbishop Theobald of Canterbury. "Have we met, sir?"

"N-not yet, my lady." His voice was cultivated, his stammer disarming.

"You're going to see a lot of him." Henry sat on the corner of my table. "This is Thomas à Becket, archdeacon of Canterbury."

I was satisfied. I had met him—I pride myself that I never forget a face—when we first arrived. Strange he didn't remember.

"I just appointed him to be my chancellor," Henry said.

Blood pounded in my head. "Your *chancellor*? How can that be? Arnulf of Lisieux is your chancellor!"

Henry's large teeth were still on display, but not smiling. "At the express recommendation of Archbishop Theobald, I decided on young Becket instead."

Young? He was in his mid-thirties and Henry was twenty-one. And Arnulf—my hope for freedom.

"Bishop Arnulf is a w-w-worthy man," Becket murmured.

Henry laughed. "Worthy he may be, but he can't hunt! Listen, Joy! This fellow can track a spore six months after it was dropped."

"Which is an essential skill for a chancellor!" I snapped. "I'm sure you'll find great piles of dung around the court, Thomas. Look under the throne for a start."

Henry leapt angrily from the table. "I refer to hunting game in the wood, as you well know! We scoured the New Forest while I was here in England earlier."

Suspicion leaped. "When did you decide on young Becket, my lord?"

Becket looked at Henry humbly. "My lord Henry suggested the office shortly after King Stephen succumbed. Though I might be unworthy, I had to accept. To work for the new king of England is to serve gr-gr-greatness. He is one of the wonders of the world. I'm astride the north wind."

You can read a man by how he handles flattery: Henry's icy eyes melted—he had succumbed to the first honeyed tongue to lick his backside. But his vanity couldn't justify duplicity. You can also judge a man by his word. On this very first crucial test, Henry had revealed himself as a manipulative liar.

"Another wonder of the world is a snake curled on a rock, and we know how the serpent's tongue doomed the world," I pointed out.

Henry's voice dropped to the deadly pitch I'd heard before. "Thomas is my choice, Eleanor. Do you understand?"

"You might have told both me and your mother of your choice, my lord, at the time that you agreed to appoint Bishop Arnulf." Another question answered, whether Henry was worthy of her trust. "Write to her now and say that you never lie, despite this strange contradiction. But what can you possibly tell Bishop Arnulf? That you thought the icy crossing on the whale path would improve his health? That you forgot that the post was already occupied? That you were experimenting with *dangling*?"

"I'll wait outside," Thomas said.

Henry stopped him with a wave of his hand. "Never use the word *lie* with me again, Eleanor."

"Never lie again and I won't."

I studied Thomas anew. "Well, my lord, if you are to be our liaison with the Church, tell me about yourself. When did you take orders?"

Becket's brown eyes slid to Henry. "I've not taken orders."

"But you're a priest? Or at least a monk in some order?"

"No, I began my career as a banker's clerk."

I was stopped; a secular commoner—very common, very secular. Yet Henry was not a total fool—why had he appointed him? "Since you hunt, you must engage in tourneys. When did you take your spurs?"

"I would have liked to be a knight, but I had no patron to arm me, or to give me a horse."

In short, he had no connections. Henry had protested appointing Richard de Luci because he was a commoner, though he was very knowledgeable, and then taken an unqualified commoner as his chancellor. Unheard of!

"Not a knight, and obviously you had no calling for the bank, so you went into the Church as a last resort?" I tried to be charitable, remembering Suger's ascent in the Church.

"He's not interviewing to be keeper of your larder, Joy," Henry said testily.

"Yet he will be an intimate member of our household. Have you a wife, Thomas?"

"N-no." He shuddered.

"Have you taken the vow of celibacy?"

"No."

I felt an ominous foreboding; I'd seen his like before. "And do you have a mother? Sisters?"

He looked pained. "Of course, though I no longer see them."

"And why is that?"

"Though I have not taken the vow, I avoid the contamination of females."

"You have surely noticed, my lord Becket, that I am a female, and we will be associates."

Henry took Becket's arm. "Time for an inquisition when we get back, Joy."

"Back from where?"

Becket answered. "During King Stephen's reign, ruffians built castles all over England and called themselves nobles. They terrorized the n-natives and stole everything in sight. We're going to raze these illegal c-c-castles."

"With pickaxes," Henry said brightly.

"For the first time, I see your argument, Henry: I'm certain that poor Bishop Arnulf can't follow a spore, nor can he chop, though he has a good knowledge of fauna. How many of these illegal fortresses are there, my lord Becket?"

"A th-th-thousand."

A thousand stone castles to be lowered with axes, surely a thousand months. "And to be personally razed by the king and his chancellor. A mighty enterprise for two men."

Henry caught my drift. "I need Thomas's long nose to sniff out the rogues."

"They have the sulfurous stench of demons," his new chancellor agreed.

I slapped my table. "Even a bank clerk, Thomas, knows the difference between religion and rank superstition! I will not tolerate vulgar chicanery in my court! Never speak of demons in my presence again! Do you understand?"

Becket's long jaw dropped.

"Thomas takes his orders from me, Joy," Henry interjected angrily.

"You can order him to place an arrow in a deer's rump, or to chip at a castle's foundation, but in my court, he will do as the queen says! Or I will dismiss him!"

Henry's eyes bulged; he breathed deeply, then tapped my nose playfully. "*Your* court, my beauteous queen? Very well, I'll leave you to form the government in *your* court while I'm away."

"Henry, I know nothing of England!"

"Nor do I. But Becket does. I'll send daily runners with his advice."

"England is your responsibility!"

"Indeed it is; I'm glad you recognize that fact. As a novice king, I'll seek advice from Becket, and you will execute my orders."

"As a novice king, my lord, you will be closely watched by your subjects. How do you think they will judge your long hunt in your New Forest? Will you have to prove yourself a second time? And, if so, do you think you can wave your genealogy again and be accepted? Have you no sense of your royal office?"

He turned red at my tone. "England can't be ruled at all so long as these renegade nobles exist! I'm doing my duty, by God!" He calmed down. "While we're away, Westminster Palace will be renovated. That should please you." His eyes glittered. "Thomas has already drawn up the designs. You'll have twenty ovens in your kitchen, a large nursery for our family, an arcade of Sienese marble, a stage in your great hall for your troubadours."

I stared at Becket. "Tell me, do you also sing? I can always use a new troubadour."

"You're insufferable!" Henry shouted.

"Not at all. I'm outraged."

"Now, Thomas, if you're ready . . ."

"Wait!" I ordered him. "Henry, you can delegate Richard de Luci to carry out your orders. As soon as my child is born, I'm leaving for Poitiers."

Henry slapped the table as I had done. "You'll stay in England, by God!"

"I'm going to Poitiers! You have England to govern, and I have Aquitaine. I'll not neglect my duchy as you do your realm."

Henry breathed deeply. "A compromise: Go to Woodstock after your lying-in. Young William will enjoy the menagerie Stephen collected." He pushed himself off my desk. "That's an order, Joy. You'll be very happy in Woodstock."

"Henry, wait!"

He stopped.

"Name William as your heir before you go."

"I already named him!"

"Name him in the Church, before an archbishop."

His face was as red as his robe. "I'm getting angry."

"So am I," I said coldly.

He turned away abruptly. The two men tramped out of the chamber.

Amaria put her hand on my shoulder. "God's breath, calm yourself, darling. You'll give birth right here on this table."

"Fine, the sooner the better."

"Now, now, sweets, perhaps Becket won't be as bad as you think."

"I've lost Arnulf, Am. Do you realize what that means? Do you think he'll release me from this marriage when he learns of Henry's betrayal? I'm defeated!"

"You're confused, I would say. Didn't you tell me yourself that Arnulf tended to glorify Henry? Now he'll have his own reason to see the truth. You should be grateful!"

I gazed into her clear green eyes. "You have a political mind, Am! Of course this works in my favor. And in more ways than one! Help me rise."

She took my arms and pulled me up.

"Listen, Am, Henry's addicted to hunting, and Becket will supply the drug. While the king's away, my dear, I'm going to summon Rancon."

My second son was born in February, and this time I named him Henry, to be known as Young Henry for clarification. I sent word at once to Petra so she could inform the French court of the second son born to the "barren" queen. Henry was delighted beyond measure, proud as a cock, devastated that he had missed the great event, couldn't wait to greet his new prince in person—but he did wait. I ordered Ivo the Builder to leave his work at Westminster Palace and go to Woodstock to prepare a project of my own design in the park there. Finally, I was ready to write Rancon, though I still couldn't bring myself to mention Young Henry.

The winter gloom of England, I discovered, was preamble to the most glorious spring I ever remembered. I bundled my charming Prince William into an open litter with his baby brother, mounted my own charger at the head of my burgeoning household, and rode out of London under a canopy of apple blossoms. Blithe songs filled budding trees, the sward bent silver-green in a soft breeze, and brooks trilled like music. I laughed at lambs gamboling stiff-legged in the meadows, startled fawns who appeared innocently in the bushes, and mares suckling their foals in the middle of our path, where the grass was richest. The very earth was giving birth, and I was part of the fecund cycle. I rode to the back of the line again and again to look down on my two little princes.

Yet spring is a fickle season. Huge puffy clouds formed on the horizon: I was nervous at the prospect of seeing Rancon.

At midday, we crossed the Glyme River, passed a small church dedicated to Saint-Madeleine, and were soon winding through a forest of giant wych elms. The slant of light through the trees reminded me of Saint-Denis, and I felt a spasm of homesickness for Suger. How I had loved the old man.

A wall of high palings enclosed Woodstock, and we could hear the roar of animals behind it. By this time, William rode on my saddle in front of me.

"Was that a lion, Mama?"

"No, I don't think there are any dangerous beasts at large."

"It sounded like a lion."

He was right; I recalled the animal park in Constantinople.

The gate swung open and I saw at once that Petronilla had already arrived; since she had become a widow, she was happy to be with me. Then, beside my sister's litters from Vermandois, a huge black charger with the metal studs of Taillebourg shaping a lion's head on the saddle. My heart raced; my breath grew tight.

"Let's find Aunt Petra, darling."

William was staring with terror at a bristling animal in the compound.

"Come." I lifted him down. "It's only a porcupine."

With Amaria, the nurses, and the servants, we entered the huge rustic structure. My sister and her children ran lightly down the stair to greet us.

"Oh Joy, I'm so sorry to have missed your coronation."

"You were there when I became queen of France, and this was much the same. How is young Raoul?"

I looked at her son, still a sickly boy, standing close to William. William was squinting at a man behind Petra.

"Ra?" he said uncertainly.

Though I'd not yet looked directly at him, his presence filled the room, filled my heart.

He knelt beside William. "So you remember me, eh? But you're a big boy now and should say my name better. Call me Richard. Can you say Richard?"

"Richard de Luci?"

Rancon grinned. "The same name, but I'm simply Richard."

He looked up at me.

"Richard," I said. "Rancon."

Young Henry gurgled behind me and Rancon's eyes moved, then darted back to me.

"My new son," I said, "born in February." And, though he was Henry's, I was proud of him. He was the fattest, the most dimpled baby I'd ever seen.

"Yes, I know. The bells rang all over Aquitaine."

We strolled on a mossy carpet starred with small white flowers. Perfumed chestnut blooms dropped to our shoulders.

We'd walked more than a mile in absolute silence. Much preoccupied, Rancon kicked at tufts of May bells.

"Are you angry?" I asked. A moot question, for I knew he was.

He looked up. "Do you know where we're going? We're deep in a wood."

"Are you speaking poetically?"

He stopped. "Henry's new son is very handsome."

"Thank you." I grimaced. "I wanted to write you, Rancon, but I was afraid."

Two elephants walked slowly in the distance. Ears flicking, they didn't glance in our direction. I froze until they disappeared into the trees.

"Married people produce babies," he said without expression.

"I feel married to you!"

"Do you?"

"I couldn't help it, Rancon."

He gazed at me as if I were a strange beast, perhaps one of those elephants. My heart pounded with dread.

We'd reached a small wooden hut. Ivo had wrought a wonder, I thought, for the proportions were perfect. "Oh look!" I cried.

"Is it the gamekeeper's quarters?" Rancon asked.

"Let's go inside."

He followed me, then fought to close the door—the green boards had warped. Sunshine from a large window flooded the small room.

"What a beautiful garden! They've built a fence to keep the animals outside," I cried.

Rancon glanced without interest. "We're trespassing, Joy; this is someone's home."

But I was examining the quarters: a fireplace large enough to roast small game, a bed, two benches, a chest, and a desk. I turned back to the window.

"Look, a stream meandering among the flowers."

He peered over my shoulder. "Christ, it passes almost directly under the foundations! In a storm, the cottage will be swept away!"

"Listen! Go into the garden, Rancon. There, at the back, in the grove of pines. I want to show you something."

To my relief, he went, fought his way around a few saplings, and disappeared into the pine grove. He hadn't yet touched me once.

"Throw a pinecone into the brook!" I called.

He obeyed. The cone bobbed forward, caught on a snag, broke free, and danced to the window.

"I have it!" I cried.

He started back.

"Do you understand the significance?" I asked when he entered again.

"I'm not sure."

I chanted:

> Behind the castle of Tintagel/
>   a fine orchard was fenced
> With stout and pointed stakes;/
>   under a stalwart pine ran a stream.
> From the garden and grove/
>   to the chamber of the queen;
> Tristan cut twigs and cast them into clear water.
> When Iseult could see their coming/
>   she met her friend.

"Tintagel!" Rancon grabbed my shoulders. "Are you proposing that we be Tristan and Iseult?"

"I thought you'd be amused."

"*Amazed* is a better word." His dark face reddened; his voice was rough with anger. "How dare you ask me to live like a mouse summoned from his hole when the cat's away? What happened to our vows in Angers? For you to escape your marriage? Did Henry beat you to submission with a golden crown?"

I shouted in my own rage. "If you're referring to Young Henry, I had to submit! Henry had heard the truth about us in Angers—probably from John of Salisbury! He threatened to kill both me and William, Rancon! I had to more than submit; I had to convince him he was wrong! I still think he knows the truth about us!"

"Kill William?" Rancon sat on the bed with a thump. "If he ever attempts such a thing, I'll run a spear through the bastard myself! Yet, if he knows, why aren't you both dead? Why aren't I?"

"I wish I were," I said bitterly. "Better the gallows than this marriage prison."

A heavy silence fell.

He spoke first. "This is Hell."

"Not for you. You don't live with Henry!" It was an ugly jibe and I knew it. I, too, was sick with jealousy.

He looked up reproachfully.

"Well," I said as brightly as I could, "let's get back before William goes for his nap." His love for his son, at least, was unchanged. "He's a charming fellow, Rancon, astonishing in his speech."

Rancon turned back, again angry. "Suppose you explain why William isn't heir to Aquitaine as you promised, *Duke William*. Did you bargain with Henry about that as well? You'd say you loved him—and prove it, by God—and disinherit my son!"

"Hardly disinherit! He's to be king of England!"

"We agreed, I believe, that he would be Duke William of Aquitaine."

I argued strongly that the king's first son must be his heir, and that the duke of Normandy and the duke of Aquitaine couldn't be one and the same person and that my boy had to be duke of Normandy in order to claim the English throne. He listened, unimpressed.

"You broke your word," he said. "He's Aquitaine."

I rose and paced, again pleading about my vulnerability, Henry's determination, adding the dashed hopes I'd had about Arnulf and I know not what.

"All of which we knew long ago, Joy. Let me ask you a few direct questions." When I didn't reply, his voice became steely. "I believe I've earned the right."

I nodded.

"What are your feelings about Henry?"

When I began to rant, he stopped me.

"Think carefully. You don't behave as you did with Louis."

He was touching on an area I well knew to be fraught: I would never forgive Henry many things, the rape above all, but I had to be fair. Henry benefited from comparison to Louis—he was a rational man, unfettered by rank superstition or cowed by the Pope and he had no sanctimonious hatred of the female sex. Though he didn't share his power, as he had promised, he assigned me to carry out his instructions. None of this interested Rancon, I knew; he was hurt that I'd produced a child by Henry.

"You must know, Rancon, how easily I become gravid. So far in our marriage, Henry and I have been separated most of the time. We've been man and wife very little, but—"

"You enjoy it! Tell me the truth! Rumors say he's a lusty king, and just as uxorious about his beautiful queen as Louis ever was."

I looked directly at him. "Very well, Henry is lusty—do rumors also tell you of his many mistresses? In any case, lust isn't love, Rancon. Oh, it's better than being reviled and threatened with death. As for his feelings for me, who can tell? And what does it matter?" Tears sprang to my eyes. "You've taught me what love is. When I'm with Henry, I feel only loneliness."

"Except what?" he insisted. "Besides your lonelines, you have another reservation."

How well he knew my mind and heart. "It may be a digression from your question, but I'm repelled by Henry's chosen chancellor."

He was surprised. "Did Thierry of Galeran come to England?"

I shrugged without humor. "Not such an extremist—at least I hope not. Becket's not so coarse in his methods. Bernard sought power; I'm not sure. . . ."

Rancon waved a dismissive hand. "You're not sure and I don't care. Stop evading the question. You're sleeping with Henry, not Becket. So, continue. If it's not love, how does he hold you?"

"If you mean in marriage, I should think you'd know the rules as well as I do. If you mean in emotion, he doesn't! I'm with you at this moment, aren't I?"

"Is it the crown? Have you grown accustomed to being queen of some country or other?"

"If I wanted to be queen, I would never have left France!"

"Then what?"

I tried to reply. "Despite my divorce from Louis, it's virtually impossible to dissolve a marriage. I had the good fortune in France to have the help of a prestigious lunatic to exploit my 'evil affair' with poor Uncle Raymond."

I continued to talk of Raymond, whose death had benefited me in a gruesome way, at the same time that I tried to be honest with myself about Henry: his stimulating intellect combined with an insatiable desire to learn, his sense of humor, which, though at others' expense, was always amusing. No need to dwell on his negative character, which was obvious: his restless ambition, his duplicity, his brutality, his use of people, even those he ostensibly liked. Nor could I tell Rancon my most basic reason for accepting my position: Henry was the legal father to my children and my children would always come first.

"As I say, I am with you," I finished.

"You have your little Tristan fantasy."

I told the truth. "What else do you suggest? What else can I do? I write to Marie and Alix every day, and I couldn't bear to lose my sons."

"Then you should understand how I feel. William is my only child. Take him to Aquitaine, Joy; let me know my son."

"I told you I would, and I will."

"But you'll still stay with Henry."

I didn't answer.

"You talk in circles, but the truth is that you love him, love the life he gives you. Love *him*!"

"No, I do not! Nor does he love me! *Dex aie,* Rancon, you speak of love as if it's commonplace between husbands and wives. That's because you're from Aquitaine! You were nurtured on troubadour poetry and believe that all couples are joined by affection, but you're wrong! Ask any nobleman in this country if he loves his wife and he won't understand the question! Men 'love' God; they marry for expediency—don't you know that? If they use the word *love* to a woman, they mean lust, and rarely for their wives. Listen! I told you I was lonely. For you, Rancon. Perhaps you don't want to hear that I love you."

"Are you suggesting that we're inventing love? Or that it's only a poetic conceit? Suppose you explain—I want to be clear."

I struggled. "Very well, beginning with my grandfather's poems, which I believed as absolute truth, love is spontaneous. It begins in the eye, is sudden, overwhelming, and forever. Since, as I said, marriages are arranged for dynastic purposes, love tends to be adulterous. It's both passionate and spiritual, earthy and transcendent, and its power rivals loyalty to family or Church, which makes it antisocial. Lovers are anarchic, often destructive." Now my tears flowed. "It's irresistible. With you in Angers, I was transported. Beyond self, in an ethereal state I can't describe."

His black eyes were unreadable. "Strange words from you. You make love sound like a religion."

"Yes! A love religion! Louis said something like that once—that love rivals religion."

"Perhaps you'll be transported by Henry one day."

"You're jealous."

"Of course."

"So am I."

We stared at each other.

"Except that you have no reason. Away from you, I'm an abstinent man, and I have no other children."

"Of course, but as a man, you can choose your own fate."

"If I could, I would not have chosen you now."

"Then why did you?"

"I don't know. It seems to go back forever, during a Saint-Radgonde festival, I believe; you couldn't have been more than five and—"

"I rode with Grandfather on a float designed as a ship. I looked down at you—you were bouncing on a wine bag."

Our eyes mixed, remembering.

"Can it begin so young?" he asked.

"Yes."

He walked back to the window. "I should return to Aquitaine, and yet . . ."

The sun had set; the afterglow filled the room with a rosy purple. Rancon reached his hand behind him; I took it in mine. For a long time, we stayed motionless, like figures poised on the edge of a cliff, the tension almost unbearable.

"If you knew how I've suffered," he said softly. "I've been on the rack."

"I do know. So have I."

"That's also part of your damned love religion. Next, we'll be hanging from a cross." He turned. "Joy, I can't resist," he groaned. "I can't leave you!"

I was in his arms, on the bed.

Love had its own feckless will.

Lai of Amaria of Gascony

The queen on her palfrey passed close by,
More dazzling than the jewel-toned sky;
Tristan, watching from his branch above,
Sent a silent message of undying love;
She touches a leaf of his hazel tree,
And sighs; "Here you must leave me";
The knights quickly did obey,
And she looks upward, "Now what do you say?"
He leaps to her side, "You are my honeysuckle vine!"
She puts her arms around him, "And you are the tree I do entwine."
"I am yours, you are mine."
On the grass they know rapture of a special kind.

I moved my father's library into Tintagel to justify my retirement if anyone should question my absence; I needed to work alone on administrative problems, to study and write. Despite the danger—or because of it—our pleasures deepened. We were free of the constraints we'd felt in Angers, both the pressure of Henry's court around us and a baby forming between us. We were like new lovers, exploring and discovering in wonderful bursts of ecstasy.

May gave way to an even more beautiful June.

"When Henry gives up lowering his towers and begins acting like a responsible king, I'll be able to go home with you," I told Rancon.

It looked, however, as if Henry would be on his merry chase forever. Rancon and I sank into the same false security we'd felt in Angers; we couldn't—wouldn't—contemplate the end of our tryst.

Then Louis attacked the Vexin, and a runner announced that Henry was on his way to Woodstock before he left for France.

Rancon prepared to depart.

"When will you come back?" I asked.

"When will you come to Aquitaine?" he countered. I recognized the warrior taking over in his steady gaze, his tensed jaw. A true Aquitanian, I thought, he loves war; a true Aquitanian, he loves me.

No doubt, but we had no absolute date for meeting again

I watched him melt into the bucolic greenery.

"Damn your ex-husband!" Henry exploded in greeting.

"Don't you want to see Young Henry?"

"What? Oh, God's eyes, yes! Where is my new prince?"

Young Henry was shaping into an extraordinarily beautiful infant; everyone said so, and even Henry was impressed.

"Do you think he looks like me?" he asked.

"He will in time." Surely he knew he was the father of this boy.

Henry lifted the pink-and-gold baby gingerly onto his shoulder, with the usual result. He gave him back to his nurse.

"Becket and I must talk to you, Joy."

I looked at the chancellor with distaste, but I followed them meekly to Henry's quarters. Becket was dressed like a dandy.

"My l-l-lady," he began, "we must impose on your good offices to rule England while we are away."

"Why are you going, my lord Thomas?" I asked. "You said you didn't fight."

Becket explained his reasons and the general strategy as Henry stared silently out the window. Was Becket making the decisions?

I addressed Henry through Becket. "You can assign your justiciars to rule. I haven't been in Aquitaine since you sailed for England the first time. I mustn't be absent another summer."

"Don't concern yourself. I'll be riding through Aquitaine," Henry assured me.

"That's not the same thing!"

Becket smiled, displaying even brown teeth. "The king will do everything you could do, I promise you."

He promised me? *He* controlled Henry's actions? The chancellor, whose task was to sniff spores? To hack at the foundations of castles? Oh, I knew that Henry claimed Becket could teach him the laws and customs of England, and thus expedite his much-vaunted aspiration for the rule of law in his island kingdom, but Becket's present promises concerned Aquitaine. The mystery had less to do with politics, however, than with the relationship between the two men. I studied Becket's pale features to penetrate his mask. How had he gained so much authority in a single spring? I considered the two men, the age difference above all. Though I'd rightfully scoffed at making Thomas Henry's chancellor, he had been the deacon of Canterbury, and he was a student of law. Becket was cunningly exploiting a situation created by Henry himself. Henry, though different in style, resembled Louis in his heavy dependence upon advice from more experienced men. Of course, Louis had been vulnerable to religious fanatics, and Henry was not, but the heavy weight of a crown made both men reach out. Henry, barely into his twenties, had depended on his father, then his mother, and even me. Despite his vaunted bravery and his remarkable mind, he had never governed; he needed help. I could hear Suger's whisper: *"Take him in hand, Joy; he's a gifted apprentice."*

Becket continued: "We're impressed at how you've brought the dissenting justiciars into accord, a most commendable feat. Therefore, we want you to travel around the country and meet with the local justices and mayors."

"You mean take a *chevauchée?*"

"Exactly, only here it's called a 'progress.'"

As I listened with disbelief, he laid out my route, the names of the various officials and their importance, the fairs and market days in the towns, just as my father had done years before.

When he'd finished, I addressed Henry. "Do you think that the English lords whose castles you've just razed will support your adventures against Louis?"

Henry glanced at Becket. "Thomas has devised a tax, a scutage. I'll use the money to hire a professional army, which will make it unnecessary to call upon the English."

It was an ingenious scheme; Henry wouldn't be limited by the forty days' service a knight owed, nor would he have to depend on dubious English loyalty.

"Well then, your summer is arranged, and so is mine. I'll be in Aquitaine."

Becket smiled. "I think not, Queen Eleanor, not if you want your son William recognized as your heir."

I whirled on Henry. "Do you permit your chancellor to blackmail me?"

Henry bared his teeth. "I want you in England, Joy; you invited the blackmail, as you call it, by showing us your vulnerable spot."

"You call my son a vulnerable spot?"

"I want you in England."

I left swiftly, before I should say too much.

Henry was more passionate than ever, and even tender at times; I could almost believe he'd been abstinent during our separation. However, I had not been faithful, and I was able to be passionate and tender as well, so perhaps not. We were both excellent actors.

Two days before they left, Becket organized a quick ceremony of recognition in Wallingford. Henry held young William by the hand as the lords of England—most of them—knelt before my sunny boy and accepted him as their next king. I tried to hide my exultation when I wrote Rancon, and I promised that soon we would present William together as my heir in Aquitaine.

◈

I approached my progress through England with humility, for I was well aware that my years in Aquitaine and France had not prepared me for this island kingdom with its own history and mores. Fortunately for me—and for the natives—Richard de Luci offered to accompany me on the first few stops.

England was a double-layered society: the Normans on top, and the people they had conquered almost a hundred years before on the bottom. Yet, though the Saxon nobility no longer existed as a force in the land, most had survived and now lived as country gentry, or even in the peasant class. The instant we left London, we found that Norman ideas were filtered through the Saxon sieve and dripped out as Norman-Saxon. An example was the language, which I'd had difficulty learning, with good reason—it was very much in flux, mixing Norman-French, Anglo-Saxon, and Latin. I heard a little verse again and again:

C'est ma volunté
That I might be with thee
Ludenti;
Votre amour en mon questre
Brendeth as the fire
Crescento.

The same mix applied to their law. People still followed their "moot court" and "court of a hundred" with its many witnesses. Canon law, which I'd learned in spite of myself while in France, was weaker in England. The people seemed devout, and God knows London was alive with churches, but the secular spirit prevailed.

My courts proved exceedingly popular, however; was my person the attraction? My foreignness? No, the English liked all their queens. Matilda was a legend and King Stephen's queen—also called Matilda—was still popular with the masses.

The law required that each plaintive who approached me must present a writ; therefore, I was amazed at the number of women who appeared. The same law forbade women the right to present writs, but they apparently didn't care; they demanded justice.

My first case was in a town called Chatteris, where a midwife introduced herself as Dame Agatha. She was a crisp, overbearing wench of middle years, with bulbous breasts and a large wen under her right ear. After she'd kissed my hem, she stood and looked me directly in the eye.

"Master Glottenball, the smithy in Chatteris, raft the maidenhead of my sister Hincmar in broad daylight, he did. Full five gawkers looked on as he bounced belly-naked atop the poor lass."

"And you want to bring suit against him?" I asked cautiously.

"I'd like to stick a hot poker up his nether eye," she retorted, "but we both knew that when a knock-head be hit, the world will pipe."

I turned helplessly to Richard de Luci.

"She means that when a feebleminded woman is assaulted, no one cares," he said.

"Knock-head?" I repeated to Dame Agatha.

"Aye, born with water whar her brains should be, but a harmless wench withal. The pint be that she war brought befar the moot and ordered to pay the *lerewita*."

"*Lerewita?*" I asked Richard de Luci.

"A fine payable to their lords for the sin of fornification."

"When she's been raped? And lacks her fantastic cell?"

He frowned. "That's the law. My advice is to let the fine stand. Otherwise, you'll be swamped with such pleas."

"Did you understand?" I asked the midwife gently.

"My sister hae the water, not me."

"I can pay your *lerewita*. How much do you need?"

"Six Angevins."

Which was nothing.

"It would have been twice that," Richard de Luci told me, "if she'd been with child."

I shuddered. At least the poor peasant could buy her way out of punishment. I now knew I was with child again, and I prayed that Henry was the father.

After the fornicators, the most common type of women in court were recent widows. The court assigned them new husbands and men jammed the courtroom to claim their brides—often young men suing for toothless hags and their pitiful legacies. A contradictory law gave widows the right to hold their inheritances so long as they didn't wed again. To my disgust, the widows' children as well as men tried to pry these hapless women free of their security, but the mothers proved tough crones. It was a good law, I thought.

Petra and her children traveled with me faithfully even as summer gave way to winter, and Henry didn't return. We fought our way along unmarked roads obscured by snow drifts, traveling from village to village, braving wolves and even hungry bears, and often covering less than two miles in a day. After staying in a series of drafty hovels, we were grateful to move into the abbey in Reading. Our rooms were monks' cells, the heat scant, but the walls were thick and the food plentiful, my last stop before retiring to bear my child.

On one free Sunday when it wasn't raining or snowing, Petra and I took young William and Raoul to see the tomb of Henry I, Henry's famous grandfather.

"May I climb down beside him, Mama? I want to touch his mouse."

"What mouse?" Raoul leaned over the rail.

"He means mouth," I said. "No, William, we let the dead sleep in peace."

"Look at the relics above him," Petra instructed Raoul.

"You, too, William," I added, "for that chest contains the arm of Saint-James. Your own grandmother Matilda traveled all the way to Rome to get it."

"Did she cut it off the saint herself?" Raoul asked.

"Where's the blood?" William shouted.

A monk frowned.

"Listen!" I said hastily. "In that smaller box is Christ's foreskin."

William stared. "Why did He need four skins?"

"She means His prick, silly," Raoul said loftily.

But the prick I was looking at was real. Perched on the head of the effigy was my dead grandfather, naked and robust, his eyes blazing, spreading his legs lasciviously.

"*I miss you, Joy.*"

"What's wrong?" Petra took my arm.

"Does that effigy look like our grandfather, William the Ninth?"

"I don't know, dear; remember, I was only three when he died. I know he loved you—that you were his favorite."

> *The wintry wind makes merit grow*
> *Brings gaudy flowers in the snow*
> *Which into joyous jewels do grow*
> *Grant me but this*
> *And I will go!*

The image faded. Though we spent the rest of the afternoon studying the stones, I remained disturbed.

The following morning, I was back at my desk which had been set up in the nave. Amaria touched my shoulder.

"Joy, come quickly."

"In a—"

"Now! It's William!"

I was running under the arches before the words were out. Into the nursery, where the nurses clustered around William.

"Out of my way! Move, you fool!"

I snatched him from his mat. A hot coal in my arms. Fetid odor. Glazed eyes. And his breath, his breath . . .

"How long has he been breathing like this?" I screamed.

The nurses cowered.

Petra rushed in. "What's happened?"

"Get everyone out of here!" I cried. "Am, go for the leecher! And the barber! Bring me my chest! Hot bricks! Are you all deaf? I said *go*!"

I scooped furs to wrap my prince. I hugged him close.

"Mama's here, darling. Everything's going to be all right."

I might as well have talked to a green quince. He coughed, then began to choke. I heaved him across my shoulder and pounded.

Amaria was back with hot bricks.

"Are you mad? He's on fire—bring me a cold bath!"

She left again.

Two women sloshed a bucket of icy water between them. Another handed me cloths. I put William on his bed and slowly stroked cold water onto his skin. The cloths steamed, but the skin remained the same.

Now I wrapped him in blankets and placed hot bricks around him as if he were in an oven.

"He'll sweat soon," I said.

Shapes moved around me. No one answered.

The leecher arrived. With long tongs, he fished for squirming black leeches and placed them in clusters on the temples, under the arms, inside the thighs. The little devils sucked away.

The barber arrived. He perched a bowl of water on William's bed. He lifted my prince's arm and sliced it open. Blood spurted into the bowl.

"To reduce the fever," he said.

I watched, sick.

The apothecary came. He sniffed the breath, the armpits, the crotch.

"Tertian fever."

"I don't care what you call it!" I screeched. "Cure him!"

He pasted leaves on the temples close to the leeches. He placed mint on William's upper lip.

I looked at the black snails, the leaves, the bandage, the bricks, the red water.

"Everyone leave!" I ordered.

I was alone with my boy. Whispering and crooning. I spread a hot plaster of pimpernel on his chest. I rubbed oil of dittany on his throat. I replaced the leeches with lemon balm.

I traced a finger under his nose. It was wet! Now even his forehead glistened. He was perspiring.

His eyes opened. "Mama?"

"I'm here, sweets."

"Thirsty."

I stretched my hand and someone put a cup of broth in it. William sipped it slowly.

"Take more," I coaxed.

"I hurt."

"You'll soon be better."

"When?"

"Tomorrow."

"Tomorrow never comes."

He closed his eyes.

"That's right, darling. Sleep."

I looked over my shoulder at my sister and Amaria. "He's better. Hear? No rasping."

Petra moved forward. She put her arm around me. "Joy, oh Joy."

Amaria hugged the other side. "Be brave, dear."

"What . . . Why . . ."

I looked down at my sleeping prince. No rasping. No breathing.

"William!" I clutched him to my shoulder. Again I pounded. I begged. Cajoled. Screamed. Implored. Prayed.

Two days later, I stared at my beautiful son where he lay in his coffin next to the effigy of Henry I.

"Peace be with you in love. Peace be with you in the glory and bliss of paradise."

Familiar words, faintly comic words. Where had I heard them before? Ah yes, in my wedding ceremony with Louis.

They were comic no more.

Levis insurgiit, William.

I went back to the nursery after a night of prayer. Young Henry's wet nurse turned in alarm.

"Be somewhat amiss, milady?"

She held fresh swaddling cloths aloft. My son, stark naked, sat sucking his thumb and fondling his penis. I pushed her out of the way.

"Greeting, young prince." My voice trembled.

His sunny face broke into a smile; he removed his thumb and held his arms high. "Mama!"

I wrapped his satin folds close and paced to and fro. "I love you, baby."

He drooled on my shoulder.

"Four children, and you're all I have left. Never leave me. Promise. Grow up strong and well."

"Mamamamama," he chanted.

20

$\mathcal{M}$y daughter Matilda came squalling into the world on the hottest day of the year. We pressed wet cloths to her copper skin to cool her, until we realized that red was her natural color, just as choler was her humor. Henry's child, no doubt at all. I wrapped her against her cradleboard to still her beating arms, though nothing would stop her loud squawk, and, holding Young Henry, boarded my ship at Queenshithe. We were going to Poitiers.

My own knights met us in Barfleur, and at last I headed home, where I hadn't been since my fateful marriage three children ago. The land rose and fell gently, the forests bloomed, the bogs oozed, and the familiar silver tiles gleamed atop the joined houses, but the people regarded my passage with a grim reserve that bordered on hostility. No more the streaming tears, the signs of the cross, the throwing of kisses. With a shock, I realized that I was more beloved in England. Instantly, my spine tingled. What was wrong?

In Poitiers, Petronilla left me to return to Vermandois. Raoul had again evinced disturbing symptoms, a flaking of his skin and growths on his joints, and Petra planned to summon a Jewish doctor she trusted from Paris. My beloved grandmother Dangereuse had died in my long absence, my aunts hadn't been in Poitiers in years, and I was alone with my memories. Henry wrote that he must postpone seeing his beautiful daughter until September, or even later; his fighting had distracted him from pressing court matters, to which he must attend when his bellicose brother finally withdrew, not to mention the mooncalf king of France. I sent a missive to Rancon.

Four days later, he arrived.

Rancon led me quickly to a deserted hermit's cave on the far side of the Clain. Without a word, we clutched each other close and sobbed without restraint. Nothing could stop us so long as we had energy to cry out, to moan, to tremble. Only exhaustion brought quiet. Leaning against the cool stone wall, speaking in half phrases, we recalled William's conception, his growth in the womb, his incomparable drolleries, his sweet embraces in Woodstock. And finally, I spoke alone of his death.

"Did you use your book by Galen?"

"Of course; I'd memorized every page."

"And you say he seemed to recover? "

"Oh, Rancon, I was so sure! When he said, 'Tomorrow never comes,' I . . ."

We returned to Maubergeonne Tower in moonlight, still recalling, still disbelieving. That night for the first time, we had no passion except grief; we talked all night of the dear whimsical child we had lost, for it was *our* loss, no one else's.

The next night, however, in the feral dark, silent as animals, our bodies began the healing process and I realized that—Church teaching notwithstanding—carnal love has a profound spiritual dimension. Love's solace took on a new meaning: it was no longer Tristan's love and death; it was love over death.

Poitiers was too visible for prolonged intimacy, and so we decided to ride south. Leaving my children with Amaria, Rancon and I left on a sunny summer morning. In the next weeks, we passed manors and abbeys with sweet espaliered gardens, splashed through bogs, passed through tiny hamlets called Chamignac-le-Rivière, Ladinac-le-Long, and Ruines-Gallo-Romaines, crossed parched plains, entered densely wooded country, and forded dangerous rivers with their craggy green furry depths, moving farther southward into grape country. Together, we swallowed salty river oysters, ate fois gras, sausage spiced with flame. With shepherds, we danced with scarves to the wheeze of bagpipes, leaped the *gambades* with each other, drank deep of the grape to the tambourines, clappers, viols, bells, psalteries, and trumpets.

I was home. I was with my beloved. And, almost invisibly, I began to heal.

We spoke little of love; we experienced it. We rode on one horse across water meadows, along verdant paths in country that seemed unreal in its perfection. And we slept in close embrace.

Yet I was haunted. I woke screaming in my sleep.

Then in her sorrowful sleep/
  did a vivid vision come to Iseult;
She was in a dense wood and two lions leaped to fight/
  in deadly struggle for the queen's love!
With roaring and snarling, clawing and tearing/
  did they vie for her pleasure.
She gave a cry and woke!

"Oh, Rancon, I'm so frightened!"

"Hush, darling, you're safe; you're with me. " He stroked my hair. "We still have each other. We have memories"

I settled into his arms, not daring to tell the import of my dream, yet the fear stayed with me. Rancon sensed my apprehension; his love grew more intense, more protective. Whether it was grief or fear or our ever-deeper experience, I didn't know, but we loved as we never had. We both grew pale, and although we laughed at our condition, we couldn't stop. Perhaps being so close wrought some positive change as well, for the people along the way seemed friendlier.

"People in the south haven't suffered as much," Rancon confirmed when I asked him.

"Why? Suffered in what way?"

"I told you, around Poitiers, north to Angers, but not yet to the south, Henry's mercenaries ravage the villages. As to why? The excuse is King Louis, or the Lusignan brothers, or no excuse at all." He seemed reluctant to continue. "They may blame you—your neglect of your duchy."

"I thought the fighting was strictly between Henry and Louis."

"Not strictly. In fact, Louis may screen Henry's real purpose." He grimaced. "Both kings want to control Aquitaine, and, since you're away, several barons have the same idea. Henry is determined to demean the Lusignan brothers and Aimar of Limoges, and they're equally determined to drive him out. He lowered the walls of Limoges—did you know?"

Of course I did not. I was shocked. "Surely the barons realize I'm not behind Henry's policies!"

Again he was slow to answer. "You seem to have deserted Aquitaine; you stay in England."

"But my uncle Ralph and Archbishop Geoffrey, not to mention you . . ."

"Govern well, I grant you, but it's your presence more than your governance that they want."

"Henry must know that," I said slowly. "He keeps me in England deliberately, doesn't he? It's a political tactic."

He glanced. "That's my opinion, yes."

And keeps me pregnant as well. I smiled bitterly. Another political tactic.

September came and went, then October; still Henry remained in Normandy, and I in Aquitaine. In November, far to the south, I asked Rancon to take me alone to see an ancient Roman ruin in moonlight.

We dismounted in a riverbed between two scarps, where a dark aqueduct loomed against fast-moving clouds.

"I didn't know you were an antiquarian, Joy."

"Oh, yes, I worship the ancients."

"I thought I knew all about you."

I faced him. "You don't know that I'm pregnant."

"You mean . . ." He gasped. "But that means . . ."

"Yes, Rancon, our second child."

He had a violent fit of coughing. "Sorry, I'm so happy!" His cough turned to laughter. "Oh God, thank you!" He hugged me tightly. "Oh God, I'm so happy." He hurled a stone at the aqueduct. "Hear that, Romans? I'm about to become a father!" He hugged me again, more gently. "Do you feel all right? Aren't the early months the most dangerous? Should you be on a horse?"

"Listen! The horse could ride me and I'd be fine!" Except . . . my dream came back. "Henry's dangerous, Rancon."

"Henry's fighting somewhere in the north. Just write him and—"

"Henry can count. Remember how he threatened me in Rouen?"

"I won't let you!" he howled, reading my thought.

"If I arrange a Christmas Court in Bordeaux, he'll accept a slightly early birth."

Rancon picked up another rock and hurled it against the aqueduct viciously. I shuddered. Where would this end?

Henry was delighted to come to Bordeaux. He would bring his court from Angers, some of his greater nobles from Normandy, and his mother of course. He wanted to grieve in person for our irreparable loss—an afterthought.

He came, I suffered his attentions as I must, and he left to hunt. Within the hour, Rancon arrived.

"My God, Rancon," I cried in alarm. "Henry's still here. He just—"

He slammed the door behind him. "Are you all right?"

I shrugged. "I survived."

His face twisted angrily. "Henry abducted two of my nephews."

I jumped in panic. "Does that mean he suspects?"

"I don't think it has anything to do with us. He's been taking children as hostages all over Aquitaine. He snatched the boys from my uncle Bric's hunting preserve and demands that my uncle swear homage, recognizing Henry as duke of Aquitaine."

"I'll get them back, I promise you."

Rancon's eyes blazed "If he hurts you, if you should have a miscarriage, by God, I'll . . ."

"Stay close, Rancon, and do nothing. I'll send word yet today."

I watched him leave with less confidence than I pretended.

Becket answered my summons. "How may I s-s-serve you, Queen Eleanor?"

"By releasing the children of Angoulême."

His eyes were dull brown turf. "I'm s-s-sorry, but such orders must come from the king."

"Lord Angoulême is my vassal, this is my duchy, and you are my chancellor as well as the king's. See that it's done within the hour."

Henry appeared in the allotted time.

"You'll return to England at once!" he roared.

"Child-killer!" I burst into furious tears. "You even threatened William's life once!"

He stopped cold. "Never!"

I ranted bitterly. "In Rouen, you threatened both him and me! You don't care a fig for children—the most vulnerable creatures on earth!"

"Don't ever speak to me like that!"

"You lost a son and now you strike terror into the hearts of innocent parents. Have you no pity? No shame? I'll never forgive you!" I rushed from the room.

In my own chamber, I dried my tears and waited. The bells rang twice before he knocked.

"They're free," he informed me. Then, to my surprise, his shoulders began to shake. "Oh Joy, he was such a lively boy. I never saw his like. What can I do to make it up to you?"

I held his bulllike frame and stroked his coarse bristles. Henry was a superb actor, but these tears seemed real.

"There is one thing you can do," I said softy. "I need help with Petronilla."

He smiled through his tears. "Again? Who's her lover this time?"

"Raoul has leprosy."

Henry gasped. "There's no cure!"

"No, he must be sequestered."

"I'll build him a lazar house in Caen. I swear to you, a private setting where his family can visit."

"Thank you, Henry. You're a generous man." I hoped he was sufficiently generous to ignore the premature birth of my next child.

I told Henry that I planned to have my next baby in Poitiers, and, for a change, he seemed supportive, but his generous sentiments were short-lived. When Louis attacked after Easter with Henry's brother at his side, Henry responded with his usual fury. Since his intractable enemies distracted him from his real work, he ordered me back to England.

"But you promised, Henry!"

"I should think you'd understand my situation! God's eyes, I've tried to tame that wild brother of mine! Haven't I offered him a fine estate?"

"You gave Anjou to Geoffrey?"

His face reddened. "Not Anjou! An estate, damn it, which is more than he deserves! Why should I part with my inheritance?"

It was an argument I didn't wish to enter; Geoffrey claimed that his father had left him Anjou to compensate for Henry's having Normandy and now England, which sounded reasonable. On the other hand, Geoffrey was a malevolent man, proved so by his association with Louis.

"I need you in England, Joy."

"You have Luci and Leicester! Or send Becket! It's important that I stay in Poitiers, Henry. This baby will be my heir. I should think that for once you'd understand!" I insisted. "Do you have no respect for my wishes?"

"Your first wish should be to help me. You have an excellent understanding of the English."

If Rancon was right about my people, this was no idle matter. I must pay heed. I argued with such heat that Henry became suspicious, and I retreated. Rancon had said that both Louis and Henry coveted Aquitaine, so I asked Henry why he thought Louis was so persistent in his attacks. He burst into such an insane volley about Louis's frustrated love for me that I feared he would go into one of his fits; yet I had learned that his blusters were often calculated to change the subject. Rancon's suspicions were probably correct. After all, Louis had been wed this year to Constance of Castile, who would certainly be perplexed if the battle were simply for an ex-wife. Behind all the sentimental outrage, Louis, too, yearned for Aquitaine, something Suger and I had discussed years ago.

Of course, behind my political outrage was the sentimental motive: I longed to stay with Rancon.

After Henry left, I lingered in Poitiers just long enough for Rancon to visit. His determination disturbed me: He *would* be with me when his child was born, no matter where I was or what the circumstances. There would be no maneuvering, no capitulation to Henry's schedule, did I understand?

I did. And began to calculate frantically.

We had our usual excruciating farewell, and I rode to Barfleur. In London, I worked with Leiceister and Richard de Luci until June. With the summer and the fighting season ahead to distract Henry, I felt safe; I retired to Oxford, and summoned Rancon.

Before he could reply, I heard from Henry: His brother Geoffrey was dead; Louis had retired. As my heart sank, I read on: "There's still time left in the season for me to take Wales. Thomas and I are preparing to sail to Southampton and will assemble our army in Winchester, so you must remain my regent." No suspicions concerning my new baby. Nor any interest.

Rancon arrived in late July.

It was the second time he'd seen me with child, though I was much more advanced than I had been when he'd come to Angers. I was embarrassed at my girth, until he put his hands at my middle.

"Bel Vezer, you should always be with child!"

Which made me laugh. When was I not?

There followed a hundred questions about my symptoms, my appetite, my energy—had I stopped riding? Could I immerse myself in water? Under his barrage, I felt a spiritual weight lifting. God knows I'd been pregnant often enough to know the stigma and loneliness of the condition. He made it a fulfillment, a celebration.

"Clean this place," he said upon viewing my quarters. "I don't want my babe exposed to dirty rushes on the floor."

"They're changed every day, Rancon, and they guard against typhus. Your baby will be safe." I was delighted.

"Have you hired a wet nurse?"

"I've interviewed several," and tentatively settled on a dame called Nurse Mincia.

Rancon rode to the neighboring villages and returned with Hodierna of Albans, who was that rarest of wet nurses, a woman who could read. Her son, called Alexander, had already been born. Now we waited together for my confinement.

For prudence, Rancon was not permitted close to the birthing room, though Amaria kept him informed. In less than three hours, I gave birth to a son. Rancon entered, haggard with anxiety. Amaria held candles so he could study his boy.

At Rancon's insistence, he crawled into my bed and the tiny infant was placed between us. He had a theory about two heart-beats, blood smells, and voices that made up the world of his new son, and must not be disrupted. We lasted that way a week, during which Hodierna had to disturb us every few hours to feed her lusty charge. If she was shocked, she made no sign. Then, suddenly, as I grew stronger, the new father agreed to let the infant sleep with Alexander and Hodierna. My poor baby was left to fend for himself in the strange world.

Rancon continued to share my bed, though he still woke at regular intervals. Only now it was to an appetite of a different kind. Love sprang like a hidden animal between us.

"Why Richard?" Henry wrote from Chester. "Why not William again?"

"I'm superstitious about naming him for the dead," I wrote back. "Richard for Richard de Luci. It's a nice name, native in both England and Aquitaine."

Henry changed the subject. He'd split the Welsh north and south but lacked a clear victory. A later letter swiftly followed, announcing that he intended to make a progress through England himself to examine the legal system. He would ride north as far as the Scottish border, where he hoped to quiet King Malcolm's whines that Henry had promised him Northumberland. Were the Scots so dense that they took "dangling" seriously?

Would I care to accompany him?

No. After the loss of William, I would not expose my baby to an English winter on the road.

In that case, Henry would come by Oxford to see his new son before he ventured on his progress. His stay would be short: Rancon retired to Tintagel.

Becket arrived late that very same day. I remarked on the chancellor's appearance, which was indeed astounding.

"I never saw orange leather before, Thomas. Is it from a tiger?"

He laughed. "It's from Master Willie's dye lot. Do you like it?"

"Very much, especially in combination with green satin. You've become quite the dandy."

"I try to dress in a manner fitting to my st-st-station."

"And what is the station of this charming fellow?"

A small bright-eyed monkey perched on his shoulder, dressed in the same costume exactly.

"You have a new son and I have mine," he announced. "Rolfie, meet the queen of England."

"A fertile season," I said dryly.

"Even in France, if the gossip be true. King Louis's queen is said to be with child."

My heart jumped. "If he has a son . . . he'll be king of France!"

"Perhaps the queen will produce a she-monkey."

"I'll give you a bucket of diamonds, Thomas, if you put my daughter Marie on the throne of France."

"A worthy incentive."

Henry arrived the next day full of vigor and complacency, as if he'd just conquered someone's bed, which he probably had.

"Where's my new son?" he cried.

He bounced the squalling infant.

"The best ever, Joy! I never beheld such a handsome boy!" he shouted.

I reached for the babe. "Except that this is Richard's milk-brother, little Alexander Neckham."

At that moment, Hodierna entered with my darling, fresh from his morning feeding. And he *was* the best ever, my thought always upon having a new baby, except in this case it was true. His dark blue eyes already focused; his fat legs kicked vigorously. Even his square hands were like Rancon's. Would he play a lute? Be a great warrior?

Henry peered at his son. "A fair lad, eh? Though I still say that Richard's an odd name. Why don't we exchange? Alexander's more fitting for a duke."

I took Richard from him. "Count Richard of Poitou, Duke Richard of Aquitaine, I like the ring."

Three days later, I rose before dawn to see them off. The men in Henry's train, weary from the Welsh campaign, were carrying only the basic amenities; they expected to receive hospitality along the way. In their drab, dispirited company, Becket was a parrot flying among sparrows.

"I'll pluck a few of his gaudy feathers for your bonnet," Henry whispered, with a malicious glint in his eyes.

As the last cart lurched around the bend, Rancon returned.

Henry was gone for almost six months, a marvelous gift.

Such domestic bliss is rare in great households, for we all live peripatetic lives, always on the road in order to govern, always on display. We knew it; we cherished this interval. We doted on Richard as he learned to smile, to roll over, then to sit up straight. We guarded him carefully from Young Henry, now three, a tun of Greek fire hurling himself widdershins over babies, and whatever else crossed his path. I would have guarded his sister, Matilda, as well, except that she could strike sparks of her own. Both loved the animal world, he the world of birds and she that of insects—which was unfortunate, since birds devour insects.

Of course we continued our administrative work. Both of us were in constant touch with Aquitaine, Rancon with the military sector, I with the trade, the incomes, the political appointments. I also received daily runners from London, but one of the benefits of Henry's constant absence was the independence of the English government. It reminded me slightly of Aquitaine: Great barons were virtual kings in their own territories. Of course, as I well knew, this had a negative side as well as a positive.

When Henry trumpeted his return in late March, Rancon prepared to return to Aquitaine. Our agony was extreme. When would we have such a long sojourn again? Have another child? All of our tranquillity turned in an instant to poignant uncertainty.

"Find a good instructor for Richard," he ordered. "Let him learn several languages simultaneously, Latin, French, and langue d'oc."

An instructor was years away. "And not English?"

"Of course not!"

"It might be politic."

"He won't need English in Aquitaine."

"True, my lord."

The sure knowledge that we would meet again usually made our farewells bittersweet instead of tragic, except now there was Richard. And I had no definite plans. We were both edgy.

Henry's train of decimated ghosts returned looking as if they'd been on a crusade instead of a simple *chevauchée*. Their pinched faces, dripping noses, hacking coughs, and haunted eyes attested to a miserable journey. Worst was Becket. Though wrapped in Henry's own fur-lined mantle, the chancellor shook with ague and his cheeks were hollow as a hermit's.

I served a magnificent feast to celebrate their return, and took maternal pleasure in their voracious appetites.

"I miss the worms in the meat," Peter Smythe said facetiously.

"Or the gas in the turnips," said another wag. "And the week-old fish."

"Where were you served these luxuries?" I asked.

"Everywhere," Becket replied. "Barons outdid themselves to provide variety, which meant carrion off the roads."

"Yet you're not eating, Thomas," I pointed out.

"I have a cold stomach."

I called for fresh orange laced with vinegar to relieve him.

"Where's your monkey?" I missed him.

"Lying atop a sheet of ice on some godforsaken moor." Tears sprang to his red eyes. "I couldn't even bury him."

"Because of the cold?"

"Because we didn't have time. We slept only four hours each night." He began to cough helplessly.

Henry, of course, had thrived on the hardship. He'd set the killing pace and dragged his mesne lorels to remote shacks for hospitality. Now he was filled with hearty good humor, but his men responded warily. The many japes he'd made at their expense showed plainly on their faces, especially on Becket's. He'd obviously suffered most.

The following day, Henry asked me to attend him and Becket in the great hall; they had a proposition to make.

Becket smiled when I entered the *salle*. "Where's my bucket of diamonds, Queen Eleanor?"

I didn't know what he meant.

"You said that if I put your child on the French throne, you would reward me."

I gasped. "Has Louis's child been born?"

"A female," Henry replied.

"Then Marie must be his heir!"

"I'm afraid not, Joy. She's been sent to Champagne to wed Count Thibault's son, Henry."

I simulated surprise, for Marie had already written me about her Henry, the gallant knight I'd known on the Crusade. She'd assured me that he was nothing like his prudish father, that she planned a great court of troubadours. Henry knew, of course that I corresponded with both my daughters, but I was curious about his scheme, especially since Marie had confessed that both she and her sister had long ago given up hope of inheriting the French throne.

"There's still Alix," I submitted.

"She's been sent to Blois to marry. And disinherited as well, remember. No, Louis's new baby princess has been named his heiress."

"So I keep my bucket of diamonds?"

Henry rested his rough hand on my shoulder. "You asked me to put a child of yours on the throne of France. If not a daughter, what about a son?"

"What son? How?"

Becket grinned. "We propose to claim the new princess as a bride for Young Henry."

Young Henry was only three.

"Becket's idea," Henry said. "I wouldn't have the gall myself."

I envisioned Louis's intransigent face.

"Yet, I want you to be happy. That's my only aim in life. Can you suggest how we might persuade the monkish king?" Henry wore his predator's grin.

I met his marble eyes. "I take it, then, that you're ready to declare Young Henry as your heir."

Henry raised pale brows. "Was there ever any doubt?"

"You had your barons recognize William at this age. Why don't you do the same for Young Henry?"

"The succession is assured," he barked.

"You have to convince Louis, my lord. Suppose we tell him that we'll symbolically put aside our crowns in deference to Young Henry and the French princess."

"Marguerite," Becket offered. "Her name is Marguerite."

"You haven't answered me, Henry."

He threw up his hands in mock submission. "We'll go through the motions. Three heartbeats and we resume our power. Will that satisfy you?"

As if Henry could ever satisfy me.

Henry removed my name from the negotiations, convinced that Louis must still be obsessed with me. The note, when it was finally sent, asked humbly if the royal chancellor, Thomas Becket, might visit the French king. Louis agreed to receive the good friend of Theobald, archbishop of Canterbury.

"I will put on such a display as the world has never seen!" Becket cried.

I winced. "Louis hates show."

"For himself perhaps," Henry argued, "but I trust Thomas's instincts. Louis must be convinced that England is not some poor country province. He must think of the advantages his little princess will enjoy when she becomes an English queen, rather than the advantages our prince will have on the French throne!"

By the time Thomas left for France, we'd amassed every bauble in England for him to take with him. The piles of gifts stacked in Westminster were staggering. How would he transport them?

"You can have the royal *Esnecca*," Henry offered grandly.

"Thank you, my lord. My own fleet of ships will suffice."

I was astonished. "What fleet?"

"I have six vessels for my own use," Becket said modestly.

I stared at Henry. "And you have *one*?"

He grinned.

We went to Sandwich to see Becket off, then turned our mesnie northward to Worcester, where we planned a ceremony to put aside our crowns.

We had to be leisurely, as I was again pregnant.

A week later, Becket entered Paris. The procession was led by 250 footmen bellowing forth Welsh and English madrigals, followed by eight huge wains carrying fine English ale. The golden liquid was dispensed to the awed French crowds. Behind the footmen came rare birds from Africa, an army of saddled mastiffs ridden by monkeys costumed with shields, helmets, and banners. Behind them, slinking wolves and lumbering bears created havoc among the burghers. Teams of eight creamy oxen pulled longcarts loaded with gold and silver coins, packhorses loaded with rare antiquities from Arthur's time, Excalibur held by an English squire, and a plank from the Round Table.

Becket himself was preceded by two hundred servants in tunics that glittered with gold and silver. And finally, there came the great Becket himself, dressed in a long tunic embroidered with jeweled flowers. He scattered gold coins to the eager crowds. Becket was a bolt from Heaven, and all France split asunder at the golden fireflash. How could Louis resist? He couldn't.

Within days, the baby Princess Marguerite was promised to Henry as Henry's marriage ward. The English king was now expected to come in person and collect his prize.

Henry groaned. "How can I top Becket?"

"You should ask where Becket accumulated such wealth. Has he been robbing the treasury?"

"No, he's honest. I've advanced his riches to him."

Yet Henry was known for his parsimony. "Advanced against his salary? And six ships? He can never repay you!"

Though he grinned, his eyes remained cold. "Which gives me power over my ambitious chancellor, eh? Falcons think they fly free until they feel the tug of the jesse. When the time comes, I'll ground my gaudy bird."

Through Becket, Henry had made his point of his largesse and would go to France himself as a penitent. Soberly dressed, he carried money only for the dedication of a list of abbeys I provided.

Once in Paris, he insisted on attending Notre Dame every day with Louis; he wrote me: "If Louis's tears are the measure, then I must count myself a great success. The French king is the most mournful man I ever did meet. He weeps that he loves me as a brother; he weeps that he adores me as his fellow king; he weeps that we are to be joined forever in one family. My tunics are tinged with green mold from all this dampness."

I stopped, remembering.

"The French princess has black eyes and a tuft of black hair, and she comes with the dowry of the Vexin! Does this mean I won't have to fight every summer? Does King Louis finally accept the loss of his beauteous wife to the better man? We are carrying Marguerite to Rouen to be put in the custody of Robert of Newburgh until the nuptials. Your former husband demands that under no circumstances are you to care for her."

I burst into uncontrollable laughter.

"What's wrong, dear?" Amaria took me by the shoulders. "Did Louis change his mind?"

She thought I was weeping, and indeed I had a few tears. I tried to speak and couldn't; I pointed helplessly to the parchment where it lay beside me.

She read it, puzzled. "I see nothing amiss."

But I was doubled in mirth. The very thought of these two men sitting atop Mont Saint-Michel, which is where they were, as the tides swished and sucked below them, these two pretenders to my bed discussing whether I was fit to tend an infant was too rich to endure. I was not to care for poor Marguerite? When her own mother had apparently let her go to a stranger without a whimper? When her father was discarding all his daughters as fast as he could? And to be exerting a promise from Henry, which was like asking the wolves not to attack the sheep. And to have traded away the Vexin once more, the very land Henry had once given up for me.

Was I fit to care for young Marguerite? Who else did she have but me? A pox on her father for denying me my own daughters and thrusting this poor waif into my lap, then trying to control her fate.

As for Henry, his hypocrisy was no surprise, but his success as a religious pilgrim was either a tribute to his formidable acting talents or to my ex-husband's gullibility, or perhaps both. No matter. Young Henry would be on the French throne, and thereafter it would be only a short time before I had access to my daughters again.

Give credit to Henry. Much as I despised his person, he was finally turning out to be a protective father, as his father had been before him, even if I had to remind him of his duties.

21

$\mathcal{A}$s I was waiting both for the approaching birth and Henry's return, I was barraged with notes from Rancon. Most of them concerned Richard, which I dutifully answered with honest assurances that he could lisp a few words in langue d'oc and Latin, that he had most remarkable physical coordination, and that he was entranced with music. His second kind of note was more difficult, for he sent me poetic love notes as fast as the runners could deliver them.

> Love cannot be killed
> When it is mutual;
> Love cannot be willed
> Just by the taking.

An obvious reference to the manner in which Henry had captured me in the first place, now long ago.

> I would not pray to God
> To escape my love's enthrallment
> Though every day she brought me pain,
> With faith and hope I would remain
> Her devoted lord.

Yes, he was devoted, in the sense that he didn't cohabit with his wife, or so my spies informed me. Yet I remained jealous. What Aquitanian baron doesn't rove as he rides the heated roads in summer? And though Rancon was two years older than I was, he was still a young man, while I . . .

> Though far from my beloved
> I have no fear—
> So long as I can keep her wishes dear—
> It seems Christmas every day
> Her soul-filled eyes turn my way.

And that was the crux: When could I turn my eyes his way again? How many of Henry's children would he tolerate?

Nevertheless, true to my word, I wrote him about my coming child. He answered—not in verse—that I must not neglect Richard, despite my new duties. In fact, this might be the propitious time for Rancon to assume Richard's education. Would I send him to Poitiers? Then he wrote in langue d'oc a small addition:

> Bele amie, si est de nus
> Ne vus sans mei, ne jos sans vus.

Though I wept, I wrote only that Richard was too young to leave my household.

I named my third son Geoffrey, after Henry's father. The baby looked nothing like Henry or his father, however, though certainly he couldn't be Rancon's. Wizened and dark, small and nervous, he was a stranger in our midst.

I wrote to Henry, who was still on the Continent, that I would be able to travel in time to hold our Christmas Court in Rouen, so he could view his new son. I sent a letter the same day to Rancon—I would meet him in Poitiers after the Nativity. Richard would greet him in Latin.

Henry's response was curt: "I am delighted that my father finally has the namesake he deserves. I shall have to defer the pleasure of greeting my new son, however, till well after the Yule. Please continue your fine work in England."

To Rancon, I wrote: "*Asusée!* Henry must be enamored with some Norman hussy, for he's keeping me at bay. I am leaving at once for Barfleur and hence to Poitiers."

I received letters from both men exactly two weeks later.

From Henry: "I'm foregoing any but the most perfunctory observation so that I may devote myself to military plans. I have a great project in hand."

From Rancon: "Stay where you are. Henry is planning to march on Aquitaine again. The threat is serious—even Hugh and his brothers have stopped fighting everyone else to join in the general defense."

Furious, I wrote to Henry: "My spies inform me that you are going to invade Aquitaine! Have you utterly lost your senses? Answer at once."

He shot back: "Dismiss your spies, my lady; you are misinformed as usual. I am assembling a huge force for the purpose of invading Toulouse for you. You told me that it's yours by the right of your grandmother, who was countess, that your grandfather lost it by going on a foolish Crusade, and that your father wanted you to take it. I hope I understood your family history correctly, because I now plan to do so. Our burgeoning family requires more territories: Normandy and England for Young Henry; Aquitaine for Richard; and now Toulouse for Geoffrey."

I wrote acidly: "Are you utterly without discretion? You have just succeeded in calming Louis's wrath by arranging a marriage between our two children, which would make Young Henry king consort of France. Yet you know well that Louis considers Toulouse one of his own fiefdoms and that by invading Toulouse, you will be invading France. Furthermore, Louis's sister is wed to the count of Toulouse. Do you want to risk our son's future? At least seek Louis's permission for this act."

I didn't hear for a month, after which Henry wrote: "You were correct: Louis is incensed by my plans. Does that make you happy? And why do you say that Toulouse is his fiefdom? The count of Toulouse, Raymond by name, should do homage to Aquitaine, not

France. As for Louis's sister, I should think she'd be grateful if I killed her husband, who is said to be the greatest lecher in Europe."

I prepared to sail at once, but somehow Henry got wind of my intentions and sent a stern message that I was to stay where I was: He needed me to keep the peace in England while he was engaged; I was his other self.

His other self—I moaned aloud when I read the words—yet I knew exactly what he meant. Henry was incapable of sentimental phrases; he referred to his royal self. With a kingdom split down the middle by a sea path, he needed to be two people, and while I had no actual power in England, I was perceived as Henry's other self, which was all that mattered.

During the next four months, Henry assembled the largest army ever seen in Europe except for the Crusades, and there were no pilgrims among Henry's men. King Malcolm of Scotland alone required forty-five ships to carry his troops across the channel. Relying again on the loathed scutage, Henry levied a fine against every man of fighting age—even the clergy—who must give military service or pay the tax. Here in England, the monks and priests turned against their king to a man. Oblivious to criticism and rage, Henry borrowed from the Jews, from his lords, from every family who could be tapped to purchase his army.

When the mercenaries began to march in June, Henry sent me his usual daily bulletins: they'd taken Cahors, then Quercy; then he was lowering castles in the neighborhood of Toulouse itself, then silence.

The thick of battle, I thought; impossible to write. Another month passed, and I knew something was wrong.

In August, I heard from Rancon: He was in Woodstock! Never before had he come to England unannounced. I left London at once.

He was waiting in Tintagel, sitting at the desk. "Did you bring Richard?"

"Of course." I leaned to kiss him. "What a marvelous surprise."

He looked up with cold, triumphant eyes. "Henry lost Toulouse, Joy."

I gasped. "He never loses!"

His lips tightened. "The invincible Henry. Terror of the north. Well, the red comet's fallen from the sky and everyone now knows it was just a beet with a wispy tail after all, and it can even bleed."

"You mean he's wounded?"

His eyes became more chilly. "Don't worry, milady. His body is sound; I was speaking—as you say—metaphorically. But he did lose the battle."

I sank opposite him. "The count of Toulouse must be stronger than we thought."

Rancon then recounted the most incredible tale I'd ever heard. Henry had marched with his massive mercenary army southward, taking castle after castle without losing a single man. At last, he could see the red tiles of Toulouse in the distance. In the meantime, Louis had been riding like an arrow from Paris to Toulouse, and he reached it a few hours ahead of Henry. When Henry charged through the city gates, therefore, Louis was waiting for him. Louis didn't want to fight; he wanted to parley. The two kings had talked earnestly, though no one knew what was said, only that Henry had turned his army back and ridden away without a single arrow being shot.

"*Louis—talked—Henry—out—of—his—attack?*" I gasped in disbelief. "By holy Saint-Denis, how?"

His eyes gleamed. "By offering something in return, a deal—I don't know what."

But wait, still another anomaly. When Henry left the scene, he ordered his army to retreat with him. Becket, however, circling Toulouse with his seven hundred knights, refused to obey. He continued to fight, taking castle after castle.

"Becket disobeyed his king?" We both knew what that meant.

Rancon pushed from the desk. "It's my chance, by God!"

"To do what?"

"Why, to defeat Henry of course! Every aggressor from Caesar onward depends on his reputation as an infallible general! The first lost battle punctures the myth! Every baron in Aquitaine now knows that Henry can—and will—lose!"

"The fact that you might win is hardly an excuse to attack, is it?"

His eyes sparkled with gold points. "Absolutely! I haven't attacked before precisely because Henry was supposed to be invincible."

"Or because he hasn't yet justified your suspicions."

His brows lowered. "How quickly you've forgotten your forced marriage."

"I've not forgotten, nor do I refer to it. I'm speaking of the kind of scorch-and-burn tactics he used against the people of Maine, and later of Normandy. I want to spare my people that fate, and if we attack first or Henry attacks, they will suffer."

He jumped to his feet and grabbed my arms. "Christ, are you so opaque? The fight will come whether you want it or not! All I'm suggesting—no, demanding—is that we pick our own time, which is now!"

"You can demand nothing of your duchess. Nor can you command. I say we will wait until Henry strikes, if he ever does, at which time we will respond, and even then when I give the signal, not before."

His hands dropped as if he were burned. "I apologize; I forgot my place." He returned to the desk. "I've written a report of the events I just described, as well as the suggestion for immediate attack. Of course you will do as you like." He didn't look at me.

"Rancon," I implored, "I'm sorry if I offended you. Surely you don't want my people to suffer." I thought of Suger's observation long ago. "Our barons are incomparable in battle, even against Henry, but they're disorganized, quarrelsome."

He glanced up coldly. "Another criticism, my lady? As your captain, I have the responsibility of holding your troops together. If I've failed, perhaps you should replace me."

I was dumbfounded; I was also deeply aware of Rancon's hands on the desk. His glance held.

"Rancon, please."

To my infinite joy, he rushed around the desk and took me in his arms.

Our love had never been more impassioned, perhaps because for the first time a real difference remained between us.

Henry wrote from Rouen: "The French queen is with child. If it's a boy, what say you to Matilda becoming the queen of France? Come at once to Rouen so that we may confer."

I groaned.

"Don't go," Rancon ordered.

"Oh God, Rancon, I'll be back within two weeks, I promise you."

"Come away with me." He was serious. "This is the time, Joy. Forget Henry for once. This is the time for Richard, the time for you and Aquitaine. Toulouse was a distraction from Aquitaine, but only that. We'll fight together next summer."

I didn't remind him again that I was his overlord. I wanted to go, wanted Richard to be with his father, but what of my other children? "As soon as I have my children placed. Young Henry's taken care of, but Matilda and now Geoffrey . . ."

"You can't stay any longer." He plucked one of my hairs from the pillow and wound it around my throat. "You're my *prisoner*, Joy, and I won't release you."

He sang softly against my ear:

> Like the lark which flies into the sun,
> I soar in love till I'm undone;
> For love summons me to sing,
> To rise on high on burning wing,
> I will love her with my last breath,
> Love the joining which brings me death;
> Worship her burning face,
> Her body, and encompassing embrace,
> Where no act ever fails,

Where Nature herself pales
To behold her skill in love,
  A lark consumed in fire above,
  Forget Tristan and Iseult the fair,
  Antony and his Cleo,
  Aeneas and his Dido,
  Who were there
  Before us.
I swear that their erotic claims
Were mere embers to our flames.

"That's the finest troubadour song I ever heard," I said truly.

"Because I had the finest inspiration. I love you, dear Eleanor."

I stayed as long as I dared. We sailed together from Sandwich, then separated in Barfleur as he turned south to Aquitaine. I watched him on his huge black destrier until he was lost in the mists. I felt the usual wrench, and much more: With all our love-making and protests of transcendent feeling, the politics of our situation had finally driven a wedge between us. I fought the urge to call him back, or—even more compellingly—to follow him.

Henry waited in the chilly courtyard of Rouen, eyeing me with a show of forced levity. "Holy Saint-George, you're a ripe plum. What's your secret?"

For a moment, my heart squeezed. Then I saw that Henry was referring to himself. He looked ill.

"My secret is chastity," I said brightly.

"We'll change that. Christ, I've missed you."

He glanced at his brood. "What a challenge, eh? Normandy and England for Young Henry, Aquitaine for Richard, and now we have Geoffrey." He grimaced. "I'd thought to put Toulouse on his platter—maybe I'll get Brittany for you instead. As for you"—he pulled Matilda's red braids—"what say you to becoming a queen, Squirrel?"

"Mama is the queen."

"Of England, to be sure, but there are other countries in the world."

She took my hand. "I want to stay with Mama."

"So do I, but we can't always have our way."

I saw she was frightened. "Don't worry, darling. Your father means far in the future. I promise we'll never be separated."

Henry's mother was present, of course, as was Becket. I watched the chancellor curiously. He was dressed as richly as ever, and I could see no sign of distress between him and the king. I was even touched when Becket knelt to talk with Young Henry, until I realized that he ignored my other children. Of course, because Young Henry was the heir.

Henry wanted to retire early, but not for love, as it turned out. He'd been kicked by a horse and wanted my advice on treatment. "I've had my Jew and my leecher, but I prefer you."

I placed the candle tree near, then took one taper in my hand. The wound was directly on the anus.

"Gangrene?"

"I believe not." Though serious.

"Hurts like the Devil. Can you cure me?"

I called for a warm salt bath, and while he was sitting in his wooden tub, I prepared a plaster of wheat boiled in oil, which were materials we had at hand. The next morning, I added a little lye, linseed, and black nightshade to the mix. Although at first Henry noisily resisted his syrup of fennel roots, parsley, horseheal, radish, and honey, he finally drank it. He began to improve at once. Everyone remarked that I had cured him, though he was far from perfect and couldn't sit on his horse. I knew and he knew that I'd raised his vital spirits more than anything.

He trusted me, God help him.

Six weeks later, Queen Constance of France retired to the birthing chamber. Henry, Becket, Empress Matilda, and I were huddled tensely in Rouen tower, awaiting our own spy in Paris to bring us the news.

"S-s-someone's crossing the moat!" Becket called from the window.

The runner was sweating despite the cold. "A girl! Called Alais!"

Henry did a little jig. "Four daughters! Four riders of the Apocalypse! Poor 'barren' king!"

The runner finished his cup. "The queen died in childbirth."

"Of mortification, no doubt," Henry japed.

I felt a faint chill off the river. I prayed that I wasn't pregnant again.

The runner offered his cup for a refill. "King Louis is getting married again."

All levity melted.

"Married to whom?" I asked sharply.

"Adèle of Champagne."

"God's feet," Henry said quietly.

I knew exactly what he meant. Suger had always advised Louis to marry southern women to offset the power of his ducal lords in the north, especially Thibault of Champagne, and twice he'd done just that: first me, then Constance of Castile. Adèle was Thibault's daughter, which meant that Louis was allying himself with his former enemy, and thus he would be a greater threat throughout Europe. Beyond the political implications, I was aware that Adèle was also the sister of Henry of Champagne, the future husband of my Marie. What a tangle: Louis would be both father and brother-in-law to his own daughter. I didn't try to determine what Young Henry would be when he entered the family.

"How many daughters can you have before you produce a son?" Henry wondered aloud to his mother.

"I had two sons," she answered, "and dear Eleanor has had four." Which didn't answer the question.

"Louis is putting the issue to trial," I answered. "However many times it takes, he'll keep trying."

We were subdued. The name Champagne revived many memories for me; Marie would soon be creating her court. The next time

317

Petra went to France, I would send Marie copies of my grandfather's poems. Let her set her standard high. Would I dare to
include Rancon's song of the lark?

"When Louis has a s-s-son," Becket began, "he may renege on
our arrangements for Young Henry."

Henry stared. "Why?"

"So he won't have to give up the Vexin as Marguerite's dowry," I
answered for Becket. "England becomes less attractive, certainly
not worth the loss of his favorite Vexin. In fact, my lord, he may
withdraw from our marriage contract entirely."

"The Vexin is mine!" Henry roared. "I gave it to him as a gesture,
but I never meant to lose it forever! And he promised it, by God, as
Marguerite's dowry!"

"Queen Eleanor is right," Becket opined. "He may not permit
the marriage at all."

"Listen!" I grabbed Henry's arm. "We could have Young Henry
marry Marguerite now, while Louis is distracted. Then the Vexin is
ours! Let's do it!"

Henry was quick. "God's eyes, I like your spirit, Eleanor!"

Becket frowned. "An excellent suggestion, except that we must
attain a papal dispensation permitting the marriage between children."

"Pope Alexander is a notorious prig," Henry pointed out.

Becket's smile broadened. "Prig or not, he'll see it our way."

Three weeks later, we had our dispensation.

Henry and I went at once to prepare Young Henry. We found him
and Richard playing tournament in the nursery.

Henry roughed his son's curls. "Young Henry, how would you like
to be married?"

"Very much, I *would*," the boy said with surprising conviction,
"but my eagle won't let me."

Henry looked at me, puzzled.

"His eagle is his invisible counselor."

Henry knelt. "Listen! I'm going to tell you a very important
secret, Young Henry. Your mother is your eagle."

"No, she's not! My eagle has wings and claws."

"So does your mother, but she shows them only at night, a strong bird from Aquitaine. Did she ever tell you how she hunted gazelles with eagles on the Crusade?"

"Did you?" My son's eyes widened. "What's a gazelle?"

"A very small deer."

"And you're going to marry a little dear," Henry said. "Her name is Marguerite."

"Mah-geet," Young Henry repeated. "When can I have her?"

"Soon." Henry rose, satisfied.

That same day, Robert of Newburgh delivered the French princess to our care. At two, she was a bewitching black-eyed baby with long, straight lashes. Young Henry, however, did not find her charming.

"She's not a gazelle! And she stinks!"

He gave her a hard push to the floor, where she started crying. I picked her up.

"I want to marry a gazelle!" Young Henry bellowed. "You promised!"

"Your father was japing." I patted the little princess. "My hunter will find you a fawn as a pet, but you will wed Marguerite. She'll be like your sister."

"Sister." Richard reached for her boot.

I kissed her wet cheek. "And I'm your mama, dear."

She drew back and stared at me. "Ma-ma."

I wondered how she recognized the word, since she'd never known a mother.

The day Louis left France for Troyes to be wed, I put my children and Marguerite in a litter to be carried the short distance from our palace to the Cathedral in Rouen, for the winter day was bitter cold and windy. Wrapped in furs, Becket and Henry and I crossed the Church Square to the portal of Saint-Etienne. In the vestibule, Becket carefully removed his sword and spurs. We then stepped silently into the great gray edifice, where we huddled under the hurl of massive stone ribs. Suger's style of architecture had swept all across Europe, but here in Rouen, in the pale silvery light of the winter, a frosty God entered the tall windows.

"Where are they?" Henry asked irritably; his voice echoed hollowly in the cavernous space.

"There," Becket replied.

Archbishop Rotrou of Rouen walked slowly to the altar with the two papal legates. At the sound of the sacring-bell, we shuffled unevenly from the door to meet them. I carried Marguerite, while the other children marched behind me. Young Henry wore a scarlet cape embroidered with three golden lions and a small golden band atop his shining curls. He was incredibly beautiful, like a gilt angel, and his sweet face imbued the cynical occasion with dignity.

Matilda held his hand throughout the ceremony and once kissed his hair.

Now almost three, Richard had blond hair like mine, but I could see Rancon in his profile. He stood perfectly still, like the good boy he was, and fondled his sword.

We'd left little incorrigible Geoffrey in the nursery, for he could be as disruptive as an otter.

The ceremony was meticulously legal; Henry answered for Young Henry; I answered for Marguerite; the legates confirmed that the Pope blessed the union between children, waiving all restrictions. The contracts conferring the dowries were produced and we guided the dimpled hands to make their marks. Everything went well until I put Marguerite to the cold floor to prostrate herself before her husband. She screamed mightily until I lifted her again, then fell promptly to sleep.

The deed was done, our oldest son was prince of France, and we had the Vexin—well, almost, for we must take quick possession. Again, we paused at the portal so Becket could arm himself; he was to lead our army in lieu of Henry, who was not yet recovered from his wound.

The Church Square was now crowded with Becket's seven hundred knights, and Henry's mercenaries awaited him outside the gate.

"Are there any restrictions on my attack?" Becket asked Henry.

"Take the Vexin, take the string of castles that goes with it, then ride to Paris if you like!" Henry slapped the chancellor's arm.

"I go, too!" Richard cried.

"Not to fight against an anointed king, darling," I said. "Your father wouldn't permit such a heresy."

Henry burst into laughter.

Yes, very good-humored. My son was guaranteed the throne of France and I was expecting another child. Even with his wound, Henry had done his duty.

Becket cut a bloody swath across Normandy, becoming legendary for his brutality; he slaughtered every living thing in his way, peasants and their cattle, even chickens on their roosts, while women fled with their children to the woods. He was stopped only when he fell ill.

Henry rushed to Saint-Gervais, where Thomas was bedded. By coincidence, he arrived the very day Louis came from France to visit Becket as well. Henry wrote jubilantly that Louis agreed to forfeit the Vexin and the castles as part of Marguerite's dowry. He did demand, however, that Henry crown Young Henry and his bride as king and queen of England at once in the manner of French monarchies, to assure their proper succession to the throne.

I could have kissed my ex-husband; he'd accomplished exactly what I wanted for my son.

By the time my daughter Eleanor was born in Domfront in early spring, Henry and I had shared the same household for seven months, the longest we'd ever been together, though not as long as Rancon and I had been together in Angers. Of course I wrote Rancon of the new baby, but I received no answer.

On the eve of the fighting season, Henry announced that he'd invited all the Aquitanian nobles to Domfront for baby Eleanor's christening.

"Even the Lusignan brothers?" I asked. Henry hated the Lusignans, and even I was wary of Hugh, but that was not my real question.

He rattled off names from La Marche to Gascony, including the Lusignans, but not Richard of Rancon. I had a growing malaise, even guilt. I would have suspected some ulterior purpose in Henry's party concerning Aquitaine, except that the great families of England and Anjou were also included. Still, Henry hadn't noticed when his other children were born; they'd been christened in privacy.

"Life ahead is a broad golden ribbon," he said proudly when I asked, "and I want all our subjects to enjoy it with us."

At the rear of the palace, I transplanted blooming bushes and potted trees from Anjou, then decorated them with bright red hearts to celebrate Saint-Valentine of Rome and Saint-Radegonde of Poitiers, saints dedicated to love. Let my namesake begin her life in love. Yet I summoned the famous troubadour of the moment who despised love, the acerbic Marcabru. Let Baby Eleanor also be exposed to a first-rate cynic.

The same papal legates who'd made Young Henry's marriage possible agreed to officiate; Bishop Arnulf was to hold the infant. The day before the ceremony, our first guests arrived. Among my women friends, only Mamile was able to attend. The four Lusignan brothers arrived with a large entourage, as if ready to attack, and Hugh greeted me for all of them. He was bald as an egg, and—like Mamile—double his former size.

"Greeting, my lady," he said stiffly. "You haven't changed, at least not on the surface."

"Nor in my heart, Lord Hugh. I've missed you sorely all these years."

"If so, you knew where I was."

I nodded. "I plan to go to Aquitaine this summer."

"Oh?"

No wonder he was dubious.

When the bell rang for None, Henry and I led a solemn procession to the garden altar, which was constructed of lilies and roses. Bishop Arnulf carried Eleanor on her cradleboard to the waiting legates. The company formed a semicircle on the grass in front of us, and the sanctification began. Eleanor's tiny fists opened and closed as she squinted at the men in front of her.

A single lute struck a plaintive chord and people began to move and talk. Henry and I thanked the legates and Arnulf, who gladly gave his charge to her waiting wet nurse. As we were still engaged in this ceremony, Mamile nudged me sharply in the back.

"Joy," she whispered urgently in my ear, "Rancon is here."

22

*A*s Mamile spoke these fateful words, a thousand starlings blackened the sky and descended into my potted trees in a noisy, poisonous cloud, dropping their sticky rain upon us.

"Help!" Henry cried, laughing. "Bring us cover!"

In short order, we retired to the palace and sent our beaters to frighten the birds away. In the confusion, I pulled Mamile to one side.

"Where is he?"

"In the stable, when last I heard. Soothly, he's here, Joy!" Her black eyes sparkled and her matronly flesh quivered like pudding.

"Does he plan to come in the open?"

"I don't know."

A soft wooden horn from the garden signaled that peace again prevailed. The company, laughing and wondering at the strange happening—was it an omen?—moved back to the altar. Now muted horns gave way to clackers, the merry tambourines, the signal for the *estampe*. I took my place on the platform beside Henry and we watched for a few heartbeats before he leapt to the grass and disappeared among the guests, then returned and sat a few moments, then was off again, restless as a flea. The dance ended and Marcabru appeared.

"Who's that mangy cur?" Henry asked.

"The most talented man in Aquitaine, I'm told." Told by Rancon, who'd been his mentor.

"Then you should give him better rags to wear."

Marcabru affected an artfully ragged robe. He strummed and the crowd fell silent. In the background, the rebec began its groan, then the dissonant viol, and I thrilled to the familiar beat. Such energy, such anger and passion.

'Tis April and the streams run clear;
Lovers roll sans fear
   In ditches deep with green
   Where they can't be seen.

Watch the lady of lilies and the stud in her bed.
Her lover, though not her husband 'tis said;
Yet she's not so evil as snake's construct
For her husband also fucks in the muck

   And dares not reproach her with a belt
   Until Hell can make his own sins melt;
   Ugh! Enjoy your helling,
   While the tongue probes the swelling
   Where pain is felt.

I coughed into my hand to conceal my gasp. Could this be deliberate?

"Salisbury, you old rascal!" Henry called, sighting a friend. Apparently, he hadn't listened to the lyrics, though I noticed that John of Salisbury approached with a knowing smirk.

Marcabru continued his scurrilous way for three more verses, but the theme no longer seemed so directly applicable to me. Perhaps I was too sensitive.

The long twilight mellowed; the light became diffuse, as if filtered through linen. I ordered that torches be lighted so the dancing could continue.

"Come, Joy, we're not too royal to dance." Henry stood before me with his hand extended. "The lily of Aquitaine! No, by damn, the lily of the world!"

I stepped off the platform. The musicians changed their rhythm to a more stately cadence and the other dancers stood back. To my astonishment, Henry began to sing in a low growl:

Whoever beholds Joy in her fame
As she sways in the dance,
Must grant that she deserves her name
As Queen of Romance.
Were the lands all mine
From the Elbe to the Rhine,
I'd count them as little case
If the queen of England
Lay in my embrace.

The viols soared; our guests sighed.

"When will that be, Joy?" Henry asked softly.

"Soon, very soon."

"Tonight? I have a wooden leg."

"You're incorrigible, my lord." I laughed lightly.

Once on the green, I continued dancing as one after another of my Aquitanian friends took my hand. I was with Hugh, dour Hugh with his glistening pate, turning in circles against the hibiscus tubs, when we lost touch. He took my hand again, pulled me into the shadow, and I was crushed against Rancon, kissing as if life were at an end.

"I thought you weren't coming," I said breathlessly.

"When I saw that rapacious goat mooning over you, I almost wished I hadn't."

"You're mad."

"I grant you."

"Joy, are you there?" Henry called from nearby.

We managed to pull apart just as the bushes were swept aside.

"Ah! They're beginning a royal dance just for us, and I—who's with you?"

326

"Rancon of Taillebourg," Rancon said, cleverly omitting his Christian name. "Captain for the duchess in Aquitaine. At your service, my lord." He bowed slightly.

"Taillebourg," Henry repeated slowly. "Part of the Angoulême dynasty."

"Yes, my lord."

"I've heard of you."

"Rancon led my troops for me on the Crusade," I said hastily, taking Henry's arm. "We're like brother and sister."

Henry shook me off. "I thought you weren't coming."

"I changed my plans. I hope you don't mind."

"Not at all. Did I interrupt a conversation?"

"We hadn't yet begun to talk," Rancon said suavely. "I had just given her the kiss of peace."

"How is that possible," Henry asked in a dangerous voice, "when such kisses are exchanged only between warriors?"

Rancon was equally steely. "And from vassal to lord; Eleanor is my duchess, the ruler of Aquitaine."

Before Henry could respond, I stepped between them. "Now that you've greeted me, Rancon, won't you join our frivolity?"

"Yes, but first I want to make a request of the king."

Henry paused. "Go on."

"I wish your new daughter's hand in marriage."

I stiffened. "Rancon!"

He turned an innocent face in the flickering light. "Am I too late? I rode as fast as I could—surely she's still available."

"If this is a jape, sir, I find it in poor taste," Henry said icily.

"I assure you I'm serious. Of course we won't consummate until the damsel is at least three; and I can offer you a good portion of Aquitaine as my dowry, which will save your having to conquer it."

"Rancon, that's enough!" I scolded lightly. "I know your bizarre humor, but Henry thinks you're serious."

"I am serious, deadly serious. One must move rapidly in your family."

Henry dropped my arm. "Joy, I'll await you on the dancing area. Dispose of this captain in your own way." And he left.

"Rancon, you truly are mad. Why did you goad him so?"

"I'll give you my reasons tomorrow. Find a time and place; tell Mamile."

I was strangely hurt. "You didn't mean it about baby Eleanor, did you?"

He laughed softly. "Of course I did. Have you not heard the tale of Oedipus, who fell in love with his own mother? If I'm your son, I'll have constant access, eh?"

And he disappeared.

Henry was talking now to Patrick of Salisbury, no relation to John, and seemed to have forgotten his invitation to the dance. I took the hand of one of his knights and continued until the last musician had folded his instrument. When the torches were nothing but glowing embers, I walked with Mamile to the palace in moonlight.

Henry called to me from the great hall, where he sat with John of Salisbury, Becket, and Bishop Arnulf.

"Joy, come inside. We've just received bad news. I need your advice."

My stomach tightened. Now convinced that Salisbury had not only gossiped about me long ago at Angers but that he'd surely put Marcabru up to his scurrilous lyrics, my mind moved frantically to find a defense. Perhaps he'd even witnessed the "kiss of peace" between Rancon and me.

Henry patted the bench beside him. "Archbishop Theobald is dying at Canterbury and summons Becket and me to come say farewell to him. Do you think we should go?"

I was so relieved that it took a moment to absorb this unexpected news. "You must!"

"Yet what could I do?" Henry argued. "I'm not a physician."

"Nor did he ask you as a physician! You're his friend, my lord! He asked you, which is reason enough. God's heart, Henry, you owe him so much; he virtually put you on the throne."

Henry snapped his fingers under my nose. "I put myself on the throne."

Arnulf shifted on his bench. "You deserve the ultimate credit for your meteoric rise, my lord king, but no star shines in the heavens alone. Archbishop Theobald was a most excellent friend." He turned to Becket. "Surely you agree with me."

Becket looked only at Henry. "Archbishop Theobald backed King Henry's rule as all good Englishmen did; he didn't lead an army."

"So you don't think I should attend him?" Henry asked.

"No, my lord king, I do not. Once you were in power, he showed himself your implacable foe. Did Canterbury not refuse to give up Church jurisdiction over criminals? Is that not the very opposite of the law of your grandfather? Priests can murder and steal at will, providing only that they repent. Or what about the rentals of Canterbury, which lawfully belong to you!"

"For shame, Thomas," I rebuked him, "to talk of policy at such a time. The man is dying. As he enters the roll of necrology, he deserves to be surrounded by good friends."

"Let him be a good friend in return; let him give the king his rightful incomes," Becket replied, ignoring me.

I glanced at Arnulf. "You have my opinion. Now if you will excuse me . . ." I rose to take my leave.

Henry rose with me. "I'll accompany you, my dear."

On the stair, he clutched my waist. "Say yes, darling Joy, I quite l-love you."

I pulled free. "Why, Henry, you've caught Becket's stammering disease."

"No, I'm diseased with love, like a puling boy. Must I beg?"

"Soon, my dear. This has been a long day and I'm still not fully myself."

He stepped back. "Say you love me."

I was alarmed. Henry never spoke of love except in jest. "Of course, you're my husband, the father of . . ."

"Love, damn it, between a man and a woman."

Lust, damn it, of a man for a wench.

"You know I do."

"I hope so." He buried his face against my breast. "I'm glad that baron from the south came tonight—the one from Taillebourg. Now you have some faint idea of the hostility I face every day on your account. Your former husband and every would-be count in Europe wants you and your lands and wants me dead. I must talk with you tomorrow."

And he ran down the steps to the great hall.

Wants you *for* your lands, except that that didn't apply to Rancon. I sank to a step, too weak to go on. Henry must suspect—what else? The reference to Taillebourg couldn't have been accidental. How could Rancon have been so indiscreet?

At dawn, I joined Rancon in a dew-drenched thicket behind the Benedictine abbey. Without speaking, he pulled me down a steep path toward the Varenne River, where he'd hidden a small boat. Still silent and not looking at me, he bent over the oars, cleaving through tree shadows reflected in the water. Fish leapt with startling splashes; birds shrilled above. He turned into a cove a mile below the palace, then jumped knee-deep into the water. I followed.

He secured the boat, glanced up the river, then beat into the woods to a game blind.

"Here," he whispered, and we sank behind the stakes.

For the first time, he met my eyes. "Joy, Henry's struck a deal with the count of Toulouse."

It was the last thing I expected—or wanted—to hear. Always policy!

"Yes?"

"That's what he gained from Louis: Toulouse will give homage to Aquitaine instead of to France."

"As it should," I said irritably. "It always did until my grandfather lost it."

His eyes gleamed like a fanatic's. "Listen! Not just to Aquitaine, but to Henry, the duke of Aquitaine."

I heard him. "You mean Henry the duke consort!"

"Not anymore, not in the eyes of Toulouse. I told you when Henry turned away from Toulouse that he'd struck a deal."

"I remember what you said," I admitted slowly. And I did—at Tintagel, but the words hadn't registered. "My God! What sort of deal?"

"What does it matter? Henry won't keep his part of the bargain anyway, depend on it, and the count of Toulouse is hardly any more trustworthy. But at least we know he recognized Henry as duke. What does that make you, my lady?"

I stared into his hard eyes as memory rolled: Suger in the valley of the Chevreuse, revealing that France had occupied Aquitaine. But bloodlessly, and Suger had been willing to listen to reason, to protect me. Needless to say, Louis had probably never known, and, as we'd all noted many times, Louis wasn't Henry.

Rancon smiled cynically at my silence. "I'm glad you finally understand. We're going to fight Henry this summer on your behalf. And now you can't remind me that you're the duchess, since that title has become meaningless."

I winced, as I should.

"I hate to see you fight Henry."

"Why? Do you want him to assume your title? If so, tell me now!"

I couldn't answer. If he didn't know how much I dreaded losing him, no words could inform him now.

"Well? I'm waiting."

I shuddered. Of course I wanted to retain Aquitaine, my title, the source of my incomes, my connection with the past, my very person. But to fight? I recalled Rancon's own description of Henry in Normandy. Or, better, in Toulouse. Couldn't I, too, strike a deal?

"No, but . . ." I became distracted, as strong feeling warred with reason. Rancon was treating me as if I were another man. Of course my position dictated that I act as a man, but not with Rancon, not after all this time. Was I losing my beauty? We hadn't seen each other for two years, when he'd sung to me then about a lark ascending into the sun. Had I changed so much? Had he forgotten his love letters? What had altered?

He went on. "I'm wasting time and words. Joy, you must come to Poitiers now, at once, with us. You have no choice. We have a large enough force to protect you—Hugh brought over a hundred men."

"What will I tell Henry?"

"Why tell him anything? He knows the facts; he'll realize that you do, too. Or if you must dissemble, tell him you're going to visit your family. He can't stop you."

"No, I suppose not."

"Or say that you want Richard to begin his training. I'll be his tutor in arms." For the first time, his face softened. "Tell me about him. Is he here with you?"

"Of course, in the children's quarters with his nurse, Hodierna."

As I described Richard's abilities, I became heartsick at the prospect of attacking Henry. What if we lost? Would my people live under an iron heel, as Rancon described the Normans? And if I weren't duchess, if Rancon were no longer my captain . . . I racked memory for Suger's counsel: *compromise.* Henry'd often told me how he hated to fight, how he never killed in battle; surely I could persuade him to spare Aquitaine—in return for?

Perhaps I could invoke family feeling. Henry had been kind to my sister's leprous boy; he was kind to his own brothers and sisters (except for impetuous Geoffrey—I still didn't know exactly how he'd died), to his mother—in fact, to his entire family, including his bastard children. I came back to the salient truth: He controlled the destinies of Geoffrey, Matilda, and now little Eleanor, yes, of Young Henry and even Richard. Could I make him their enemy? Wouldn't it be better to play on his kindness? Rancon might want to protect Richard, but Henry was in a better position to do so. And he was certainly in a better position to harm him.

"I'll join you within the month," I said.

His brows drew down. "You'll ride with us tomorrow! God's spurs, Joy, the man is stealing your duchy! You can't risk staying here another day."

I touched his arm. "I have a conference with Henry this afternoon—I'll talk to him then."

He suddenly pulled me awkwardly into his arms. We sank onto the dank earth.

"Forgive me, I shouldn't, promised myself I wouldn't, but I can't help myself! Oh God, Joy, if you knew how I suffer!"

I was wildly happy. Oh, how I loved him. I would do anything he asked. Anything!

And yet . . . Rancon, too, might have an ulterior motive. If he couldn't persuade me with words, was this another strategy?

"**God's teeth, you** have wet leaves all over your tunic!" Henry brushed my backside vigorously. "Did you fall?"

"Ye-yes." I cleared my throat My heart drummed—could he hear it?

"Where? Down by the river? Wait, you're muddy."

My mind flew. "I thought to take an early-morning ride and my horse reared. I'm sorry; I should have changed."

He took my arm. Now I was aware of Rancon's odor on my person, not only his manly fragrance, but the smell of sex. Henry seemed not to notice, nor could he possibly intuit the invisible impression of love on my body. My senses were still soaring.

Servants were folding trestles, and sweeping ashes from the torches as Henry led me to a rocky overcrop above the river.

"A happy occasion, eh?" He guided my hand to his lips. "I enjoy domestic life," he continued. "Each day smooth as an ox's eye." He turned my hand over, and ran his tongue along my lifeline. "You're driving me mad, you know."

"I hope I'm fully recovered before the fighting season begins."

He released my hand. "I'm not going to fight this summer. I want to remain here with you."

"But Louis—"

"Didn't I tell you? When I visited Becket's sickbed in the Vexin, when Louis came at the same time, we agreed on a truce."

"No, you didn't mention it." How very odd. "However, there's always Wales, or Ireland." My eyes asked, Or Aquitaine?

"I've done as much in Wales as I can for now, and Ireland will wait."

I smiled. "Since you're free, then, go to Theobald in Canterbury, I urge you. I pity the poor man."

"Save your pity. He's been my enemy, as Becket pointed out; I'll not tolerate an archbishop who defies the king's law, even if he's dying. My task now is to find someone to replace him, someone who will do my will for a change. You might help me on this score; I value your opinion."

As he had with Arnulf? "Someone to crown Young Henry and Marguerite," I said automatically. "Nevertheless, go to Canterbury; say farewell, Henry."

"I've already sent my farewell, and my regrets. I'll stay exactly where I am."

"You're not planning to ride south?"

His eyes studied me. "Do you want to be rid of me?"

"On the contrary, I hoped we could go together. I want to show the children Aquitaine. And I have business."

"What business?"

"My uncle Ralph tells me that the salt mines near La Rochelle need rebuilding."

He cracked his knuckles. "Then use runners to confer; send them twice a day if it pleases you. I won't have you exposed to those mad barons again."

We both studied a swoop of gulls over the water. A strong breeze dissipated Rancon's odor on my body, though I still felt waves of passion in my person.

Suddenly, Henry pushed the snood off my heavy hair. "Turn your face—I love to study your profile. Would you believe that I adore your nose?"

Was he japing? I'd never seen my nose, of course, but noses are rarely objects of adoration. I smiled into his frosty eyes. "You're a troubadour, my lord." Though a nose was hardly an ascending lark.

"Yes, we'll have a domestic idyll. Enjoy the children, enjoy each other." He licked his lips. "When did you say you would be ready?"

"Perhaps in two weeks, which gives me just time for a rapid visit to Poitiers."

His face flushed. "I just told you—"

"But I am the duchess of Aquitaine, and I take my responsibility seriously. One of those responsibilities is to make a personal appearance, something no runner can do." I looked at him directly.

"I relieve you of your responsibility."

"Then I relieve you of England!"

"England is not in constant turmoil. And I did give you autonomy there, you admit."

"Autonomy to execute your orders, for of course I'm not a birthright queen."

His eyes narrowed. "Speak your mind."

"I am a duchess, my lord. The turmoil in Aquitaine may be the result of my absence."

"According to whom? You've been conferring with someone."

The man was a wizard—I must be careful.

"Hugh of Lusignan asked me to return—and to bring Richard." Poor Hugh had stood in for Rancon on the Crusade; let him do so again.

"Richard?" Henry frowned. "Why Richard?"

"To be trained for his future role. Why, he hardly knows the language. I would find a tutor."

Henry rumpled my tumbled locks. "I want you with me this summer. We deserve a little domestic tranquillity, Joy, both of us."

I shook my head playfully. Of course, if Henry were with me all summer, he couldn't do mischief in Aquitaine, a fact that should mollify Rancon. Not that he wanted domestic tranquillity; I'd heard him yesterday ask the master of the hunt about the game, and I doubted not that he would seek carnal comfort in the local taverns. Yet, even with his hypocrisy, I gave him credit for his shrewdness, for he must sense that I was weary of court duplicity, weary of the confusion of policy with personal sentiments. At the same time, he'd reminded me that I was queen of England, no small position, and I took pride that I did do well with the English. Wouldn't Rancon understand? After all, he'd said many times that he wanted to avoid Henry in the field, and if he had Richard . . .

"Then I'll send him on his own. He's eager to begin his training—I have a most excellent tutor in mind."

"Who?"

"My own captain, Rancon. He was trained by my father."

"The man in the bushes? Your father must have omitted courtesy. I wouldn't want Richard to confuse sarcasm for civility."

"You don't know Rancon. Take my word—"

"Where the preparation of my sons is concerned, I'll make the decisions, my lady, which brings me to the reason I asked to speak with you. I've arranged to put Young Henry in another household."

"With Louis?"

His eyes bulged. "Louis!"

"His father-in-law, after all, and his overlord."

"God's eyes, I want the boy to learn something about England! What could that French eunuch teach him except to be a monk? No, I plan to put him with Becket."

"Becket!" It was my turn to gasp. "That cold, grasping sycophant?"

"Is that your notion of Becket?" He seemed amused. "Perhaps he is, yet you can't deny his intelligence. And he knows the English law better than I do myself. Becket is the perfect choice."

"I'll agree if you permit Richard to return to Aquitaine."

"Do you take me for your lily Louis? Or for your adoring father? I don't bargain my decisions away! You don't know how to live with a strong man, milady. I am a slave to your charms, as much as any man could be, but I make the decisions for my sons, every single one of them. Is that understood?"

"No, it is not! I conceded that you should supervise Young Henry's education because he'll be the English king, but with Richard—"

"Good, then that's settled."

Far from it.

"Will Becket take him to England?" I asked, leaving the dangerous subject of Richard.

"I doubt it."

"Before he expires, Archbishop Theobald could crown Young Henry and Marguerite."

"When the next archbishop is in place, that will be his first duty, which I'll make him understand if he wants the appointment." He put his arm around my waist. "Sorry if I barked at you. Of course you have an important role to play in our sons' futures, but you offended me by suggesting that rude churl from Taillebourg. Forgive me?"

I had to—or I'd reveal too much. I accepted his kiss at the same time that I realized I'd been outfoxed. With all his "domestic idyll" palaver, Henry was simply waiting for Archbishop Theobald to die so that he could make his move.

Not daring to trust anyone, I rowed the small barque alone to the woody trysting place to await Rancon. He was there before me.

"Don't say anything. I can tell by your eyes that you're not coming." He didn't embrace me.

"Listen! I have good news: You don't have to fight in Aquitaine! Henry plans to stay here in Domfront all through the summer. He's not going to take up arms—he told me! He and Louis have a truce!"

"Why? Tell me the truth, Eleanor."

"Why what?" I grew angry. "Why should I lie?"

"Stay in Domfront and do what? What is his motive?"

"He says he wants to be with his family—he's in a domestic disposition."

"You mean he's in a fucking disposition."

"Rancon!"

"And so are you, my lady! Admit it!"

I reached for him. "If you believe that, why are you leaving me?"

"We could win this summer, depend on it. This is our moment! And especially when Henry prefers to distract his beauteous queen with love! But we can't win without you as our rallying point! So exactly what are *you* accomplishing? Or are you destroying?"

"I never claimed he loved me!" I said hotly.

"God, Joy, how he knows your character!"

"No, I know *his* character! His motive isn't lechery; he's staying this summer because he's waiting for the archbishop of Canterbury to die."

"A good excuse. What's yours?"

He crashed into the woods.

Becket and Young Henry left two days later to live in Becket's residence in Bayeux. Though my son wept at leaving me, he was attached to Becket.

Henry and I then settled into our "idyll." He conducted court business as usual, hunted, and waited for Theobald to die. I saw no sign that he thought of Aquitaine.

Nevertheless, I was in a good position for daily missives from my uncle in Poitiers, and I kept close governance on my duchy, as I had when in France. Amaria visited Aquitaine to see her sisters and carried a list of directives for my own curiosity. When she returned, she reported that my barons were riding the roads in their usual high-spirited manner, though actual clashes had been few. Rancon was cloistered at Taillebourg; his wife was rumored to be dying.

23

$\mathcal{A}$s I had anticipated, the death of Archbishop Theobald of Canterbury brought Henry's preoccupation with domesticity abruptly to an end. He summoned Becket back from Paris, where he'd taken Young Henry, to discuss a replacement.

Still as beautiful as an angel perched on his saddle, Young Henry, now six years old, sat with cocked head and squared shoulders; he ordered his servants like a miniature despot.

I ran down the steps. "Did you enjoy Paris, my darling?"

"Oh yes, Mama; Father took me with him to sing with the choir in Notre Dame."

Father, meaning Louis.

"And did you see your sisters?"

He frowned, puzzled. "You mean Princess Alais? She's Mahgeet's sister, not mine.

"Marguerite's," I corrected him. "I meant Marie and Alix, your older sisters."

"They're not my sisters."

"More so than Princess Alais, for I'm their mother."

He wasn't interested. He looked down at Richard. "I'm a duke now and you're not. I did homage to Father for Normandy!"

I put my arm across Richard's shoulder. "You're also older, Young Henry; Richard will soon be duke of Aquitaine."

I tried to remember myself at Young Henry's age: Had I been so arrogant?

339

Henry ignored both boys. "The archbishop of Canterbury is the most important appointment I've yet made, Thomas, and I need your advice. I don't want another Theobald to be intransigent about the laws and customs of my grandfather. Never an archbishop who puts the Church above me!"

"Absolutely correct, my lord. Canterbury must defer to royal prerogatives rather than Rome's; you know my position on this. Do you have s-s-someone in mind?"

"No need for haste, is there?" Henry replied. "So long as the see is without an archbishop, the crown can collect the rentals."

"And insist on secular law," Becket agreed, smiling, two friends again in collusion. "Accustom the monks to the king's rule."

I stroked Young Henry's hair. "Your new man must crown our prince at once! Louis is anxious on the matter and, frankly, so am I."

Becket smiled. "I share your concern for my boy, and I have a thought. Though the archbishop of Canterbury traditionally crowns the king, could we not send an emissary to the Pope asking permission to use some other archbishop in extremis? Then we would be free to choose the new archbishop at our leisure."

"Do it, Henry!" I cried. "Let our prince be crowned!"

Henry squeezed my arm. "I'll send an emissary this very day to Pope Alexander. Will that make you happy?"

"Oh, yes, thank you." For the first time I ever remembered, I voluntarily kissed his cheek.

"The archbishop of York could do it," Becket assured me. "Perhaps the king should write him, as well."

Pope Alexander sent back his assent at once, though he hoped that his most beloved king would expedite the appointment at Canterbury with all haste. On the other hand, he wrote, Henry should remember that the election of the archbishop lay in the monks' hands, although he could suggest his preference.

"I'll see that they vote for my man," Henry promised blithely.

Becket returned to Bayeux with Young Henry; Henry took our

family to Falaise to winter with his mother. We were becoming a fixed domestic unit.

I had no word from Rancon.

It's hard to send runners through winter drifts, but as soon as the spring thaw came, I sent a message: "To Rancon, baron of Taille-bourg, greeting. I hope all goes well with you, my lord, and that you're still performing your duties as my captain in Aquitaine. Please send your reply with my runner, who will await your convenience."

The answer was swift. "To Eleanor, duchess of Aquitaine and queen of the English, greeting: until you tell me otherwise, I will continue to look after your military affairs, as well as the commerce. As you can see by the enclosed records, the wine harvest was excellent, likewise the cheese and salt. The weather has been kind; no major fighting has taken place." There followed sheets of reports, most of which I'd already received from my uncle in Châtellerault, and the archbishop of Bordeaux. There was no personal message, not even a query about Richard. I tried not to care.

We remained in Falaise that spring. I'd been married to Henry for many years, but this was the first time I thought of him as a fixture in my life, not that my feelings for him had changed, but Rancon's had apparently changed toward me. I struggled, with moderate success, not to think about it. Henry was probably no worse than most husbands, and better than many: His idea of domesticity was to hunt from dawn to dusk, and though he killed many animals, he gave most of his game away. He read by tallow light well into the night, brought scholars from all over the Continent to instruct him, and conferred with runners from his vast empire. He dropped any pretense of the sentimentality he'd displayed in Domfront and visited my bed on the nights he wasn't studying or—more likely—in the bed of his mistress Belle-Belle, who was ensconced in the village. Though he was a jocular father

341

to our children when he noticed them, and even though Empress
Matilda doted on all of us, it was a strange contrast to my family
life in Poitiers with my father and mother, my many aunts and
cousins; I remembered games and festivals almost daily, songs and
gaity.

One rare day when the family was together, lolling beside the
river, Henry threw himself lengthwise on the grass and informed
his mother and me that he had something of import to tell us. I
became alert; politics was the one subject where Henry and I could
communicate.

"I'm going to make Thomas my archbishop of Canterbury," he
said.

Gulls' screams mixed with the cries of children.

"Am I supposed to laugh?" Empress Matilda rejoined with
incredulity. "I'm not amused, Henry fitzEmpress!"

"I'll not be dissuaded, Mother."

"Since I remember how you appointed that popinjay once
before despite my advice and despite your false promises, I'll not
even try. Let me just say that, frankly, you're a fool, Henry fitz-
Empress."

Henry's voice was deadly. "Fool I may be; I'm also king."

My skin pricked in the hot summer air.

"It won't be the first time that a fool wears the crown. This man
Becket is neither a priest nor a monk, and therefore not fitted for
the title. Nor will the monks of Canterbury ever accept him."

"What do you think, Joy?"

"Why not keep him where he serves you well? Though I, too, dis-
approved his appointment as chancellor, he's proved capable."

"Who said I would discharge him as chancellor?"

I started. "But you must! How can he represent the crown and
the Church at the same time?"

"He can resolve contradictions. Canterbury will abide by my
grandfather's laws as every other see must do." He sat upright. "You
should be delighted—he'll crown Young Henry."

I was suddenly on guard. Was he *dangling* my son's coronation to gain my approval? This plot had surely been brewing in Henry's mind as he'd waited for Theobald to die.

"Richard, not so far!" He was close to the current. My mind opened to the truth: Had Henry *dangled* domesticity and love to me as an excuse to await his moment? As Rancon had said how well he knew me, I felt sick with shame. How could I have been so susceptible?

"He will give me the rents, enforce the law of your father, Mother, protect me from the dictates of Rome." This was what he was *dangling* to his mother.

As Empress Matilda argued—for she was not so easily enticed—Henry studied me. "You haven't answered, Joy."

I smiled slyly. "I would say it's a perfect appointment, Henry. It matters not if he's a priest or a monk, or even if he believes in God at all. He has his nose to the ground, sniffing out demons, which is all you ever wanted."

He burst into laughter. "How well you understand me!"

Unfortunately, I was beginning to. Thank God Aquitaine was still intact—why hadn't I listened to Rancon?

A week later Henry told Becket, who was more excited than I'd ever seen him, though he made the same arguments against his own appointment that Henry's mother had; he appeared apprehensive about passing the scrutiny of the monks of Canterbury.

"Nonsense," Henry cried. "The monks have been conditioned by Theobald to oppose me—I could never permit them to select from among their own ranks."

Becket took me aside. "Does he know wh-wh-what he's offering me?"

"Do you understand what he's asking of you?" I countered.

"Y-yes, and I'll never disappoint him."

"Not if his offer and your understanding are the same thing."

"You're too subtle for me, my lady."

No I'm not, I thought. Fortunately, Canterbury was not my concern; I would probably see less of Becket, which was a positive aspect. Even more important, once Young Henry and Marguerite had been crowned, I could arrange for Richard to be sworn in as duke. Should I write Rancon?

Becket prepared to leave for England at once, with Young Henry beside him. We planned introducing the boy to the barons for their approval—then send Marguerite, then the crowning.

Young Henry explained the honor to his wife. "I'm going to England to become king, Marguerite."

"I thought your father was king."

"My father is going to make me king."

"How?"

"By telling the barons to accept me."

His father, meaning Becket.

Marguerite asked reasonably, "What will become of King Henry, then?"

"He'll continue to rule in Aquitaine."

My heart chilled.

Thanks to the preparations of our justiciar, Richard de Luci, our plans in England went surprisingly well. Young Henry was accepted by the barons, while the monks of Canterbury, grumbling because they saw through Henry's ploy to put his own man in place, grudgingly accepted Becket. Young Henry, as king-elect, graciously gave his consent to accept Thomas as archbishop as well.

On the Saturday before Whitsun, Thomas Becket was ordained as a priest, although he'd never studied orders; two days later, he was consecrated as archbishop of Canterbury.

In Falaise, Henry and I toasted each other at cross purposes, he for the appointment, I for our son, and I planned to leave for Aquitaine.

I was determined to see Rancon.

Just hours before my departure, a runner arrived from England with two missives. Henry opened the one from Becket first: It returned to Henry the Great Seal of England and Becket's resignation as chancellor: He couldn't serve two masters.

"Who's the other master?" Henry cried, bewildered.

"Remember God?"

"Not as Becket's overlord!"

"Open the other packet."

It was from Richard de Luci and full of alarms: the duke of Clare reported that Becket had claimed rentals and lands the king had given Clare for special favors.

"What favors?" I interrupted, puzzled.

"Wait, there's more." Becket had seized Henry's own castle at Rochester and dismissed hundreds of clerks working for the king; he'd seized lands of Kent to gain new rents for the see's coffers.

"And he says nothing about crowning Young Henry," I cried. "You must bring him to task, Henry. This is serious!"

"Get the children ready; we're leaving for England."

My concerns about Aquitaine dissolved in the greater issue of protecting my son's interests. We sailed within a day.

Southampton was gripped by fog. Henry hung over the rail to seek Becket below while I protected my bevy of children and attendants on the slippery boards. By the time we moved forward, Henry was already on the dock, talking to Becket.

"I see my husband!" Marguerite cried.

Young Henry was huddled in the folds of Becket's resplendent fur cape. We made our way cautiously down the plank.

I bent to hug my son. "Greeting, my darling. What a big boy you've become."

He smiled up at me, his new front teeth prominent in his pinched face. "Greeting, Mama; I'm going to be king."

"So you are."

"Look, Young Henry, I have a new sword, and it's real steel!" Richard tapped his brother on the shoulder.

"I have ten steel swords bigger than that," Young Henry replied with disdain.

I stood upright. "Greeting, Archbishop Thomas."

"My lady." He kissed my hand coldly; his glistening face signaled that he no longer had use for me in his new world; I was the enemy, a woman. It was an attitude I knew well.

Later that night in Winchester, I questioned Henry. "How does he justify himself?"

"For which offense?"

I grew irritable. "For not crowning Young Henry, of course."

"That's a small part of the larger question, which is his resignation as chancellor. He claims that the office is no longer needed."

"Is it?"

"Not on a daily basis," he conceded. "Of course, I need a chancellor to represent my secular interests."

"Perhaps Becket no longer considers himself secular."

He stared at me. "How did you know? He's full of pious nonsense about his devotion to God and His great representatives in Rome."

I heard echoes of Bernard of Clairvaux. "Careful, Henry, the man wants absolute power."

"You mean he wants to be a Pope himself?"

"From his acts thus far, I would guess he wants to control England. Listen!"

Henry had never shown much interest in my experience in France with Suger and Clairvaux, but now he listened attentively.

"I see what you mean. And Young Henry is his hostage."

"Otherwise, why dally? He thinks you're impotent because of the boy."

"In the morning, I'll order him to crown the boy at once! If he resists, I'll know his intentions. Damn the traitor!"

In the morning, however, Becket had returned to Canterbury with Young Henry.

"By God, I'll show him who's king! Saddle my horses!" Henry roared.

"Don't follow him," I cautioned. "Use your cunning, Henry. Summon him to us; force him to openly disobey."

Henry instantly cooled, "I should make you my chancellor; you give excellent advice."

Good advice for Henry, perhaps, but counter to my own wishes, for I yearned to put an end to this struggle and go to Aquitaine. I wrote Rancon that Henry's preoccupation with his archbishop might permit us a short meeting in Tintagel where we could discuss our differences, if he could come to England; but before I could send the letter, Henry announced that we would settle in Clarendon.

Once there, Henry summoned learned men to instruct him on England's laws, and laboriously collated them in writing, calling them the Constitutions of Clarendon. Thus he coiled himself under a bush, waiting for the right moment to strike. While he plotted, I rode with my children along the high paths of forests, overlooking the old Saxon donjon called Old Sarum.

Then I had a letter from Rancon and forgot Henry and Becket. He understood the protocol that put Young Henry ahead of Richard in my consideration, but I must now ignore hierarchy and return at once with Richard. Aquitaine was burning, and even my presence—or Richard's—would not cool the embers unless I acted swiftly. Burning where? Who was behind it? Not Henry surely—he was here. I reread the missive, to no avail.

There was not a word of affection.

How could I react swiftly? My runners couldn't even deliver an answer quickly, and then my answer had to be no, I couldn't come. I hated Becket for forcing me to remain in England. I was also in a rage at Henry. What I'd formerly seen as deliberate prudence on his part now appeared as passive dithering. Why should I be audience to his endless moves? Life was not a chess game!

"I understand your strategy, Henry, but for God's sake, take your son off the gaming board! Get Young Henry crowned."

"Try to see the larger picture."

"There's nothing larger than succession," I reminded him acidly, "as you should well know."

That same day, I acquired an unexpected ally. Empress Matilda wrote me from Normandy:

To Eleanor, queen of the English and dearest daughter, greeting:
You must force King Henry to crown his son without delay. Tell him that to do otherwise is dangerous folly, as he should have learned from his own experience. The matter is equally urgent for you, dear daughter, for a different reason. You are a gifted ruler, even as I am gifted, but we are both cursed with our female sex. We can rule in this man's world only through our sons. Heed me, Eleanor, cultivate your boys; see to their educations, their understanding of loyalty both to their countries and to their mother. Do as I say and you will be queen for so long as you live.

Good advice, and an echo of what I'd first observed between herself and Henry. Not that I needed goading, nor was I thinking of my own governance. I pressed Henry daily, risking his increasingly short temper, forcing him to think of Young Henry at every ringing of the hour, but he was just as stubborn as Becket. The law was the issue, he insisted, not any single application of the law, and he met with Becket again and again in public forums, where Becket promised to recant his hard stance. Becket seemed to give in until he added the maddening caveat that he would obey, "saving my order," meaning in every place except the See of Canterbury, which included the better part of England.

"You're earning the contempt of all Europe," I warned Henry. "Even Bernard of Clairvaux was not so openly defiant."

"I don't give a fig for all of Europe, by which I suppose you mean that lily-livered king of France. Becket is disobeying the law of the land and he's close to treason. By entrapping him in some legal manner, I'll prove that even an archbishop is not above the law."

"Prove to whom? Be strong, Henry!"

He struggled for control. "Very well. I've set another meeting with Becket in London, where he's promised to accept the laws according to my grandfather. If he reneges this time, I promise you I'll act."

I wrote again to Rancon that same day that I would return to Aquitaine sooner than I'd indicated. Then I swallowed my pride—or my sanity—and added, "I come because I must, not because of the fires you mentioned. I burn with another flame." At the same time, I cursed myself for my weakness. Had he not made his choice clear? And one thing everyone knows about love is that the fire can't be blown alive from dead ashes. How often would I humiliate myself? How long could I sustain this unrequited long-distance passion? And at what cost?

Moot questions: I had no answer.

Henry and I attended the meeting in London; once the confrontation with Becket was finally accomplished, I planned to leave directly for Aquitaine with my children. As it turned out, the monks objected to a woman attending a Church conference, and for once Henry bowed to their wishes. While Henry was gone, I sat close to a fire with Richard and Matilda to teach them chess. They retired; I sat alone.

The instant Henry entered the chamber, I knew that Becket had again defied him.

"Send for Sir Joscelin," he snapped at the page.

He sank silently beside me and cracked his knuckles. When the young knight arrived, Henry leapt to his feet. "Do you know the whereabouts of Archbishop Thomas of Canterbury?"

"Yes, my lord. He's in residence at his palace here in London."

"Go to that palace at once. Tell the archbishop that he's to bring me my son Young Henry."

Sir Joscelin hesitated. "Bring him when, my lord? On the morrow?"

"Now, at this moment, and I'll brook no delay." When the knight had departed, Henry met my eyes for the first time. "I've reached my limit, Joy."

349

"You're going to pour the hemlock?"

"I'm going to pull back the jesses. Our high-flying friend has forgotten that there's a falconer in control."

While he waited, he recounted Becket's transgressions in detail; formerly, Becket had quibbled about what the laws of Henry's grandfather might be, but this time Henry had presented a written document, his Constitutions of Clarendon; every law and precedent was listed.

"He read them; he wrote me beforehand that he would accept them," Henry told me. "'I accept the Constitutions of Clarendon as writ,' he stated before the monks, then added 'saving my order,' which is a good part of England!"

By the time we heard horses below, a gritty dawn lightened the windows.

Becket entered with a belligerent air. "May I ask on what grounds you dare pull me from my bed, my lord?"

"Where's my son?" Henry answered.

"I'm here," Young Henry whined from behind Becket, "and I'm sleepy."

"He's frightened," Becket added.

"I am removing Young Henry from your care."

"My son!" Becket gasped. "B-but you can't."

"Young Henry is not your son, Thomas," I said. "You have my word on it."

"I'm his spiritual father. Y-y-you put him in my care to instruct him, and I love him."

"You love him as a hostage!" I accused him.

"Hostage? Hostage for what? I swear that I have only his best interests at heart."

"Then why haven't you crowned him?"

"I will—I intend to."

"When he's grown a hoary beard perhaps," Henry said. "You've proved, Thomas, that your intentions are writ in water."

Becket knelt beside the boy. "Tell them what you want, Young Henry. Don't be afraid—be honest."

"I want to stay with Father Becket," my son announced.

Henry took the boy's shoulder. "You belong with your real father."

Young Henry flew into a tantrum worthy of his real father. "Leave me! I hate you! Hate you! You hurt Father Becket!" He stamped on Henry's boot and bit his hand.

Just as quickly, Henry struck the boy violently across the face, then pushed him toward me. "Is this your idea of spiritual guidance?" he roared at Becket. "How dare you turn my own prince against me?"

Becket cried out, "May the Lord forgive you!"

"Best ask for forgiveness yourself, you hypocrite! Now leave, before I strike you, as well."

Becket, pale as a ghost, knelt by the prince. "Calm yourself, my dear; the Lord is always with you, and so am I in spirit. No one can ever separate us."

"I can," Henry reminded him. "Must I call the guard?"

"I'm going." Becket rose. "I'll pray to God to forgive you for tearing my boy from me." To my amazement, tears flowed down his cheeks. "Be merciful with him." He turned to me. "My lady Eleanor, you have a tender heart."

"Oh, Thomas," Henry interjected, his voice now tinged with its familiar jocularity, "best seek refuge in the archbishop's residence. As of this moment, I'm revoking all privileges you held as my chancellor. Your palace here in London, your estates at Eye and Berkhampstead, your fleet, your armor and all your horses, your wine cellar and wardrobe herewith return to the crown."

Becket might love Young Henry—though I doubted it—but this loss wrenched his very soul. I thought he might faint.

"H-Henry, my l-lord, those estates were given me in perpetuity, and I—"

"Sacrificed them when you decided not to be my perpetual chancellor. I'm waiting for you to leave."

Becket threw one more tender glance at Young Henry, then walked through the door. Henry closed it after him.

"Can you prepare the household to ride within the hour?" he asked me.

"Of course. Where are we going?"

He laughed shortly. "What say you to a Christmas at our new estate in Berkhampstead? Do you think you can bear such luxury?"

We made slow progress through a heavy winter rain, arriving at Berkhampstead after dark. My younger children and Marguerite had ridden in a wagon covered with oiled barrels, but Young Henry, Richard, and Matilda had trotted on ponies beside me. All were drenched and chilled, but none complained. Though Berkhampstead was called a manor, it loomed as big as a cathedral when our torches penetrated the driving rain.

The knights pounded on the tall oaken door. "Open in the name of the king!"

After a time, the portals slowly gave way and Henry rode inside on his dripping horse. Quickly, I dismounted and followed him.

"A worthy hovel for a bank clerk's son," he said, his voice echoing, then joined me on a thick Eastern carpet. "We've made ourselves rich this day, Joy."

Frightened staff appeared in the gloom.

"Bring torches!" Amaria ordered.

"The steward!" I called.

A short, fat man bowed before me.

"Prepare us a hot supper at once and show me to the upper chambers."

I told the children and their servants to follow me up the stair, where we would establish a nursery.

"I'll not sleep in a nursery," a thin, imperious voice announced from behind me.

I turned on the step. "Must I carry you like a baby, Young Henry?"

"I'm not a baby! I'll sleep in my father's office, as befits my station."

Henry seized him from behind and ran up the steps. He dropped him at the top.

"Henceforth, you'll obey your mother in all things. Furthermore, the barons may have accepted you, but I haven't. A prince must earn his inheritance. I mean that, Young Henry."

The boy muttered, "I hate you!"

We ate a morose supper in the company of our knights, Amaria and my ladies, Matilda, Young Henry, Marguerite, and Richard. The younger children and their nurses were already upstairs. The dining tier was under a lead roof and the drum of rain made conversation impossible. Young Henry played with his gold plate and refused food. His father sipped his broth grimly. After a time, I excused the children; the rest of us retired to the great hall, where I listened to arguments about the next gambit with Becket. An hour later, I went quietly up the steps; I paused in the door to observe the children.

Young Geoffrey was astride a chair carved like a dragon; Marguerite—still dressed—dozed on a high bed; Baby Eleanor dozed in a cradle; Richard and Matilda were crouched on a fine carpet, where they'd emptied boxes of snails, which Matilda carried with her everywhere. Young Henry, holding to a carved bedpost, watched them.

"This red square will be the princedom of Antioch, where our great-uncle Raymond fought," Richard instructed Matilda. "My army will come from the sea."

He placed a row of snails along a jagged emerald border.

"This big snail will be Raymond." Matilda emptied another box onto the rug.

"That's a stupid game," Young Henry scoffed. "Those snails are dead."

Matilda look up. "They're not! They're just cold."

Young Henry stamped on her line of slugs. "They're dead now!"

"You're mean!" She rose and tried to hit him.

Young Henry scooped a few remaining snails and pushed them onto his fingertips. "Look, I have fat nails!"

Matilda began to cry. "Stop that!"

"Can't make me!" He wiggled his hands in front of her.

"I can make you!" Richard struck his brother on the nose.

Young Henry reeled, but Richard was no match for a boy a head taller than he was. Within moments, Young Henry had forced him to the floor.

"You'll do whatever I tell you to!"

"Won't!"

"We'll see!"

Twisting Richard's arm, Young Henry managed to pull at his own tunic and display his bare member.

"Suck my cock, Richard. Go on, suck it!" He twisted harder and straddled Richard's head. "I'm waiting. Suck it!"

I felled my oldest son with a single blow.

From the floor, he looked up in outrage. "How dare you strike me! You're nothing but a woman!"

I kicked him in the ribs with my heavy boot. "Apologize."

"Woman! Woman!"

I kicked him again and again. "Apologize!"

He tried to roll away, and I stepped on his golden curls. "Apologize!"

"You're hurting me!"

I raised my boot.

"I'm sorry!" he screamed.

"Now to Richard. Say you're sorry!"

"Don't bother!" Richard cried. "I'll never forgive him! He's foul!"

By the time Young Henry uttered his apology, he was weak with pain.

That night, I told Henry what I'd observed.

"I'll beat his arrogance out of him! Damn Becket!"

Neither of us addressed deeper concerns. "Let me work with him, Henry; I'll bring him around."

After the worst Christmas I ever remembered, we went in separate directions, Henry to Woodstock, the children and I to Northampton, a remote castle.

To my children, the bleak approach over flat wastes and frozen rivers seemed an adventure. They cried out at sheep with their wool encrusted in ice, waved at the occasional shepherd, and claimed they heard wolves howling at night. The castle amazed them from a distance, because of its low bulk across the horizon; then, as we entered the circle wall, because of its deer park. Northampton, constructed of local freestone, was our best fortress; it was also our snuggest domicile. Surrounded by a fine stand of oak, the manor was an ancient structure of small rooms and low ceilings, perfect for heating, especially since I'd added modern fireplaces.

Each of the older children had his own closet, which isolated Young Henry. I quickly established a routine: Young Henry was to go forth each day with our master of the hunt, no matter what the weather, while I taught the others from books. When my prince returned in late afternoon, his eyes bright, his cheeks red, we sang and recited poetry. After supper, if anyone was still awake, we played games.

The children thrived. Their exalted position in the world was forgotten and rivalries among them seemed to melt away. Young Henry became the sweet child I so loved, and I was relieved to see that he was especially kind to his pretty young wife, Marguerite. They became inseparable. As for me, despite my combined duties as mother and teacher, I had too much time alone. No matter what the political strains or personal estrangement, Rancon's silence was inexplicable. He'd never withdrawn from me. I berated myself that I was becoming like Louis, but I couldn't help wondering if Rancon had found someone else. After all, he was a widower, a handsome man. . . . And, when I wasn't suffering my personal loss, I worried about Aquitaine. Was it possible Rancon was fighting too hard to write?

Then I had a jubilant letter from Henry: He'd finally trapped Becket in a legal infraction. A man named John the Marshal had summoned Becket on a civil suit concerning rents, and Becket had failed to appear. The archbishop was therefore in contempt of court, which gave Henry the right to bring him before a council of bishops. He'd called the council to gather in Northampton.

I threw the letter to the floor. God's heart, after all my labor with Young Henry, to bring Becket back into his life, especially in another confrontation with Henry. I was confounded.

24

*H*enry greeted me warmly, his children indifferently—it occurred to me that he might not recall their names, though he knew each of his seventy hounds—except for Young Henry. He gazed on the boy coldly.

"You'll sit by me on the bench during Becket's trial," he told the boy.

"No, he won't," I countered. "He has no knowledge of the case. Why be cruel?"

Henry's brows rose. "Cruel? He called Becket 'Father' and kicked at his real parent. Let him learn the true measure of this criminal archbishop."

I slipped an arm over my prince's shoulders. "Then I'll sit beside him."

Henry grinned jauntily. "You anticipate me; I need your support."

When Becket arrived with his entourage of forty, Henry sent him out of our courtyard to stay in a barely habitable Clunaic monastery, a blow to his dignity. A fine beginning.

On the morning of the hearing, I bundled Young Henry and myself in furs to withstand the clammy chill of the chapel where we were assembling. Unlike the great hall, this room was open to the northern gales and the stone floor was often puddled with melting snow. When my boy and I took our places on the platform facing the monks, we confronted a sea of blue faces, red noses, and stamping feet. After an interminable wait, there was a rustle at the back, then an audible gasp.

Becket dragged slowly up the aisle wearing a jeweled miter, a silk and velvet episcopal pall, and he held the heavy silver cross of Canterbury. Then the gasp became vocal: With all his splendor, Becket trod on bare feet!

Someone cried out: "Bread!"

Indeed, Thomas had pinned a crust of bread on his sleeve, a sign to ward off sudden death, as if Henry had put him in mortal danger.

"God's balls," Henry muttered, "He forgot to bring his apes."

My thought exactly.

Young Henry, however, turned deathly pale as he watched his "spiritual father" approach, then sit directly below us. Becket raised shadowed eyes and fastened his hypnotic gaze on the boy. I took Young Henry's hand.

After prayers, a clerk stood to present the case of John the Marshal, who was not in attendance. When he finished, Henry spoke pleasantly: Becket had been remiss in ignoring the plea, but he was held not guilty for the original offense. A sigh of relief swept the chapel as the bishops realized that the king was going to be lenient.

Henry continued, his tone no longer so soft. "However, I must address a second matter, my lord archbishop, of the gravest importance. According to the royal pipe rolls, you spent in excess of three hundred pounds on your former estates of Eye and Berkhampstead when you were chancellor. What say you?"

Becket stammered, "You d-d-did not summon me here to render accountings. I don't remember."

"I have the figures here. Let it be noted that this amount is owing to the crown, and I hereby demand payment. But there's more." He read from a scroll the cost of Becket's seven hundred knights on the Toulouse campaign, and in the fight against King Louis in the Vexin, and money borrowed from the Jews in the king's name, a sum over a thousand marks.

"That money was a gift!" Becket cried aloud. "How can you demand a return of what was freely given?"

"I never said it was a gift," Henry replied. "To continue: The See of Canterbury was without an archbishop for over a year, during which time you collected all the rents and revenues, an amount of forty thousand marks. That money is owed to me."

Becket rose to his bare feet, his face wet with perspiration. "No man could repay such a vast sum."

"I could," Henry said.

"But I'm not the king."

"I'm glad to hear you admit it."

Their eyes held.

"I need time to prepare my answer," Becket mumbled.

"And I would give it if you'd agree to my Constitutions of Clarendon, for my grandfather granted such time, but you've refused to admit his laws. Therefore, I'll proceed according to the current custom; the bishops will decide."

Abruptly, Becket turned to those present, who clustered around him.

"Are you all right?" I whispered to Young Henry.

His eyes filled, but he managed not to weep. I squeezed his hand.

Suddenly, the bishop of Worcester broke free of the group. "My lord king, we cannot judge impartially! The archbishop has threatened to excommunicate us if we vote against him."

The bishop of London joined him. "He wants to excommunicate men of God when he's never even administered the Eucharist!"

Another shouted, "And he's sent to the Pope for help!"

Henry jumped to his feet. "To the Pope? That's treason! The Constitutions prohibit coercion! Not by excommunication or by going over the king's head to the Pope!"

"Treason!" The cry went up.

Becket turned a distraught face. "Tomorrow! Give me till tomorrow to bring my answer!"

Henry sat again. "Tomorrow. I'm a fair man."

The meeting dissolved; I pulled Young Henry across the courtyard and to our upper chamber, where the other children were watching events from a window.

"They're throwing horse dung at your father," Richard said to Young Henry.

"Where? Let me see!"

With a vexed look at Richard, I crowded behind the others to look down on the courtyard below.

Becket, his cross still held high, was making slow progress across the cobbles. The bishops, filled with pent fury, hurled rushes at him, and indeed, they also threw dung.

"Traitor! Liar!"

Becket turned a pale face. "If I had my sword, I'd show you who lies!"

"Catamite!"

Young Henry leaned against the wall, as if he might faint. I gripped his shoulder; he trembled like a poplar leaf.

"Take a deep breath," I ordered.

He looked at me with shadowed eyes. "The king wants him dead, doesn't he?"

"Of course not! This is a matter of law, but—"

He ran to his own closet.

The next morning, we were all in place for the resolution of our drama. One tense hour passed, then two. Suddenly, Henry leapt to his feet.

"Send a guard to the monastery!"

In short order, the guard returned. "I couldn't find him, my lord; he—"

"Close the ports!" Henry jumped off the platform. "After him! Gold to the man who stops him!"

In the melee that followed, I again pulled Young Henry free. This time, there was no gathering at the window, for a heavy rain obscured vision. The rain continued for nearly three weeks, as if God had provided a second flood to aid Becket in his escape. On the fourth week, we learned that the Archbishop had reached the Continent; both King Louis and the Pope supported him. Nor were they alone. Scattered nobles in France, Flanders, and even Anjou and Maine rallied to Becket simply to defy Henry.

"So the shark swims into the tunny net," Henry commented. "Good riddance for England."

"Except for Young Henry's coronation."

"Ah, yes, that. Well, it will be postponed. As for me, I'm off to Wales to fight the white-robed tree men, a vacation after what I've been through." He turned at the door. "Which reminds me, I'm sending you to Angers to see to our holdings there. I don't want to be on the Continent with Becket."

And Rancon. I could have kissed the archbishop for giving me this opportunity.

"I'll leave at once with the children."

"Take only the older ones. This won't be a long sojourn; I'll want you back by spring."

"I'll put the babies with my sister in Winchester."

"Leave Young Henry with her, as well. I want to work with the boy alone."

I started to protest, then thought better of it. Petronilla was kind to all children, and it might be more prudent to keep Young Henry away from Richard. My young prince hated his brother still; I don't know how Richard felt, but I sensed a wariness.

When I told Young Henry, however, he broke into bitter wails. "You want Richard and not me."

"That's not true! You know that I love you; you know it. God's heart, Young Henry, when your older brother, William, died and I had only you—"

"I know, Mama, only I hate to be away from you. You love me, but the king doesn't."

"Of course he does."

He wiped his eyes on my tunic. "No, he doesn't, and he doesn't want me to be crowned."

"Why do you say that?"

His nine-year-old face was almost tragic. "You always say it—he doesn't. Father Becket said he was jealous of me."

I lost my breath. "How dare Becket speak to you in that manner!"

"I asked him; he told me. He meant no harm, and he did love me."

"You must forget Becket."

"I love Father Thomas; I'll always love him."

"What about your real father, Young Henry? Do you love him?"

Again that young-old face. "I understand that I must obey; my future depends on him. I wish he were dead!"

I couldn't reply. Of course he spoke with the hyperbole of the young, and Henry and Becket both had been grievously wrong to insert him into the center of their argument. I could only pray that our sojourn together would now sustain Young Henry.

When the time came, I had mixed feelings about returning to Europe after so many months. I was aching to go but . . . Should I write Rancon that I was coming? I wrote instead to my uncle Ralph in Poitiers.

Before I left, Henry took me aside. "I know it's useless to tell you not to visit Aquitaine."

"Yes, useless."

"When you go, then, summon my uncle, Earl Patrick of Salisbury, and his young protégé, William Marshal, to escort you. You're never to ride out without their company; that's an order."

"Very well, if you insist."

"I do."

Before he left, Henry banished all of Becket's relatives from England, no matter how distant, even the very old and young. They had one week to leave or else face death. Four hundred braved the storm-tossed Channel; we never learned how many survived.

Henry departed from Northampton with Young Henry and the younger children in his train, who would be left in Winchester; I then rode to Southampton with Matilda and Richard. Once on board the *Esnecca*, I stood by the rail, gazing to the east; I couldn't wait to be home.

I had one secret reservation: I was again pregnant.

I stayed in Angers hardly long enough to change horses, then set off to Aquitaine, accompanied by my escort, as Henry had demanded, but nothing could diminish my joy. The earl was a pleasant, avuncular man who took his assignment to guard me seriously, as did his young knight William Marshal. Since we'd made a late start, we decided to spend the night in the Lusignan Castle before pressing on to Poitiers, so we had no need to hurry. William Marshal sang to rival the troubadours as we traversed the flowered paths. The instant we crossed the border between Anjou and Aquitaine, my spirits lifted. Even Earl Patrick remarked on the beauty of the land, which he said reminded him of Sussex.

The Lusignan brothers were not in residence, but their widowed mother made us welcome. The day was still bright, the air filled with spring perfume, and I couldn't stay indoors. Patrick and Marshal agreed to accompany me on a ride into the hills before supper. Followed by a few servants, we chose a narrow path enclosed with hedgerows that led to a vantage where we could overlook the scene.

Suddenly, to our right, two scrofulous knights brandishing swords charged across the meadow. Earl Patrick and Marshal quickly pushed in front of me.

"Who goes there!" Earl Patrick shouted.

"We demand the queen of England as our hostage!"

I recognized the voice. "Hugh!" I cried. "God's heart, you frightened me! I thought you were serious."

Hugh and his brother Guy watched me coldly.

I smiled, genuinely pleased to see them. "Did your mother tell you where we were? Come, ride with us."

How Hugh had changed! Except for his bald head, I might not have recognized his newly lean face, now grooved and hawk-nosed.

"Dismount!" he ordered Sir Patrick.

"Put away your swords in the name of the king!" Patrick retorted, staying where he was.

"We want the duchess."

"Nonsense, Hugh," I said sharply. "What ails you? What possible gain can come from such a mad scheme?"

He glanced from malicious dark eyes.

"Come peaceably, or you may be hurt," Guy threatened.

"Come with me back to your castle," I countered, "and I'll forget this incident."

Hugh menaced Earl Patrick with his sword. "Get off your horse."

I rode between them. "Stay where you are, Sir Patrick. Hugh, this is treason."

"Is it? I now do homage to the king of France."

"Which is homage to me, since he's my overlord."

Jostling his steed, he placed his sword's point against the earl's stomach. "Dismount!"

"What do you want, Hugh?" I demanded.

Hugh's lip pulled up. "I'll tell your husband what I want."

"Let me handle this, Queen Eleanor," Earl Patrick interrupted. "We're not armed, sir. You must give us the opportunity to defend our lady on equal terms. Chivalry demands it."

Guy laughed shortly. "We respect chivalry, eh, brother? By all means, send to the castle for your arms."

Earl Patrick grabbed my bridle. "Queen Eleanor goes with us; if we lose in fair battle, she's yours. You have my word as a knight."

Hugh jerked my reins again. "The duchess stays here and so do you. Send your men for the arms."

Earl Patrick's keen eyes warned me. "As you wish."

The terrified servants galloped away.

"Hugh," I pleaded, "I beg you to reconsider. I know that you're disaffected, but try to think of your future. Why do you think I've returned to Aquitaine? I beg you, in memory of our many good times in the past, don't do this foolish thing."

"Stop whining!"

I recoiled from the raw hatred in his voice. Overhead, the sun passed behind a cloud, then reemerged; flies bit the horses and tails flicked. The cloud again, a shadow. Finally, the servants appeared, followed by mounts loaded with armor. When they were almost upon us, traveling single file between the hedges, Earl Patrick and Marshal slid to the ground.

"There you are!" Earl Patrick called with obvious relief. "My armor is on the lead horse, I see."

He raised his arms to receive his mail, and in short order he was armed, all except for his helmet. Hugh and Guy watched silently. Now too heavy to mount easily, Earl Patrick reached to Marshal for help.

Then I heard a whack. A needle cut my cheek. "What . . ." A bloody chip dripped on my finger.

Incredibly, Earl Patrick's head lolled forward on his chest. A single thread of skin held it upward, so his dead eyes gazed into mine.

Marshal raised his sword. "Ride!" he shouted at me.

Before I could move, Guy buried a dagger in Marshal's thigh.

"Ride!" the wounded knight cried again.

I whipped Hugh's face and took off! Behind me, his horse closed in. I ripped my steed with my spurs. "Hoyt! Hoyt!"

I was inside the courtyard.

"Lock the gate!" I shouted to my guards. "Take Lady Lusignan into custody!"

I sent my best knights to help Marshal, but he and the Lusignans had disappeared without a trace. All they could find was Earl Patrick's body.

I wrote a note to Rancon and ordered him to come at once.

I waited in a highly agitated state, hardly knowing what worried me the most: Aquitaine, young Marshal, or the prospect of seeing Rancon. One concern was decided when a runner arrived from Taillebourg; Rancon was in touch with the renegades, who would release Marshal for gold. If I would give the ransom to the runner, Rancon himself would effect the trade. Summoning a strong guard from my uncle, I left immediately for Poitiers, where I could find such a large sum.

In a few days, Marshal returned, dangerously weak from his unattended wound. His manner was so courteous that I asked him his background: He was descended from knights but not of nobility, and he'd made his way upward through the tournaments. I'd already rewarded him with a fine horse and armor, but now I had another idea.

"If it please you, Marshal, I would like you to become the military instructor for my oldest son, Young Henry."

His eyes widened. "The future king of England?"

"The same."

He was overcome with gratitude. Marshal was therefore safe and happy, but what about Aquitaine? My uncle Ralph delivered a somber report. The fighting among our barons, once a playful summer diversion, had become deadly in the absence of a respected overlord. The Lusignan brothers were determined to seize the entire duchy for themselves. Henry exploited the fighting as an excuse to subdue one and all to his will, and his methods were brutal.

"How could that be?" I protested. "Henry's never here."

"He has mercenaries. They've been given carte blanche."

"Would it help if I returned?"

He considered his answer too long. "You have a residue of affection, I believe, but your marriage compromises you. The barons can't understand why you permit Henry to raze your lands. Your first obligation should be to your subjects."

I accepted his judgment with outward stoicism, but inside I was wounded. How could anyone believe I wanted to hurt Aquitaine? I knew now why Rancon had withdrawn from my person. At least I hoped I knew.

I didn't return to England that spring as planned. Instead, I governed my own duchy via runners from Angers and waited for the birth of my baby in October. Henry was still engaged in Wales, at the same time that he waged a political war in Europe against Becket via his representatives. That fraudulent archbishop was still determined to return to Canterbury. I was at war with everything, mostly my expanding belly, which inhibited freedom. At least my pregnancy was a perfect excuse for avoiding a confrontation with Rancon.

Then Henry sent a runner with monumental news: Louis had finally produced a son! A son. Marguerite would never take the throne, nor my own son Young Henry. I bent my head a long period. At least the Vexin was still ours.

My baby was born, another little holly berry, and Richard and Matilda named her Joanna. With Amaria, I did my usual exercises to coax my waistline back to normal as I prepared a Christmas Court. The Nativity feast had just been cleared away and I'd retired to my chamber with Richard and Matilda to play parchisi before the fire.

Richard suddenly looked up joyfully. "Rancon's here!"

"Where?" I rose from my bench.

"Here," Rancon said from the door.

"Rancon!" I could hardly speak.

"Have you supped?" Richard ran toward him.

"Yes, have you?" I echoed.

"No, I forgot about food."

"That's terrible, to miss your repast on the day of the Nativity," I said breathlessly. "I'm certain we have sweetmeats and pudding."

"I'll get you something," Richard offered proudly.

"Me, too!" Matilda squirmed from the corner.

They rushed out and I was alone with Rancon. The last time I'd seen him had been in Domfront, when he'd crashed into the wood.

"You have a new child," he said courteously.

"Yes, a girl, Joanna."

"Congratulations."

"Won't you rest by the fire? You must be cold."

"Thank you." He leaned against the hearth.

I was as tongue-tied as a young girl. Thank God Richard and Matilda soon returned. As Rancon ate, Matilda cuddled against him while Richard sat at his feet.

He ruffled Richard's thick hair. "I've missed you, Richard. Tell me what adventures you've had."

Richard described his conquest of the entire world, for he was still Alexander the Great. Rancon asked him pointed questions about his campaigns; both became excited.

"Don't you want to know about me?" Matilda fretted.

"I can see that you've grown very pretty."

She cocked her head. "I have a suitor."

"I'm not surprised. Do you like him?"

"I've not met him. He's very old, but said to be kind."

"Who is he?"

"Leo, duke of Saxony."

"Ah, a worthy choice. He has a famous library."

As Rancon listened and the children continued to tell of their exploits, my excitement sank slowly to a dull depression. I'd been with Rancon since childhood; I didn't need a stone cast to my head to know something was gravely amiss. This was no casual estrangement.

After an eternity, the children retired.

"I brought you a Nativity present." He groped inside his pouch. I accepted a thick scroll. "Troubadour songs?"

"A copy of your genealogy next to Henry's. You're cousins to the third degree, closer than you were to Louis."

"I know our relationship."

"Your barons intend to dissolve your marriage."

"My barons?"

"With your signature, of course. We'll send this to the Pope."

"And if I don't sign?"

"They'll send it without your signature." In the flickering firelight, his black eyes were opaque.

"Was this your idea?"

"Yes."

I dared ask no further—was this also an attempt to renew our relationship? Could I? I'd made a mental resolve to stay with Henry, and yet . . . Oh God, how I loved Rancon!

He continued in a noncommittal voice. "You've always said that you wanted to be free—this is your opportunity. Oh, I know we once spoke of claiming that Henry had abducted you—forced himself upon you—but the evidence has grown unconvincing in view of . . ." He gestured toward Joanna.

My head throbbed. "The same might be said about consanguinity. It may have been my legal argument against Louis, but the case was won because I was barren. Do you think the Pope would accept such a claim with Henry?"

"You won because you allowed yourself to be demonized! Too bad your Becket isn't at hand to do the same!"

"I permitted the calumny because—"

"Henry's destroying your duchy! Is there any greater cause?" His first display of emotion. "When did Louis ever invade Aquitaine?"

"Invasion isn't against canon law!" I beseeched him. "The barons don't know what they're doing, Rancon. God's heart, I spent years trying to escape Louis. I know the laws!"

"So do we. Your last hope, Joy."

"Be specific. My last hope for what?"

"Saving your title."

"Do you have some other ruler in mind?" I asked slowly.

"Anybody but Henry. If you won't fight against him, do your duty; we'll find someone else."

I chilled to the bone. I didn't know this man.

"I have five children by Henry. What happens to them?"

"We're not against your children."

"Yet if this annulment is granted, my children become bastards."

"Your daughters in France are still legitimate."

"And disinherited," I added bitterly. "And I fought for their legitimacy in the divorce court."

"Surely Henry would never disenfranchise his sons."

"Can you guarantee that? And what about his daughters?"

He didn't reply.

"You don't know Henry," I said, thinking of how he'd fought for Young Henry, meaning that Henry loved his children as I did, a point I felt it better not to make. In pressing for divorce, I would deprive my sons and daughters of legitimacy, future success, and a father's devotion.

"Better than you do!" he snapped angrily.

"How?"

"How often do I have to tell you that I've seen him on the field?"

"And how often do I have to reply that a few playful barons in Aquitaine can never bring down the greatest army in Europe?"

"We're not alone; we have allies."

"Name them."

"Join us first."

"Before I join."

"Three, then: Philip of Flanders, King William of Scotland, and Louis of France."

I was beyond speech.

"Come home to Aquitaine!"

"Be forthright, my lord. If I don't, what will happen?"

"Aquitaine will explode!"

"And that's your purpose for this visit—to save Aquitaine?"

"Isn't that sufficient reason?"

In spite of my effort, my voice trembled. "A political gambit."

"You are still our duchess, my lady."

"And that's all."

His brows shot up. "Our queen?" He laughed shortly. "We do not accept the king of England, nor his queen. We do homage to France, remember?"

"Your ally, France."

"That's correct."

"Though France is an enemy to England."

"Always. Please don't pretend ignorance. And even more so since the Becket affair. May I be blunt?"

When hadn't he been? "Please, speak your mind."

"Very well, you can hardly be shocked at anything I've divulged. God knows, I've written you often enough. But it's obvious to me, and to others, that since you understand, you deliberately obfuscate your excuses."

"And do you know my real reasons?"

"I think I do." For the first time, he hesitated. "Please don't take this amiss; I speak as a friend."

He then proceeded to outline my character as he saw it. Though I claimed that my allegiance to Henry was my entrapment to the marriage vow and devotion to my children, in fact my motives were less exalted. Henry could offer me the throne of England, no small thing for a woman so keen for power; furthermore, he provided me with said children, and here was the process that enchanted me. I wanted—had to have—a virile man in my bed.

How dare he say that of me?

Worst, he went on, Henry knew how to exploit my weaknesses. He flattered me on my beauty, saw to it that I remained pregnant, though he took no interest in children, deceived me as he did everyone else.

"I never asked him to be faithful!"

"I'm not speaking of fidelity. Henry is extremely intelligent, *cunning* might be a better word. No one, but no one, can trust him. He offers prizes, then doesn't deliver."

Dangling, I thought.

"He turns against beloved friends with no warning. Witness Becket."

"Becket betrayed him!" But I remembered Henry's betrayal of Arnulf.

"He's even hypocritical about his vaunted law. If he believes in the rule by law, why doesn't he accept the customs of Aquitaine? Why invade us? He's highly selective in the laws he respects; in Aquitaine, he thinks he's Alexander the Great!"

I took a breath. "You're speaking of him solely as a political figure."

"Because that's what is he, nothing more."

"And except for my preoccupation with carnal love, I'm the same."

"Henry shares that preoccupation, but, yes, the last few years would seem to say so, yes."

I tried to control my growing rage. Had he forgotten the time we'd spent together?

"Then let me address you in exactly the same language, as a political entity. You're setting yourself up as an unsullied model of chivalry, sans ambition, sans deception. But let me ask you: Were you not thrilled when my father approached you years ago to be my future husband? Wasn't I with you when he pointed to the towers of Toulouse and suggested that some day you would take the duchy for me? You were to be the duke of Aquitaine!"

"Duke consort, yes."

"And what did you lose when I married Louis? Or again when I married Henry? Though you were already wed to Lady Arabelle, you clung to your dream, eh?"

"Stop it, Joy!"

"No, I won't stop! You say Henry plays on my 'weaknesses,' which I call a need for love. What about you? Have you not 'fucked' me for years? At the same time that you justify it with sentimental poetry? At least Henry's not a hypocrite in that area! If I succumb to your wishes, you have everything to gain! What about me? What are my ulterior motives?"

"Oh God, stop this, Joy! Stop it!" He pulled me close to his chest. "Christ, Joy, I've pined after you all my life like a puling boy. I want you; I deserve you. We deserve each other. Haven't I suffered enough for love?"

"I don't know," I said. "Where is the limit writ down?"

"You call me Tristan—show me another living man who plays the role! Show me a lover who permits his beloved to produce another man's children by the dozen! Even the Iseult in the poem never became a mother!"

I pulled away.

He went on. "You use children as an excuse—we could have children! I want an heir! Come home to Aquitaine."

I heard another threat. "Or you'll what?"

He kissed me deeply, murmured against my lips. "Is this not a sufficient reason to come?"

My body said yes, but my mind said no. Too much had been spoken.

"My wife died, Joy."

"Yes, I heard. My sympathy."

"I'm free."

"Are you asking . . ."

"Not to be Tristan, no! Listen, Joy, you know the poem well. Even Tristan became disenchanted with his situation and—"

Married someone else, Iseult of the White Hands.

"Who is she, Rancon?"

"She is you. Come back to Aquitaine, annul your marriage to Henry, and we'll marry."

"Despite your analysis of my character?"

"Christ, you know what I feel!"

"I did once. I haven't seen you in years."

"Come back, Joy!"

"Who is she?" I asked again.

He paused significantly. "There's a lady in Guyenne."

If he hadn't been holding me, I would have fallen. I waited until hurt was replaced by fury. "Is she also a religious fanatic?"

He drew away. "What do you mean?"

"Your dead wife, Arabelle, the lady who starved herself. Oh, I know about the Perfecti, a new religious cult that denies the body in every way. Was that why you were available?"

"I was 'available,' as you call it, because I loved you!"

"And your wife refused you solace!"

"As Louis did you, you may remember! Is that why you sought me?"

"Louis wanted to kill me!"

"And me!"

I took a deep breath. "And now you claim that Henry is doing the same!"

"Yes, I do! He wants to destroy Aquitaine, which I hope you still consider your own person!"

"And you're offering your body to save Aquitaine!" My voice trembled. "If you were a woman, we'd have a name for you!"

"What about you? Aren't you selling your body for a crown? Or do you simply lust for Henry?"

I slapped him. "Henry raped me! What did your lady of Guyenne do to you?"

He laughed. "By God, you're jealous! Good! Now you know how I feel when I see you dancing with that murderous worm!"

"I prefer to dance with Henry than to dance alone! I've written you again and again, with no answer! Must I grovel?"

"Just leave him!"

"Oh, Rancon, you know in your heart that I can't. It's gone too far for an annulment. Don't torture me!"

His grasp went slack. Very gently, he bent and kissed me. "That was farewell."

"Just tell me, do you love—"

"I love you, the lady of many loves."

"And I love you!"

"More than your children?"

"I can't destroy them for you."

"Then you destroy everyone."

And he was gone.

25

The following morning, a servant announced a visitor.

"Who is it?"

"A stranger, my lady."

My heart stopped—Rancon had returned!

So agitated that I could hardly speak, I said, "Show him in."

A lean, ragged figure leaned against my door.

"Thomas!"

"We were ever f-friends, my lady Eleanor. May I speak to you privately?"

I instructed my servant to permit no one entry, and to bring my guest a cup of broth. I watched as Becket sipped slowly, recalling his wracked appearance when he'd returned from the progress with Henry.

"You understand my h-heart, my lady."

"I believe I did once." Hardly a compliment. "I'm not sure I do now."

I caught the echo of my words to Rancon.

He proceded to rant about God in a manner worthy of Louis, but this was mere show. I waited for the favor I was certain he would ask.

"Could you speak to my lord Henry on my behalf?"

"What would you like me to say, Archbishop?"

"That I love him as a brother, as I always h-have. That I b-beseech him to permit me to return to Canterbury."

"I have no part in the differences between you, my lord Thomas, but I believe you must accept his Constitutions of Clarendon."

Becket's eyes streamed. "I cannot live without his love!"

For a moment, my flesh trembled. Did I not feel the same about Rancon? Yet I'd sent him away.

"I fear you confuse sentiment with policy. A king cannot forsake his power."

"No king has power over God!"

Which in our world meant over the Pope. And it was true, as I'd experienced all my life, that rulers must succumb to Rome. Yet we fought, and on this score, I supported Henry.

"You've said this often, Thomas. Henry feels differently, and just as strongly as you. I can only advise you to submit to the law, then work out your differences."

Though he persisted for the rest of the morning, he knew I wouldn't help. When he left, he begged that I keep his visit a secret, and I agreed.

After he'd departed, I mused on the comparison Rancon had drawn between Becket and me, but, as I saw it, my loss was Rancon, not Henry. Like Becket, I now gave in to tears. All the rest of the day, I sank into a deep melancholy, unable to rally even for my children.

But slowly, I became more sanguine. In a week's time, I began to survive abandonment. I sent to Chartres for a copy of *Meditations,* by Marcus Aurelius; let me be a stoic. I submerged myself in motherhood, in administration, in constant anxious letters to England concerning Young Henry. I learned, in short, that I could live without happiness, without hope.

Henry arrived just before Easter, in pursuit of Becket. He stayed only a week, and though he was gruff in humor and distracted by coming meetings with Becket, I became pregnant. Well, this is my life, I thought, the queen bee. So be it. I'll be a great queen and a great mother of great children. I decided to return to England for the birth; I wrote Henry that I was rejoining my family in Winchester for the Nativity. Could he come to us?

Henry was returning to the Welsh fray, and I was to remain in

Angers. I argued that I hadn't seen Young Henry, Marguerite, Geoffrey, or little Eleanor in over a year. Could he please send them to
me? I had no reply; he was in battle somewhere.

I taught Matilda German in preparation for her coming nuptials,
taught Richard langue d'oc for his coming induction as duke,
taught Joanna to clap her hands, wrote all my children in Winchester daily.

Becket had failed to have Henry excommunicated, because of
Matilda's future marriage with the duke of Saxony, who had influence with the Pope. After his Welsh campaign, Henry wrote that he
longed to return to Woodstock, where he'd set up his English
court, but he was forced to take his troops to Aquitaine. There was
a new eruption in Angoulême.

Angoulême, where Rancon's family held sway.

He was also upset—belatedly, I thought—at the birth of Louis's
son. I must realize that the birth quashed any hope that Young
Henry would become king consort in France.

I replied that the fact that Young Henry was married to Louis's
daughter made his ascendancy to the English throne a certainty—
Henry and Louis both wanted it. However, and I didn't write this.
I was more concerned with my expanding middle. The autumn was
short, the winter early, and I began to prepare for my second
Christmas Court in Angers. By my reckoning, my present baby
might arrive on Christmas Day.

Another letter from Henry again upset my plans.

To Eleanor, queen of the English, et cetera, greeting: You have
warned me for years of the instability in Aquitaine, and I admit that
I was remiss in not heeding your advice. Now that I'm here, I find
the entire duchy falling into tribal factions, with no central authority
whatsoever. Therefore, I propose to hold my Christmas Court in
Poitiers, where I will combine the festivities with a political ceremony. I'm bringing Young Henry from Winchester and the barons
will be asked to swear allegiance to him forthwith, which will make
him a central rallying point in that troubled land.

I wrote back at once: "I am overjoyed at the prospect of spending Christmas in Poitiers and I yearn to see Young Henry again. However, Young Henry can't be the center of Aquitaine's government; ask the barons to do homage to Richard instead, their future duke. They don't know Young Henry, nor do they have any reason to serve him." I didn't add that Rancon especially would lead the support for Richard, his own son.

Henry shot back: Had I forgotten that Richard would have to do homage to Young Henry as his overlord when our older son was crowned? Surely I understood the urgency of establishing Young Henry's future position with my nobles, especially since Becket was delaying the coronation; this was a good gambit for establishing Young Henry as the heir apparent in lieu of a crowning.

I didn't completely follow his argument, but I forgot that issue when I read on: I was not to attend the Christmas Court, nor was I to send Richard, his letter continued. If Richard and I were present, the whole purpose would be undercut; Young Henry must be the center of this event, with no competition, especially from Richard or me. As a matter of fact, it would be better if I were not even on the Continent. I should prepare to leave for England at once; I could have my desired reunion with my family in Winchester after all.

My baby gave me a sharp kick. I pressed my hands to my abdomen, breathing deeply, until the spasm passed. Yes, England was where I wanted to be, not Poitiers, where Rancon was sure to be in attendance; he didn't even know I was again pregnant. Perhaps his new wife was with child as well. I told Richard and Matilda that we were returning to England.

Che Channel churned wildly, spinning our ship like a leaf in a winter gale. We reached England by a miracle, only to learn that the road to Winchester was impassable.

Richard and Matilda were bitterly disappointed. Both children hated the huge drafty Westminister Palace Becket had constructed for us.

"Couldn't we go to Woodstock at least?" Matilda begged. "It's not far."

"I could gather holly in the woods," Richard interjected.

"My monkey is there! Please, Mama, this is the last Christmas I'll ever have with you."

I kissed her red hair. "Never say last, darling, but you're right; it will be different once you're married."

My scouts reported that the way to Woodstock was clear enough to be safe, so we left the following morning. We arrived in late afternoon, and I knew at once that we'd made the right choice. The sun, already low, cast golden streaks through gray clouds. A steady north wind cracked ice in the branches and shaped the purple-shadowed crests in the snow. The friendly staff seemed especially warm. Amaria carried little Joanna for everyone to admire, while Richard and Matilda ran in circles. I took a deep breath. Yes, this was a wise choice.

"Can you see to the unloading, Am?" I called. "I want to walk a little. One of my legs is cramped."

She turned worried eyes. "Wait, I'll come with you."

"Nonsense; I'll be careful."

I left before she could stop me. Once away from the lodge, the woods were darker, the wind stronger. God's heart, I would be glad when this baby was delivered. How deceptive the turf was under the glistening surface, how heavy my legs were, impossible to pull my feet free of the snow; I turned one ankle, then the other, and staggered slightly. Easy, easy. High steps made me short of breath. I stumbled, lost my balance, and fell on my side. My head hit a tree.

I must have lost consciousness for a few heartbeats; the shadows were now longer. I pulled on the tree, and collapsed again, my legs weak as water.

I closed my eyes. A steady sough moaned in the wych elms, then a *clackety-clackety-clackety* like giant clappers signaling a song. An omen? A cosmic festivity?

"Richard! Richard!" I called weakly. He'd said he was going to gather holly.

No answer.

The hollow clatter around me intensified, a death rattle. Memories flooded back; I couldn't bear it. Tears turned to ice; my cheek stuck to the trunk. Once I'd heard a tale of twins who, though separated by a great distance, fell ill and died simultaneously. I was a severed twin. Without Rancon, I'd ceased to exist. Rancon, Rancon. Was he suffering as well? How beautiful the opalescent streaks across the snow.

A naked man on a white horse galloped under the black branches. Silently, smiling, he came closer.

"Give me your hand, darling! Tonight the branches will creak in the ice, and tomorrow we'll wake to sunshine."

"Not yet, Grandfather."

He laughed soundlessly and galloped toward a lady of feathers in the distance. She soared like a bird onto his saddle. *"Love! Love!"* they sang together, then disappeared in a white froth.

A small boy walked on his hands across shadowed snow. Although he wore a mask, I thought I knew him.

"Tomorrow's come, Mama."

"William, wait!"

"The dark is coming," his voice said from the shadow.

From inside me, another child gave a strong kick. I called out with pain. A mother of great children, *live* children, not dead. I must stand. I rolled so I was facing the tree, took off my gloves so I could grasp the bark, and clawed myself upward. Panting with the effort, I took my bearings. I was closer to Tintagel than to the manor.

Slowly, I limped, until the small hut was in sight. Amaria would know to look for me here. Holding the rail, I pulled myself up the icy steps. The door gave way at once to my pressure. What was this? A fire was burning brightly; candles flickered on the chests and sills. Who had put glass in the windows? Was I still hallucinating?

A real figure rose from the bed. A woman's voice called, "Who's there?"

"Eleanor, only Eleanor." What a relief. I was truly safe.

The figure waddled to the fireplace I had built. How bulbous she was in silhouette.

"Eleanor!" Incredulous. Frightened? "The queen?"

"Yes, I wrote you from London. Didn't you—"

"No!" She hugged herself.

I stopped, puzzled. This was no member of the staff that I'd ever seen. Was she an intruder? A young woman swathed in furs. *My* furs, *my* ermine, which Henry had given me! And she was pregnant! I felt giddy. Hadn't I just thought of twins? Here was my very other materialized from nowhere. I must be having a vision after all. Had I lost consciousness? Was I still lying in the snow at the foot of a tree?

"I'm sorry," she stammered breathlessly. "I would never have . . . I shouldn't except . . . Henry—the king—assured me you were going to Winchester. . . ."

Henry had told her? *Henry?* Rapidly, I counted backward and, unlike either of my husbands, I calculated accurately: She was carrying Henry's child, conceived within a week or so of the baby I was carrying.

"Henry was right; I *was* going to Winchester," I said affably, "but the roads were closed." I smiled disarmingly. "I don't know your name."

"Lady Rosamond of Clifford," she announced with childish pride. "You've never heard of me?"

"Should I have?"

"Yes . . . I mean, Hen—the king said he'd told you about me. Maybe he didn't mention my name. When I was staying in Westminster Palace, everyone knew me well."

Westminster! I pulled up straight; my baby thrashed, and I tightened my muscles to quiet it. Let this infant learn to be royal. "When were you in Westminster, Lady Rosamond?"

"Most of last year, and even after Hen—"

"Call him Henry, dear. I don't mind." Call him the Devil. I don't mind.

"After Henry left, I came here because I knew you were riding through London."

"That was considerate of you." God's balls, considerate! My mind was hot as a coal. "Do you mind if we sit? I'm weary after the long ride."

We both sank on the edge of the large bed, where we had obviously both known passion. The boards groaned under our combined weight. I was careful to sit so the light struck her face, which gave me an advantage. Her features were ordinary in isolation, brown eyes and hair, straight nose, average mouth, but the whole created an ethereal beauty of great sweetness and innocence. My anger found its true target: Henry.

"How old are you, Lady Rosamond?"

"Fifteen, milady."

"How long have you been with Henry?"

I might have pitied her, except that she'd stayed in Westminster with Richard de Luci, with Robert of Leicester.

She glowed. "I met him when I was only thirteen, and Cupid struck us both at the same time—it was a miracle. He was returning from Wales—I'm Welsh, you know—and I was on one side of the stream, he on the other. We couldn't even speak—we were under a spell."

"How charming." A lecherous king in his mid-thirties, a virgin of thirteen.

"He said that I was the love of his life and that he'd dreamed of someone like me even when he was a small boy. He called me 'the rose of the world.'"

Rose of the world versus the lily of Aquitaine; I'd not known Henry was such a horticulturist. But I wasn't amused. This child was naïve. What was my excuse? I flushed with shame; when he'd recited his flowerly spell to me in Domfront, I'd felt *guilty* because of my assignation with Rancon!

"That's why I'm surprised he didn't tell you; he said he would because . . ."

"Because?" I nudged her.

She lowered her eyes and whispered, "Because he wants to marry me."

"Marry!" I couldn't conceal my shock. Marry? He had a wife, and a large family—what did he plan to do with us?

"Oh, he told me about his mistresses," she babbled on, sensing my shock. "Trollops along the road, but some ladies, as well. Isabel of Clare—he built this cottage for her—and Avisa of Stamford. But I'm different because . . ."

Isabel of Clare, the mysterious favor Henry had given to the duke of Clare—in exchange for his daughter?

"Because?" I again prompted her.

Her eyes were unsure. "Do you think I should tell you? Perhaps Henry would prefer—"

"But he isn't here, and you're with child. We shouldn't wait." My logic was faulty, but she nodded.

"Yes, the child. You see, Henry is very young to have sons as old as yours. You're older, of course, so perhaps you don't realize—"

"Realize what?" This was profound—I didn't want to miss a word.

"That he isn't ready to sacrifice power to his princes. It's much too soon for him to abdicate his own hard-won titles to his successors. Besides, they're spoiled and soft, nothing like he was at their age."

Which sounded like Henry. "That's clear enough, Lady Rosamond."

"I don't want to make him seem cruel—he said he would grant your sons adequate incomes—I think that's what he meant, although I know little of such matters—so that each would be independent in good time, but that my . . . our . . . son would be king of the whole. Of that I'm certain."

A smug little smile.

"Yes, your son will be much younger than mine," I agreed, then waited for the recognition that was sure to follow.

"Except for the one you're carrying now." Her pretty face became perplexed. "He also said that you were no longer . . . that you didn't . . . couldn't . . ."

"Have any more children?"

She nodded.

My son would be the same age as hers. But hers had the father's blessing, whereas Henry's rejection of our sons was quite real. Of that I had no doubt. Rancon had hinted, but someone else had told me—ah yes, Young Henry had claimed his father didn't want him crowned. Could that be true? Had Becket known more than I did? I was cold, and not because of the elements.

"I daresay this will be my last child." Absolutely my last. "However, Henry was wrong to mislead you."

A tear rolled down her cheek; she wiped it on my ermine sleeve. "My mother warned . . . but my father was sure he was honorable."

Because Henry had met his price.

"Then when everyone at Westminster seemed to know . . ." Her voice rolled on.

Yes, very serious. He wouldn't discard me until he had Aquitaine—my insurance. Yet Henry must have lied to her, because even now he was establishing Young Henry as overlord to Aquitaine. My barons were swearing fealty to him for—

My mind raced. I recalled verbatim Henry's letter about Young Henry, the argument that I should not attend, which had confused me. The barons of Aquitaine were recognizing Young Henry as Richard's overlord at this very moment. *But Richard's overlord should be the king of France!* God's heart, where was my reason? If the barons acknowledged Young Henry now because he would one day be the English king, they were in effect acknowledging Henry himself, the present king, as their overlord instead of Louis! Once they did so, *Aquitaine would be Henry's.* Not mine, never Richard's, but Henry's!

A thousand sharp glinting shards showered about me—my shattered illusions.

". . . said you wanted to retire to Fontevrault," the simpering, damning voice went on.

"I must return to the lodge." I rose stiffly.

She stirred as well. "Do you prefer that I leave?"

Leave for her father's protection? Besides, I was finished forever with Tintagel.

"No, my dear. I didn't plan to stay. I'm going to Oxford for my lying-in. I have excellent support there; it's where my son Richard was born."

She continued to hold me. "You won't tell Hen—Henry what I said?"

"Never. In fact, this entire meeting never happened, eh?"

She released my cloak. "You're much younger and more beautiful than I expected. I don't know why he wants to leave you."

But I did: because he'd finally gotten control of my lands.

It was difficult to move, but now my problem was strictly in my awkward body. My spirit was revitalized with purpose.

I dragged across my former love nest and left. A thin moon illuminated the steps just enough for me to see. As I reached for the rail, a form stepped from the shadow.

"Amaria sent me to find you," Richard said. His tight voice revealed all.

"Did you hear?"

He nodded.

"We'll talk later." I took his shoulder.

Standing under the eaves of the stable, my children and I watched by flickering torchlight as the porters slipped over the ice to heave our chests onto the waiting longcarts.

Amaria put her arm around me. "Won't you reconsider, Joy? This is madness."

"No."

"Will you at least tell me why?"

"No."

"Ready!" the coachman sang.

Richard and I climbed into one longcart while Amaria, Matilda, Joanna, and her nurses got into one behind us. I eased myself onto the shallow wooden bench, legs pressed against Richard's as he faced me. The servants wrapped us with furs; the torchbearers mounted their horses and took their places at the head, the rear, and to the sides of our longcart; the knights joined them as we lumbered down the drift-covered path in the dark.

The peculiar clack of whipping branches rose in volume. Our cart slipped into gullies; wheels spun. Grunting men and horses pushed from behind.

Richard flung his arms around my impossible bulk. "I love you, Mama!" he cried, sobbing in his breaking boy's voice. "I hate him forever! I'll take care of you!"

I stroked his fur hat. "Hush, sweet boy. I'm all right."

"She wore your cloak! How could she? How could she think she could ever take your place? I'll kill him!"

"You're only a child, Richard."

"I'll be a great warrior one day."

"Then I speak to the warrior, not the child. Do you fully understand what you heard?"

"Of course. He's stealing Aquitaine from us. Her b-baby will be his heir."

"Good boy. Now we must be cunning. And secretive."

Richard straightened himself. "Do you have a plan?"

"In embryo." I smiled grimly, a fit image. "What I want from you is silence, with your life as forfeit. Promise?"

"Yes."

"I'll confide in you when I can, but trust me—and be silent. Will you take an oath?"

He swore on my soul.

With my free hand, I felt under my fur to my crotch. I was bleeding.

At dawn, I had to be lifted from the cart to enter our manor at Oxford. Hodierna, Richard's nurse, quickly took charge. The day passed, then the night, then another dawn. My pains tore me asunder—I heard myself scream—I was on the rack. I slept with deep snores.

On the third day, I fell into delirium, in and out of consciousness, heard voices but couldn't reply. The fetus clung like a spider to my "gateway to Hell." We were trapped together in an iron web.

The midwife, Ulviva, gave way to a woman misnamed Angela.

"Angela's an expert on difficult births," Amaria told me.

"So am I!"

A snakeskin girdle was fastened to my waist, an eaglestone forced between my teeth, a lodestone thrust up my vagina—at great pain.

Then I heard, "We'll have to use the hook or she won't—"

I heard a baby cry. When I woke, it was dark.

"Is anyone here?"

"I'm right beside you, Joy," Amaria answered.

"Bring a torch. I want to get up."

"In the morning. You're too weak."

"Must I rise in the dark?"

I sat on the edge of the bed.

"You had a boy," Amaria told me, "born on Christmas Day."

"Does that make me a virgin?"

"What do you want to call him?"

"Boy."

"Will John be all right? That's what the children suggest."

"Fine." They had narrow imaginations—first Joanna, now John. "Bring me ox broth. We're leaving for London."

"Now?"

"At dawn."

I checked my new son methodically, small but perfect. Odd, he'd felt like a tarantula in my womb. We climbed into our litters again and slid down the roads to London.

I wrote to Petronilla: "To my beloved sister, countess of Vermandois, greeting: Please pack all my personal possessions in Winchester for immediate shipment to Poitiers. This includes my wardrobe and hounds as well as loftier items, and see that they're sent as soon as possible. Once done, you and the children are to join me here in London."

The roads were still dangerous, but I paid a runner triple to get the message through.

I then sent similar letters to my residences in Northampton, Woodstock, every manor we used in all of England—even Eye and Berkhampstead—and to the guard at my dock on the Thames, Queenshithe, to assemble ships. The packing would take months, and the transportation would have to wait until summer, but the process had begun.

My last letter required six efforts before I was satisfied:

To Louis, king of France, from Eleanor, queen of the English and duchess of Aquitaine, greeting: After such a long silence between us, I find myself overwhelmed with all I would like to say, but I will confine myself to the urgent matter at hand. You and I have a mutual interest in the fortunes of our married children, Young Henry and Marguerite. Less directly, we share a concern for Richard and Geoffrey, who will be your vassals in Aquitaine and Brittany, respectively. My lord, I have just learned on the best authority that King Henry intends to supplant you as their overlord in these duchies; worse, he intends to rob Young Henry of his inheritance. He plans to carve out an Angevin empire, over which he will rule as sole emperor, sans heirs or any other threat to his authority. His present method is to persuade your vassals to swear allegiance to his sons as his surrogates; he will then claim that homage as his right.

As your loyal subject, as a concerned mother, and as your former friend, I hereby offer my services, arms, and riches to help subvert the English king in any way possible. This letter would be construed as treasonous by my lord Henry, but I have a higher loyalty to my own ancestors, to the vows I made in my duchy, to my beloved children, and to you as my respected overlord.

You now know my intentions. Henceforth, I shall reside in Aquitaine, where I shall await your instructions. You may contact me through my sister, Countess Petronilla, who will carry this letter.

God preserve your health and that of all your family. Your devoted subject, et cetera.

I affixed my seal.

Rebellion
1173

26

To my infinite relief, the Christmas Court at Poitiers never took place. I suspected that Rancon had seen through the ruse and aborted it, but I never knew for certain.

For the first time since our marriage, Henry no longer governed my moves. He summoned me to Rouen when his mother died; I sent condolences. He summoned me to Angers during the summer; I was occupied in England, so sorry. When he summoned me to his Christmas Court in Argentan, he dangled Young Henry as the lure; I accepted.

Unlike Woodstock the previous Christmas, the snow was sparse as we began our climb from the confluence of the Argentan and Orne rivers up the peak where our castle was perched. The children and I had been singing to the sound of the pipe as we crossed the plain of the Vendée, but now everyone fell quiet. The younger ones were tired, and Richard was tense.

"You promised me," I reminded him.

"I won't say anything."

"With that face, you won't have to. Vikings, I am told, smiled before the kill."

He didn't smile.

"Your father can smell a nuance."

His lips drew upward into a snarl.

"Never mind."

The fortress was high on a windy crag, the approach steep, like Taillebourg. We'd barely dismounted in the small courtyard when Henry ran down the steps to greet us.

He hugged me against his furs. "God's eyes, what took you so long? I was ready to send out a regiment."

"Greeting, my lord." I turned to avoid his kiss.

"Mama!" Young Henry engulfed me. "How I've missed you!"

"Young Henry, you're beautiful!" My angel boy, as perfect as a Greek statue. I tried to match his dignity. "Tell me, do you like William Marshal?"

"He's the best knight who ever lived! He says I'm gifted in arms."

"Of course you are!" We gazed, mutually entranced. That sweet smile went back to babyhood.

"Greeting, Mama."

"Ah, Marguerite! Another beauty, and so grown-up!" The French princess blushed, glanced slyly at Young Henry, seeking confirmation. We embraced; I could feel her nubile breasts through her tunic.

Henry squatted before a terrified Eleanor. In disgust, he turned to my toddler Joanna, who danced saucily out of his grasp. Geoffrey tugged on his tunic, but Henry didn't notice—a mistake, for Geoffrey was quick to resent a slight.

"Geoffrey, show your father Baby John, will you?" I suggested.

"God's eyes, yes!" Henry cried.

While he and Geoffrey bent over the cradleboard, I took Richard's arm.

"Speak to your father," I said between my teeth. "During the festivities, watch after Geoffrey."

I greeted Henry's sisters with commiseration for Empress Matilda.

We dined, we danced. Eleanor cried, Baby John cried, Richard and Geoffrey both glowered; only Young Henry and Marguerite seemed oblivious to the tension. The music played, the troubadours sang, Henry smiled too much, spoke too loudly, and unconsciously arranged his crotch.

"Tell your ladies to sleep in the corridor tonight," he whispered.
"I need to speak with you, Henry."

"In our bed."

"No, in the hall."

His smile was forced. "For what reason?"

"Meet me by the fire when the bell rings Matins."

"Matins it is."

From the stairs, I paused deep in the shadows to study him. Silhouetted before the flames, he stoked the fire pit, a hedgehog with fiery spikes. Using his fists for ballast, he pulled a stool to sit on, rather than crouching, as was his wont. Was it his old wound? The inevitable stiffening after years in the saddle? No wonder he'd sought out young Rosamond as the "love of his life"; she must have encouraged his self-image as the boy wonder of Europe, the perpetual boy who didn't want to be the father of growing sons, eh? I was grateful to the charming Welsh wench for sharing her perception. Her own son would never threaten his father; poor mite had died soon after birth, and Rosamond was now in a nunnery, all but forgotten.

"Greeting, my lord."

Henry jumped to his feet. "God's eyes, I thought you must have fallen asleep! What's kept you?"

I sank to the faldstool he placed before me. "You're too eager—Matins just rang."

"Yes, I am eager, and why not? I'm overwhelmed by my wife's beauty! No wonder troubadours dedicate their love poems to you! I never saw your like!"

And he continued to rave in a way I'd once almost believed.

I finally raised a hand. "May I remind you that I patronize these troubadours? It would be both churlish and indiscreet for them to dedicate their poems elsewhere." Seeing that he was about to argue, I hastened on. "But you didn't summon me to chatter about my beauty."

He tried to be gallant. "No, I was simply overwhelmed. And I did intend to say that I've missed you sorely, Joy; that I need your friendship." His voice thickened. "Christ, how I need you!"

This sounded true. "For some special reason, Henry?"

"Surely you've followed events. This has been a most trying time, Joy, the most dreadful year I ever remember."

It had been dreadful for me as well—were we thinking of the same events?

He glanced, read my thought, then hastily launched into a long diatribe against Becket, Louis and the Pope, the monks of Canterbury, and the king of Scotland, who still demanded Northumberland, while I waited patiently. The hours struck, the fire had to be stoked twice, and still he droned on about his difficulties. I remained absolutely quiet.

"Why are you moving all your effects to Aquitaine?" he asked abruptly.

Ah, here it was—he was worried about Rosamond. I admired his gall, and smiled gently.

"I'm past childbearing, Henry; this last birth finished me. Since I can no longer serve you in that area, I plan to live a regular domestic life of retirement in Poitiers. The children will be happy there, and I can educate them myself."

The children, my excuse with Rancon. Though I recognized the irony, I was not amused.

Henry's eyes fixed, like the snake head on the prow of his own *Esnecca*. "What do you mean 'beyond childbearing'?"

"Why, Henry, you amaze me. Surely you know that all women go through a period of change, during which they suffer delusions and after which they're barren. I'm growing old, my lord."

He pounded his fist. "Don't take me for a fool! I know your age; I know your condition! You're avoiding my bed, and I demand to know why!"

He might know my age and condition, but he underrated my wit. As if I would sob on his shoulder of how he'd betrayed me with his

Welsh rose! "Very well, I didn't want to make you feel guilty." His face flushed. "But this last birth quite undid me. My midwife used tongs—she was a butcher!" I covered my face. "If you knew how she tore at me—I may never recover!"

After a time, he patted me awkwardly. "Hush, Joy. God's eyes, I've never seen you cry before. Give me her name and I swear I'll put her on the rack!"

I smiled through tears. "I have my Galen book—I'll make myself well, I promise you."

Now his arms were around me, his voice close to my ear. "I need your love, damn it! If I'm very careful, can you share my bed?"

"No."

"If I swear I won't . . . until you say?"

"No."

I pulled away. Our eyes locked, snake eyes to snake eyes. His gave way first.

"Inner wounds take the longest to heal," I murmured—amen to that.

Henry was no fool; I'd just told him about Rosamond and he knew it. He chose to bluster. "Why didn't you tell me when it happened? I would have been considerate. No need to hide in Poitiers as if you were a nun. Damn it, Joy, I need you as my wife, my friend! My mother didn't stop ruling just because she no longer produced children."

"Nor will I. I'll rule Aquitaine."

"Ah."

Again our eyes locked, but this time his pupils were dancing in speculation. I daresay mine were as well; this was the crux. How much did I know, and not just about Rosamond? Could Aquitaine be my real reason? Henry was clever—more than clever, duplicitous. I didn't underestimate him anymore.

He finally burst forth. "Aquitaine? After you were snatched by those mad Lusignans? I can't permit you to risk your very life!"

I bowed my head. "You were correct, my lord, and I light a candle every day for poor Patrick of Salisbury. However, the incident served as a warning, eh? I assure you I'll take care."

"Have you forgotten that you're my wife? I'm forbidding you, damn it!"

For the first time, I showed my fangs.

"I think, Henry, that it is rather you who have forgotten: I'm the duchess of Aquitaine. A title, I might add, which I'd held for years before we married. I've made my decision; there will be no more discussion."

"I will set the rules of parley, my lady. Your title in Aquitaine has been superceded by the fact that you're queen of England. I need you there!"

"I hope that I've served you well in England, and I love the country, but I'm not native, nor was I born a queen."

There followed more argument, in which he flattered my abilities and I pointed out that Richard de Luci and Leicester were capable seneschals. Besides, if I was so effective in England, why could I not rule Aquitaine?

"God's eyes, don't play the fool! You know that England is a peaceful island, obedient to the law! Unruly barons don't prowl the roads looking for victims!"

"Thanks to your strong rule, Henry. Give yourself credit."

He changed his gambit. "Don't desert me, Joy. I can't do without you." The ice in his eyes turned to a suspicious glitter.

Christ, don't let him cry.

"You forget, Henry, that out of our fifteen years as man and wife, we've been together only three. You did very well during the twelve years apart."

So I was jealous, his eyes said. What else had that foolish Welsh bitch disclosed?

Your plans to disinherit my sons, my eyes answered.

"I never left you alone from choice! Your former husband attacked within hours after we were wed and every summer thereafter! Do you think I wanted to be separated from you? From my children?"

Exactly what he had wanted. How clear it was after the fact.

"You must have become accustomed to separation, as I have, Henry. Nothing will change, except that I'll now be in Aquitaine."

"And you'll no longer share my bed."

We stared at each other in firelight, the truth sparking between us.

"That, too," I repeated.

"Forever?"

"Oh no, not forever." I, too, could dangle.

"I'll keep my officers in place to guard you."

He'd conceded.

"As you wish."

He sighed. "I still can't fathom your spending all your days prattling in the nursery."

"You anticipate me," I said brightly. "I have an exciting project in store, my lord. I'm planning to gather young people from all over Aquitaine to attend my court."

He leaned back into the shadow. "Are you establishing a school?"

"Oc, a school for love!"

"What?" His shocked face was comical, and revealing. He obviously thought I knew nothing of the subject. "I suppose you'll teach your grandfather's nasty songs, invite your troubadour protégés?"

"Oh, no doubt the troubadours will participate, and the romancers. Is it not strange, Henry? Our lives are composed mostly of love— except for men when they're at war, of course,—and yet our society never talks about love, can't even define it!"

"Most people would disagree. I certainly know that I love you."

"I'll wager that every person in my court will have a different definition of what that means."

His snake eyes returned, full of suspicion. "What people specifically? Whom did you invite?"

I spoke rapidly. "Mostly women, of course, the countess of

Flanders, the baroness of Maine, even ladies from England, and they will present cases to the court."

"Eleanor, do you want to make me the laughingstock of Europe? How dare you dally in the trivial complaints of dissatisfied wives! You'll insult every lord in the country! I forbid it!"

Though this was an ideal moment to fight him openly, I kept my wits. "Can you forbid Marie, duchess of Champagne? Alix, duchess of Blois? They have permission from the king of France!"

Again his face was comical. "Your daughters? Louis gave permission for a school of love? I don't believe it!"

"Be calm, my lord, this is not instruction for the physical act. While we recognize the role of lust in love, our concern is more political."

"Politics? How? What has love to do with politics?"

"It shouldn't, I grant you, but you must admit, Henry, that most marriages are politically motivated for the man's advantage."

I read his choler and hastened on before he could stop me. "Remember how your own brother tried to seize me? Visualize, if you can, what such a marriage would have been. Husbands and wives are 'lovers' and mortal enemies." I placed a soft hand over his arrow-scabbed fingers. "Don't be misled by our own ideal union; what I say is true. We plan to educate young men and women in the happier aspects of carnal relationship, and to discover rules that will ensure such happiness."

"Like Ovid?"

"Yes, insofar as we'll deal with love; no, insofar as he addressed only men, and taught them how to exploit women; it is our hope that we can change society."

"In short, you want to start a revolution."

I laughed lightly. "That's a provocative word for what we intend. Remember, I lived in France, visited the Byzantine Empire, each with its own societies. I would like to make the world more like Aquitaine in its attitudes toward love. Is that revolutionary? We won't use arrows or catapults, only music and stories. Marie is bringing her famous romancer, Chrétien de Troyes. I will supply troubadours."

He cracked his knuckles. "You know, Joy, you may have me to thank for Marie and Alix."

"How so?"

"Just this: I suspect Louis permitted them to come to you because of me."

"Did you ask him?"

"Not directly; I think the effect is more subtle. I permitted Young Henry to attend him in Paris; Louis was so grateful that he made him seneschal of France. Quite a feat, eh?"

Yes, *my feat,* my letter; Louis had replied that he would honor my son as his pledge of conspiracy.

"Furthermore," Henry continued, "we're meeting in a few weeks' time in Montmirail to grant my other sons the duchies I fought so hard to win. They'll swear homage to Louis for them, a real coup! I'll gain in a single day what I've wanted for years!"

Except that he'd wanted his sons to swear homage to England, not to France—and he would probably realize his error in time. Clever man, but not clever enough. I made the appropriate gurgles.

He laughed. "Yes, you might say I'm the patron of your courts of love!"

"Indeed you are, my dear. Patron and teacher, for you've taught me all that I know of love."

A mistake. His eyes narrowed.

"You said women will complain of their husbands' treatment. What will be your complaint?"

I laughed. "Absolutely nothing; I'll be the judge, not the plaintive. These are women who've been taught to loathe themselves."

He was still uneasy. "Have I taught you to loathe yourself?"

For the first time, I spoke the absolute truth. "No, my lord, you have ever flattered my person and my abilities, witness this conference. Yet I have loathed myself, I admit, because of my own real faults. Why I have them, I don't know, but I'm trying to recover."

"Recover?"

"Did I say that? I meant *discover*."

He took my hand. "You may take my word, Joy, you have no faults. You may be right, however, about going through that period in your life when women often lose confidence, even loathe themselves, as you say. Remember, I had a mother. I'm not insensitive."

"Thank you, Henry."

He then went back to the conference of Montmirail. Louis was eager to forge new ties with Henry; he would not only recognize our sons, he would tie them closer with marriage prizes. Best of all, he'd invited Becket, who had agreed at last to recognize the Constitutions of Clarendon, a banner occasion! After that, there could be no excuse for not crowning Young Henry! All this would take place in only two weeks, at the feast of the Epiphany.

"Doesn't that remove your self-doubts, Joy? Make you feel like the victor you are?"

"It's your victory, Henry, not mine."

"Don't be so modest! You share my victories, every one! Accompany me to Montmirail, Joy; stay with me. I can wait for the bed, only I need you. And I want you to witness your sons' ascendance. You'd like that, wouldn't you?"

"You know it's what I yearn for more than anything, to see my sons settled. Well, if you're certain, I'll come."

I wouldn't miss it.

I rose to retire, but he held my hand. "Wait, Joy, don't go. You're a sly creature—what's your real reason for going to Poitiers? The truth, please."

A final test, to see if I would mention Rosamond.

"I've told you the truth. To teach love; to show that love itself is a teacher."

His gaze was a mix of pity and perplexity. "Such a waste of your abilities. However, in time, and I admit that you're the expert. God knows you've taught me—I love you, Joy; you can't know how much."

Before I could avoid him, he kissed me ardently. I tried to respond.

Like another kiss given long ago in Beaugency, when I'd said farewell to Louis.

The meeting in Montmirail took place below the city, in a low field where benches were set up to accommodate the guests. A January mist swathed the area in penetrating cold, which forced everyone to huddle in forced friendship. Wrapped in marten, I sat in the first row for an unimpeded view of the platform where the dignitaries would conduct their business.

A hush fell over the crowd; the abbot of Saint-Michel climbed up the steps, followed by Louis of France with his small prince beside him. Others followed, but I watched only Louis. Had I ever been intimate with this stranger? When had he grown a long beard? Where was the shy boy who'd doubled in shame on our wedding night? The abbot began his prayer and we all bowed our heads. I couldn't resist—I looked upward, and met Louis's dovelike eyes. The look vibrated and there he was, the same boy, the same mixture of yearning and panic. But no, there was a new confidence born of years in the saddle. Louis had become a fighter, not a brilliant man in the field perhaps, but he had endurance. And courage. His faint smile acknowledged our new alliance.

My eyes slid to Henry, the first time I'd seen him next to Louis since that fateful parley when he'd come with his father. Now thirty-four, Henry was in the insolence of manhood. His slanted smile and shining eyes bespoke an oozing sensuality, which enthralled even this company of celibates and eunuchs. For an instant, he, too, looked at me, and sent a distinct message: See? I'll win the peace just as I won the war.

The third most interesting person to me was Louis's young prince, Philip, a sallow, undersized boy with one slightly milky eye. I pride myself that I can read children, and this boy was disturbing. Frail he might be of body, but I sensed a dull determination in his character. Determination toward what? Then he raised his gaze to Henry and I knew; he hated Henry with the fierce fanaticism that Louis had once displayed in his love of God. I felt cold beyond the elements.

The peace parley began, in which Henry solemnly swore he would fight no more in Aquitaine, Brittany, or any other of his Continental possessions that were under Louis's sovereignty.

That portion ate up the morning.

By midday, a dull, sulfurous sun glowed through clabbered clouds. Henry, solemnly facing Louis, asked that his sons be permitted to swear homage for those lands that he, Henry, had assigned them.

"My princes bring you their loyalty even as the three kings brought gifts to our King of Kings on this day of Epiphany."

I cringed. Henry should avoid religious imagery. Louis smiled sweetly. "Since Jesus Christ inspired your words, likewise may your sons receive their lands in the presence of the Lord."

A felicitous reply, avoiding Henry's false analogy, which would compare Louis to Christ. It also made the transaction inviolable before God. Clever Louis.

Young Henry stepped forward first and knelt before his father-in-law, the French king. Palm to palm, they gazed with mutual love. For a moment, I was disquieted to see my own flesh and blood so openly acknowledge Louis as his father. Solemnly, my boy received Maine, Touraine, Anjou, and Normandy and swore homage to Louis for his new possessions. Louis again pronounced him seneschal of France.

Henry couldn't resist a flash in my direction. My son was on the throne of France.

Next came Richard. Louis studied him with interest on this first meeting. Seeing him through Louis's eyes, I was aware of Richard's gravity, purpose, and tensile magnetism. Young Henry was charming; Richard was dangerous. He swore homage for Aquitaine.

"As a special gesture of friendship between our two houses, Prince Richard, I hereby offer you my daughter Princess Alais as your future bride. She will bring with her the county of Berry as her dowry."

Again, Henry glanced at me with satisfaction; he'd long coveted Berry. The rest of us were watching an exceedingly pretty young girl approach Richard. She looked much like her sister Marguerite, except that Alais's nature seemed more tremulous and vulnerable. Richard observed her warily, then with interest, then fascination. For the first time, he smiled.

My throat grew tight. Joined, I thought, like dragonflies.

Last came Geoffrey, whose position was less certain. He'd been betrothed at five to the countess of Brittany, but the count of that wild country was still fighting against Henry. Now Louis gave this dark, wiry boy the land without a struggle.

Henry had his empire—except that it belonged to his sons.

The sun disappeared, the mist returned, and priests descended from the town, leading Thomas Becket. The main event had arrived.

Of all the people on the platform, Becket had changed the most. Lean as a hermit, he reminded me of Louis in the days he'd worn sackcloth. He knelt before Henry.

Henry raised him to his feet and embraced him, tears visible on his cheeks. Henry, of course, could summon tears as readily as Louis ever had.

Again, Thomas knelt. He spoke directly to Henry in low, rapid Latin: He was sorry he'd left his see, deeply regretted his separation from Henry, the man he loved best in all the world, and he begged forgiveness.

He ended with an imploring look: "I now submit the case to your judgment."

Henry, overcome, said, "I grant you clemency," and extended his hand.

"Saving the honor of God and my order," Becket added in a loud voice.

Henry's hand froze. Shocked horror resounded across the field. The same damning caveat? What was the purpose of the meeting? Hadn't he promised France and the monks that he would give in to Henry?

Henry lost control. He whirled on Louis and shouted of "heretical depravities!"

As he went deeper into a fit, the horror shifted. Could this be the famous king of England who ranted like a spoiled child? Abruptly, Henry stopped in midhowl. "Tell the archbishop," he said, "that I will review the English laws to see where they may offend canon law."

Louis and the legates surrounded Becket, arguing hotly.

Becket would obey God's law, and saving his order.

"Who's going to define God's law?" Henry shouted. "Thomas Becket? Tell him to give me the power of the weakest king England's ever had and I'll settle!"

Becket refused.

With that reply, Becket lost the king of France, lost the abbots and prelates, lost the entire audience. Henry was suddenly a hero. For the first time, everyone understood the tribulations he'd endured from this power-mad archbishop.

I went to collect my sons—now assured of their inheritance— and to continue my journey to Poitiers. Richard was in a corner with the French princess, explaining the strategy of Alexander the Great.

Henry, of course, had already forgotten his vows: He called loudly for arms! He would attack Brittany at once.

Though I had my own guard of knights, I was forced to accept Henry's escort, as well. Riding at a good pace with my sons in the van, only slightly impeded by heavy mists and a light snowfall, we made excellent time and had no difficulty until we reached a rise above Mirebeau, close to Poitiers. There I called for a halt; I thought I'd heard a human cry.

Moving carefully through a small copse with a single escort, I gazed down on a confused scene in the meadow below. The snow and mists had increased, but so had the wind, offering glimpses of mayhem before the visibility closed again. Horses and cattle mixed in circles, obviously disturbed. Then I heard, rather than saw, an arrow whiz, and at the edge of the field, a bowman raised his head. Again, and a cow sank to its haunches. Since when did humans fight cows? Then I saw that the horses in the herd wore saddles and, yes, there was one knight still in his seat. An Aquitanian? Hard to see, but I thought he wore our colors of blue and white. The army in the hedge ran forward, not really an army, but a group of ruffians. Were they local *routiers*, pillaging the countryside? What did they want? Then smoke rose in the distance; a woman and three children ran screaming into the clearing. They were hacked to the ground and screamed no more.

"*Dex aie*, who are those swine?" I cried to the knight nearest me, one of Henry's men.

"Quiet, my lady, or you'll be heard. We'd best move on before we're discovered."

We trotted down the hill to safety, though I could see now that our safety was a mirage. *Routiers*, ruffians, perhaps—for there were always many about—but I suspected they were mercenaries. Our knights do not fight thieves. Nor did they customarily fight at all during the winter months. Well, this was what I'd come to change, eh?

I entered my palace at Poitiers briskly, ready to take up arms myself. And yet—I climbed the steps to my grandfather's chamber in Maubergeonne Tower, which had not been altered since my grandmother's death. A haunted tower, I thought, as I touched the dent in the center of the high bed where the illicit lovers had once been entwined. When I turned, the Crusader's mirror reflected my image.

I sank before the glass. As the sun struck my face from the right, I could see that my skin was still smooth as a polished apple; my heavy braids, highlighted with jewels, were still a dark Oriental gold, no streaks, thank God. My lips curled mysteriously in the manner Henry so often remarked, and my eyes—mirror to the soul—glittered a blue obfuscation. Good, I had no wish to be known.

I reached for my quill.

"To Richard of Rancon, baron of Taillebourg, greeting: I have resumed residence in Poitiers. My son Richard needs to be trained in the military arts in preparation for his induction as duke. I'm herewith appointing you as his master and mentor. Please respond at once. Eleanor, queen of the English, duchess of Aquitaine, countess of Poitou."

I pressed my seal, my own image holding a falcon aloft, designed at my request after my hunt with Rancon on the Crusade. Such a tiny waist I'd had then—was I still so small? I stood so that the mirror caught my middle, turned as far as I could. Flat in front, rounded in back, all of it still firm to the touch. Youthful for forty-four.

Very well, forty-five.

I sat once again. Was that spark a flaw in the glass? I rubbed with the heel of my palm, then leaned closer. I removed the spark by touching my own cheek; for a long moment, a single tear trembled on my finger, then fell.

Cwo weeks had passed with no answer to my letter. Then, on Ash Wednesday, he rode into our courtyard.

The first person to see him was Richard.

"Heigh, Rancon!" the boy shouted.

From the entrance, I watched them greet. Rancon's hair was still dark, his figure trim, but there was a dignity in his bearing that bespoke a mature man. A married man.

He ambled easily up the steps. "Queen Eleanor, greeting."

No touch of hands, no kiss of peace.

"Rancon, thank you for coming."

"I obey my overlord."

"I'm not compelling you, Rancon," I said coldly. "I could find someone else if you prefer."

His eyes narrowed. "Obedience and pleasure are one." He greeted Amaria, my sister, young Geoffrey and Eleanor, then was

introduced to Joanna, Princesses Marguerite, and Alais. Young
Henry was with his father, and I'd put John with the nuns in
Fontevrault for a few weeks.

After interminable civilities, I suggested to Rancon that we confer, some safe place where we wouldn't be observed.

"You go first," I ordered. "To the cave by the river—you know
where."

The hermit's cave where we'd sobbed all night in each other's
arms.

Memory, confusion, reluctance crossed his face in rapid order. "I
will do whatever you say, my liege, but I remind you that it's raining—almost snowing—and the great hall is quite private."

"Please do as I say."

He bowed, put on his heavy cape lined with miniver, and, with
some excuse about tending his horses, left. At my signal, Amaria
pulled the children up the stairs to the women's quarters, and I,
too, donned my marten cape.

There was no one about for good reason. The weather was chilly
and damp, the mud underfoot dangerous for man and beast alike.
At first, I thought Rancon wasn't in the cave after all, until he
spoke from its depths.

"I'm here, my lady."

I stepped inside. "Thank you for responding to my summons."

"I've told you often that I want to teach Richard." He paused.
"I'm curious, however, as to this secrecy. Is training Richard such
a dangerous undertaking?"

"Your work with Richard will serve as cover to your real work,
Rancon."

"Which is?"

His cold tone compelled me to say what I'd hoped to avoid.

"You must wonder what I'm doing in Poitiers."

"Not at all. It's for the sake of your children, always your moti-
vation. Except, Richard is obvious; I'm not sure about the others."

"Yes, you're right, but it's more complicated than a bucolic interval. May I explain?"

"Please do."

"At our last meeting, we both spoke harsh words concerning the connection between policy and our intimate lives."

"I remember vividly. You compared me to a strumpet."

"Hyperbole spoken in the heat of anger," I said evenly. "You said—which you've just repeated—that I put my children above all else, above you, above Aquitaine."

I waited; he didn't comment.

"You also accused me of being . . . physically obsessed with Henry."

"Hyperbole spoken in the heat of anger," he said dryly.

"You were only partly wrong," I admitted. "I was obsessed with only one aspect of Henry, however: his ability to help my children or his ability to destroy them."

"Before you continue, perhaps I should tell you that all Aquitaine is gossiping about the fair Rosamond and how your lord wants to discard you."

All Aquitaine? I lost my breath for a moment, then, in a dispassionate monotone, recounted the scene with Rosamond as it had actually happened.

Rancon was ahead of me. "He was going to disinherit Richard!"

"As my heir, yes. He was actually disinheriting me, since I still hold the title."

"And Richard heard?"

"Worse, he understood."

"I shouldn't say that I told you so."

"*Mea culpa* for not moving sooner. But listen! I've now done everything that you asked: come back to Aquitaine permanently; left my marriage."

He didn't reply for a long period, then took a deep breath. "Lady Eleanor, may I speak plainly? Your *mea culpa* should be said to a priest in the confession box, not to me. Your marriage, though perhaps personally estranged, still has the same legal status. Come, I'll escort you back to the hall."

"No, wait, please!" I held his arm. "Hear me out! I've joined the rebellion, Rancon!"

He pulled away. "What rebellion?"

"The rebellion against Henry's rule in my duchy. Is there any other? I've joined with Louis; we're planning together."

At last, I had his attention. In a soft, rapid voice, I described my letter to France, Louis's response, the meeting at Montmirail. Rancon was astonished that I'd approached Louis, though still not convinced.

"Why are you telling me all this?"

"Because you're in touch with France as well! Louis told me—I know it!"

"We all do homage to France. Of course I'm in touch."

"Don't pretend! You're conspiring against Henry! I'm with you, need your help, Rancon! And you need mine—you said so! Listen! I have a scheme—I'm going to converge a court of love here in Poitiers."

His dismay almost matched Henry's. "Love? Is this another Tristan scheme?"

I felt as if I'd been slapped. "Not at all." I rubbed my brow with my rough mitten. "Perhaps I should clarify any misapprehension. The last time we met, you said a final good-bye to our intimate relationship. This is not an oblique strategy to renew our friendship."

"But—a court of love?"

"As a diversion! God knows I have a reputation for illicit love— let me use it! Now, listen to the ladies attending my court." And I repeated a long list of names. "Do you see anything remarkable?"

He hesitated. "Are you referring to the noble ladies of England and Scotland?"

"*Oc!* These are the wives of the nobles who've joined our cause! Their lords will come as well, only in disguise, and will hide in places we'll provide. At night, we'll make our plans. Love will serve as a perfect cover!"

Before I could stop him, he pulled me outside the cave into a freezing rain. "I absolutely forbid you to go forward with this *mesclatz* and dangerous scheme! And why are you even contemplating bringing strangers from England into our local problems?"

"Local if I'd moved when you asked me to. Now Henry is an enemy to England, and much of Europe as well, his Pax Angevina gone awry, eh? But, to be particular, he betrayed the king of Scotland and he *dangled* rewards to the aristocracy, promises he never fulfilled. At the same time, he bled both Scotland and English lords to finance his battles here in Europe. Finally, just as he finds it difficult to rule with his feet spread on two shores, he will find it difficult to defend himself on two fronts," I concluded triumphantly.

"This is dangerous folly, Eleanor. My God, you're asking for a death sentence!"

"Were you offering me a death sentence when you asked me into the conspiracy?"

"Never! You were to annul your marriage before you joined us! Not for the queen of England to rebel against her own husband, the king of England! Have you forgotten the rule?"

Rain coursed down his cheeks, dripped off his nose, while behind him I saw again the black crags of Mount Cadmos in sharp silhouette. Oh God, let it not be an omen.

"Does he suspect what you're doing?" he insisted. "Why you've come to Poitiers?"

"He believes—along with much of Aquitaine—that I'm jealous of Lady Rosamond."

"And if you're discovered, that's what Aquitaine—all of Europe—will still believe. Except Henry. He probably knows the real reason you left even now and may have spies watching you. Never underestimate the bastard!"

"Louis seems to have done remarkably well."

"Don't delude yourself. Henry's playing with him."

"My life as sacrifice to my sons' futures, then; I accept the outcome."

"How will you help them by dying?"

"I won't die, Rancon; I'll win—with your help. Please, for my father's sake, we have to fight!"

"For his sake, I should protect you. I forbid you to go forward with this deadly scheme!"

"Forbid all you like!"

Like warriors in the field, we faced each other in locked gaze.

"You say these English lords are with our cause—how do I know?"

"You have my word." I heard myself echoing Abbot Suger long ago, though I meant it. "Henry's permitted his English nobles to fend for themselves. They have little need for him."

"In short, they're disloyal and dangerous. These same nobles may use you!"

"Use me how? Only to destroy Henry!" I turned away. "Do as you like, but you now know my position. You once asked me to fight for Aquitaine, but I was afraid that doing so would destroy my children. Now I do so to protect them. Ironic, isn't it?"

He held my arm. "I'm going to see Richard inducted as duke of Aquitaine, by damn!"

"Not before Young Henry is crowned. Henry would never permit it."

"And Becket still controls Young Henry's crowning?"

I nodded.

"Christ!" He gathered a handful of mud and flung it into the river. "Damn Becket! Damn the whole wretched quarrel!"

"Becket approached me in Angers, as if I would help him. He's manipulative, intransigent, and the crowning is a powerful tool for bringing Henry around, if anything can."

"Rosamond told you that Henry doesn't want an heir! If she's right, Becket may be his excuse to avoid what he doesn't want to do anyway."

"But he appointed Becket specifically to crown Young Henry."

"Test Henry," Rancon said intensely.

"How?"

"Suggest that some other archbishop do the honors. If he refuses, you'll know he doesn't want the boy crowned."

"Canterbury always crowns England's kings."

"Are there never any exceptions?"

I stared at him. "God's heart!"

"Tell me!"

413

"After Archbishop Theobald died—in the interim before Becket was assigned to Canterbury—Becket himself wrote to the Pope asking for dispensation in the crowning of Young Henry, and the Pope granted it. Any archbishop could do it! I wonder if that dispensation is still in effect—I'll write Henry!"

"If Henry refuses?"

"He won't. Even if Henry doesn't really want the crowning, he'll go forward to thwart Becket."

"A deadly game, Joy."

"No, an endless game. Both men get perverse pleasure in their power struggle."

"Not endless. Henry will win. Watch Becket's fate, and see your own."

"I would settle for Becket's success."

"Becket is a dead man, if you count that success."

"I'll write Henry now!"

We both sloshed through the mud as quickly as we could, eager for hot claret and a dry room. I didn't deceive myself about my own feelings—hadn't I thrilled when he'd called me Joy? Hadn't I even taken solace that he didn't want me dead? But I was satisfied that I'd maintained my dignity. That single tear was all I would ever shed.

Within a week, I had a triumphant reply to my letter: No, the Pope's dispensation had never been lifted! Henry would write Louis at once to send Young Henry to Calais; I should meet him there with Princess Marguerite. He had already written Roger, the archbishop of York, to request that he crown the young couple as future king and queen of England. Archbishop Roger of York had accepted his assignment; most of the lords of England had approved.

I immediately wrote Louis that the first step of our plan was virtually accomplished. And I informed Rancon that on this issue, at least, he had been wrong about Henry.

Then, announcing that I must visit a new abbey in Caen, I left with Marguerite for Calais, there to prepare for England. Only Rancon knew my real purpose.

We found Young Henry so elated by his prospects that he had to be shut away, lest he bray his triumph and ruin everything. Marguerite joined him in his secret room, and I had a strong suspicion that they shared a bed for the first time, a double celebration.

Henry arrived; I ordered Marguerite's coronation gown to be hastily stitched. The excitement grew as the hour approached for them to sail. I would remain to guard the ports against Becket and his spies. We moved from Calais to Barfleur, where the *Esnecca* waited.

I kissed Young Henry good-bye. "The last time as prince," I said happily.

Then I embraced Marguerite, who seemed my real daughter. "England is fortunate, and Young Henry even more so," I whispered.

Henry interrupted us. "Joy, keep the young princess here with you."

"What?"

"We'll crown her later."

"How dare you betray France!" I was furious.

"I can do exactly as I please!" he blazed. "She'll stay with you!"

"Then I stay as well!" Young Henry cried. "I'll not have my wife demeaned!"

Henry snarled, "Get on board, or you'll never wear the crown at all."

There followed a scene of unprecedented acrimony while Marguerite wept bitterly and I despaired of anyone being crowned. I pulled at Henry's tunic.

"Your reason?" I demanded.

"I don't have to explain!"

"Tell me, Henry, or no one goes."

He grinned disarmingly. "I have to play with Becket a bit, tell him that I had no alternative about the coronation, but that I can still yearn for his blessing on my boy."

"You're planning a second crowning?"

"Let's say I'll *dangle* a second crowning, this time including the princess. Fix an arrow in him and Louis in one thrust, eh?"

"You're too shrewd, Henry." Too duplicitous.

At last the ship lurched out of the harbor. Keeping the princess by my side, I called on Sheriff Humet to guard the ports without me.

A runner arrived from Paris demanding that Marguerite return to her father at once. Louis was beyond fury at this insult. Another English betrayal—would he never learn? I despaired for our recent partnership, which already had such a weight of history to overcome, but Marguerite assured me she would tell her father that Henry was the villain, and that I'd argued on her behalf. I could only hope she prevailed. And I must admit to Rancon that I'd been at least partly wrong.

Four days later, when I walked into the great hall in Poitiers, I stopped in confusion; Rancon was conversing with a pretty young woman. His new wife? And she had a child beside her. All three rose.

"I'm sorry," I said weakly, "if I interrupt. Is this Lady Rancon? And your daughter?"

"Don't you know me?" The lady came toward me, arms outstretched. In an instant, I took in her heavy gold braids, her polished skin and intense blue eyes, my very younger self.

"Marie? Marie? You're a grown woman!"

"Mama, you haven't changed!" She threw her arms around me.

In close embrace, I recognized my little girl's fragrance, the touch of her petal skin. We swayed back and forth, crooned snatches to each other as the real little girl watched.

I knelt. "And who is this?"

"I'm Scholastique, Grandmother," she said plainly.

"A most appropriate name, I'm sure."

"Scholastique, go with Amaria. I want to speak to Mother alone."

"I'll leave you as well," Rancon said tactfully.

"Wait, Rancon, I must tell you about the crowning. We have new problems."

Marie smiled. "I didn't know, Mama, that this famous troubadour was your captain."

"And you didn't tell me that Marie was helping with your court of love, Lady Eleanor," Rancon said significantly. "She says you will change the social face of Europe."

"This is my year of change," I replied.

"And all for the better." A brutal comment, considering our new relationship.

"However, we need not disseminate. Marie is also part of our conspiracy." Her eyes sparkled; Rancon looked away. After our first meeting in the cave, we'd never spoken again of the rebellion. I didn't know whether he'd withdrawn, or simply wanted to exclude me.

At the moment, however, we sat in a conspiratorial huddle as I described the sailing.

"What's his reason?" Marie asked, puzzled. "Doesn't he like Marguerite?"

Rancon watched me. "It has something to do with Becket."

"True." And I explained.

"Dangling," Rancon commented.

I concurred. "Yes."

He then insisted upon leaving us alone.

Marie hugged me again. "Oh Mama, how I do love you! I feel we've never been apart! Your letters have taught me so much about music! About love!"

By love, she meant the social rules of love, not her relationship with her husband, Henry.

We lost track of time, comparing our ventures into verse and romance. Then she startled me.

"Who is this Rancon, Mama?"

"I told you, a troubadour, my captain in Aquitaine—"

"A special friend?" she asked, interrupting me.

"Why do you ask?"

"I have a sense . . ." She saw my expression. "I didn't mean to intrude."

"Tell me about Louis," I said brightly. "Is he well?"

Marie found him a kindly but distant father. He seemed truly enamored, however, of his son, Philip.

"He looked sickly," I commented.

"Don't be misled by his small stature or pinched expression. He lacks a great nature, but he has absolute concentration on what interests him, like a hound on a scent. He hates King Henry."

The question was, would that hatred extend to Henry's sons?

We tried to cover the years that had separated us, and when was Alix to arrive? Servants came and went, food was offered and withdrawn, it grew dark, and still we talked.

Then she went back to Rancon. "He seemed reluctant to speak of the rebellion."

"Did you ask him about it?"

"Shouldn't I have? Since he's your captain—"

"It doesn't matter."

"Isn't he part of our plot?"

"He will be. At the moment, our movement seems split into two factions."

"You mean England and Europe?"

"That, too, but there's another group, in the south of Aquitaine, around Angoulême, who've been fighting for years. They fear giving up autonomy. But come, enough of politics!"

We began again with the day we'd parted in Beaugency.

Once I heard from England that Young Henry had been crowned by Roger, the archbishop of York, I went forward with Richard's induction as duke. To placate Aimar of Limoges, who still smouldered about Henry's lowering his walls, I planned the ceremony in his city, to be presided over by his bishop, and I invoked the Limousin saint, an obscure virgin called Saint-Valerie. By coincidence, the monks of Sainte-Martial discovered a life of Sainte-Valerie buried in their archives, which seemed to everyone an omen of good fortune. I also took great care to include Princess Alais in every step of the ceremony. She and Richard were not yet married, of course, so her presence didn't have the significance of Marguerite's to Young Henry, but Louis had to be placated.

Henry begged to be excused from the ritual; he was instructing Young Henry in Winchester, which was just as well. A blind man would have sensed that Rancon had a special interest in Richard; he couldn't keep his eyes or hands off the handsome lad, and Richard responded with unabashed love. I looked forward to the day when I could tell Richard the truth, only not yet, not when we were moving into such dangerous times.

Nevertheless, as I rode on one side of Richard, with Rancon on the other, down the narrow streets of Limoges, I pretended that we were a family bound by blood and love. With Rancon watching us, I led our son up the aisle to the limestone rood screen, where we knelt, facing each other. Playing the role of Sainte-Valerie, I placed a ring on his finger in holy matrimony; he promised to cherish me forever, then prostrated himself before me. Thus was Richard symbolically wed to the people of Aquitaine. Involuntarily, I met Rancon's eyes, and for one blessed moment, we were not changed at all.

From Poitiers, we rode out on a *chevauchée* so that I could present the new duke to his people. Here my euphoria dimmed; Rancon, accompanying us, introduced Richard to the barons as their future military leader, and I was reminded of my own father introducing me in like manner. The sense of loss stabbed me like a knife: We *should* be a family; it was unendurable to be so apart. So alone.

I was glad when we returned to Poitiers.

Henry suddenly sailed back to Normandy to resolve the Becket affair once and for all. To everyone's astonishment, he conceded to all of Becket's demands: He canceled his debts, he compensated Becket for the income he'd lost while in exile, and he offered to escort Thomas back to Canterbury himself, using the royal *Esnecca*.

Most important, he scheduled a second crowning for Young Henry, with Thomas officiating and Marguerite in her rightful place.

"The rebellion can go forward!" I cried to Rancon.

"Henry's learned something," he worried. "This tactic is calculated to take the wind out of all the rebels. Some form of dangling."

"Do you believe the rebels are so shallow? That they'll be willing to forgive years of injuries just because Henry seems conciliatory?"

"People are fickle, Lady Eleanor. Rulers tend to be judged by their most recent acts."

"What do you think he's learned?"

"I don't know."

Since Rancon's work with Richard was finished, he was returning to Taillebourg. I was keenly aware of former partings, when we'd clung desperately, whispering agitated promises to meet again soon. Now he said only that he would be in touch, then rode out the gate.

Except for the one slip when I'd seen him with Marie, I'd not mentioned his new family, nor had he volunteered anything.

Rancon proved correct about the reaction to Henry's generosity. All Europe was impressed, except for two people: Becket and I. Thomas sullenly refused royal largesse, until pressure forced him to accept. He went to Barfleur to meet Henry.

Then Henry's true purpose emerged. Instead of going to Barfleur himself for the appointed rendezvous, he suddenly dashed to the Auvergne for an imaginary battle; instead of giving Becket income or even the *Esnecca*, he left his old friend begging for passage back to England. Someone finally lent him a few coins to board a merchant ship just before Christmas; even the monks of Canterbury were not alerted of his arrival.

Henry had made his point, however. He might renege on his promises, but that didn't raise Becket in anyone's estimation. They were sick of his ceaseless whining, his borrowing, his unforgiving stance.

Once Becket was safely out of Europe, Henry summoned all his greatest nobles to join with him in Bures to celebrate this most propitious year at his Christmas Court. Hadn't he crowned his prince (though not his prince's wife)? Hadn't he disposed of Becket at last? There was much for which he might be thankful.

Reluctantly, I agreed to join him.

My entourage stretched almost a mile along the road. Not only did I have five of my children—all but Young Henry—with their attendants, as well as the two young princesses of France, Lady Constance of Brittany, who had recently become betrothed to Geoffrey, Amaria, and a dozen personal attendants for myself, but I carried my cook with his staff, my vintner, pots, braziers, my own bed, linens, live chickens and pigs ready to slaughter, two bands of musicians, my personal troubadour, and a large guard of knights to be sure we arrived in safety. We left Poitiers with bells ringing fore and aft and a merry pipe piping, but we were soon overtaken by a strong wind, followed by snow flurries. With our hoods pulled low, our scarves across our noses, we plodded on the narrow path in silence.

The snow was heavy by the time our man in the front shouted, "Bures! On the horizon!"

Thank God. We crossed the narrow bridge above the moat; though I'd tried to arrive before the guests, the courtyard was filled with horses and grooms. Inside, the dim great hall was crowded with stamping men and a few ladies. The temperature was close to freezing, and yet the fire pit in the center of the room was a gaping gray hole without wood; the smoke hole in the roof above was open to the storm, though there was no smoke to escape, only clouds of icy breath. I didn't see Henry.

"Make way! Make way for the queen!" my pages sang out.

I called for my steward, then my keeper of the flames, my woodman, and a dozen burly knights to help. Servants scurried into the storm, up the stairs to the kitchen court, to the cellar, and within an hour, flames roared, sparks shot onto wet furs, where they sizzled briefly, the hole in the ceiling was snugly shut—smoke hung like a choking fog, but no matter—and most of the guests held wooden methiers filled with hot grog. The festivities had begun.

Henry grabbed me from behind. "God's eyes, I was worried about you in this storm! I might have lost my entire family."

He was swathed in marten, and his hard gray eyes and red nose glowed in welcome.

"That would indeed be a disaster," I commented dryly. "You could never replace your sons."

He'd turned and didn't hear me.

People were still arriving, though darkness had fallen, and I went to check my supplies. Christmas used to be a happy season in Poitiers, and was so even now when I was alone with my children, but these huge courts required the administrative skills of Caesar leading his army. I'd just arrived and was already counting the days until I could depart.

In the morning, I was able to see who was in attendance. There were the usual lords and clergy from Anjou, Maine, Touraine, and Normandy, a few from the low countries, but I was surprised to see so many from England. Even more surprising was the fact that not a few of the visiting Englishmen had signaled a willingness to rebel: Robert of Leicester, Hugh of Chester, Hugh Bigod of Norfolk, and William of Gloucester. Could Rancon possibly be right? Had Henry's blandishments to Becket cooled the ardor of these hotheads? I had no time or inclination to explore the question; that day, I was able to serve a fair feast of roast capon and spiced cakes, and the hall was now hung with holly and pine. Behind the echoing chorus of rough shouts, music sounded sweetly and my troubadour sang my grandfather's songs.

Although I had to delegate servants to care for my children, I noted with pleasure that Richard, at least, was enjoying his first Christmas with pretty Alais, and Joanna was the center of admiring ladies who clapped as she danced. Henry carried young John on his shoulders as he moved with jocular charm among his old friends and enemies. Even the weather became an asset; snow and sleet hurled against the walls, and winds growled in startling contrast to the bibulous warmth inside.

By the third day, I was exhausted—mostly from smiling—and it was only Christmas Eve. The pine branches had to be constantly changed so they wouldn't burn; one of my dinners had been a disaster with spoiled fowl; Lady Constance of Brittany—a sour child with pouched eyes—was torturing Joanna; my troubadour had developed a sore throat. Perhaps it was my own exasperation, but it seemed to me also that something was wrong with Henry. I was reminded of the Christmas celebration in Argentan, when the party had been askew; now he was edgy, boisterous to the point of insult, as if he were courting disaster.

The day was almost done and several people had retired, when there was a dull pounding to our left.

"Quiet!" Sheriff Humet called. "Quiet, everyone!"

"Quiet!" Henry roared, and the room fell silent except for the children.

The pounding was now clear and we could hear faint shouts. "For God's sake, let us in!"

"Who's there?" Humet called against the oaken boards. He looked around, amazed. "He says he's Roger, archbishop of York."

The crowd began to buzz. From York? How had he crossed the Channel in this blizzard? Why hadn't the guards stopped him at the curtain wall? Why wasn't the moat bridge raised?

Henry himself swung open the door. A very fat man in black sables fell to his knees.

"My lord king, God preserved me that I might bring you tidings this Christmas Eve."

"Go for the mulled wine," I ordered my porter. Two other bishops had followed the archbishop and looked near collapse.

"Take your time," Henry told York. "Care for your own needs first."

We could now see that the other bishops were from Salisbury and London, the cream of English clergy. Gently, knights escorted them to stools by the fire.

"Take the children to the nursery," I told Am.

"Not me," Richard protested at my elbow.

No, he was now the sworn duke of Aquitaine. I nodded.

Finally, the archbishop of York began to speak. "I bring you news about Becket, my lord."

Henry stooped on his haunches, so he was close to York. "Becket? Is he not in Canterbury?"

"He may be by now. We turned him back with Young Henry's guard."

My stomach tightened.

"Start at the beginning," Henry ordered.

Becket had landed at Sandwich on December 1, twelve miles from Canterbury; he'd ridden the distance among adoring crowds, then dismounted to walk on bare feet into the abbey. There, York and the bishops before us had met him to demand that he lift their excommunications for their roles in the crowning of the Young King. He'd refused, saying that the Pope had excommunicated them, not he, which they knew to be a lie. He'd also censored the monks of Canterbury who were equally outraged. Then after a week of celebrating and a pious distributing of alms, Becket had shown his true colors.

"He canceled the Constitutions of Clarendon," Henry guessed.

"Worse, my lord king." York spoke in a low voice, which carried in the hall like a drum. "He called for a hundred armed knights and rode on Winchester, declaring that Young Henry had no right to be on the throne, since he'd not been properly crowned. Along the way, he tried to rouse the rabble to insurrection!"

I gasped along with everyone else in the hall.

Henry jumped to his feet. "Do I hear aright? This recipient of every honor I could confer has turned traitor against me? An army, you say? Insurrection?"

York nodded.

With a mighty howl, Henry yanked a strand of holly and whipped it like a rope at his amazed guests. "You, you there! Have you no loyalty? No shame? How can you stand here like so many scuttle fish when your king is attacked? To arms! Take the traitor! Will no one rid me of this turbulent priest?"

I'd now witnessed Henry's rages a dozen times, but never one like this. He grabbed a knight's sword and swung it wildly, gnashed, stamped, made animal sounds of terrifying volume. Thank God I'd sent the children away. Then Richard tugged my tunic.

I looked where he pointed; outside the fray, four men were calmly arming themselves. Making a wide swath around the howling king, Richard and I moved in the direction of the four knights. I recognized two of Henry's bastard uncles, Tracy and fitzUrze, and two barons, Morville and Bret. Paying no attention to their frothing monarch, they spoke quietly among themselves. Once armed, they added heavy furs and edged around the crowd in the direction of the door. Where could they go on such a night? In deep shadow, Richard and I followed them. At the door, they paused and looked back; we ducked behind a knot of Angevins and watched.

FitzUrze raised his hand. Looking where he looked, I saw Henry pause in his rampaging and meet fitzUrze's eyes. He, too, raised his hand and nodded abruptly, a break in his insanity. The door opened to a gale of snow, but we could see destriers waiting, saddled and ready to go.

I clutched Richard's hand; he squeezed back. Together, we returned to the front of the crowd. Slowly, Henry became his normal self. He called for a table, parchment, and his secretary to write a note.

"To His Holiness, Alexander, Pope of the Christian world, from his faithful servant Henry, king of the English: We have just learned of most treacherous acts committed against our own person and that of our son the Young King Henry by Thomas Becket. With fraudulent deceptions, he has stripped our clergy of their rightful prerogatives and has attacked our prince with an armed host. We beg you to stop the aggressor in his unlawful acts."

He signed and called for runners, two extra ducats for any men who would brave the storm. Many volunteered; runners were on their way to Rome within the hour.

Now Henry ordered a council of secular men. An officer named Mandeville was put in charge of a second contingent, who were to leave for Canterbury as soon as weather permitted.

But four men were already on their way to Canterbury. For what purpose?

Mandeville and his men were to deliver an ultimatum to Becket: Either he must desist from all hostile acts against the young king and the old king or they were to put him under arrest. More was discussed, but I'd heard enough. Richard and I retired.

Richard stopped at the top of the stair. "What do you think those four knights were going to do?"

"They had their orders to confront Becket before legitimate officers reached him."

"Yes."

I couldn't read his eyes in the dark, but our thought was the same. We were remembering another Christmas with Lady Rosamond at Tintagel; the context of perfidy might be different, but they had the same source. Who knew how low he would stoop?

Christmas Day was somber; the guests were subdued. Archbishop Roger led our Nativity worship, then blessed the members of Mandeville's council, six in all. Snow or no snow, they were determined to ride that same day. Henry's tears ran down unshaven cheeks and his voice broke. "I beg you to wait one more day, until it's safe. Becket won't raise arms during this holy season."

Mandeville, also wet-eyed, swore that he loved his king above personal safety. As the moat gate clanged after him, Richard and I looked at each other silently. His blue-gray eyes reflected my own thought: Why hadn't Henry wept to send four knights into the dark the night before? Or the runners to the Pope? Where had his compassion been then?

Christmas passed, then another day, and another. I must stay through the burning of the Yule log, but many guests left. Henry, no longer the host, worked with his sheriff, Richard of Humet; after our initial greeting, he and I had exchanged hardly a word.

On December 29, I ordered my chests be brought to the great hall for packing. The pigs, chickens, dried fruits, and cakes were gone, but much remained. As I worked with Amaria, we were interrupted by another pounding at the door.

"Let me in, for God's sake. Open the door! In the name of the king, open!"

Am and I rose from our knees, terrified. What more could go wrong? Was Young Henry . . .

I opened the portal myself. A young knight, half-dead from exposure and weariness, would have slumped to the floor if Amaria and I hadn't caught him.

"The king!" he cried weakly. "I must see the king!"

Am ran up the stair. I pulled the knight to the fire.

Henry ran briskly down the steps. "Well, sir—Sir Balliol, is it?—what brings you here in such a state?"

Sir Balliol tried to rise but couldn't. "My lord king, King Henry, I bring you—the archbishop of Canterbury is dead!"

Henry's ruddy face bleached white as the drifting snow. "Thomas is dead? But how? He had a weak stomach—"

"Murdered, my lord, cut down at the altar as he prayed." He began to blubber, so it was hard to follow. "Cold blood, by four lords, knights they were. Hacked the kneeling man with their swords. They say his scalp hung like a quoit."

My own knees became weak; I had to sit.

"Thomas dead?" No tears flowed this time, but his shock appeared real. Yet no one could dissemble as Henry did. He reached to the knight. "Take your ease."

He turned back to the stair and slowly ascended to the top, where he paused, head bent. Then he let out an animal cry of such agony that my flesh crawled. The howl still echoed in the brown holly long after Henry had disappeared.

Sir Balliol looked at me fearfully. "He seems very taken."

"Yes."

"But they say . . . they say . . . that the men came from this court. People say that the king murdered Becket."

How could I be shocked? Yet I was. Henry had committed many crimes great and small, but not murder. Also, this was the first time I'd ever known him to be held accountable for anything. Before I could ask more, Henry appeared above us.

"Joy, will you come up to my chamber, please? I must confer with you."

27

$\mathcal{H}$enry's door was closed when I reached the top of the stairs. Then suddenly, Sheriff Richard of Humet burst out and streaked past me.

"Joy, are you there?" Henry called from inside.

"Coming."

Though his normal color had returned, his face was strained. "I've sent Humet to overtake our runners to Rome. We have to be sure Pope Alexander hears about Becket's attack on Winchester before he knows of the death."

"To justify Becket's murder," I replied.

He glanced at me sharply, then rose and paced. "God's eyes, what foul luck. To slaughter him at the altar—I can't believe it."

"Who did it, Henry?"

"Christ, how should I know?"

"The knight below reports that they came from this court."

"Mandeville couldn't have reached Canterbury by now."

"What about the four men who left Christmas Eve?" I asked boldly. I was sure that was why he'd summoned me, to find out who might have observed his signals.

"What four men?"

I described them, naming names.

He stared fixedly. "Have you told anyone?"

"Why should I? However, if I saw them, others must have as well. You should be prepared."

"For what?" he challenged me.

"To deny your own role."

He came close, and spoke through his teeth. "My role was exactly nothing. Do you understand?"

"You don't have to convince me, Henry." And he couldn't have if he'd tried.

"Not you," he agreed, "but that ex-husband of yours will be after my hide."

I stroked his cheek. "You've shown remarkable patience with Becket over the years. Why would you change now? Besides, such a brutal act is not your style."

His face muscles relaxed. "No, by God, it's not. I rarely kill in battle—never if I can avoid it—and I'm lenient with prisoners. The record's there. However, this is a rare dilemma. I wish my mother were alive to help me calm the waters."

His mother had been the least calming woman who'd ever lived.

"Fortunately," he continued, "I have you. I need your help, Joy; never have I needed you so much." To my horror, he clasped me in his arms and buried his face in my neck. I almost screamed aloud. "You remember how I once said that every man needs an intimate friend he can trust? You are my friend, Joy. With God as my witness, I can't get through this without you."

Becket had also been his intimate friend. Rancon had been absolutely right: try to seize power from Henry and end in a pool of blood.

"What's wrong?" Henry drew back. "Why are you trembling?"

I hoped he read my breathless voice as anger. "Becket invited tragedy, didn't he? Offended those knights with his attack on Winchester, which put the blame on you when they took revenge. Tell me what to do, anything at all!"

He showed his teeth, but his eyes didn't smile. "Be my eyes and ears; keep me apprised of rumors, who's loyal and who's not. Meantime, I'll retire to Argentan to grieve; I'll be out of touch, except for you."

"I'll report to you regularly."

Tears spilled from his reddened eyes as his pupils darted from side to side, speculating on my sincerity.

I gathered information from my spies.

The monks of Canterbury, having no great love for Becket, left his corpse lying in its own pool of blood on the altar for two days while townspeople came to stare. One enterprising fellow scooped up as much blood as his cup could hold. Just when the festering body was becoming an embarrassment, the monks carried it to a bier, where they stitched the head wound (shaped like a quoit) and removed Becket's rich robes. To their astonishment, they discovered a hair shirt crawling with vermin and worms next to his skin. Was it possible he'd been truly devout? That his vows, taken in unseemly haste, had nevertheless been sincere?

If so, wrote my informers, he'd been foully murdered. (I admit, I couldn't follow this reasoning; he had been foully murdered, whether he was devout or not.)

The following day, the third day after the murder, Becket sat upright in his tomb and blessed his monks. Now there was open talk of martyrdom.

The enterprising gentleman with the cup offered Becket's blood for sale. Within a week, a blood-soaked rag cured dame Britheva's blindness; a priest with a paralyzed tongue regained his speech; wife Godiva was cured of swollen legs. Pilgrims swarmed to Canterbury and the word *saint* was on everyone's lips.

This much I wrote to Henry.

What irony! That Thomas Becket, a vain, ambitious, greedy toady whose only virtue was a fast, shallow intelligence should be the "saint" of another phase of our rebellion, or that he should be a saint at all. Except for taunting Henry, he'd done nothing that would be remembered; no one who knew him personally had liked him; he'd been alienated from his own family and—particularly damning in my view—disliked women almost as much as Bernard of Clairvaux had. Nor did I forgive him for hurting Young Henry.

What were the Church's criteria for sainthood? There had recently been talk of canonizing Bernard of Clairvaux, and now Becket was also in the offing, while Abbot Suger was receding into oblivion, remembered only for inventing a new kind of architecture. Well, if I were right about the importance of literature and art, Suger might yet prevail in the centuries to come.

I withheld from Henry the public reaction, of which he had no interest. From the Pope to the meanest stable lad, the people viewed Henry II, king of England as a combination of Pontius Pilate and Judas Escariot; like them, he had delivered an unarmed saint into the hands of his murderers; like them, he had delegated the bloody deed to others, "washed his hands" of the heinous crime.

I did tell him that the churchmen rose in wrath.

I certainly withheld the reaction of our own rebels from Scotland to Guyenne, who pronounced themselves ready to march, not that they cared a straw about Becket. What they did see was that the time was ripe. We had the king cornered, trapped by his own murderous folly.

Louis urged that I assemble my court of love at once—he was calling for a meeting of heads of state to be held in Poitiers that summer.

Henry, sequestered in Argentan, was unaware of the dimension of the fires licking at his tower base, and he still thought he could weather the heat. He said loudly in every forum that he was innocent of murder, of collusion, or even of the slightest desire for Becket's demise. He'd loved Thomas as a brother, had given him every favor a king could bestow. Those who visited him were impressed with his anguished tears, but, of course, not many visited. My letters, while accurate, were dismissed as hysterical.

I couldn't escape the fires, however, nor could my children. Even in the friendly city of Poitiers, my young brood was vilified as children of the Devil. It was said that Joanna rode a broomstick on nights of the full moon, that all of them attended covens in our park. Tales were revived of Henry's witch ancestor Melusine, of his grandfather Fulk the Bad, of crazy Ermengarde of Anjou, of the Angevins' well-known proclivity toward diabolical madness.

I anxiously awaited Marie to plan our court, and I hoped she could distract my poor children. I could have wept with relief the snowy day they rushed into the courtyard to greet her, only it wasn't Marie; it was Rancon. Watching him dismount one of his magnificent Andalusian steeds, I had the usual surge of joy, which I quickly controlled. No doubt Becket's death had brought him to deliver another lecture about my own danger.

"Greeting, my lord," I said warily.

He nodded without looking at me, then walked into the great hall with one arm around Richard, another around Geoffrey, while the girls danced backward in front of him.

Best disarm him before he began, deflect his attack. "How kind of you to think of us, Rancon. We're really suffering—we bear the brunt of the Becket affair, especially the children."

"They say I'm a witch!" Joanna shouted.

Rancon looked up sharply. "Becket? What about Becket?"

I lowered my wine in disbelief. The children jabbered the gory tale with delight while Rancon expressed horror and amazement in equal parts. As they talked, John climbed onto his lap, Richard and Geoffrey fingered his sword where it lay on the floor, and the girls all shyly touched his hair and person, a strange, sentimental scene. I could understand their desperate need for attention, but what was his motive? Why was he here if he hadn't heard about Becket? Where had he been? All of Europe talked of nothing else. He laughed, made exaggerated faces of shock, stroked the girls' hair in return, played the avuncular role with perfection. He didn't, however, glance once in my direction.

The afternoon gloom deepened, the keeper of the fire brought more wood, and Amaria took the children to their various servants. I drew my stool opposite his.

"Save your words!" I ordered, as if he'd spoken. "I won't withdraw from the rebellion!"

His answer was so muffled that I could hardly hear. "Christ, Becket's dead!"

"Which you predicted. Why so surprised?"

"I thought Henry would be more subtle."

"I suspect there was a mistake in the execution, killing at the altar, for example. As for the *miracles* . . ."

He seemed not to hear.

"At least it makes Henry vulnerable," I repeated for the second time.

"Forget the rebellion! For God's sake, consider your children! They need you!"

"That's strange advice, coming from you."

He touched my shoulder. "Joy, I didn't come to quarrel."

"No? Why did you come, then? The roads are closed; my court of love won't begin until summer."

"Would you believe me if I said I was just out riding?" He attempted to smile.

"Hardly."

"Well, it's true. At least partly. I assume you have room for me?"

"You know you're welcome. No one's in the military quarters; I'll have your place prepared."

"Wait!" He caught my hand as I rose. "I want to talk."

I sank to my stool.

He began with his movements at the end of last summer, after our *chevauchée,* when he'd returned to Taillebourg, where he'd fallen into a deep melancholy humor. His marriage was to take place at Christmas, and he'd realized he could not go forward with his plans. I felt a surge of joy, though I concealed it. Whatever his reason, he was still unmarried! He'd contacted his lady of Gascony and withdrawn as honorably as he could, citing soul sickness. As autumn approached, he'd decided to take a pilgrimage to Compostela.

For the first time, I interrupted. "That's more astonishing than Becket's death, Rancon! You—a pilgrim?"

He pressed his lips and didn't speak. At once, I regretted my words. Was he still melancholy? Had Rancon, of all people, suc-

cumbed to the black humor? Rancon, so naturally ebullient, sanguine, even choleric at times, but never sad.

"I am a religious man, Joy. And I had the example of your father,
who'd sought relief from the saint."

My father, not a religious man, had sought relief because
Bernard of Clairvaux had put a curse on him and my father had
been deathly ill. Oh God, was Rancon concealing something? Had
he returned because he feared for his health?

He then continued his saga. "It's a long ride to Compostela, you
know, through the great pine forests of Guyenne, red soil, the tang
of turpentine, the silver-green needles catching the sun, tremen-
dous space above—I felt light-headed, as if I trod in a different
world. Suddenly, an Arthurian tale came full-blown into my imagination—remember when Henry tried to commission me to write
about Arthur?"

And I'd sponsored Wace of Jersey, who could never produce a
convincing version.

"It's about Guinevere. You recall that she was unfaithful to Arthur
with Mordred, Arthur's evil nephew—an affair that demeans the
great queen."

How alike our minds. "He was an unworthy lover."

"So I replaced the villain with a hero."

"Who?"

"Lancelot."

Of course, the greatest knight of them all. "Go on."

With his usual compelling manner, Rancon wove his spell. One
day while sitting at the Round Table, King Arthur was informed that
his queen had been abducted by the evil Mélégant. Arthur called for
a knight to rescue her, and Sir Kay volunteered. On the road, however, Sir Kay succumbed to one terrible test after another, and quietly, without fanfare or his name being given, another knight took
over the quest. He crept across a raging torrent on the sharp edge
of a knife; he resisted the temptation of a beautiful seductress without a moment's thought. Then, to his chagrin, he was approached
by a dwarf who drove a dung cart, the most lowly of creatures and

the most lowly of transport. The dwarf promised Lancelot that he could take him to the queen, only he would have to crawl under the pile of dung to hide himself. For a long moment, Lancelot hesitated; not only was the dung a filthy cover but it was unworthy for a great knight to ride in a cart—and with a dwarf! Finally, he overcame his scruples and burrowed deep into the ordure.

Far away in the castle where she was kept prisoner, Queen Guinevere, watching her lover in a magic mirror, saw him hesitate. She flew into a rage. Did he not love her? Did he put his pride above her life?

Lancelot reached the castle, where he fought Mélégant against terrible odds, and lost. Ripped by spikes, starved and bleeding to death, he was tossed at Guinevere's feet. Obviously dying, he begged her to cure him.

"Did she?" I asked.

Rancon gazed intently. "I don't know—would you say she did?"

"It's your tale, Rancon. Tell me how it ends."

"The cure was to offer him the solace of love."

I rose in agitation. "For God's sake, tell me the truth. Are you ill?"

"Yes, sick with love."

My heart burst with joy. I was too weak to stand; I sank again to my stool. "Is your tale a metaphor, Rancon?"

He rose above me. "I love you, Joy. That's why I'm here, why I'm still alive, for I hope. If I'm wrong . . ."

"You're not wrong!"

And I was crushed in arms, melancholy no longer.

A long time later, in the darkness of my bedchamber, I came back to his Arthurian tale. If it really was inspired by our own circumstances—and I was sure it was—who, then, was the dwarf in our lives?

"Need you ask?" he answered my query. "A small man—children."

"Richard?"

"To get to my queen, I must accept all her children."

"Even Henry's?"

"They're all yours, eh?" I heard his amusement. "And three of them are probably mine."

Three? William, Richard, and—ah, yes—possibly Matilda.

My children, our children, children—I loved them, and so did he. If they had had a choice of father, they would have chosen him.

"But Rancon, perhaps I'm not Guinevere."

He laughed. "Will you be quiet? The tale is finished."

"Guinevere was a true prisoner of an evil enchanter. And King Arthur wasn't her nemesis. I could have left Henry—you begged me to—I should have left that first month, pregnant or not and no matter what the scandal. I'm guilty, Rancon! I'm the one who put you under a dung heap, not my children. Can *you* forgive me?"

"I'm here, aren't I? And don't forget, you accused me of wanting to raise my station by loving you. I needed to accept my demeaned state, go through the stages of knighthood."

"Hyperbole, remember?"

"I had to pass my test. You know what I think? The only real sin is to betray love—neither of us has gone quite that far, eh?"

How warm his voice, his arms, his flesh pressing against mine. A spark exploded in the fireplace, giving brief light.

"Ah, look, Rancon, beautiful black wires on your chest."

He drew me close. "I found a gray wire on my head—do you mind?"

Smoke from the spark wafted to the beams above, weaving and hovering in ephemeral designs.

Tristan and Iseult, Love and Death, now changed to Lancelot and Guinevere, where he died and she ended in prison.

I burrowed against Rancon's strong beating heart.

"I love you," he whispered.

28

ancon lived in Máubergeonne Tower, our tower of love, where I met him every night. Though we tried to be discreet, we were also forthright. No one spoke of our intimacy and everyone benefited from our happiness. My life became a many-layered chord, like one of those polyphonic harmonies of Constantinople: child care, domestic husbandry, the governance of Aquitaine, messages to England, to Louis, to Henry, to the conspiratorial lords all over the Continent and Britain, and through all the contrapuntal complexities ran the pure melody of love.

Henry descended from his eyrie and learned the truth about his reputation. With typical craft, he sailed the Irish seas, on the attack, where no one could follow. Unintentionally, he cut himself off from all intelligence of what we were doing.

My daughter Marie returned, and this time Alix was with her. Alix had her father's features, alas, but her deep, throaty voice was mine, the never-ending mystery of the mixture of blood, and she possessed her own breathtaking intelligence. This was my moment of total happiness, and I knew it. Over and over, I would stop under a willow, or on a bridge, or on a stair and say aloud, "I'm happy!"

Rancon's troops rode forth, singing his *sirventés*:

> *In March and June*
> *I do just as I will!*
> *War is my tune*

And my theme is the kill!
I live only for war—
That creed is my star!

Barons skirmished as they did every summer, La Marche against Angoulême, Limoges against Poitou, everyone roistering, broiling, shouting, and raging. Under the cover of these mock battles, the leaders of our rebellion quietly came to Poitiers. Still other lords from Scotland, England, Maine, Normandy, France, and Anjou rode the quiet paths under cover of dark, then entered the town disguised as monks, jongleurs, tradesmen, and farmers. Poitiers also burgeoned with their ladies, ostensibly to attend my court of love.

On the Feast of Saint-John, young people were gathered in the dazzling sunshine of our garden to talk of love, while the conspirators bided their time until nightfall. When my young students were assembled, I sauntered to the grassy circle at the center of our assemblage. They immediately fell silent at my appearance, partly, no doubt, because of my position and partly because of my choice of costume. I wore the troubadour green, with a long cape fashioned of Byzantine silk embroidered with scarlet hearts; my pearls of great worth hung in triple strands to my knees and my small crown was of gold and rubies.

"Welcome, young lovers!" I said softly, reaching my hands. "Welcome to our court of love, where we intend to change your lives— *oc,* to change history itself. We are latter-day Noahs, sailing on an ark to preserve life itself, to abjure the brutality that is disintegrating our very natures." I held my hands aloft in pretended shock. *"Dex aie!* Am I too late? What means those circled eyes? Tell me truly—are your bedclothes rumpled? Did you suffer from insomnia last night? Were there raging beasts in your sheets? Shafts of desire?" At each question, I touched the blushing cheek of some embarrassed youth and waited for laughter to fade. "Are you gathered to hunt in the night? Do you fear that our court will tame

Cupid's pigeons as they soar to ecstasy? That we counsel celibacy? On the contrary, we approve the rushing heart, except that we will force it to beat to our own commands. However, until that domestication has taken place, I advise the young virgins among us never to sleep—knowing that pudendal things befall an unwary maid." A gasp of delighted shock.

Slowly, I strolled among the pimply youths, twisting locks of hair, patting cheeks, and speaking saucily of lust, while Rancon sang softly in the background:

> *Remembering now*
> *The despair when we were apart:*
> *Remembering*
> *The emptiness inside my heart;*
> *Then remembering*
> *The softness when I put my hands*
> *Under her cloak again,*
> *Remembering that, I pray to God*
> *That never more shall we part.*

I raised my hand for attention. "Ah, our lord Rancon has reminded me once again that we are here to teach you of love, not to encourage your animal lusts, which need no instructor."

I turned so I could see Rancon under a leafy lacework. "This is a revolution, my dears, a rebellion against Ovid and all the mayhem he has caused through the ages in our inner lives. Men are not by nature rapists, nor are women mere animal game; we are created as two aspects of the same species, yearning for completion. All feel the truth of our longing at your tender years, but the culture gradually coarsens our natures, and we become hunters and prey, always sensing that we have betrayed the central meaning of life. Only artists have remained true to our instinctive feelings and then, I fear, few artists except those here in Aquitaine. I invite you to listen once again to Lord Rancon's song and note the longing that speaks to each human heart."

I bowed my head as he played.

"Thank you, milord. Very well, then, since love as a central theme of life is so alien in these rapacious times, we have codified a few rules that will help you defy your culture. These rules of love may be found in this slim volume"—I held up a bound book— "which we have copied on manuscript sheets for your perusal. We call our laws the Constitutions of Duke William the Ninth, to honor my great troubadour grandfather. These laws will govern us as we explore our cases in the court of love, and our first case is based on our first law: 'Marriage is no excuse for not loving.' Come forth, my lady Marie, duchess of Champagne, to preside as judge!"

I withdrew as Marie took my place.

Once out of sight, I removed my crown and walked swiftly up the steps of Máubergeonne Tower to meet Rancon. He was already before me, poring over a map spread beneath the mirror.

I placed a hand on his shoulder. "Before we begin, my lord, I thank you for your song. Every word was perfect—though it almost undid me." I kissed him lightly.

He covered my hand with his. "We should strike in Normandy and Suffolk simultaneously, the first move to make Henry split his troops."

Though we'd been over this a thousand times, we repeated our strategy blow by blow.

"I wish Young Henry had been knighted," I argued as I began to pace.

"It makes no difference."

We disagreed about Young Henry: I believed—as did Louis— that Young Henry must be ready to assume the full responsibility of the English crown by the time we went into open warfare. We couldn't depose Henry and leave a vacuum of power both in England and in Normandy, which would tempt every scoundrel in Europe. Rancon agreed about the necessity of leadership, but he had strong misgivings about Young Henry. He preferred that a senseschal be assigned to my prince. Either way, we couldn't strike for another year. It would take that long to assemble our armies.

Below our window, we could hear singing and laughter. The court of love was going well under Marie's guidance. And why not? From her own court in Champagne, she'd brought many fine performers to assist her. Shadows fell, torches glowed in great luminous circles, and the court of love continued into the evening.

When it was completely dark, Rancon and I crept down the tower steps, made a wide swath around the garden, then stole through the orchard down to the Clain River, where my sons Richard and Geoffrey were waiting. Wordlessly, we followed a path by the river along a muddy bank to the Chapel of Saint-Radegonde, close to the bridge and just inside Poitiers. The ancient church seemed dark, but inside the narrow nave with its low ceiling, a dozen men awaited us by candlelight. This was our first official meeting.

Duke Philip of Flanders introduced each lord with proper deference; an agenda was set forth concerning the division of responsibility, the leadership, and—most important—the timing. In general, we agreed to foregone decisions: We should fight on both sides of the Channel to keep Henry off balance; we should wait until Louis had conferred the Great Seal of England on Young Henry (with Rancon dissenting). Then we came to the dispersion of knights.

Suddenly, an unknown runner burst through the door. Someone snuffed the candle, plunging us into tense darkness.

"I'm from Paris!" the runner whispered. "King Louis sent me to warn you!"

"Your identification," Rancon's voice demanded.

The man sang hoarsely, *"I live only for war!"*

"The message!"

"King Henry's in Chinon! He may be here by midday tomorrow! And he's bringing Young Henry!"

A gasp ran around the room. When had he returned from Ireland? Why was he coming to Poitiers? Had someone informed him? And, I agonized to myself, did he know of Young Henry's role?

Swiftly, Rancon took charge. Everyone was to return to his lodging place and don whatever disguise he'd used to travel. Do nothing—with luck, Henry would stop only briefly and move on. Let the queen question him subtly as to his purpose.

We all fumbled our way through the low arch; shadows quickly disappeared in the dark. Back at the palace, the court of love had finally come to the end of its first day and Marie and Alix were waiting anxiously to hear our report. We told them; then Rancon escorted them across the dark meadows to Fontevrault Abbey, after which he followed his own advice and disappeared.

"Have you utterly lost discretion?" Henry roared.

"Hush, the windows are open." We were sitting in the great hall with our children.

"Why should I be quiet when you're braying your scandals to the world?"

"What scandals? Why do you take all this personally?"

"Do you think I haven't heard about your Constitutions of Love? Is that not personal, milady? Do you think I'm such an illiterate bumpkin that I don't grasp the allusion? Listen! Listen carefully! I won't tolerate ridicule! My Constitutions of Clarendon are sacred, yes, and so are my grandfather and his laws."

"I had a famous grandfather as well!" I countered. "He invented love as we know it! Did your Henry the First do anything more important?"

"Father is attacking you so that he may forget his humiliation in Avranches," Young Henry said, sneering. "His Constitutions didn't matter much there."

"What happened in Avranches?" I asked quickly.

"Merely a public show to appease the Pope, nothing more," Henry barked.

Young Henry glared with malice. "Why, my father recanted the Constitutions of Clarendon, despite his protests right now. He then bared his back for the monks to flagellate, and confessed to the murder of Thomas Becket!"

Henry's fist shot out.

Young Henry clutched his ear. "Strike me all you want, but that's the truth!"

Henry again raised his hand, but I caught his wrist. "Stop at once!" He pulled free.

"Was Young Henry telling the truth?" I demanded. "Did you confess?"

"Yes, I accepted responsibility for Thomas's death; no, I did not confess direct guilt, for I am not guilty! Yet a king is always responsible for acts done in his name; I said what was right. I had to put this behind us." He then launched into a bitter account of his return from Ireland, where he'd defeated the many Irish kings without a blow. Instead of being welcomed as a hero, however, he'd been greeted with hatred.

"If you'd prosecuted the four knights who were responsible, people might believe you," I commented. "Since you rewarded them, my lord, you're considered guilty."

"When did you become a judge, milady? You were in Bures; you know damn well I didn't order Becket's murder. Yes, I was angry, I admit that, and why not? Didn't he raise an army against my own son in Winchester? Those hotheaded knights thought they were doing me a favor; they acted *pro* my welfare, but not *per* my orders. Too bad the subject isn't love, for then you might grasp the distinction."

"Nevertheless, they murdered a man as he prayed. Wasn't your quarrel with Becket based on the right of the king's court to punish civil crimes? Shouldn't a king prosecute murder?"

"I never quarreled with Becket!" He gazed at Young Henry. "Thomas refused to obey my orders, which I will tolerate from no one. Do you hear?"

Young Henry bristled. "When have I disobeyed?"

"You beg, like Becket, for more power, more autonomy. You forget who's king."

My son rose. "It's you who forget, my lord. I've now been crowned twice. All I ask is a chance to be knighted, and to sit in the councils."

"I'll let you tend the kennels. When you can keep the hounds in check, we'll talk again."

Quickly, I took Young Henry's hand before he could say something damning. "Tell me more about Ireland."

As Henry talked, I studied Young Henry. He appeared physically more mature, although dangerously angry. I wondered if I dared introduce him to the men who were in Poitiers for the rebellion.

Henry paused. "You're looking well, Richard. Have you been studying the military arts?"

"Yes, sir."

Another son to worry about; he couldn't meet his father's eyes.

Henry glanced at the adoring Alais. "And do you plan to marry this French bonbon?"

Richard's jaw shot forward; he would not take any ridiculing of his beloved lightly. "Yes, sir."

"Good, glad to hear it." Henry looked at me witheringly. "Be sure you instruct him in your code of love. This princess is too gentle to live with a lecherous rogue."

I smiled brightly. "How long will you be with us, Henry?"

"Longer than you want. A few days."

What did he mean?

"On the contrary, I'm delighted. You can attend our sessions."

"I intend to. Love is all my concern."

He stayed a full seven days, one of the most grueling weeks I ever remembered. The court of love went well, thanks to the irresistible subject and the age of our audience, but our night meetings had to be canceled. Rancon remained out of sight, but through Richard, I learned he was suspicious. He wanted to know how Henry had gotten wind of our plans. I had to be careful in my questions, but my tentative answer was that he hadn't; his visit had other motives—perhaps my court of love?

Henry suddenly departed to see the count of Maurienne, that same Maurienne who'd gone on the Crusade, to arrange a marriage between our John and Maurienne's baby daughter. He would be gone about ten days, he announced, but would return to Poitiers on his way to England.

"I'll leave a small guard here to protect you," he said.

"Protect me from whom? I need no protection."

"You are my queen, and all my children are here. I can take no chances."

"As you wish." But my heart skipped. Rancon was right; he did suspect—we were under surveillance.

The first night after Henry left, we didn't risk meeting in the chapel. Instead, one of my knights took Henry's men to the local stewe, where we had a spy placed among the harlots. She reported that they were all Brabantian mercenaries who'd been told to keep their eyes open, but had little interest in policy themselves. Of course, it takes only one dedicated spy to discover the truth.

The second night, we invited the same soldiers to attend the court of love, which lasted well into the night, and served them drugged Poitevin wine. As they reveled, I led Young Henry to address his future subjects.

Rancon met us by the river. "Anyone see you?"

"No," Richard answered. "Alais kept watch."

The atmosphere in the nave was charged with apprehension and excitement. Everyone was eager to greet their new king. The single candle picked up their awed expressions as, to a man, the lords went to their knees.

Young Henry accepted the adulation graciously. "My lords and future subjects, I am delighted to meet with you."

"And we with you," a dark figure replied. "We have many complaints."

"This is not the time to ask for favors," Rancon said sharply.

Young Henry waved his hand. "No, the lord's quite right. I want to put myself on record. I can't see too well—you're Matthew, count of Boulogne. Yes? When I'm king, I shall return your rightful marriage portion, which my father seized, the county of Mortain and the honor of Hay."

"Oh, thank you, my liege."

Young Henry went easily to the next suitor, Matthew's brother, Philip of Flanders, to whom he promised the county of Kent; then the castle of Amboise to Count Theobald of Blois; Northumbria south to the Tyne River to Malcolm, king of the Scots (who was represented by Bishop Hugh of Durham). Then he addressed the English representatives, Norfolk, Leicester, Chester, and Derby; then those from Anjou, Brittany, and many from Maine, Henry's birthplace. I was amazed at his grasp of their grievances—no wonder Henry tried to keep him from power.

Hugh of Bigod expressed the general feeling in an emotionally charged voice. "I never thought I would live to see civility restored in my land after your rapacious father stole our castles, our preferments, our very hearts away!"

"Hear! Hear!" others joined.

Robert, lord of Leicester, turned to me. "Why do you think the king came here at this time, milady? And why did he leave a large guard?"

"Because I'm here," Young Henry interjected.

Leicester was unconvinced. "Does he suspect that you're meeting with us?"

"No, he has no inkling of your presence, of that I'm sure. He does know, however, that I'm more popular with the people than he is. He commenced to guard me whilst we were still in England."

Earl Robert studied him. "I can't help being uneasy."

"No time for wondering. We've met to prepare ourselves," the bishop of Durham said testily.

Again the subject turned to strategy and timing. When the armies were ready to engage, and only then, Young Henry would ride directly to Paris, out of Henry's reach. Once Louis knighted Young Henry and gave him the Great Seal of England, Henry would know that he was betrayed. Then, and only then, the rebellion would start.

We talked all night, then the next and the next, pushing ourselves to complete this first round before Henry returned. He'd said he'd be gone for ten days, but at the end of the first week, one of my spies ran into the palace.

"He's at the gates!" he panted. "The king! He's here!"

"Warn Rancon!" I pushed Richard out the door. "Tell him that I'll distract Henry with the court of love today so that our guests can escape. Go now!"

All of Henry's former spite seemed to have disappeared as he rode into the courtyard. He called greetings from his horse, smiling broadly. He thumped his sons on the back, kissed all the girls, then put his arm heavily over my shoulder.

"Congratulate me, Joy. Our John Lackland has just become John Hasland. Maurienne was delighted to sign away his county—he sends his best to you, by the way—as dowry."

We could hardly believe the shift in Henry's humor; in fact, I'd rarely seen him so buttery soft. He agreed to attend my court that afternoon, just as soon as he'd refreshed himself. I prepared the most outrageous program I could devise—anything to make our rebels' escape possible.

Jugglers and trick dogs frolicked on the grass when Henry took his place beside me at the court of love. The king beamed at the fresh faces gazing in awe at his famous person, and he lifted his glass to the merry musicians strumming under the trees.

On signal, Marcabru strode forward, garbed in a silver tunic slit to his hips, a golden crown of thorns atop his shaggy mane.

"God's eyes, who's that old man?" Henry asked.

I winced; Marcabru was my age. Of course, his hair was prematurely white. "He sang at Eleanor's christening. Don't you remember?"

"Oh yes, a poor representative for love, I would say."

Mamile stepped into the space the jugglers had vacated; she was draped in dark robes like a judge and she carried a heavy book.

Ignoring Henry, she addressed our young guests: "My lords and ladies, jury in our court of love, we have such a perplexing case before us that we have decided to act it out in a pantomime. Our contenders have chosen to remain anonymous, so I will recite their writ while the young people dance."

As Marcabru plucked the rhythm of the *trotto*, Geoffrey undulated to the center of the green. Masked and garbed in dark red, he looked older than his thirteen years. His movements were sure, his timing skilled.

"This is the young husband who's just been wed to an exquisite damsel of the south, a lady filled with passion and joy," Mamile announced.

Geoffrey's affianced wife, Constance of Brittany, ran to join him. With her sour expression, she was an ideal choice for the role, and she, too, could dance. They moved in unison, though without touching, imitating the carnal act.

"God's eyes," Henry whispered.

Marcabru began to sing:

I swoon with lecherous delight
Though I'm sure her beauty's a lie—
Oc, she paints, she laces, pads her samite—
Yet God! If she prove false, I'll die!

At each line, Geoffrey touched Constance lightly on her face, her waist, her bosom.

Lord!
God!
She's better when unlaced!
Piece by piece I strip her clothes—
Ah, a milky breast and night is day!
Ah, below! Below!
Here the sun doth glow!

Henry's hairy finger tapped in rhythm. Suddenly, Marcabru's entire group of musicians burst forth in a deafening coarse beat.

Young Alais ran toward Geoffrey and Constance. I'd chosen her because of her beauty, grace, and to please Richard, who was smiling in the third row.

"This certain man," Mamile intoned, "found another lady and made her his mistress. He declared that he loved her with all his heart and persuaded her to award him the solace of Venus. He'd married for strategy, he declared, but this maiden was his true love, the rose of the world."

Henry's finger stopped.

The dancing became more intricate as Alais mimed the steps and moves beside the couple. Her lips parted in pleasure, her cheeks flushed, and she truly did make poor sallow Constance look like the weed beside the rose.

Now the dance became graphic. Alais fell to her knees; her back arched as Geoffrey knelt above her. They didn't touch—didn't have to—for the meaning was plain.

"Because of his tricks, he obtained the second lady's favors," Mamile crooned superfluously.

Marcabru crashed his cymbals and sang:

> See him in the mawkish wind
> Take his slut down to the ditch
> Place his nail till she is pinned
> In her gloomy smelly itch.

Geoffrey slowly stood upright, made a vulgar gesture, then looked around to Constance.

Mamile spoke again: "Once the married man had accomplished his goal, he sought to return to his wife."

Constance rose from her collapsed position, then danced backward before Geoffrey's imprecations.

Marcabru sang out:

> You married man, you act the goat;
> You pump your cushion to a peak,

The cunt winks and jumps aboard,
Pretty fatty little stoat!
You commit your folly 'til you're weak,
Until your upright wand can't be shored,
And furthermore you're bored.
Is there a moral in this tale?
Oc, when the lecher begins to wail
"My sons had no respect for me!
What have you done, dear wife?
To create such strife?
What can the matter be?"
She replies:
"Look in the mirror, little starling;
You've misused your lance, my darling;
Hunt around, little birdie,
Hurdy-gurdy
Hurdy-gurdy
There is no word-ee
For a stud gone jay-dee."

The dancers left the stage. "I invite the Queen of Love to judge our case," Mamile said.

To applause, I pressed past Henry and joined Mamile.

Mamile took my hand. "The question comes from the wife, dear lady: What can she do to punish her husband?"

I waved to the young people. "She cannot accept him back to her bed, since he's ruled by lust, which is the enemy of love. Never, *never* become the object of lust—even if you're married."

"Should she feel shame for marrying him?" Mamile asked.

"If she was forced to marry, the question is moot. Even if she once loved him, she should still feel no shame. When we love, we are easily deceived."

"How should she feel about her rival?"

"She should pity any woman who becomes his victim. Such men, trained by Ovid, are superlative in the arts of seduction and betrayal; they wake to the sun each morning and cry, 'To rape!'—the same nightmare for all."

Mamile signaled that we would now take questions from the audience.

"What makes a man become unfaithful?" a pretty young girl asked. "Do you think that separation from his wife is the reason?"

"No, though it may be his excuse. Such men are driven by lust, not love; they need to attend our court!"

There was laughter.

Marie called, "We await your answer to the question, milady: What punishment can the betrayed wife inflict?"

"The only power a woman holds over a man—whether he's her husband or not—is his desire for her. She can either grant her favors as a reward, or withhold them as punishment. If he feels no desire, she loses control. In this case, we don't know if the husband feels remorse or desire for his wife."

Richard called out, "You said he married for strategy—what about withholding her lands?"

Henry stiffened.

"She lost that power when she married," I said easily. "I would say she should withhold her favors for her own self-respect. He may not care."

A young woman from Niort waved. "Your answer seems so crass, Queen Eleanor, almost as if wives sold their bodies."

I half-talked, half-sang:

> *Service and gifts and fine clothing and riches*
> *Nourish true love as does water the fishes!*

More laughter.

"That is the current cynical ethic, and our ladies forget it to their peril; we aim for:

> *Joy and prowess and good behavior and worth*
> *Bring rewards of which there is no dirth.*

But until that glorious day arrives, I grant you that my solution is crass. Only love can change this situation; that's why we're all here, to learn a new method of love. This wife's error was to be born in the wrong epoch; to withhold a favor that may have grown stale from overusage may avail little now. I beg you, young virgins, test your lovers thoroughly—even cruelly—before you succumb. Demand a long courtship; make him suffer in order to appreciate you." I walked slowly among the tables as Marcabru sang:

Baseness beats the walls
And Joy guards the enclosure;
Beware the goat who bawls
For entrance! Say to him, "No sir!"

He takes his honey
Morning and night;
Letches for money
Until the light.
Or until his cock hurts.

Kah—how explain this culture?
Dominated by the vulture
Who feeds on cunt?

I'd succeeded: Henry was in a rage. "You dare pretend that this 'case' came from some unknown suitor?"

"Unknown to the young people—we wanted to be discreet. Lady Beatrix of Montferrat proffered the question."

"Not discreet enough, milady. Your so-called case was a display of your own jealousy! Didn't I warn you that I'll not be ridiculed?"

"How are you ridiculed?" I countered. "I'm amazed! Does this case fit you?"

"Stop the hypocritical cant!"

"You first," I said evenly.

"Very well, Rosamond of Clifford. She's the canker in your craw, eh? Can't believe that your rough, rapacious Henry might be capable of tender love."

"As you say, that's not the side of your nature you show me."

And we launched into one of our sillier arguments about whether Henry could love or not, especially silly since I knew he'd discarded the fair Rosamond. I listened for bells tolling away the hours, watched the progress of the sun across the floor. Henry's soldiers should be happily employed in the stewe by now, and surely my noble allies were on their way.

"That first time I saw you after Rosamond," he roared, "your eyes had turned bright green, and they still are, by damn!"

"That was seven years ago, Henry. Even I can't sustain jealousy that long."

"Don't be modest; you have the persistence of a cobra."

"Why should I be jealous? You convinced Rosamond that you loved her, then stayed out of England for years. What kind of love is that?"

"A cobra, by God, who's poisoned our children!"

"The children have nothing to do with this!" I said sharply.

"Why did your troubadour sing about the sons' anger, then?"

"I don't know—ask him!" Damn Marcabru—why had he included that verse?

"Too bad you don't have a lover."

I froze with apprehension. "Why?"

"Then you wouldn't be so obsessed with love, parading around like an old witch dressed in silver hearts, hiring troubadours to praise your declining charms. By God, I sympathize with Louis."

"You sympathize; I recall him with nostalgia."

"Yearn for his flaccid balls? There's a word for women like you."

"Don't tell me; I'm sure it's not in my vocabulary."

"Playing the hypocrite still, eh? When I remember how you attacked me on our wedding night, my God! You once mentioned that we've spent years apart. Maybe it's because I didn't want to lose my ramming rod."

I was weary of this rondelet, but not so weary that I would stop. "Yet you forced the marriage."

"You married a great king, milady; I've put you in the annals of fame."

"I married the duke of Normandy, my lord, not a great king, and I was already famous. Only with Aquitaine in your pocket did you have the power to attack England, and then Toulouse, and Wales, and Ireland. You call yourself a king? *Thief* would be a better word."

He stared at me glassily, as if considering a fit, decided against it, then left. The bell rang Compline; I'd kept him occupied long enough for every lord and bishop to leave in safety.

Despite his anger, Henry had news from Maurienne, which he needed to impart. Marie took over my duties in our court as Henry met with me and our sons in the great hall the next day.

"In order to complete a contract for John's future, I gave Maurienne as a marriage portion the castles of Chinon, Loudun, and Mirebeau," he began in a cold, crisp tone.

"Those are my castles!" Young Henry cried. "Given to me at Montmirail!"

Henry looked at him stonily. "You will inherit them when I die."

"How can I inherit them when you gave them to John?"

"Maybe John will put you in his will."

"You're stealing them!"

"Dare you say steal to me?"

The familiar signs of a fit threatened.

"Ask anyone! Everyone in Europe says that you steal!"

Horrified, I moved between them. "Young Henry, you must apologize." How could he be so indiscreet? Next, he would reveal all our plans.

Henry pushed me aside. "Who's everyone in Europe?" His voice was deadly.

There was a long pause as Young Henry grappled with his blunder. "I don't know—Richard says so." It was a weak effort to recoup.

Henry turned bloodshot eyes to Richard. "Is that true?"

Though Richard was furious to be made the scapegoat, he handled the situation tactfully. "He's confused about what I said. He accused me of stealing in a game, and I replied that he accuses everyone of stealing, everyone in the entire world. He's always been jealous of me."

"He's jealous and you'll lie for him." Henry turned back to Young Henry. "Who's everyone? Name names, damn you!"

Young Henry was white. "I misspoke, my lord. Richard is right; I tend to lash out when angry."

Henry looked from one son to the other, then pushed a parchment in my direction. "Sign this, if you please. No need to read it—it releases the castles to John."

I pushed it back. "I don't have the authority to release castles that were never mine."

"As my queen, you share all my prerogatives."

"I am your queen consort and own nothing but Aquitaine."

"I order you to sign this release, Eleanor."

"With your great legal mind, my lord, you surely know that I can't."

He turned away. "Richard, here's the place for your signature."

"The castles are in Anjou," Richard replied. "As overlord to Anjou, I can't betray my vassal."

"Don't betray your ignorance, Richard. I am count of Anjou, just as I am duke of Aquitaine for the rest of my lifetime, but you will show your intention."

"When you die, my brother will be count of Anjou."

"How is Young Henry the count?"

"Since Montmirail," Richard said.

"Montmirail." Henry beat his forehead. "Montmirail."

Was it possible he was just realizing the implications?

"Geoffrey?"

"Montmirail," Geoffrey answered. "I swore homage to France, not to England or Anjou; I can't sign without consulting my overlord."

Henry glanced at Young Henry. "I already know your answer.

Well, I've hatched a nestful of lawyers." He looked at me. "Or should I say eagles? Reaching for my entrails. However, it doesn't matter; I was just trying to give you a sense of inclusion. God help me for being a trusting fool. In fact, the castles are my possessions; I don't need your signatures." He rose and looked down on us with significance. "I do demand loyalty."

He walked to the door. "I was going to push on to England, but I'm intrigued with your court of love, Eleanor. I'll stay on a few days."

After he'd left, we looked at one another, appalled. I put a finger to my lips; we would talk later.

Never had Henry's jocular presence been so galling. We were all forced to perform, and nothing is so draining. Only the girls in the family—and John—were spared his unremitting gaze. The worst test was for Young Henry; his father taunted him constantly, trying to make him lose control. My son behaved magnificently after that first major slip—I was proud of him. Rancon hovered in the wings, and occasionally we talked late at night, but he dared not come forward.

Then, almost casually, Henry announced he was leaving. Again we dissimulated, pretending that we wanted him to stay.

He grinned mirthlessly. "You flatter me. If you really feel so strongly, Young Henry can ride with me. I'm celebrating my birthday in a week, and I'll need company. Meantime, we'll hunt, eh?"

"That would be wonderful." Young Henry's face was ashen.

"Yes, wonderful." Henry's grin widened. "Perhaps you'll be able to remember the names of all those men who say I steal from them."

"I never said there were men—only Richard."

Henry nodded. "Furthermore, I'll dismiss your retinue. Why do you need guards when you're riding with me?"

"Those men have been with me for years!" Young Henry cried. "You can't dismiss them!"

"I already did—yesterday," Henry said coldly.

He glanced slowly around the room, relishing our stricken expressions, then ambled into the garden to play with the children.

"Hunting!" I cried when he'd gone. "Without your own guard and with his huge army? He's putting you under arrest, Young Henry. Richard, go tell Rancon that we must meet tonight by the river."

"It's dangerous!" Richard protested.

"And imperative! Tell him!"

I took Young Henry's hand. "Listen! You made a blunder, but he can't be sure. This is a test—he's isolating you!"

"I know."

"Whatever you do, admit nothing, say nothing. He'll press and use tricks, but he can't make you speak."

"I know him better than anyone," he said bitterly. "Oh Mama, I'm so sorry." His head rested on my shoulder.

I stroked his back. "Remember the thousands of people who are depending on you. We all trust you, my darling."

"I want to be a good king."

As soon as it was dark, we crept to the river.

Rancon reiterated what I'd already said.

"He may suspect, but he doesn't know," he insisted again and again. "Be quiet, be docile, hunt and drink, and talk as normally as you can. And don't speak of politics."

"Say nothing of Louis, of France, England, or Becket," I implored.

"We have to maintain this farce at least a year," Rancon reminded him.

Young Henry listened, his head bowed, his hands trembling. Yes, he would do exactly as we instructed, he said again and again; he was profoundly frightened.

Rancon sensed his fear. "Don't worry; I'll be close by," he said suddenly.

Startled, I asked where.

"I'll follow the army as a hermit. Signal me, Young Henry, if you need me."

Young Henry's voice broke. "Thank you, Lord Rancon."

The hunting party, the regular mercenaries in Henry's army and his faithful contingent of knights, gathered in the courtyard at dawn. Young Henry held Marguerite in his arms until his father called him impatiently. The young people kissed as if for the last time.

Then my son embraced me. I was suddenly reminded of the naked baby sucking his thumb in terror after baby William had died.

"Take care!"

He kissed me again.

When he was on his horse, I called, "Remember your eagle!"

"We're hunting with falcons!" Henry answered.

But Young Henry nodded. His eagle, his name for me when he'd been a child.

Four days later, Rancon galloped full speed into the courtyard.

"Young Henry escaped!"

"Escaped where?" I cried. "Why?"

"A spy told me that Henry probed about the loyalties of one person after another, our allies to a man, and Young Henry panicked."

"To where?" I begged.

"France! Luckily, Louis was holding his court in Chartres and the boy didn't have to go far to safety."

"Oh God," I moaned.

He led me inside. "Listen! Henry received no hard confirmation of his suspicions."

"Young Henry's bolting is confirmation enough."

"Yes," he conceded. He locked the door of the great hall. "Joy, I don't want to alarm you—"

"Something's happened to Young Henry, and you haven't told me!"

"He's perfectly safe; I didn't lie. I'm worried about Henry. He knows more than we think."

"You just said he had no confirmation."

"He may have a spy among us."

"No!" I cried strongly. "Henry knows the rebels because he knows whom he's cheated. He could have named them before they even thought of insurrection."

"Go to Paris today, Joy."

"If I leave, he *will* know there's a plot."

"He knows it anyway. I'm concerned for your life."

"Henry would never touch me!"

"He murdered Becket."

I pressed my head to his shoulder. "I can't leave you. We're fighting together."

"Only if we both stay alive."

29

I lingered in Poitiers, pleading for a few more days. Louis knighted Young Henry at once, then cut a new Great Seal of England in preparation for war. Meantime, Rancon worked daily with Richard and Geoffrey, honing their skills for knighthood—and what lay beyond.

I rode out to the military field every day and sat on the sidelines, watching. Sometimes the young princesses came with me, though I discouraged Princess Alais, who wept all the time. I appreciated how difficult the impending separation would be for the young lovers—who better than I—but her grief was hard on Richard. Young Joanna, however, was an asset to her brother. Cheering and waving her hands, she never tired of screaming his praise.

Geoffrey was training as well, of course, and he was adroit, lithe and elusive in his tactics, brilliantly so. Nevertheless, it was Richard we all watched. Handsome, strong, and well coordinated in his person, he seemed totally different when he was mounted and armed. I became aware of bulging muscles on his arms and thighs—almost grotesque—and his face under his helmet lost all human sensibility. His chin jutted sharply, his brows scowled over his intent eyes, and his nose guard cut his face into two parts. He sat quietly on his huge destrier as Rancon talked to him, then selected his weapon.

What I saw became doubled with memory. Richard was Rancon, never more so than now. A quintain was placed at the far end of the field, a mock human for Richard to attack. His first weapon was the lance, a long iron piece, so heavy that it took two men to lift it to Richard's hand. Rancon signaled, and Richard shot as if on a catapult, raced furiously down the field, head low, hand lifting the metal shaft as if it were a twig, then thrust it down! The quintain fell to the ground, completely shattered.

Three veteran knights then confronted him, wielding their broadswords, Richard's favorite weapon. He clashed with one after the other, with eyes in the back of his head, turning on a hair, striking in long, metallic slashes. Again, the boy outmatched them all with his combination of uncanny strength and equally uncanny heart. He was rage personified, a killing machine nonpareil. Thrilling. Chilling.

Then the quintain was resurrected, this time with a dead pig hanging by its feet. Now Richard took the morning star, a particularly loathsome weapon, with its iron ball studded with spikes. The purpose was to rip his opponent to ribbons, and Richard did. With one deadly pass after another, he shred his opponent into sausage.

Memory was sweet and nostalgic, but this exercise pointed to the future. I had to leave.

I began to organize my children for departure. I urged the French princesses, Marie and my younger daughter, Alix, especially, to ride for Paris while the road was still open. Marie wouldn't go without me; Alix left only because she was expecting her first child. Princess Marguerite, though anxious to be with Young Henry, wouldn't leave my side. Alais was a vexing problem. I warned her she could become a hostage if she lingered, and that Richard would be leaving soon, but the girl could only weep. She withdrew into a deep melancholy, which in turn made Richard wild; he hovered over her every moment he wasn't in the field, whispering and pressing her hands, or just watching hungrily.

Young Eleanor had wed the king of Castile in September, so she was spared, as was Matilda, safe in Saxony, but Joanna and John were still with me. In some ways, Joanna was my most remarkable child. Though fully aware of our situation, she kept all of us diverted by her many pranks and games. She and John entertained us with droll travesties of our court of love; she brought a badger into the palace, which drove us mad; she talked incessantly and forced everyone to answer. For me, her greatest contribution was calming John, not an easy task.

John was a mercurial little boy, brilliant and strange. He was poor in sports and games, and would dissolve into foolishness when he failed. "I'm just a fool!" he would hoot, beating himself about the ears. "Come on, thwack my bottom, everyone! Kick the silly boy!" No one touched him, of course, but only Joanna could tease him out of such demonstrations. "Have dignity, John," she would scold. "You're a great prince, and besides, you're my brother." Then she would put her arms around him until he returned to normal.

Constance of Brittany was the most obnoxious, though I don't think she cared about our danger. She was gripped in resentment about her marriage to Geoffrey, whom she obviously despised. Indeed, Geoffrey was difficult to like, though he was gifted in both mind and body; he lacked character. On the other hand, he was much kinder than Constance concerning their marriage; she was a homely, spiteful child with no redeeming grace, and Geoffrey treated her as he did everyone, with good-humored indifference.

Mamile and my friends left after the court of love, but Amaria stayed, of course.

Henry's presence—though removed—hovered over all of us like a pall. Rancon was right; for the first time I was experiencing Henry as an enemy, and I knew well there were no limits to his spite—we all knew. Where was he? What did he know? When would he strike? Each day was shorter, more intense, more jittery.

Rancon and I were caught in both spring and autumn: We loved with the ardor of youth, and the poignancy of maturity. We talked almost not at all.

In October, Amaria touched me with an icy hand. "Joy, come quickly! I'm worried about Princess Alais."

"Yes, she's despondent, and I'm afraid—"

"She's ill!"

Something in her tone . . . Baby William!

Pamela Kaufman

"Take me!"

Together we rushed to our new dormer, where our guests were housed. The instant I saw Alais, my heart shriveled. I touched her fevered face.

"Can you hear me, dear?"

Tears coursed down her cheeks as I asked her gently about her symptoms.

I looked up at Amaria. "Tertian fever?"

Her green eyes didn't waver. "I'm afraid it's cholera."

I made a fast decision. "Call for a litter. I'll remove her to Fontevrault."

Her eyes widened. "Do you think the nuns—"

"Aunt Mahaut will see that they accept her. You accompany her, Am; you can explain."

"Should I stay with her?"

"No." Again our eyes communicated: If Henry should attack, I wanted Am with me. "You can return yet tonight."

Within the hour, we'd carried the sick child to a bed litter, where I tucked her damp hair under a shawl.

"Don't be frightened, Alais. I'll visit you very soon."

She turned her face away. We tied the leather flaps and the long-cart rolled slowly out the gates, with Amaria riding behind it.

I now had to handle Richard; he was due to leave for Paris the next night, where Louis would knight him.

When he returned from the field, he asked at once, "Where's Alais?"

I told him that I suspected she had tertian fever; she was sequestered in Fontevrault Abbey for her safety and ours. The disease was highly contagious.

"I'm not afraid! I want to see her!"

"Richard, take hold. You must put your journey to Paris first— you can't expose yourself!"

"I won't go without seeing her!"

"You'll see her in Paris."

If he could get to Paris and if she could. Runners arrived that

464

same day with the news that Henry had left Normandy and was headed south.

"The main road to Paris is closed," Rancon reported. "The boys will have to use the back road through Berry."

He informed Richard and Geoffrey of the change in route that same evening, when they returned from the field; they would leave the following night, accompanied by a mercenary from the south named Mercadier. Their weapons would be packed in a farmer's cart with pots and dried vegetables on top; they would dress as food-mongers. Richard turned very white.

The next morning, he had disappeared.

I ran to Rancon. "He's gone to Fontevrault!"

Blood drained from his face; he breathed quickly. "He'll be here in time—don't worry."

When Mercadier arrived in midafternoon—a brutal-looking man with knife scars on his face—Richard had not yet returned. I heard him ride to the stable just before dusk.

As the dark closed in, rain began to fall in a steady sheet. We all crowded into the vestibule to say good-bye. Richard and Geoffrey were dressed in the brown motley of foodmongers, their brimmed hats pulled low. I could see only Richard's mouth and jaw; his lips appeared blue in torchlight.

"I've sent your weapons ahead in a cart," Rancon told them crisply. "Your horses are smeared with mud and wear common bridles, but your own saddles are in the cart. Everything will be behind a hawthorn at the first crossroad behind the first hill, guarded by your squires. Mercadier's squire will step out when he sees you coming. You're to ride in the dark, without torches. When possible, stay off the road—Mercadier knows the way."

"Yes, sir," Geoffrey said, his voice shaking with excitement.

Richard said nothing.

"I doubt if you'll meet anyone on that lane at this time or in this weather, but if you do, say as little as possible."

Mercadier interrupted in the rough argot of Marseilles: "Here are daggers for your belts. If you're challenged, don't bother to talk—slide the blade under the ribs on the left side. I sharpened them for the job."

Joanna burst into loud wails; Geoffrey grinned; Richard's blue lips didn't change expression.

"You'll come to my estate in Troyes," Marie crooned, stroking Richard's cheek.

I embraced Geoffrey. "I'm so sorry that it's come to this, my darling."

"I'm not, Mama!" His eyes blazed under his hat. "I'll fight bravely for you, you'll see."

I was touched with guilt; this was a son I'd never known.

Then Richard, moist and cold to the touch.

I put my lips to his ear. "Did you see her?"

He nodded.

Rancon took him from me. "Take care of Geoffrey, Richard—he tends to be reckless." He put his arms around his son, and his voice broke. "Most of all, take care of yourself. You're very talented—you know it—but you're young. There's time."

The embrace knocked Richard's hat back; for the first time, I saw his eyes, glazed as marble. "I'll be careful, Rancon. And I'll take my time."

His innocuous words were foreboding.

Rancon kissed his lips.

We all crowded at the door, staring into the dark. We heard a few scuffling sounds, then nothing. Everyone left except Rancon and me.

I pitied him. "He'll be a great knight, darling."

"If he survives, he'll be the best. Oh Joy, I wish I could spare him!"

"So do I."

The following morning, we were wakened at dawn by a shout from the courtyard. "Eleanor, are you here?"

Uncle Ralph from Châtellerault fell from his mud-spattered horse.

"Henry reached Chinon last night! He's headed this way right now! Right on my heels! You must leave!"

"Get the women!" Rancon ran to the stables.

I roused the household. By the time they were dressed and in the courtyard, Rancon had their horses ready.

"Not you, Joy." Rancon held me back.

"Are you mad? I'm going with them!"

"It's too late—they can't get through to Paris—not so many of them."

"But Marie, Marguerite—"

"They'll ride to Niort. I've sent for Princess Alais to meet them there—and then to the south."

"Then I'll go with them! You told me—"

"That you should go to Paris. Don't argue—we're wasting time."

"For God's sake, Joy, do as he says!" my uncle cried.

My children were already mounted; I waved at them as they trotted away. Then I followed Rancon to the knights' dormers, where he threw fustian and bits of armor at me.

"Put these on—and hurry. I'll take you as far as the border; from there, you'll go on with my knights!"

"Without you? But—"

"I'm your seneschal, remember? I have to protect Aquitaine."

Rancon fastened my breastplate, and crushed a helmet over my braids.

"Follow me!" Uncle Ralph shouted over his shoulder. He turned abruptly right, onto a river path along the Clain. Bent low behind the shrubs, we galloped along the muddy path. Bushes whipped our faces.

We reached the Vienne River, took a broader path toward Châtellerault, the same route my grandfather had used when he'd abducted my grandmother many years ago. We rode without pausing or speaking. Shortly after midday, we fell into the courtyard of the castle. Grooms quickly took our exhausted horses out of sight. Still without a word, we followed my aunt up the stairs to the women's quarters, where Rancon, his two knights with their squires, and I collapsed on mats.

"We'll bring you food and wine," my aunt said.

When she'd left, Rancon groped for my hand. "Can you rest?"

I lay quietly, my grainy eyes memorizing Rancon's face, as if I needed to. He lay on his side, watching me, as well. Voices below came and went; then horses and other men talking with Norman accents.

When they'd ridden out, my aunt entered the room fearfully. "They were here—they're looking for you."

Rancon was already buckling his sword.

We climbed down the stairs in the dark. Fresh steeds were saddled and ready to go in the yard. Rancon's knights, Sir Guillem and Sir Saurostre, who would accompany me all the way to Paris, led the way.

We'd removed the bells from our bridles and rode in absolute silence. When we came to the bridge that crossed into the village of Chinon, dogs barked wildly. Men shouted, and the dogs quieted. We withdrew deeper into the wood.

Just before sunrise, we stopped in a tiny clearing. The ground was rimed with frost, but we dared not build a fire. Rancon and I lay on the cold earth, our heads on our saddles, our bodies curled around each other for warmth.

Soon it was dark again. We ate a little dried venison washed down with wine, then mounted our steeds.

Avoiding roads and rivers where we might be seen, we inched our way slowly through the forest. The growth changed in character, more oaks than maples, with less underbrush to impede us. We were making good time. Dawn came warm and golden.

"Look." Rancon pointed to a lane winding below our small incline. "Around that next bend lies France."

"Can't we rest until evening?" I pleaded.

For one heartbeat, he pressed my head to his shoulder. "Now, Bel Vezer, every moment counts."

Oc, every moment I had with him. Our eyes met briefly; we'd said everything and nothing. I couldn't bear it.

The knights rode down to check the road. They separated in opposite directions, then came back together.

"It's quiet," Sir Guillem reported.

Rancon turned to Sir Saurostre, his brows raised.

"Nothing."

Rancon's horse pawed. Rancon frowned. "I don't like it—I feel something in my bones."

Suddenly, he half-slid down the steep slope himself in a shower of pebbles. His helmet appeared through the thicket to our right, then our left, and he was back. "A shepherd is approaching from the French side. Otherwise, you're right, there's no one."

Sir Guillem took my bridle.

"Wait!" Rancon stopped me. "If anything goes amiss, deny and deny and deny. No matter what spies may have said, they have no proof about you. Promise!"

"Yes." I was losing him to a cloud of tears.

"Don't write me—your letters will be read. Send a runner with a verbal message."

"Yes."

"And lower your nose guard."

I pulled the metal piece down from my helmet. Slowly, I edged my steed down the steep embankment. Though I had to keep my eyes to the ground, I managed to glance up twice: There he was on his magnificent black. We reached the lane, and I looked once again: Rancon had disappeared, had become a memory.

I trotted rapidly toward the bend in the road, with one knight before me, one behind. Four knights suddenly pounded from the trees in front of Sir Guillem.

"Stop in the name of the king!" shouted Henry's knight, Sir Joscelin.

"What king?" Sir Guillem asked.

"King Henry of England!"

"Ah, good, we're on our way to join his army."

"You're riding toward France!"

"I thought I was leaving France."

"You didn't quite reach it, traitors!"

Betrayed! We were betrayed!

"Your names, if you please," Sir Joscelin demanded.

Sir Guillem moved between me and Henry's men. "Why should we give you our names? We've done nothing wrong!"

The English drew swords. Sir Guillem reached for his hilt, when a dozen more men appeared from the bush.

"We have a right to ride into France," my knight insisted.

"The king will be your judge. Again, your names."

My knights and their squires each replied with false identifications.

Sir Joscelin stared over their shoulders. "Your name, sir."

I coughed into my hand.

"That's Sir Raimbault of Berry," Sir Sausostre said quickly. "He has a sore throat."

Sir Joscelin leaned close. "It's the queen! My God, it's Queen Eleanor!"

"*Asusée!*" Rancon shouted. He slid downward through dust and rolling rocks.

"Leave!" I cried. "Save yourself!"

My arms were grabbed and I struggled like a tiger. A small army of Englishmen charged up the slope. Then my nose guard slipped and blotted half my vision.

"Go back!" I screamed.

I caught a brief flash of Rancon, sword upraised, before I lost all sight. I could hear everything crashing and twisting. Knights slashed furiously, weapons clanged, and horses reared. I screamed, and the scream surrounded me.

Someone tied my hands, jerked off my nose guard, tied a rag across my eyes. In that brief moment while my eyes were free, I glimpsed a tangle of horse and man at the foot of the slope—Rancon.

We began to jog.

When my blindfold was removed, we'd just crossed the moat of Chinon Castle. I was jerked rudely from my steed, yanked through the military court, the domestic court, to the dungeon at the far end. With a violent push, I fell into the cell and the door clanged behind me.

Amaria caught me. "Oh God, they've captured you! We've lost hope!"

Blinking, I counted my entire household—even young John—and the French princesses. I gasped when I beheld poor Alais, transparent as a specter.

"Who betrayed us?" I cried.

"I believe it was the count of Toulouse," Marie answered. "He's been Henry's spy ever since the aborted invasion."

We were kept in Chinon for less than a fortnight. No one came; no one told us anything. Our conditions were foul—we were treated like the worst criminals.

Then one bitter morning, we were dragged from our pallets into freezing cold. A line of huge horses were saddled in front of us. Without ceremony, guards helped us mount.

They pulled a long chain from a box and clamped our ankles.

Next, they hung heavy balls of iron to our clamps.

John began to cry.

"Have you no shame?" Joanna screeched in her high voice. "To chain us like common criminals? I promise that you'll be sorry someday!"

I recognized the road to Barfleur, of course, and by the end of the day, we were in the familiar horseshoe, once again cleared of any inhabitants. The bay was crowded with ships of every description, as if Henry were planning another invasion. Sand whirled in a fierce wind; waves sucked and crashed.

A guard ordered that we dismount. We fell to the sand, still imprisoned by our metal balls. At least John and Joanna were free to run to me.

Soon I was on board a square-sailed smack with my ladies. We were on our way to England.

The White Tower in London is almost ideal for incarceration. After all, didn't I design it myself? Nevertheless, after four dreary months of enforced imprisonment, I was relieved when Ranulf de Glanvill, the royal justiciar, appeared one morning shortly after the Nativity and told me to pack a single longcart; I would be leaving in the morning.

"One longcart apiece?" I asked, gesturing at my ladies.

He hesitated, his thin lips pressed like white worms. "You may take one attendant with her own longcart."

"I'll go, Joy," Amaria said at my shoulder.

In spite of the fact that I had a young daughter and the French princesses in attendance, there could be no doubt: Amaria must be with me. After all, she'd been my handmaid since we were both fifteen; we were practically a single person. The others would soon follow.

30

The first morning in Old Sarum, after we'd survived the winter gale, we surveyed our wind-whipped motte. The snaky black vine that held up the tower blew in and out, as if it were breathing, and sooner or later, it would collapse along with the crumbling corpse it contained. There was no doubt whatsoever as to our fate, only whether exposure, or disease, or starvation would take us first. Neither Welsh gruel nor sheepskins could save us.

When another Welshman brought us our morning *lagana,* he had difficulty opening the door against the snow. We asked for our longcarts, where we had more furs, but he didn't understand. We explored our space as best we could. Two more nights? A week? How long could we withstand the elements?

Ciarron appeared after darkness had fallen. Though he spoke gruffly in Welsh, we understood that we were to follow him. Outside, wind blew the snow in stinging clouds against our faces. Holding each of us by the arm in the dark, Ciarron half-slid us down the motte, past the treacherous moat—now solid ice—and across the arctic compound, along the curtain wall, where a few wooden structures leaned, and into a tiny wattle and daub hut.

The dwelling was a single low-ceilinged room with a dirt floor covered with straw. A flame sparked from a fire pit in the center, where an iron pot bubbled with more of our stew. Ambrosia, I thought, and these thick walls are as beautiful in their way as Suger's thrusts of glass.

A bare-footed servant looked at us in amazement; I was just as amazed at his lack of shoes. Lord Ciarron grunted in thick French that the churl's name was Davvyd; and then he called for hot wine. He indicated that we should sit by the fire, a timely suggestion, since we could no longer stand upright.

"Lord Ciarron, if ever I can reward—"

He waved a hand to stop me.

"I'll do so," I finished.

"No. No, nothing."

Meaning he wasn't doing it for a reward? No matter, if I survived . . . If? What a distance my thought had traveled since the previous day. Yet, if we could get through the winter, we might yet be rescued. Would this dour captain offer us hospitality that long?

Even with the fire and solid walls, the cold was penetrating. I worried about conditions for our rebellion in Europe, where the weather was even more severe, or were they waiting until the fighting season next summer? Or would they strike off-season? How I hated to be so far away. Yet I was in England—not so far, eh? And I'd survived the first night—the worst, I hoped.

Ciarron pointed. "You'll sleep on my bed."

Bed? A pile of faggots covered with a thin layer of brechan, but better than our sheepskins.

I lay down on the far side, with Amaria next to me. I assumed that Davvyd and Ciarron would curl around the fire—but no, they lay on the bed beside us, close as planks on a deck. I squeezed Amaria's hand; she squeezed back. I felt I was on the Crusade again, all niceties subsumed in an effort to get through the next hour. Fire shadows jumped over the beams above; coals cracked in the pit. I had always heard that the dying sometimes laugh at the absurdity of their situation. Well, we're all dying all the time, so we should all be laughing, eh? Except, for the moment, I was blissfully aware that I was alive—that there might be hope.

We settled into Ciarron's hut as permanent guests. The risk for him was enormous.

"You should put us with one of your men," I suggested. "If the king or one of his officers returns, there's little I could do for you, Lord Ciarron."

His thin lips set. "No one's coming."

It was the first confirmation I'd had of our permanent isolation.

A slow flush touched his cheeks. "You would be safe with my men—you're a queen—but I must protect Lady Amaria."

"For both of us, then, I thank you."

Later, I asked Amaria if she minded his attentions, which at the moment were saving our lives. I cautioned her, however, that in the future, he might demand repayment. Was she ready?

She, too, flushed. "He's lonely."

I took her hand. "Look at me."

She did.

"Listen! I'd rather take my chances with the elements than think that you're sacrificing yourself."

Her clear green eyes didn't flinch. "I'm not sacrificing myself."

I looked deeply. I'll never know, I thought.

We still couldn't reach our longcarts, so my book would have to be postponed. I watched Ciarron carefully, for he seemed a contented man in these narrow circumstances, though his clothing and demeanor indicated he knew something of the world. Twice he picked up a crude string instrument called a cwyth from his corner and strummed it in a wild blur. Was he also a musician? Then, one evening, he bent his head close to the firelight and scratched out a few letters on a piece of sheepskin.

"My Lord Ciarron, what do you write?"

He looked up defensively. "Verses."

"Soothly? Troubadour verse?"

Amaria rushed in. "All the Welsh are poets, Joy."

I doubted it. "Well, you should have much in common, then."

"Is the Lady Amaria Welsh?" Ciarron asked.

"No, I meant she's a poet. Hasn't she told you? She writes *lais*, short romances in verse, and very pretty, too."

"She flatters me," Amaria protested.

Well, I'd done my part to further their friendship. I paced restlessly.

"Lord Ciarron," I began again, "do you think you might get me some writing materials? Something a little finer than your sheepskin?

"You can't write letters, you know."

"I daresay I can write them, my lord; I just can't send them, eh? No, I have another project in mind."

He went back to his sheepskin.

Time may come and turn and go
Through days and years, sun and snow,
While I am dumb
With desire, ever new;
My senses numb,
I so want you!

I groaned and woke myself with my sobbing. Quickly, I wiped my cheeks and forced memory away: another morning, another month, another year. Yet I couldn't contain another groan. Wednesday, August 12, 1184; I was about to celebrate my tenth year of imprisonment.

What should I celebrate? When I'd departed from Poitiers, I'd had four sons; now I had two, Richard and John. When I'd left, we'd challenged Henry with a major rebellion, now a barely remembered skirmish, which had been lost before it started. The duke of Boulogne had been killed the first week, and everyone had lost heart. My sons had knelt before Henry and begged his forgiveness—even the furious Richard. Henry had resumed power with his usual generous spirit. My sons' allowances had been cut in half, and Richard—as the acting duke—had been told to put down the rebellion in Aquitaine.

Disastrous for Richard, worse for Young Henry.

I turned my cheek against the brechan to absorb my tears. Don't think, I commanded my heart sternly. But the hour was early, and I couldn't stop. Young Henry—the young king of England—had been stripped of all prerogatives. Like his mentor, William Marshal, he'd been forced to make his mark in the tournaments. Then, actually envious of Richard, who at least had a legitimate—if odious—assignment, Young Henry had gathered a few of the tournament renegades and attacked Richard himself, declaring that *he* was the duke of Aquitaine. In this chaotic situation, Henry had entered the fray on Richard's side, much as they hated each other.

Henry had approached Young Henry in Limoges, seeking peace. Young Henry had graciously invited his father to enter the city so they might parley. As Henry had crossed the moat bridge—the same bridge we'd crossed when Richard had become the future lord of Aquitaine—an arrow caught him on the neck, and only a rearing horse deflected the shaft, or he would have been killed. Young Henry had denied culpability, so Henry had tried twice more, and twice again he had been attacked.

Soon thereafter, my beautiful Young Henry had pillaged the churches, then sneaked from the city at night with his ragtag army, while Henry had followed relentlessly. Deep into the south the armies rode, when suddenly the young king had fallen mortally ill. He'd begged Henry to come to his tent to grant absolution. At first, his father had refused, fearing a trap, but when it became clear that the boy was dying in great pain, he'd relented.

Young Henry's last wish had been that his father release me from prison. Obviously, Henry ignored this request.

My daughter Matilda had managed to get a letter to me, telling me the gory tale, but I already knew. The day my beautiful son had died, it had rained blood in Old Sarum.

Marie had informed me about Geoffrey's sad end. King Louis had gone to his beloved God a happy man, for his son Philip—also crowned—had easily become the new king of France. Well did I recall Marie's describing him as a hound with a single purpose: He meant to conquer Aquitaine and England and to destroy their ruler; that was the sum of his character. Except that he had loved Geoffrey. He and Geoffrey had doted on each other, had been inseparable. Odd, to think that my small dark son had finally found love from such an unlikely source. When Geoffrey had been kicked by a horse in Paris—the cause of his death—Philip had tried to jump into the grave with him. Marie had described the scene with her usual vivid prose: the howling grief, the swooning, Philip's loss of consciousness for four days.

Then the French king, who hated Henry and all his sons, announced his love for Richard. Could it be because they shared the same hate—namely, Henry? The true bond, I would guess, was their mutual dismay that Henry had refused to permit Richard to wed Princess Alais, which would have brought peace to both countries. Richard, however, had his own reason for outrage: Henry would not name Richard, now his eldest son, as his heir to the throne. In fact, in a parley with Richard and King Philip at the famous oak in Gisors, Henry had indicated that he intended to name John, not Richard.

Richard—no fool—fell to his knees and did homage to Philip, shades of Montmirail.

So, the king of France and Richard fight together against Henry. Though Philip has the persistence of a hound on the track, he must depend on Richard, the most formidable warrior within living memory. Marie, Alix, Matilda, and Joanna all write the same: The mention of Richard's name strikes terror in everyone's heart. He's becoming a legend. Richard doesn't write or—more likely—he can't get letters through. Ciarron would be lenient, but there's always Henry at the gate.

One day soon, it must end.

Meantime, I lounge, physically at my ease within my newly constructed prison-palace, but mentally in turmoil. Ciarron and Amaria have been happily married for years; our compound is a bustling little village with its own trade, chapel, and orchards.

My daughters console me that I'm fortunate to be spared the ravages of the Black Death that swept across England last winter, killing thousands who couldn't be buried in the frozen earth. But I've also missed the birth of my grandchildren by Matilda and Eleanor. Joanna was crowned queen of Sicily and I wasn't there.

I finally pulled myself from the slough of memory. Outside, a sunny day, a few white clouds rushing across deep blue; I walked briskly across the compound toward Amaria's daub hut, then stopped. A lamb's bleat? A bee? No—royal fanfare! The Welshmen—already aware—stood like cattle in a field, all facing the same direction. The gates swung open and here came a blaze of color; standard-bearers, pennants of the three lions, brass horns raised high, resplendent knights.

Even with all the panoply I was unprepared to see Henry himself. Mounted on a magnificent Belgian white, his bridle covered with jewels, he sat with all the splendid regalia of his office, very unlike his usual carelessness. His hair hung to his shoulders under a narrow gold crown, and he was dressed in a yellow silk tunic trimmed in scarlet, falling in full folds to the tops of his studded boots.

To his right was Ranulf de Glanvill, still baleful. On the other side—I gasped—William Marshal, also more elegant than when he'd rescued me. William Marshal, Young Henry's mentor and companion in the tournaments, now an officer with Young Henry's worst enemy. Accustomed as I'd become to cynicism, I was shocked. Are all knights such opportunists?

Henry sat quietly in his saddle as he took in our bucolic arrangements: swine in their pens, chickens on their roosts, sheep roaming freely. His eyes fastened on my commodious stables with my best hunters, my falconry, my barking hounds, then my chapel, built five years ago to my specifications, hardly Saint-Denis, but gaudily painted in the Saracen style. Finally, he gazed on Old Sarum, which was barely recognizable. The vine was gone, the holes filled with daub, the moat drained, and on both sides stretched long wooden additions, my great hall on one side, my living quarters on the other. The tower itself was reserved for storage.

Sir Joscelin leapt to the ground and, to my astonishment, helped Henry dismount. Now that the king was at my level, I beheld a different man. No wonder he'd draped himself in royal trappings; he was trying to disguise the ravages of a hard life. Though only fifty-two, he looked to be a hundred, but age alone couldn't effect such a change. Too many years in battle had produced a deep gouge across his brow where his helmet rested, another under his chin where his strap cut, another along his nostrils from his nose guard; two fingers on his left hand curled unnaturally; his legs were a welter of broken veins, knotted muscles, and nicked bones. Beyond battle, disease had made inroads. My first impression was that he'd doubled his weight, but now I saw he was filled with liquid. His burned freckled skin lay in bloated folds; his eyes were jaundiced and swollen to narrow slits like a lizard's; his paunch hung as if he'd just given birth.

Finally, he turned to me. Silently, he examined my blue wimple, my pale linen tunic, my face.

"You're flourishing, I see," he growled. His voice was normal. "No wonder, in this little paradise. How did you do it? Seduce my guards? Conduct another court of love?"

"In a way, yes," I answered evenly. "My handmaid, Amaria, married the captain here, Ciarron ap Dwyddyn. I'm still profiting from love, you see."

"Uh," he grunted indifferently. "Where can we parley?"

I pointed to the great hall and Marshal took his arm.

"Greeting, William," I said. "You've come up in the world."

"Thanks to your generosity, my lady," he replied courteously.

I walked beside Glanvill.

"Tell me, Lord Glanvill, have you come back to torture me?"

He looked at me warily. "I never said aught of torture, my lady."

"Perhaps I misunderstood."

When we reached the great hall, Henry told his men to leave him. He then managed the steps alone. Once inside, he lowered himself slowly onto a padded bench and spread his arms along the back.

"Yes, you look better than the last time I saw you," he said. "Preserved like a mummy."

"Mummies live in tombs. I would rather chance aging in the outside world, Henry."

"Uh."

"May I offer you some wine?"

"Just water."

I clapped for my porter and spoke a few words in Welsh.

Henry's yellow eyes watched me.

"Ironic, eh? You're safe in this little Eden and I'm exposed to Hell."

"Safe in my person, perhaps, but I share your Hell."

He heard my anguish. "How much do you know?"

I became guarded. "About what?"

"About anything you choose. About love, life, death."

"Be more specific. You came here for a purpose?"

"For information." He tried to shift position. Real pain crossed his features.

"Then I must plead ignorance. I have no information."

The water arrived. Henry drank long and avidly.

"Oh yes, you have, my lady, deep, traitorous secrets. I know your guilt; I want to know your motive. My scholars tell me there's never been an instance in all history of a queen trying to overthrow her lawful lord. Why did you do it?"

"I didn't, unfortunately, for I like to be first."

"They postulate that you were jealous of other women, which you and I know cannot be. No king—not even Louis—so doted on his lady as I did you. Then why?"

"I repeat, I had no part in the rebellion. Nor do I accept your claim to devotion. You loved Aquitaine, not my person."

"No, my lady, not so; I'll not repeat here the uxorious words you heard so often, but you remember." Again, a long silence. "As for Aquitaine, I recall that I told you when we married that I could have taken it whenever I wished."

But he still wished for it, and he still hadn't taken it. Unlike William Marshal, Aquitaine didn't toady to a powerful king. He could destroy it, however, *was* destroying it, according to my latest intelligence.

"Whatever you heard, you never had reason to be jealous. However, love is different for a man than it is for a woman. Despite your court of love, you never grasped that simple point." His eyes—no longer like ice, more like moat water—appraised me. "You may think it odd, at your age and in this setting, that I dwell on the theme of love, but I know now—knew then—that the rebellion was connected to your court of love."

For the first time, my heart hammered. "Why do you think so?"

"Rebellion." His eyes fixed in their familiar snake gaze. "You were teaching women to rebel. You were rallying your troops."

I laughed. "You sound like Louis on the Crusade; he accused me and my ladies of being Amazon warriors. Are you fighting women in the field?"

"I've wondered. Your sons, for example, fight for a woman. And they attended your court of love."

"My son—the only one still in the field—fights for his hereditary rights. Since he already has Aquitaine, he hardly need fight for me or against me."

"The point could be argued. However, the rebellion is more widespread than our own family. I have noted that the lords who defy me are the husbands of your love-contenders."

I said nothing; he'd known that since he'd ridden away with Young Henry on the hunt.

He shifted his position, then his attack.

"However, that's merely the preamble, as you would say in one of your romances. Here is the heart of the matter." His husky voice dropped to a whisper. "I'm going to kill your favorite son."

I couldn't control a soft moan.

"Yes, Richard, once to be duke of Aquitaine, now slated for an untimely death."

"Why?" I gasped. "Henry, how could you even contemplate such a crime! A sin against nature!"

"I don't relish the act, believe me; I'm a peaceful man, a benevolent king, which is why I'm confiding in you. Tell him to desist, Eleanor; tell him to withdraw his troops from my county of Anjou, to accept peace, and I'll spare him."

"God's feet, Henry! I have no contact with Richard! You know that! Nor do I control actions in the field! You're a reasonable man, and a just one, I hope! Please don't torment me!"

"You forgot that I'm also an intelligent man!" he roared. "Call off your son, damn you! Call off your troops! Must I do warfare forever?"

I felt drained—I'd forgotten what it meant to be put on my mettle. "What makes you think that I have any influence? Or that, if I had, I would exercise it to please you? You've hardly won my fealty by putting me in a prison, my lord, a prison where I was intended to die an early death."

"A lapse in my intelligence. You're an evil phoenix: you just keep rising from the ashes. I was too lax in keeping you alive in the first place. I should have had the knights finish the job there on the road to France, where we slayed the others. "

His golden image blurred; his voice retreated. For the second time in my life, I fainted.

Voices spoke in the distance; I tasted salty blood, or perhaps tears, and knew where I was. Amaria administered damp cloths; Henry's voice rumbled. I pushed back my vision and opened my eyes.

"Are you awake, darling?" Amaria's face appeared briefly.

When I opened my eyes again, Henry, clinging to a chair for support, bent over me. "God's eyes, what happened? Are you ill?"

I felt such loathing, I couldn't speak. Taking Amaria's hand, I struggled to my feet, counted my breaths until my mind was again blank.

"Bring me some wine, please."

"Get the wine! Hurry!" The porter ran.

I sipped a fine Bordeaux, biding my time. My head was clear, but I was unsure that I could speak. Another breath. "I'm sorry, perhaps something I ate."

Henry stared. "Was that a real swoon? Or are you evading me? Your eyes—sliding to the side—evasive. Like that first time you came to Barfleur."

His comment braced me. "You said elusive and mysterious then, more complimentary adjectives."

"Evasive, by damn! Rebellious! From the very beginning! And you taught your sons your petty resentments! By God, two are gone and Richard will soon follow! I'll kill your favorite son, Eleanor."

I dropped the wineglass to the floor. *Take hold,* I cautioned myself; *this is serious.* "So you said. Tell your scholars to look into history for a king who murders his heir!"

"Richard is not my heir! I've named John!"

"No! Richard is your eldest son!"

"And hopelessly twisted by sucking at your eagle teats. John loves me because he escaped your talons! I brought him up alone!"

"Stop sliding from Richard to me! Or to John! Now you tell me the truth."

"Because if I don't, Richard will murder me, as you well know. Young Henry tried, Geoffrey planned to, and Richard means to finish the job! Call him off, Eleanor, and I swear he can live. Christ! You can do it! You are behind everything that happens! You're the instigator, the perpetrator, the evil force—nothing would transpire without you!"

"Then kill me instead of Richard."

"Oh I will, my lady, I promise you."

"And I believe you. After all, you murder your sons and your archbishop—why not your queen? You will indeed be first on many counts in history."

He gave a travesty of a smile. "You're out of touch. I'm completely exonerated in the Becket matter, and no one mentions Young Henry or Geoffrey. You'll die of 'natural causes'—such as old age, or perhaps a fatal fall. As for Richard, history will record that an ungrateful son rose against his own father." His husky voice thickened.

I lowered myself into the seat opposite him. "You're right as usual, Henry; Richard will kill you."

He stared, startled, then sighed. "I thought you loved him—why give him this ghastly assignment?"

"I have nothing to do with it."

His massive head drooped. "God's eyes, for a moment I hoped—"

"Richard has his own reasons."

He looked up. "Which are?"

"You can't guess?"

He stared phlegmatically.

"You just accused me of starting the rebellion against you."

"I had it on good authority—the count of Toulouse."

"Your favorite informant—though he's consistently wrong. The uprising was launched well before I even returned to Poitiers."

"You didn't tell me, which you know is treason."

"You had all the information I did."

"Stay with Richard."

"Very well; the seeds of your problems began in Montmirail. Of all our sons, Richard had emerged particularly well, since he'd also gained Princess Alais as his future bride, now your hostage."

"He wants to marry her now; tell me something new," Henry interrupted petulantly. "I've heard that demand from both Richard and her half-brother, Philip, but you know enough of policy to see that that's impossible. She's the only sword I hold over France's head. King Philip is no milksop like his father. He claims the Vexin belongs to France, now that Marguerite has returned to Paris, but

485

I say it belongs to Princess Alais as her dowry. He counters that if I will name Richard my heir, which would make Alais queen of England, and let them marry, he would return the Vexin. On the other hand, what bargaining point do I have with him except Alais? He would do almost anything to put her with Richard, perhaps even cease this foolhardy war. That's my hope."

When he stopped railing, I continued. I described the love between the two children on the edge of adulthood, the alteration the relationship had wrought in Richard. I then described our fears when Young Henry escaped from his hunt with Henry; everyone in our palace had known that we were approaching catastrophe.

"Young Alais was the most terrified," I told him. "Richard tried to reassure her, but she sank into a slough of despair."

"Richard, stay with Richard. I care nothing for young women's vapors."

But I continued relentlessly about the day in that long-ago October when Amaria had called me to see Alais in her bed. The princess had been perspiring heavily, though she had a fever, and there was a strong sweetish odor.

Amaria had led me silently to a chamber pot. There I'd gazed down on a twisted lump of blood.

"A clot?" Henry asked, puzzled.

"A fetus."

He sat up straight. "You mean that Richard—?"

"My first thought exactly. I berated myself for not reading their affection for what it was, a physical affair."

"That damned court of love!" he shouted. "Probably the same tale's been played all across Europe!"

"I doubt it," I replied dryly.

I'd bent over the terrified girl, who'd whispered the truth.

"You were the father, Henry. You'd raped her again and again during that brief visit, and this was the result."

He sprang to his feet. "I deny it! I never gave her a child!" He sounded sincere.

"Do you deny that you raped her?"

"I've never raped anyone!"

I winced. "Do you deny that you knew her carnally?"

"Christ, what an expression! I may have—I don't remember. When you're a king—yes, we may have had a couple of—"

"I tried to protect Richard from the truth. I spirited Alais to Fontevrault, but he escaped me and visited her. She told him about you. That was the end, Henry, of any hope between you and Richard."

"I'm sorry I asked. Of course you would imagine the usual romantic fantasy, the jealousy—"

"What about King Philip? He claims that you are still cohabiting with his sister after all these years—she's now twenty-five. Is he jealous? Romantic? He's written the Pope, who's taking action. Is he romantic as well? How can you defend yourself?"

"You held a court of love! I thought you believed in love!"

"Oh, I do, Henry. Love, as in Eros, a transcendent experience, heaven upon earth. My court was not about vulgar debauchery."

He sat again with his hands clasped before his face. "That's right, Eros, precisely the word. Well, let's put the record straight. Yes, I found Alais in Fontevrault and took her in my custody. Yes, I loved her that summer, but I never heard she had a miscarriage—if she did. Did I rape her? Do I keep her now against her will? No, I assure you that Alais lusted for me fully as much as I ever did for her. I am the love of her life, as she is mine."

The same words I'd heard from poor Rosamond.

"Since when did you become the seducer of children, Henry?"

"I married you, and you were hardly a child."

"You killed the count of Pohoet in Brittany, eh? He tried to defend his ten-year-old daughter from you! After he was dead, you raped her repeatedly!"

"Where did you hear such lies? Pohoet died when he tried to seize my lands! Besides, she was not ten; she was eleven, and she loved me."

"Love?" I laughed shortly. "You call it love to force yourself on a naïve child? You're a strong, brutal man, as well as being the king and overlord. Do you call abject submission love?"

"I was there, my lady."

"And I was in Poitiers, though, when Alais confided in me."

"Alais was covering for herself."

"Herself? You don't know what she said."

"Yes, I do. She told you that I'd caught her in the bowels of the wine house and threatened her with exposure if she cried out."

I was surprised. "Yes."

"We were in the wine cellar all right, a fine musty nest for a little naked dallying. Also quiet as a spider's web with the white threads dangling from the barrels, a fine site for interesting exchanges."

I frowned. "Exchanges?"

"Oh yes, a most interesting tale my young Venus whispered—how she followed you, Young Henry, and Richard night after night along the river when you met in Saint-Radegonde's. I'll give you this, Eleanor; you were right to doubt that the count of Toulouse was my informant, and I was right to suspect the court of love. Princess Alais of France was both traitor to your cause and my true love."

I cried aloud.

He rose slowly. "However, this visit has revealed much. I didn't know about the miscarriage, nor did I know that Richard had discovered the affair."

"So now you can murder him with impunity!" I shot back. "Never was there such a mad villain as you in all of history, Henry!"

He gazed with viper eyes. "Oh, I think history will record that I brought my grandfather's laws to England, despite my struggles with a power-mad archbishop, with a gorgon wife, and with a jealous son. Yes, I'll kill him with no regrets. I'll then reign in peace, and John will be my heir!"

He limped to the door, then turned. "This is good-bye, Eleanor. I have no further need for the poisonous eagle in her eyrie. I'll deal with you when the deed's done. Enjoy your luxury while you may."

Marshal helped him mount his great destrier, but he didn't move. "And take care of your diet. I never saw you faint." He smiled sardonically.

"If I understand your good-bye, my diet hardly matters."

Still, he studied me. "You were once the most beautiful creature I ever beheld, and you're still a handsome woman. But it wasn't only your physical charms that fascinated me; it was your intelligence, as sharp as any man's. What went wrong?"

I spoke honestly. "I had my life planned, my lord, when you changed my destiny. A crown never compensated for personal happiness."

"What personal happiness? A man?"

I shook my head; his image had begun to pool.

"That damned mysterious smile again." He licked dry lips. "Damned shame. Tragedy. Your beauty, talent, and all I could give—"

I smiled still. "My talent, if any, was the ability to thread my way through the many curves and blind alleys. Yet, see where I've ended?"

"Farewell." He turned his horse to the gate, horns sounded again, and the red melted into greenery. Henry was riding to his destiny, his destiny and mine, still linked, for whatever the outcome of the impending struggle, my period in Old Sarum was drawing to a close. I called for my writing materials: "To Richard, duke of Aquitaine, greeting: He's been here. Your life or his. Move swiftly."

31

oices rang from the windows of my great hall. As I crossed the threshhold, I skirted a pile of spurs and arms.

The voices hushed as I entered. Hefty knights and lords dropped to their knees, their moist eyes raised in a mixture of awe and curiosity.

"Greeting," I said. "Shall we get to work?"

I sat at the center of a long table Ciarron had hastily built for the occasion and tried to identify the strangers around me. Everyone seemed very young.

Age was forgotten, however, as we turned to the task of creating a new government. We worked crisply and rapidly, very much of a single mind. Then my secretary, Desmond, leaned over my shoulder: Lord Ranulf of Glanvill begged an audience alone with the queen.

Glanvill stood uneasily in the doorway. At my glance, he made his way toward me.

He didn't kneel. "Queen Eleanor, I came as fast as I could, but I see the news was faster."

"That Henry is dead? Yes, the new king, Richard, reached me first."

For one unguarded moment, his black eyes met mine.

I continued. "Until he can be crowned, I'm his regent."

"No!" He recovered. "England is fortunate."

"If you refer to King Richard, I agree."

He cleared his throat. "I'm delighted that you're free."

"A queen is never free, eh?"

"No, I suppose not."

"Come, I don't know the details of King Henry's unfortunate demise. Let's stroll in my courtyard and you can tell me."

He bowed, and followed a pace behind me.

I chatted inanely. "Of course I've already made arrangements for his remains to be carried to Fontevrault, where he can enter the rolls of necrology in a manner befitting his station. Henry always loved Fontevrault; he sympathized with discarded wives."

We were now walking on the path to the gate. Horsemen pulled up short upon seeing me, and men on foot ran beside me, importuning for my attention. I called Mercadier, the mercenary who'd accompanied my sons to Paris, to protect my privacy. When we passed through the gate, the cacophony behind us receded; another few steps into the forest and we were alone.

"Now, the truth, Lord Glanvill, no matter how brutal. Conceal a flaw, and I'll imagine the worst."

"Well, then, Henry retired from the fighting—which was fierce—in Le Mans, his birthplace."

"I know where he was born."

"One evening, he rode out to check the walls and, from above, saw his own fortress-home shoot up in flames. He was appalled that Richard would show such small regard for his natal city."

"Refer to him as King Richard, if you please."

"King Richard charged out of the smoke directly toward his own father. With great pain, Henry managed to flee to safety."

"Pain?" I interrupted.

"An old wound had reopened—he had a bad fistula."

"And where did he flee?"

"To Chinon."

"But why?" This was the part of the account I could never understand. "He was so close to Normandy and safety."

Glanvill looked at me with obvious distaste. "To die, milady. Why else?"

"And did he die there?"

Not immediately. Succored by one of his bastard sons who'd always remained loyal, Henry had lain in his bed, drinking broth to regain strength. During the next two weeks, as he recuperated, Richard and Philip of France had raged through Touraine and Maine, lashing and leveling everything in their wake. When the city of Tours fell, they declared a total victory over the English king and demanded that he meet them to surrender.

Against all advice—for he was too ill to ride—Henry called for his horse.

"By the time he met with the victors in a churchyard in Ballon, he was weaving in his saddle, close to collapse. The king of France begged him to lie on a blanket; Richard—King Richard—scoffed, saying that Henry was a master of deception."

Glanvill choked; he took a moment to regain his composure.

"Henry refused Philip's courtesy and stayed on his horse. He listened to their terms: All disputed territories were to be returned to France or Aquitaine; Richard was named as his heir to Normandy, Anjou, and the throne of England; Princess Alais was to be released at once to marry Richard."

"To marry him after King Richard returns from his Crusade," I amended.

"Crusade?"

"Yes, go on—Henry's death."

Now mortally ill, Henry managed to return to Chinon. Although he'd lost everything, he was still king of England, and he was determined to get revenge on those who'd betrayed him. He had a roster of the rebels, which his bastard son read aloud. He came to the name John.

Henry struggled to sit upright. "My son *John*?" He reached for the list. "No need to read the others." He lay down again. "I care no more for this world." And he died.

Glanvill burst into wrenching sobs. "His servants stole everything—his clothing, his arms; we had to borrow rags to cover him for his Mass."

He wiped his face on his sleeve and looked at me, his eyes red spots of fury. "Then Richard—King Richard—came to see his dead father. He didn't kneel, nor did he pray; he just stood, staring down. Then a miracle occurred—we all saw it—King Henry's nostrils spurted blood. A sign that he was in the presence of his murderer."

I watched him without compassion. "From what you said, I would have thought John was the culprit. Take hold of yourself, Lord Glanvill; be reasonable. Henry chose his own death."

"A bright star has fallen from the heavens!"

The red star of malice, Suger's words.

He swallowed. "Forgive me, I'm all right now."

"Your sorrow does you credit."

"Thank you."

"Loyalty is the key virtue when you serve a king." I waited for him to wipe his face. "And remember, Hector has a new heir. Though King Richard and I have little reason to be grateful to you at a personal level—for a man who so upholds the law, you ignored it in our case—we still believe you were right to be loyal to King Henry."

"Law must stand mute in the midst of arms."

"Very well expressed. Now that the Old King is dead, do you think you can be equally loyal to King Richard?"

For the first time, he lost his poise. Despite my obvious authority, he could not yet think of me as queen of England, a woman who understood well political ethics, if that was not an oxymoron. Glanvill was the most literate, the best-informed legal mind in the realm. We needed him.

"I—to King Richard?"

"Yes, the courteous count of Poitou, soon to be crowned king of England. We want to begin our reign with you as our justiciar."

He squared his shoulders. "I—would be honored to serve."

I'd called it loyalty when I'd appealed to William of Marshal as well; *opportunism* was still the better word.

"I'm immensely gratified, and relieved. You may find it an adjustment to serve the Great One"—I laughed lightly—"I mean, King Richard, who represents the flower of chivalry; his word comes from his heart. Therefore, we'll make several changes."

"Of course."

"I expect King Richard to arrive in England at the end of August, then to be crowned in early September. Meanwhile, you and I will make a progress around the country. We'll prepare the people for their new king, and change some distasteful laws."

"What laws?" he asked warily.

"First, I plan to open all the prisons. Every man, woman, or child who is incarcerated in England is at this very moment made free."

To forestall his consternation, I continued sternly. "Furthermore, you will ride yet today back to London. Once there, you are to remove Princess Alais from the palace in Westminster and place her in the White Tower."

"But not as a prisoner." He groped to understand.

"Very much a prisoner, the only one in all England."

"But—"

"Not for long," I assured him. "We'll transport her to the tower in Rouen before King Richard arrives. He's going on Crusade, you know, shortly after the coronation. She'll remain under lock there until he returns from the Holy Land."

He was bewildered; I patted his arm. "Just to keep her safe, eh?"

1 had few personal possessions to take with me when I left Old Sarum. I'd arrived with one longcart; I departed with one longcart, yet my feelings had changed. I would never forget my horror when I'd first seen it, and now I was pressing hands on every side with sorrow to be leaving. My Welsh guards wept openly, and so did Amaria. She and Ciarron would accompany me to London, but I insisted that she stay with him thereafter. I would use my sister as my confidante.

The Welsh suddenly burst into song. I held my horse to listen. Then, following the royal guard, I rode slowly along the river winding through the dense forest, back to the Winchester Royal Road, where we'd been fatally diverted so many years ago.

My steed's ears suddenly laid back, and I felt his nervous trembling beneath me.

"Calm yourself." I stroked his neck.

Then I saw what had disturbed him. Hundreds of people stood on the bridge, waiting for my appearance; the instant they saw me, a giant cheer went up, and I, too, felt a surge of panic. The forest behind me seemed to melt away; I'd left nature for the world of power and intrigue. Old habits took over; I raised my hand and smiled.

As we proceeded slowly along the wide way, the crowds grew ever larger, the shouts more manic; hands reached, tears flowed, and many people knelt, as if I were a saint passing by.

"Look at me! At me! I love you, Eleanor!"

"Touch my withered arm!"

"My blind eye!"

"I love you, Nell!"

I couldn't believe it, couldn't explain it. It had been fifteen years since that day I'd been captured in France, during which time I'd been completely out of contact with my subjects; these people were too young to remember me. I was moved, I was grateful, and I was baffled. Was it possible someone had written a tale about me? Had I become a legend? Then I heard a song somewhere ahead of me, and I listened intently.

Gaudiat Pictavia
Iam rege discate,
Tunescat Normannia
Auro coronate!

My Latin was rusty, but I translated this simple message:

Let Aquitaine rejoice
Her duke is now our king,
Let Normandy add her voice
And to his praises sing!

I wasn't the saint; Richard was. But listen!

"Hail to the queen! Queen of queens! Eleanor released all freemen from gaols! Eleanor!"

The singing continued, and again I concentrated.

Scelus datir funderi,
Scandala fugantur;
Rapinia interitum
Clero iuris aditum
Locun veritatis!

Easy:

The wicked king is dead,
His henchmen on the run;
His robbers filled with dread
For the legal battle's won
May truth prevail!

I was being given credit for not being Henry, and so was Richard. I remembered when Henry had replaced King Stephen, with a similar kind of euphoria among the populace, and I remembered how he had betrayed their hopes. Richard must do better.

I left Westminster Palace almost at once to travel the length of England, holding court, passing new laws, canceling old ones, all in the name of Richard, who would soon be king: I canceled all Henry's forest laws, opened the ports, seized all the assets of the treasury, and only when the broad outlines of the new regime had been established did I return to London. There I concentrated on preparing for Richard. I'd learned again and again how deeply England despised Henry, but I understood that they didn't yet know Richard; I knew, too, that Richard knew nothing of England. He'd never read the Constitutions of Clarendon, knew none of the nobility or officers of the court, could not speak a word of the language. All his training had been for the rule of Aquitaine. Therefore, I began a careful selection of experienced men who would help with the transition; I disposed of marriage prizes among the young nobles of England to secure their loyalty, including William Marshal, to whom I gave the duchess of Pembroke, all in Richard's name. I pleased the clergy by doing away with a hated law that they must house the king's horses in their abbeys, and I brought the archbishop of Canterbury to London to share in my largesse.

While I worked in England, Richard was making the rounds from castle to castle in Normandy and Anjou to cement his power among Henry's vassals. We were now in daily communication through scores of runners, and I kept him appraised of my plans for his entry into London. Unlike Henry, his son would be wrapped in panoply and ritual, beginning the instant he landed in Winchester. He would ride to the beat of troubadour music along flowered paths, and tapestries would hang from every window; we would create a new kind of coronation, bringing all our experience in Aquitaine to bear. England was a cold and misty isle, all the more reason to light fires in every English heart.

My family began to gather. Tears flowed unabashedly as we clasped, remarked, congratulated: Matilda, her husband, the duke of Saxony, her two sons, Henry and Otto; Marie and Alix from Champagne and Blois, my grandchildren by Marie, Henry and Scholastique; Petronilla and her daughtrers, Isabelle and Eleanor; Mamile and Florine; of the older generation, only Aunt Mahaut still lived, a venerable ancient who had retired to her own domicile at Fontevrault; everyone who could come did so. Missing were Joanna, who was queen of Sicily; my daughter Eleanor of Castile; and John, who was coming with Richard. Young Henry's widow,

Marguerite, had remarried in France; Constance of Brittany, Geoffrey's widow, had taken her children, Arthur and Eleanor, to Paris.
Also missing, of course, was Princess Alais of France.

We'd all changed physically, but we all adjusted to the change,
finding the spiritual centers, which were eternal. We put aside rage
and regret—we'd won!

Then runners reported that Richard had landed in England,
close to Winchester, and the palace became hushed. He would be
traveling the same road I'd traveled many years ago on my way to
Old Sarum. We followed his progress hour by hour: The huge
crowds were in a frenzy, the same Latin song being trumpeted
everywhere. I sat quietly in my chamber, reading his messages
delivered by his runners, trying to concentrate on the problems at
hand. I'd created a new ritual for his coronation at the abbey, formal and elegant, had ordered over five thousand dishes to be prepared for his feast afterward, but I was overwhelmed by memory: I
saw his face, white under his crushed hat, felt his kiss before he
disappeared into the dark rain. The years between were beyond
imagining.

A huge inhuman roar filled the air. He had entered London; the
roar increased as he drew nearer.

> *The age of gold returns,*
> *The world's reform is nigh;*
> *The rich man now made low,*
> *The pauper raised on high.*

Such were the hopes of the common man, now and forever. Did
Richard have such an agenda in mind? I doubted it, but he brought
change; for the moment, that was enough. Amaria came for me:
time to descend. I would welcome my son before the eyes of thousands.

Glanvill and the archbishop of Canterbury took my arms. Together,
we watched the great gates of Westminster open. Crowds pushed
into the yard, shouting, weeping, throwing flowers. Red-uniformed

guards fought them in vain. In their midst came a line of horse-men. And there was Richard!

Unmistakable on his beautiful Andalusian sorrel, both man and beast encrusted with jewels. A golden cape fastened to Richard's shoulders flowed over the horse's rump to the ground; peacock feathers were embroidered into the orofois. Magnificent! Magnifi-cent! Yet what did he need with all this decoration? His red-gold hair blazed in the sun; his smile was more dazzling than jewels; his warrior's shoulders were ready for the weight of the world.

He dismounted and momentarily disappeared, then ran lightly up the steps to a high platform, his golden cape billowing behind him. He waved, turned this way and that, tried to encompass all of London in his benevolent embrace. Then he lowered his arms and faced the palace. That was my signal: I slowly walked the long crimson carpet toward the platform. The crowd held its breath. When I reached the steps, Richard ran down to extend his hand. Our fingers clasped, and he pulled me gently upward. We faced each other and his arms were around me. The crowd went wild.

I could barely hear his whisper in my ear. "Mama, oh Mama."

Now together we smiled and waved. I glanced at him: a hand-some man of thirty-two, gray-blue eyes, full lips, even teeth, yes, very handsome, and a stranger. I couldn't find my boy in the man, except for that whispered *"Mama."*

Our combined presence drove the populace into a frenzy; they screamed half-heard words—we were holy mother and son, sanc-tified in our mutual victory, our suffering, our dedication to the right. The voices swelled and receded like the beating of a heart.

I looked upward; above the minions, clabbered clouds streaked diagonally, as if the world were tilting. Oc, time for me to slide off this world and join the even greater minions who had gone before me, my family, my sons, my husbands, and the person who in this world had mattered most. The colors under the midday blaze pooled, and I was looking out on fields of anemones as we sailed into Antioch. Then I was gazing across another sea at a silver ship as it foundered off the rainy coast of Attalia.

Richard murmured anxiously, "Are you ill?"

And there it was, Rancon's voice.

"It's only the sun. . . ."

"You're pale. Here, take my arm; I'll lead you back to your quarters."

I stepped from my mummy's tomb.

My vertigo increased. When I stretched on my bed, I had to clutch the sides to avoid falling. "Leave me, please," I whispered to Richard-Rancon. "Amaria can care for me."

"Amaria's not here; I'll call Aunt Petra."

While I gripped my pitching bed, I heard whispers and rustlings around me. Petra's voice, and Richard's again.

I sank into a my tilting universe. Once again, my father rode through the fuzzy stars on his white destrier.

"Wait for me!" I implored. But as of yore, he disappeared between Castor and Pollux.

I may have slept, may have fallen into a coma. I opened my eyes to darkness. Tapers burned beside me as if I were in a coffin, and my dizziness had abated. Smoke swirled against the low ceiling. The voices around me had ceased.

Odd, I missed my book. A false life, a fiction, for Henry had been only partly right when he'd said that I *should* have died on the French road, because, in fact, I *had* died there. When Rancon had been killed, my life had ended as well. My book, very simply, had been an effort to re-create him—more than a memory—a rebirth. Strange, we have a word for being born again, but none for going through two deaths. Was I soon to be re-dead?

I'd lost two sons since then, and I'd put my hopes on the sons still living, but there was no one to replace Rancon. On the page, he galloped forever along the Vienne on his black destrier, wrapped me in strong arms at night as he sang a new song. *Oc*, he could live in my fancy. How I yearned for illusion. Even though he was dead, he'd supported me because—isolated as I was—I could pretend he was alive.

Time to draw my book to a close. Rancon had died in France

when his horse had rolled on the hillside; now he must die on my pages. I couldn't sing the same song again and again. How many times could I return to my tent on Mount Cadmos? How many times could I evoke Tristan?

I gazed at the hazy swirls from the tapers, sought my grandfather on his white horse, yearned for my baby William walking on his hands. Somewhere in the void, they were waiting for me. Oh, please, come quickly!

The dark is coming; the dark is coming. The dark of a winter sky in Aquitaine, with its throw of sharp winter stars. The sky was a night sea, the stars bits of glistening fish bait.

I reached upward. "I take your bait, milord!"

A hand grasped my wrist. "Joy!"

"Grandfather!"

"It's Rancon, Joy. Do you recognize me?"

Rancon was here? Of course, he had been here all these poignant years. In heaven, waiting for me! Why had I delayed so long? How beautiful he was, my sun-bronzed lord! My heart raced with eagerness. Oh, let it not be a dream! Dressed in his brown, his gold lion shimmering like mustard seeds.

"Yes!" I answered. "You're the lark!"

"And you're the sun!" He leaned close and sang:

> *Like the lark which flies into the Sun,*
> *I soar in love till I'm undone;*
> *For love summons me to sing,*
> *To rise on high on burning wing.*

"I can't forgive you, Rancon," I reproached him. "You broke your word, leaving me alone all these years. We were Tristan and Iseult, remember? We promised to die together, wrapped in our flowering thorn."

"We're not ready to die yet, Bel Vezer."

A taper created a silver halo around his head. "Your hair is white."

"Perhaps yours is, too, if you would remove your wimple." He smiled.

"But you had only a single streak when . . . Give me your hand!"

I rubbed his forefinger. *Oc*, the callus. "You really are Rancon?"

"I hope you're not shocked."

I looked at him again. "Do we age in heaven?"

His cheeks were wet. "Do I offend you?"

He turned so I could see a withered arm hanging by his side.

I swung my feet to the ground. "Rancon, are you alive? Is it possible? Did you survive that—" And I burst into *mesclatz* tears. "I'm sorry, I don't believe . . . I can't . . ." I touched his cheek, his lips, his chest. "Oh God, I think I'm going to swoon!"

As I lay on my bed with wet cloths on my forehead, he explained how his horse had crushed him on one side, how he'd been taken back to Poitiers to begin a slow recovery, how he'd learned about my imprisonment, all, all, how helpless and enraged he'd felt because he couldn't rescue me. He'd summoned one baron after another, but all were engaged in saving their own lives. And my sons had been too young.

"I wanted to die, Joy, for I knew hope was finished," he whispered. "I lived only in memory."

I laughed aloud. *How alike our minds!*

"You relived your life of passion!"

"Except that life goes forward now and I'm a broken man. Perhaps I should stay with memory."

And I'd once thought of him as my twin—was I not right?

I ran my fingers through his hair. "I'll cure you!"

He placed his forehead against mine. "The solace of love?"

I wept uncontrollably.

"I was never meant to fly alone!"

"A pair of whites!"

He kissed me with sun-drenched lips. "I almost didn't come, except that Richard insisted."

"Our son, Rancon—does he know?"

"Yes."

"Did you ever see anyone so beautiful?"

"He looks like his mother."

"Kiss me again."

He did.

I touched the gold lion on his tunic. "Richard has your lion's heart."

"He needs it."

"Listen! Rancon! He's going on a Crusade."

"He must go by sea—Maurienne was right!"

"While he's away, we must rule for him in Aquitaine!"

We both laughed uncontrollably.

"Listen! Rancon, my life comes in fifteen-year-increments, eh? Fifteen in Aquitaine, fifteen in France, fifteen in England, fifteen in Old Sarum, and now—" I stopped. Why put a limit on the future?

He held me close, singing:

> *Time comes and turns*
> *Through days, through months, and even years:*
> *And unabated my desire burns,*
> *The same, unchanging; my heart yearns*
> *For Joy, to quell my tears.*
> *Her prisoner of love.*

No, I thought, for once the twins do not agree, for you are not my prisoner of love, nor am I yours; I stroked his cheek. I'd learned many times over that love was my *only* freedom; to be without love, my only imprisonment. Writing my book had made me realize just how often we'd tried to define love over the years: love in the heat of passion, in yearning while apart, in his songs, in parenthood, in my court of love, as an alternative to arranged marriages. Love was everything we had said and sung that it was, and yet until this moment, I hadn't fully grasped its significance. Not imprisonment surely. Hadn't Rancon been fettered by his broken body? Hadn't I suffered for years behind a fence of high palings? Hadn't we both survived through memory? No, not imprisonment. Nor was it death, as the Tristan poet had claimed.

Love, very simply, was life.

Testa me ipso.

Afterword

Eleanor lived for fifteen years after her release from prison, during which time she ruled as Richard's queen, then as John's. She survived her sister, Rancon, and all her children except Eleanor and John. Never ill, she retired in her last days to Fontevrault, where she lies with Henry and Richard. At her own request, her effigy represents a queen in serene repose, with a book in her hands.

1204: In this year the noble Queen Eleanor, a woman of admirable beauty and intelligence, died in Fontevrault.

—Matthew of Paris
In hoc anno obiit Alianor.

Glossary

arras: curtain, sometimes on a wall, or around a bed

asusée: langue d'oc for "upward and onward"

brach: dog, usually a hound

brechan: thin Welsh coverlet

chevauchée: an official ride into the provinces

courser: a charger, a stallion

destrier: a warhorse

Dex aie: langue d'oc for "God help me"

jobelin: a criminal trained in a professional underclass

lai: short narrative poem

lerewita: Saxon for "a fine"

mesclatz: langue d'oc for "mixed-up, confused"

milord: troubadour address with triple meaning—to a lord, to a beloved lady, to God

motte: an artificial hill on which a tower is placed

orofois: gold embroidery, often in a band

Pax Angevina: Angevin peace, meaning an Angevin empire

rufous: reddish in hue

sendal: taffeta

stewe: a brothel

subtlety: an ornament made of sugar

testudo: an awning for an officer in the military field

vair: a fur made from the gray squirrel

verjuice: the acid juice of unripe fruit

volte-face: an about-face

Waes hael: Anglo-Saxon for "Hail"

wyrd: fate, destiny

List of Characters

Aquitaine

Eleanor, countess of Poitou, duchess of Aquitaine, queen of France, queen of England

Richard of Rancon*, baron of Taillebourg, captain of Aquitaine's army

Lady Petronilla, Eleanor's sister, countess of Vermandois

Abbess Mahaut of Fontevrault, Eleanor's paternal aunt

Abbess Agnes of Maillezais, Eleanor's paternal aunt

Lady Beatrice, Eleanor's paternal aunt

Lady Isabelle, Eleanor's paternal aunt

Archbishop Geoffrey of Bordeaux, Eleanor's guardian and religious seneschal

Aimar of Limoges, Hugh and Guy of Lusignan, Aquitanian barons

Eleanor's female friends: Lady Mamile, Lady Florine, Lady Toquerie, Lady Faydide

Amaria**, Eleanor's lady-in-waiting

Lady Dangereuse†, countess of Châtellerault, Eleanor's maternal grandmother

Count Ralph of Châtellerault, Eleanor's maternal uncle and political seneschal

Marcabru, troubadour

Sir Lucain, knight to Duke William X

Aquitaine, in memory or as ghostly figures

Duke William IX, Eleanor's grandfather, famous troubadour

Duke William X, Eleanor's father

Lady Anor of Châtellerault, Eleanor's mother

Countess Philippa of Toulouse, wife of William IX, Eleanor's paternal grandmother

France

King Louis VI of France, Louis the Fat

King Louis VII of France, Eleanor's first husband

Abbot Suger of Saint-Denis, religious seneschal of France

Count Raoul of Vermandois, political seneschal of France

Thibault, duke of Champagne

Henry of Champagne, Thibault's son, marries Eleanor's daughter Marie

Abbot Bernard of Clairvaux, Cistercian abbot

Count Thierry of Galeran, a Templar, adviser to Louis

Marie de Champagne, Eleanor's daughter by Louis

Alix de Blois, Eleanor's daughter by Louis

Princess Marguerite of France, Louis's daughter

Princess Alais of France, Louis's daughter

Lady Constance of Brittany

Philip of France, Louis's son, who succeeded Louis as king (Philip August)

The Crusade

Manuel I, emperor of Byzantium

Irene of Sulzbach, empress of Byzantium

Count of Maurienne, Louis's uncle

Prince Raymond of Antioch, Eleanor's paternal uncle

Lady Constance, Raymond's wife

Bishop Arnulf of Lisieux, Henry's tutor

Conrad, king of Germany

Pope Eugenius

England

Henry, count of Anjou, duke of Normandy, King Henry II of England, Eleanor's second husband

Count Geoffrey of Angers, Henry's father

Sir Geoffrey, Henry's younger brother

Matilda, Henry's mother, duchess of Normandy, former empress of Germany

Thomas à Becket, Henry's chancellor, later archbishop of Canterbury

Patrick, earl of Salisbury

William Marshal, a knight, instructor to Young Henry

Lady Rosamond of Clifford, Henry's lover

William, Eleanor's son by Henry

Young Henry, Eleanor's son by Henry

Matilda of Saxony, Eleanor's daughter by Henry

Richard, Eleanor's son by Henry (Richard Coeur de Lion)

Geoffrey of Brittany, Eleanor's son by Henry

Eleanor of Castile, Eleanor's daughter by Henry

Joanna of Sicily (and later, Toulouse), Eleanor's daughter by Henry

John, Eleanor's son by Henry

Old Sarum

Ranulf de Glanvill, justiciar of England, Eleanor's guard

Ciarron ap Dwyddyn, Eleanor's Welsh gaoler

*Richard of Rancon was actually Geoffrey of Rancon, baron of Taille-bourg, a member of the powerful Angoulême family. I changed his name for clarity (there are other Geoffreys in the book); he was trained by Eleanor's father, served as her captain, led her army on the Crusade, was sent home by Louis, served her when she was queen of England and in the rebellion that followed. The personal story is fiction. There was, however, a troubadour named Bernart of Ventadorn who was with Eleanor for months in Angers, and close enough to the queen to make Henry suspicious.

**Amaria of Gascony was an actual lady-in-waiting, but the *lais* I have attributed to her were written by Marie de France, a pseudonym of an unknown person. The *lais* are free adaptations of the originals.

†Eleanor's maternal grandmother, though recorded in history as the countess of Châtellerault, has no given name. Several genealogies attribute various names; Dangereuse is a name of the period.

About the Author

PAMELA KAUFMAN, PH.D., has spent almost fifteen years researching and writing *The Book of Eleanor*. She visited the original sites and read all the scarce primary sources as well as the fictions and biographies of Eleanor of Aquitaine. Ms. Kaufman's career began on the Broadway stage, then moved to academia, where she taught English literature and film and created the Communications Department at Santa Monica College. She is a member of Phi Beta Kappa and serves on the board of Friends of English at UCLA. This is her fourth book.